SOUTH OF LARAMIE

Where the Trail Leads

BOOK 3
HOME ON THE RANGE SERIES

SOUTH OF LARAMIE

Where the Trail Leads

Brenda —
Through tears to
laughter — may
this be loved!
Rosie

Rosie Bosse

POST ROCK PUBLISHING

South of Laramie
Copyright © 2020 by Rosie Bosse

ISBN: Soft Cover – 978-1-64318-069-4
ISBN: eBook – 978-1-64318-071-7

**POST ROCK
PUBLISHING**

Post Rock Publishing
17055 Day Rd.
Onaga, KS 66521

www.rosiebosse.com

Like an eagle he paused, quiet and watchful.
Then slowly, he winged his way into her life.

— Rosie Bosse

PROLOGUE

South of Laramie, Where the Trail Leads is the third novel in my Home on the Range Series. I hope you will find this one as enjoyable as the first two. Again, I have tried to make this novel historically accurate while intertwining actual and fictional characters into my story line. May you miss "our friends" when you finish!

From Tent City to Streetlights

General Grenville Dodge selected the site for Cheyenne, part of the Dakota Territory, on July 4, 1867. He was the chief engineer for the Union Pacific Railroad. He chose the location based on geography.

The unique topography of the area provided a way for locomotives to cross the Rocky Mountains. The area between Cheyenne and Laramie allowed a long, easy grade from the plains of Cheyenne to the Laramie Mountains. Crow Creek was also nearby and provided a constant supply of water for the steam locomotives.

Cheyenne, known as the "Magic City of the Plains" in her early years, was chartered on August 10, 1867. The new railroad town sprang out of the prairie almost overnight and grew quickly. By October of 1867, Cheyenne boasted of two printing houses, a post office, and a telegraph office.

Like many new towns, Cheyenne had a rough beginning. That first winter, as an "end-of-tracks" town, four hundred ladies-of-the-night moved into the new city with their tents and set up shop.

Unlike many towns that sprang up along the westward-moving rails, Cheyenne survived. On July 25, 1868, she became part of the new Wyoming Territory.

Wyoming's cattle boom ran from 1868 to 1886. Even to this day, it is called the "Cowboy State." Investing money in cattle was considered a secure way to make money, and the large volume of cattle sold there brought enormous wealth. The cost to raise a range steer in Wyoming in the 1870s was around $1.50 per head. The selling price peaked at $6.47 per hundred weight (per one hundred pounds of beef on the hoof) in May of 1870. That price fluctuated over the next ten years but never dropped below $4 per hundred weight. This boom pushed economic profits for investors and cattlemen, as well as rustlers. During that time, Cheyenne counted eight millionaires among her three thousand citizens and became one of the first cities in the United States to have streetlights.

Saloons in the Old West

The word *saloon* is derived from *salon*, meaning *a large hall in a public place for entertainment.* In the United States, as in other countries, saloons evolved. Most were taking on common characteristics by 1841. Still, a saloon's appearance was much affected by when and where it was established.

While barrels and boards to hold the rotgut whiskey were common in unsettled areas, some saloons became more refined as the towns grew and became established.

The batwing doors at the entrance of many saloons were just one of their distinctive features. The swinging doors operated on double hinges and usually extended from the chest to knee level. These doors were practical because they provided easy access from either direction, cut down on the outside dust, allowed patrons to see out, and provided some ventilation. They also shielded the "shenanigans" taking place on the inside from the "proper" women walking down the street on the outside. Saloons that were not open twenty-four hours each day also had doors which could be closed and locked.

Ethnicity sometimes affected the appearance of the saloon. The Irish preferred stand-up bars where whisky was the drink of choice and decent women were not allowed. German saloons were brighter, often served food, and were sometimes oriented toward family patronage.

The West was more old-fashioned. Most saloons there did not allow women in their establishments other than those who worked there.

Some saloons offered dancing girls. Only history knows how many of these women doubled as prostitutes. With a lack of those records, I like to think some were employed by the saloons strictly as dance partners. Many saloons also offered games of chance such as faro, poker, and dice games.

Because saloons usually held more people than the other buildings in town, they were also the location of the early trials. This was a venue they all vied for. A trial meant more patrons, and people meant money in the pockets of the hosting saloon owner.

Barney Ford, Ex-Slave and Entrepreneur

Barney Lancelot Ford was a "fast-food pioneer." He was an astute businessman who followed the development of new towns, including Cheyenne in the Wyoming Territory and Denver in the Colorado Territory.

When Mr. Ford opened his restaurant in Cheyenne, he first catered to the workers constructing the new Transcontinental Railroad. Later, it was to the train's passengers.

Barney Ford arrived in Cheyenne in 1867 shortly after the new town was begun. He quickly opened his Ford House Restaurant.

His early ads offered fresh oysters. Not only were they a novelty, but they could be prepared quickly. By 1870, he was offering free carriage rides from the train station to his restaurant, saving passengers time.

The Ford House was the most popular eatery in Cheyenne during its time. While competition was much higher while the railroad was being built, five other eating establishments challenged him every day to serve the best food in town. In addition, he had to compete with other eating houses along the train's route.

The Great Fire of 1870 burned the Ford House Restaurant as well as the Ford and Durkee Hotel with its brick walls, along with all the other buildings in a two-block area. Ford was one of the only business owners who had insurance and he quickly rebuilt. He sold sometime around 1871 and moved to Denver to build his restaurant business there.

Mr. Ford returned to Cheyenne in 1875 and built the Inter-Ocean Hotel. It was lavish and was considered the finest hotel between Saint Louis, Missouri and San Francisco, California. Amenities included were a gentlemen's reading room, a billiard hall, a ladies' dining room, and a barber shop. It was also home to a popular saloon.

The Inter-Ocean Hotel became the starting point for the Blackhills Stage and Express Line (often called the Deadwood Stage) which ran from Cheyenne to Deadwood in present-day South Dakota. Many celebrities stayed at the Inter-Ocean in Cheyenne in the forty years it was open including eight United States presidents and the infamous Tom Horn.

Mr. Ford sold the Inter-Ocean Hotel a few years after it was built. After an interlude in San Francisco because of financial difficulties, he opened Ford's Restaurant and Chop House in Breckenridge, Colorado.

When the Fords left Cheyenne for the last time, the newspaper there ran a story bidding farewell to a gentleman. Barney Ford was described as "a man of unimpeachable integrity." This shows the high degree of respect he earned during his time in Cheyenne.

If you visit the state house in Denver, you will see a stained-glass image of Mr. Ford in Colorado's House of Representatives. In addition, there is a hill in Breckenridge which bears his name. Mr. Ford did become one of the wealthiest men in the West during his time. By the time of his death in 1902, he had accumulated a fortune of $500,000—the equivalent to $100 million plus today.

Barney Ford is one of my favorite historical characters. I introduced him in my first novel, *North to Cheyenne*. He also made an appearance in my second novel, *West by Rail*. In this novel, you will see an extension of the friendship created between Barney and the fictional Rocking R cowboys as well as Rowdy Rankin.

One of the things I have always loved about the Old West was men were usually judged, not by who they had been or what they had done in their past, but by who they were in the current time.

Whipple and Hay Union Mercantile

The Whipple and Hay Union Mercantile was a major goods provider for area ranchers in the 1870s around Cheyenne. The owners established themselves in the growing city shortly after it was formed. They quickly became part of Cheyenne's elite rich. Ithamar C. Whipple's mansion is still part of the walking tours in Cheyenne today.

None of the information I read mentioned a Mrs. Whipple. In this novel, she is a creation of my imagination. I can only assume a woman in a burgeoning town with a booming business would want to carry products that were of high quality and new to the market.

Most men's pants were woolen or cast-off army uniforms. Because of their long hours in the saddle, cowboys often stitched buckskin across the seat and down the inner thighs of their britches. The leather helped the pants to last longer since it handled rubbing against the saddle for long periods of time much better than cloth. Denim jeans were not available until the 1890s.

Underwear, other than long handles (long johns or long underwear), were not worn by men, so shirts were made with long tails. These were tucked in to ease the itchiness of the woolen britches.

Beckwith Round Oak Stove

Round Oak Stoves were not round but could hold an entire section of a round oak tree trunk in the firepot. There was also a foundry in England in the 1800s by the same name. No one knows why Philo D. Beckwith named his stoves Round Oak, but either or both of those things could have contributed to the name of his successful venture.

Beckwith cast his first stove in 1867 to heat his struggling foundry in Michigan. He founded his Round Oak Stove Company in 1871. Because of its functionality and durability, it was soon considered the finest heating stove on the market. By the late 1890s, there were many imitations of the Round Oak Stove being offered.

The official company name was changed in 1889 after Beckwith's death. Most of the stoves produced after 1890 carried the mark of "Estate of P.D. Beckwith" along with "Round Oak."

Innerspring Mattress

Early beds were raised off their crude frames by cross-stringing rope to support the mattresses. As the rope stretched, it had to be tightened. From that came the saying, "Sleep tight!"

The steel coil spring was invented in 1857. The springs were first patented for use in chair seats to make them more comfortable. Heinrich Westphal of Germany is credited with inventing the innerspring mattress in 1871. However, his invention was not widely used until the 1930s, after Mr. Westphal's death.

The key word here is *widely*. Who is to say one of those innerspring mattresses didn't make its way to Cheyenne in 1872? I like to think so. It was a fun addition to Mrs. Whipple's well-stocked mercantile store.

Nathan A Baker, Newspaperman

Nathan Addison Baker was a reporter, editor, and typesetter for the *Cheyenne Leader*, the first newspaper in Cheyenne. That paper is even accepted as the first newspaper in Wyoming. Mr. Baker was born on August 3, 1843, in Lockport, New York. His parents moved the family to Omaha, Nebraska when he was small. They moved again to Denver, Colorado to find gold. No gold was found, and Baker worked several jobs to help support the family when his father became ill.

He first worked in the newspaper business in Denver. He then moved to Cheyenne in 1867, hauling his printing press in a wagon pulled by oxen. His first issue was published on September 19, 1867, just weeks after Cheyenne was officially established as a town. Nearly four hundred of Cheyenne's citizens waited in and outside the newspaper office on that first day. They paid 25¢ per copy for *The Daily Leader*, and that price increased to over $1 per issue in just a few days. A year's subscription was $12 which would be over $189 today. Baker loved Cheyenne and wrote glowing articles about the city, citing the weather and the promising future of the growing town. *The Daily Leader* was the predecessor of Cheyenne's newspaper today, the *Wyoming Tribune Eagle*.

The Great Fire of 1870 destroyed Baker's newspaper office in downtown Cheyenne. A defective flue in T.A. Kent's liquor store is believed to have caused the January 11 blaze which destroyed two city blocks. The same fire also burned the Ford Restaurant. Baker still managed to publish just two days later, promising to rebuild.

In 1872, Nathan Baker sold the *Cheyenne Leader* to pursue other interests. However, his love of the newspaper business never died.

I thought it would be fun to make Nathan Baker the court reporter in the murder trial in this book. While nothing in his biography mentioned a job of that type, the descriptions of him did state that he was detailed. He also strove for accuracy in the news articles he wrote and printed.

Other Hotels and Restaurants in Cheyenne

Dyer's Hotel housed the Tin Restaurant. When Dyers first opened his restaurant, all the dinnerware was made of tin. Thus, its name.

The Tin Restaurant was located on the rough and tumble Eddy Street which was lined with saloons and houses of ill repute. Eddy Street remained active until after the turn of the century when the women of the Pioneer Ladies Club campaigned for the brothels and saloons to be shut down. The name Eddy Street was then changed to Pioneer Street.

Among the many early hotels were the Eagle Hotel and the Rollins House. The Rollins House was across the street from the Ford and Durkee Hotel and was owned by John Quincy Adams Rollins. Besides other ventures, Mr. Rollins was the founder of Rollinsville, Colorado where he allowed no saloons, gambling houses, or dance halls.

The 1870 fire burned two city blocks. It was so hot it peeled the paint from the front of the Rollins House which was across the street from the fire.

In this story, I made the Rollins House one of the nicer places to stay and to eat. The Eagle was less expensive but not as rough as Dyer's Hotel.

Women's Suffrage

On December 10, 1869, Wyoming Territory granted women the right to vote and to hold office. It became the first territory in the United

States to do so and even surpassed the established states. Women voted for the first time in September of the following year.

It was hoped that allowing women to vote would entice the fairer sex to migrate to Wyoming. More women would help balance the gender ratio thus aiding in the growth of families as well the population. It also meant women were now on the list of prospective jurors.

The first women jurors began their service in 1870, less than six months after receiving the right to vote. The women, despite pleas from the court, refused to pose for group pictures and were heavily veiled as they walked back and forth from the jury room to the court room.

As jurors, women heard cases ranging from horse and cattle thefts to illegal branding and murder. In general, they were more likely than men to declare guilt, gave harsher prison sentences, and were less likely to accept self-defense as a justification for murder. In addition, they brought a new tone to the court room. Judges and lawyers kept their feet on the floor, lawyers quit whistling and spitting, attendants and spectators came better dressed, and the room where the jurors met was kept neat and clean.

The new suffrage law also granted women control over their own property and protected them against discrimination as teachers. This led to more employment opportunities for women. However, teaching was still considered a job for single women. Since many of the schools were in rural areas, low pay often continued to be a problem.

Not everyone was pleased with the power women had gained. In 1871, newly elected judges banned women from jury duty. Some legislators even attempted to repeal the new suffrage law. Fortunately, they were not successful.

Tumbleweed Wagons

Tumbleweed wagons were used to pick up prisoners. They were most often seen in the Indian Territory in what is now Oklahoma. They were called tumbleweed wagons because they seemed to aimlessly wander across the prairie. Their tour around the Territory often took two or three months during which the prisoners were chained to the floor of the wagon. At night, when camp was made, the prisoners were chained to a tree. If no tree was available, they were chained to the wagon wheels. Handling wagons of prisoners was a dangerous job, and the men who were called on to do this were among the toughest available.

In addition to the tumbleweed wagons and teamsters who drove them, the entourage often included a cook and cook's wagon. There was also a remuda of horses for the deputies who were present as well as draft animals to pull all the wagons.

The growth of railroads throughout the West brought an end to the need for tumbleweed wagons.

I used a tumbleweed wagon in this book because of the large number of outlaws who needed to be transported. I'm not sure tumbleweed wagons were ever used in the Wyoming Territory, but I thought it was an interesting touch of trivia.

The First Rodeo

The first documented rodeo held in the West was in Deer Trail, Colorado in July of 1869. Two groups of cowboys from neighboring ranches met to settle an argument. Who was best at performing everyday cowboy work such as breaking horses and roping?

Early rodeos were mostly informal exhibition matches with nothing to be gained but pride and maybe a few bets on the side. Of course, there were always those special times when the winner walked away with a larger prize such as a saddle, a horse, or maybe even a date with a pretty girl. If her father owned a big ranch, a cowboy could end up with an even bigger pot.

The Arch

The arch on the cover of this book is a photograph of an arch built by a special young man for his bride. They were married there—minus the tombstones. The dimensions described in this novel are accurate. I changed the description of the wood from Osage orange (a type of hedge tree) to cottonwood. That made it more plausible for tree types found around Cheyenne in the mid-1800s. Of course, finding a cottonwood tree as large as the one pictured would have been a stretch in Laramie County in 1872. Crazy things do happen around water though!

If you are ever driving through North Central Kansas and decide to take a side trip on a country road, you just might see this.

******

Additional novels may be purchased through my website or from your local bookstore. Paper and digital copies are also available through various online suppliers. Of course, they may be requested at your local library as well.

Thank you for choosing to read my novels. May this story be a favorite! Please connect with me on Facebook: Rosie Bosse, Author. Your comments and reviews are welcome as well.

Rosie Bosse, Author
Living and Writing in the Middle of Nowhere
rosiebosse.com

CHAPTER 1

SLIM'S FIRST GATHER

SLIM CRANDALL SLIPPED OUT OF BED WITHOUT awakening his wife. It was May 6 of 1872. Today, he was shipping the first load of his own cattle. Pride and excitement filled the young cowboy as he thought about what the day would hold. He and Sadie had only been married one-and-one-half years. He had built their house with the help of his friends and raised the new barn last fall. Now Sadie was expecting their first child in just five months.

He looked down at his sleeping wife. Her long lashes covered her closed eyes, and she smiled in her sleep. *I don't think she needs to be up so early this mornin'.*

The cattle needed to be at the pens by nine that morning to be loaded onto the train for Denver. His ex-boss and best friend, Lance Rankin, had arranged the sale, and Slim was pleased to sell his cattle for the price Lance had negotiated.

Slim stretched his lean frame to his full six feet, one inch, and scratched his head. His blond curls were wild in the morning, and it always took quite a bit of water to calm them down. He looked back again at Sadie. Her long, dark hair spread over her pillow. Slim could see the outline of her shapely body under the blankets.

"I have the best-lookin' wife in the Wyomin' Territory," he bragged softly to himself, chuckling as he added, "And one of the best cooks too!"

Sadie opened her sleepy eyes. "Do you want breakfast before you leave?" She started to sit up. Slim paused as he pulled on his britches.

"Naw. A piece of that cold chicken from last night 'ill do me jist fine. I cin take the rest of it fer Tiny an' Smiley. But if you'd have dinner ready by eleven this mornin', that would be good. I think we'll all be mighty hungry by then!"

As he leaned over to kiss his wife, Sadie wrapped her arms around him. Slim pretended to push her away and stepped back.

"Woman, don't ya tempt me to climb back into bed. Ya know I got to have those cows gathered an' in the pens first thing this mornin'!"

Sadie smiled up at him, and Slim's heart tingled. He jumped over her and dropped back into bed. As he pulled her close and kissed her, he whispered huskily, "Sadie Gurl, I shore am glad I found ya in Julesburg!"

Sadie snuggled closer to this man she had married such a short time ago. The day Slim had wandered into her laundry area with a dirty shirt and a missing button, she had hardly been able to resist those twinkling blue eyes. When she saw the button he was holding in his hand had been cut off, she tried not to laugh. As she sewed it on, Slim did his best to win her over.

She sighed as she looked up at him. "Slim, you know I was yours from the very first day I met you," she whispered softly.

Slim pulled her closer. He kissed her stomach where their baby was growing.

"Shore, but there was so durn much competition from the rest a those cowboys. I knew I needed to move fast!" he drawled as his blue eyes shone with pleasure.

Suddenly, someone banged on their front door. Men could be heard yelling, and Slim jumped out of bed. He shouted at the door as he headed for the kitchen.

"Get in here, ya durn cayuses! Sadie left chicken fer us to grab fer breakfast. An' don't make so durn much noise or you'll wake 'er up!"

Sadie laughed, and Slim winked at her over his shoulder as he pulled the bedroom door closed.

She quickly slipped her dress on and pinned her hair in a loose bun. Sadie loved to have coffee with the men in the morning, and she wasn't going to miss it just because they were an hour earlier than normal.

As she hurried out of the bedroom, both hired hands pulled off their hats. Sadie kissed each of them on the cheek as she greeted them.

"Good morning, fellows. Ready for some coffee?"

Slim had the coffee warming and was busy shaving. He looked around at Sadie with a crooked smile.

"Now ain't she jist the purtiest thing in the mornin', boys? Eat yur hearts out 'cause Slim won her over with all his charm!"

Sadie eyed the streaks on Slim's face from the shaving soap. His blond curls poked in all directions, and his shirt was buttoned crooked. She laughed out loud as she looked from Slim to the two hands who stood grinning at her.

"Yes, he did, but he worked pretty hard at it back then!"

Slim winked at her, and they all sat down to a breakfast of thick slices of fresh bread and cold chicken. Slim led them in a short grace.

"Lord, we thank ya' fer this here food an' this fine day. Help us to git those cows gathered without much trouble. Keep the folks at this table safe an' take care a my little family while I'm gone. Amen."

Breakfast was quick, and the men were out the door shortly after five. Slim's horse was saddled and tied to the rail in front of the house. As Slim checked the cinch and tied his rope on, he began to whistle, "Oh! Suzanna."

He mounted his horse with a smile. When he saw Sadie standing in the doorway smiling at him, he changed the words to, "Oh, my Sadie, now don't ya cry fer me! I'm a goin' to gather cattle now an' home soon I will be!"

Slim leaned over to kiss his wife and doffed his hat as he rode away, alternating between whistling and singing.

As the three men turned their horses down the narrow lane, Sadie could hear them arguing about who was up first. She smiled as she watched them ride into the first light of the new day.

"How I love that ornery man."

Sadie washed the morning dishes and began to prepare dough for cinnamon rolls. She laughed as she thought of the first time Slim had tasted her cinnamon rolls. His eyes had nearly rolled with delight—he so loved cinnamon rolls.

Martha McCune had taught Sadie how to make the tender treat. The two women worked together nearly every day for several weeks as Martha gave Sadie baking lessons. Sadie also worked on her wedding dress while she was there. Unlike Molly's busy house, she could sew with no little ones underfoot.

Slim was a man who liked to know what took place in his little world. When Sadie left every morning for Martha's, curiosity got the best of him. He followed her one morning to see what she was doing there every day. He wandered into the older woman's house just as the first pan came out of the oven. Both women were concerned Slim might see the dress Sadie was making but Slim only cared about the cinnamon rolls.

"Martha is like a mother to me. I so love being part of this big neighborhood family!" Sadie murmured.

She had the cinnamon rolls raising in the pans by seven-thirty. If she hurried, there would be enough time to do her morning chores and work a little in her garden before the rolls were ready to bake.

The chickens were cackling with excitement over some grasshoppers that had hopped into their pen. The insects were dispensed quickly while all the chickens rushed around searching for more. Sadie opened the pen to let them out for the morning and filled their watering troughs. She hummed softly to herself as she moved from the chickens to her small, neat garden.

Slim had built a high, tight fence to keep the chickens out. Sadie had made scarecrows to keep the rabbits and coons away as well. She was an excellent seamstress, and the scarecrows were more a work of beauty than a shabby straw figure on a stick.

When two rabbits hopped out of the lettuce and squeezed under the fence, Sadie scowled. "I think we need a dog!" she muttered to herself as she chased them with her hoe.

Sadie's rolls were almost done baking when she heard gunshots ring out. She paused to listen. A series of shots close together sounded to the north followed by a single shot. Her body went still as she listened. She shivered but she reminded herself of the wolves. *The men must have seen one of those wolves that has been harassing the cattle.* "I hope they took care of them."

She had seen the mangled bodies of the calves and cows the last wolf pack had attacked, and it brought tears to her eyes. One more shot rang out followed by an eerie silence. Sadie pushed back the panic she felt.

"Stop it, Sadie," she ordered herself. "Stop thinking the worst and trust in the Lord. That is what Slim would tell you if he was here." However, she could not stop the panicky feeling that kept creeping up her spine.

The rolls were out of the oven and cooling when Sadie heard a horse racing up the lane. She grabbed the shotgun she kept by the door and moved quickly to the opening. When she saw Rowdy, Lance's brother and their neighbor to the north, she dropped the gun and rushed into the yard.

CHAPTER 2

DEATH COMES EASY

ROWDY'S FACE WAS TIGHT AND SADIE COULD SEE tears in the corners of his blue eyes. As he jumped off his horse, he grabbed her arm and swung her into his saddle.

"Outlaws attacked Slim and his cowboys. Give Smoke his head, and he will take you back to where they are."

He smacked Smoke on the rump and commanded, "Smoke, Trail!"

As Smoke exploded into a full run, Sadie hung on and began to pray.

"Dear God, please let Slim and all the men be okay." When she stifled a sob, Smoke turned his head and snorted. He went even faster without her urging him.

Soon, she could see the men. Slim was lying in the trail on his back. Smiley was on his face off to one side, and Tiny was nowhere to be seen. Lance was squatted beside Slim. He was talking to him softly as Smoke slid to a stop.

Sadie dropped to the ground and ran to Slim. She could see red bubbles around his mouth and his breathing was labored. His blue eyes were full of pain, but they cleared when Sadie fell to her knees beside him.

"Slim," she whispered, taking his hand.

"Sadie Sweetheart, I ain't a gonna make it," Slim whispered hoarsely as he kissed her hand.

The tears in Sadie's brown eyes spilled out and ran down her cheeks.

"Oh, Slim, don't talk like that," she whispered, her tears turning to sobs.

Lance touched her shoulder. "Tiny went for Doc. He was coming out to our house this morning. Hopefully, they can catch him on the trail to Cheyenne."

Sadie looked up at Lance with questions spilling from her face.

Lance's strong face was pulled tight, and anger was shooting from his hard, blue eyes.

"Rustlers," he spat out. "They came from behind and ambushed Slim and his men. Smiley's dead. Tiny was shot too. They stood over Slim while he was down and shot him in the chest."

As Sadie cried, she kissed Slim's face and pressed his hand to her cheek. "Stay with me, Slim. I need you—*we* need you!"

Slim's blue eyes were having trouble focusing, and his face grimaced in pain. Suddenly, his eyes cleared.

"Sadie, I want ya to move to Cheyenne an' start that sewin' business ya have always wanted to run. Sell the ranch to Rowdy. Our house has more room than his an' that big barn we built last fall will be good fer his hosses."

As Sadie slumped closer to the ground, Slim tried to hold her. He spoke softly.

"Sadie Gurl, I'm a goin' an' there ain't nothin' no one can do to stop me. I guess the Good Lord done decided it was my time."

He paused as he struggled for his breath. His breathing was ragged, and it was with great effort when he spoke again.

"I want ya to stay happy, Sweetheart. Ya—keep yur—heart—open to love. Don't—ya pine yur life—away a missin' me. Ya have—our son to raise—an' he'll need a happy—momma. Shoot, he might be as—ornery as me an' yore—a gonna do lots a—chasin'."

Slim's crooked smile was weak, and he tried to squeeze Sadie's hand. Suddenly, his eyes became large. They moved to focus on something behind his wife.

"By George, there's a gate! Why—I see my folks." He frowned and muttered. "How'd they get here? My—folks' been gone a—fierce long time."

Once again, his eyes rested on Sadie's tear-streaked face. His breathing was rough and he rasped, "Sadie Gurl, yore my one true love. Now—ya remember what I said—an' ya be happy—fer our baby. I'll always love..." Slim's hand went limp in Sadie's as his last breath sighed out of him.

Sadie fell on Slim's chest sobbing while Lance stood by helplessly. The fury inside him made his hands shake.

Doc Williams had just arrived at the Rocking R headquarters when Tiny came racing into the yard. He liked to make house calls just to make sure everyone was doing well. He was tying his horse at the hitching rail when Tiny hollered.

"Slim's been shot and it's bad. Rustlers stole the herd and shot us down!" Every hand in the yard raced to their mounts. All but two riders followed Tiny and Doc out of the yard. The remaining men quickly saddled a horse. They brought it to Molly and helped her load the little ones.

While the first group of men raced back to Slim, Molly and the two riders ran their horses to Old Man McNary's house. When the Old Man heard the riders charge up to his house, he knew there was trouble. Still, he was surprised when Molly asked him to keep Abigail as well as the little boys. He didn't know anything about babies, especially little girls. He started to protest but when he saw the anger on the faces of the riders and the tears in Molly's eyes, he took the baby from Molly's arms without another word. He caught the boys as the riders lifted them down.

"Come on in here, boys! Let's play some checkers and eat cookies while your ma is gone. I might even be able to find some sarsaparilla."

Sammy's eyes lit up. He knew something was wrong because his mommy was crying. Still, if his grandpappy had cookies and that funny-tasting drink, he guessed he would stay awhile.

Paul was three years younger than Sammy's seven years, and he clung to his mother. As his grandpappy lifted him down, Paul started to kick and cry.

Old Man McNary pulled some hard candy out of his pocket. "Why lookie here, Paul. Your grandpappy found some candy. Just maybe there is more in my other pocket!" Paul grinned at him and quit protesting as the riders left the yard in a swirl of hooves.

Lance heard the horses running. He was relieved to see Doc and Tiny leading the pack of Rocking R cowboys racing toward them. Fresh blood from Tiny's arm and shoulder showed through his shirt.

A wagon was racing down the road toward them from the opposite direction. Rowdy was in Slim's wagon and was pushing the team as hard as he dared. When the wagon and the riders met on the road, everyone was silent.

Molly pushed her way through the men and dropped to the ground by Sadie's side. Sadie collapsed against her friend sobbing. As Molly held Sadie and talked softly, tears streamed down Molly's face as well.

Doc Williams quickly dismounted and rushed to Slim's side. A quick examination told him what they all knew. Lance handed him a blanket Rowdy had thrown in the wagon, and Doc wrapped it around Slim's body.

Sadie was shaking with silent sobs. Lance lifted her up from the ground and placed her onto the wagon seat. Five of the riders dropped to the ground and helped lift Slim into the back of the wagon. They picked up Smiley's body and laid him beside Slim. Rowdy covered him with a blanket as well.

Tiny tied Molly's horse and his own to the back of the wagon. He climbed onto the wagon seat beside Sadie while Lance lifted Molly up to sit on the other side of Sadie. Lance barked orders at the men.

"Holley, you follow Tiny back to the ranch. Keep your eyes open for trouble."

His eyes moved to Tiny, and his voice grated with anger. "Tiny, you stay with the women until we get back. If a stranger rides in, don't go out. Shoot him down if he doesn't drop his guns.

"Holley, once the women are situated, you ride over to Badger's. You make sure Martha gets to our place safely."

Lance frowned and added softly, "Doc, you'd better ride into town and get Josie. She needs to know about her brother. Have Rooster hitch a buggy. You can drive her back out here. One of the boys will get you a fresh horse."

Doc's horse was already moving when Lance finished talking. The young doctor's face was grim. He wasn't looking forward to telling his fiancé that her only brother had been killed.

CHAPTER 3

ROUND 'EM UP!

ROWDY LOOKED AT LANCE WITHOUT TALKING. HIS brother nodded and Rowdy spurred Smoke toward Badger's.

One of the men handed Lance the reins to his mustang, and the Rocking R riders left in a rush of dust. Not a man in their group spoke as they raced down the trail.

Joe moved up to ride beside Lance. He glanced sideways several times and finally spoke quietly, "Boss, let's slow down. I can't trail a racin' down the road like this. I want to make sure they don't turn off an' send us on a goose chase."

Lance reluctantly pulled his mustang to a halt as Joe searched for the trail.

Joe followed their back trail until he found where the herd split. Two riders had stayed on the road with about thirty head while the larger group of cattle and four more riders had turned off into the hills toward Badger's ranch.

Lance turned his horse and grated out, "Boys, these men are killers. Don't give them any quarter. I would like to see them hung, but don't put yourself in danger. Shoot first and ask questions later."

As the group of men separated, Joe and a rider name George Spurlach moved to the heads of each of the two groups to trail the cattle. Spur, as the men called Spurlach, was a Cajun rider from down around New Orleans, and he was almost as good a tracker as Joe. Suddenly, Spur pulled up.

"Boys, they're peeling off cattle. There are only about fifteen head in front of us now. I think we need to spread out on the sides. We have to find where those cows were pushed when they separated from the main herd here on the road."

As the men moved quietly off the road to search, one rider whistled softly. The cattle were being pushed off to the side where other outlaws were picking them up. Those men were moving the herd down the hill toward a little spread not far ahead.

Pounding hooves could be heard as horses raced up behind Lance's riders. The cowboys scattered to the brush as Rowdy and Badger came into view. The men moved back out onto the road, and a plan was formed.

Badger's old eyes glistened, and his lips twitched. He stepped down off Mule, removed the saddle and bridle, and stashed them in the brush. Taking Mule's head between his hands, he talked softly and gestured toward the small spread down the hill.

Mule snorted and slowly began to walk toward the ranch. Badger gave them all an evil grin.

"Jist foller 'im, boys. Keep that that mule in yur eyeballs an' don't shoot 'im when it comes time ta fire!"

The cowboys tied their horses in the brush as they moved down the draw. They spread out and slowly worked their way closer to the small ranch below. Soon, a quiet line of cowboys was strung out around the brushy hill. Mule led the way. He would graze and then snort. As he ambled closer, he began to bray. Badger's sharp blue eyes glittered, and he laughed evilly.

One rustler came out of the house and walked slowly toward Mule. The large mule was as meek as could be, allowing the man to touch his head.

Spur had heard stories about Mule. His big, black mustache twitched, and the hair rose on his neck as he watched the outlaws. They were obviously unaware they were leading a killer mule right into their camp.

Other riders began to appear in the outlaw camp. Two had been in the bunk house while three were with the cattle. Badger held up six fingers. Badger and four of the Rocking R cowboys moved to the left while Rowdy the other four men to the right.

Mules were a desired commodity around Cheyenne in 1872, and the outlaws thought it was their good luck to have found one running loose. One of them snorted. "Heck, boys. We have us a mule an' we didn't even have to steal 'im!"

As the outlaws gathered around to inspect Mule, the Rocking R riders stepped out with guns pointed and ready. Rowdy pushed ahead and growled, "Drop 'em, boys. I guarandangtee you don't want to see that mule in action."

The outlaws looked surprised, but two of them went for their guns. Badger whistled and Mule went into action. As he whirled and kicked, men went flying. Those who were not caught in his teeth or by his feet ran, dropping their guns as they fled. Badger whistled again, and Mule walked back to his owner as meek as a puppy. One outlaw had been stomped to death and three more were injured. The rest were spread as far from Mule as they could push, their eyes wide with terror.

The Rocking R riders pushed forward, moving the captured outlaws into a tight circle. Mule stretched his neck forward, wobbled his lips at them and snapped his teeth.

One outlaw cried, "'Sakes Almighty, fellers! Keep that mule away from us! He's a killer for sure!"

Badger gave the man his deadly smile. "Shore he is. Ever been ta Manhattan down Kansas way?"

The man's face went white. "That's the mule what killed Lumpy?"

Badger stared hard at the man before he answered coldly, "Lumpy be jist one a the men Mule kilt. Mule's a notional feller an' he don't tolerate bad behavior. Now I suggest you'ins don't do nothin' ta make 'im think he needs ta straighten ya out."

The angry old man stepped back to address the tight group of outlaws. "Now, boys—here's the deal. You'ins stoled some cattle from a friend a ours an' left 'im a layin' on the road, a dyin'. Now some a these here boys rode with that man. In fact, that boy be their pard an' their foreman fer a time not ta mention a friend ta ever'one here. Ya shot 'im down like a dog, an' his hired hand as well. The hired hand's name was Smiley an' ever'body here liked that boy. Ya worthless coyotes kilt both of 'em, an' ya went an shot another rider jist so's you cin make off with some cows that warn't even yurs.

"Now cattle rustlin' be a hangin' offence in this here territory an' killin' fer sure is too. We're thinkin' 'bout stringin' ya boys up. The law is a mighty long ways from here, an' we ain't sure we want ta waste our time takin' ya in. Now, I want the feller what stood over Slim an' shot 'im in the chest. Shot 'im whilst he were a layin' on this here trail...an' Slim bein' helpless an' all."

None of the outlaws said anything, but two of them slid their eyes toward one of the injured outlaws. He was a slab-faced man who went by the name of Stone Reed.

Reed looked around the group and sneered. "Relax, fellas. These men ain't gonna hang us. We'll get us a trial in Cheyenne. These here fellas ain't got no right to do no hangin'."

The Rocking R cowboys were quiet, but their faces were hard. Several of them had their ropes out and ready. The moved closer to the clustered outlaws.

Rowdy spoke softly, "Tie 'em up, boys. Let's let the law handle this. We have some riding to do, and we don't want them getting away."

Several of the hands moved forward to tie the outlaws when a man beside Stone cursed and went for his gun.

Badger swept up his buffalo gun and fired. The man flew backwards and dropped on the ground several feet behind where he had stood.

The old man looked around at the remaining outlaws. "Any of ya other sidewinders want ta try that? Ol' Betsy here," he drawled as he patted his gun, "is jist achin' ta be more involved. Make our job a whole lot simpler if'n we cin jist drop ya here."

The remaining four outlaws were quiet as the Rocking R riders bound their hands and tied them to their horses. Gunshots broke the silence, and the riders stared toward the direction that Lance's group had trailed. Badger chuckled evilly as he looked at the outlaws.

"Looks like yur gang jist lost a few more members," he commented as he eyed them coldly.

The outlaws studied Badger, and they did not like what they saw. The old man was small and wiry. It was hard to tell how exactly how old he was although he was obviously the oldest one present. His small eyes were bright and alive. Those eyes did not miss a thing, and right now, they were as hard and dangerous as the big gun he carried.

CHAPTER 4

Bring the Tumbleweed Wagon!

WHILE BADGER GUARDED THE OUTLAWS, THE REST of the Rocking R riders mounted their horses and began to gather the cattle that were grazing or penned around the shack. The buildings were checked to make sure no outlaws had been missed.

Besides Slim's thirty head, there were more cattle wearing at least three other brands. The cowboys gathered the nearly two hundred head quickly and started them back up the trail towards the Rocking R.

Soon, they were joined on the road with Lance's group. Those riders had the rest of Slim's cattle plus two more outlaws who were tied to their horses. Lance sent Spur on ahead to open the pens and get things ready for the nearly three hundred head of cattle they would be trailing to the ranch.

"Spur, when you finish," Lance growled, "you ride into Cheyenne and get the marshal. You tell him if he doesn't send a tumbleweed wagon out to pick up these boys, we are going to hang them ourselves. They are rustlers and murderers, and presently, my common sense is a little clouded with emotion."

Lance pushed the two outlaws into the group Badger was herding, and Mule snapped at one who rode too close. The outlaw jerked his arm away with a cry as a piece of his shirt stayed in Mule's mouth.

"Watch yer step, ya sidewinder," Badger growled at him. "Mule here is feelin' the need ta chaw on somebody!"

As the riders trailed the cattle into Lance's pens, Tiny came out of the house. His friendly face was drawn down with anger and sadness. Tiny was a big man, and while he was usually gentle and soft-spoken, a deep anger was raging in him over the loss of his friends. The sawed-off shotgun he was carrying was casually pointed at the group of outlaws.

"You boys kilt two good men jist to steal eighty head a cows. You're a bunch of no-good, thievin' killers an' I'm tempted to jist cut loose on ya. Do ya even care that Slim was a goin' to be a daddy in a few months? Ya left Sadie a widow an' a little bitty ol' baby with no daddy." Tears were leaking out of Tiny's eyes as he spit those words at the outlaws. He lifted the shotgun, and Rowdy dropped quickly to the ground.

"Not like this, Tiny," he insisted quietly. "You shoot that scattergun at this range and you could hurt some of our boys too." He gently pushed the muzzle of the gun down.

Tiny's face crumpled in tears. "My best pards! They kilt both my best pards!"

Rowdy put his arm around Tiny's shoulders and lifted the shotgun gently from the angry cowboy's shaking hands. As he led Tiny to the bunk house, several of the Rocking R riders followed.

Lance knew tempers and emotions were raw. He decided to lock the outlaws up where they would not be seen.

"Get those renegades off their horses and throw them in the smoke-house. Make sure those ropes are tight. I want them uncomfortable."

The outlaws were jerked off their horses and shoved toward the smoke house. Badger slipped off Mule and looped the reins over the saddle horn. Several of outlaws started to protest the harsh treatment, and Mule charged them.

The outlaws screamed and tried to run as the mule raced behind them. He reached his head out with his mouth open. Even the Rocking R cowboys were shocked by the mule's actions and backed quickly out of his way. As the last outlaw fell through the door, Mule started to follow. Badger whistled.

Martha appeared in the doorway of the house, and Mule's head came up quickly. He brayed and raced toward the house, scattering men as he charged toward Martha. She pulled an apple out of her apron pocket and talked softly to the big mule while he nuzzled her neck.

Badger laughed and winked at the shocked men. "Mule's notional. He took ta my Martha right off, an' I knowed she were the woman fer me!" Martha smiled at Badger, but he could see the tear stains on her face and the redness around her eyes.

Once again, Badger's eyes grew hard. He loved his Martha, and he loved little Sadie. He looked around at the angry riders and winked. "Say, boys. I have an idee. Let's untie those fellers an' leave the door open. We'uns cin all jist go on 'bout our business. If'n they try to 'scape, Mule cin run 'em down!" Protests could be heard from inside the smokehouse while loud agreements came from the outside.

Two riders went in and cut off the ropes. The smokehouse door was propped open, and Mule planted himself in the doorway.

Badger said a few words to his mule that no one could hear before he hopped onto the porch and took Martha's arm. As they walked into the house, Mule took a step into the smokehouse. The men inside began to holler.

Tiny came out of the bunkhouse and shouted at them. "Shut up or I'll whack 'im so he goes on in!"

The smokehouse became totally quiet, and the Rocking R riders stood around in small groups waiting for orders.

Lance handed Joe a note. "Take five men and trail these cattle on into Cheyenne. Pin them down by the railroad tracks. Sort Slim's out and pen them by brand.

"You send this note in a telegram and wait there for a response. We might be able to ship Slim's cattle yet today." He paused and added, "Tell the deputy what brands you have. Maybe he can track down the owners.

"When you finish, get on back here. I don't want any trouble in town today."

Joe made sure all the cattle were watered. The six riders quickly pushed the cattle out of the pens and started them up the road toward Cheyenne.

When Lance entered the kitchen, Molly looked up at him. Her huge blue eyes were red from crying. Martha and she were fixing a meal, but their hearts weren't in it. Lance reached for Molly, and she fell against him sobbing. Her red-gold hair hung in a long braid down her back, and her face was streaked from crying.

Lance held his wife tightly. He looked around the room before he asked softly, "Where's Sadie?"

"She cried until she was worn out. She is asleep in your bedroom." Martha's voice was quiet as she added, "We need to prepare Slim and Smiley for burying. Maybe someone could go back to Slim's and get him some clean clothes?"

Rowdy stepped inside the kitchen and leaned against the open door. He was three years younger than Lance and could have been his twin. He cursed under his breath. The entire situation was a powder keg. If the marshal didn't arrive soon, the outlaws would be hanged.

Sammy and Paul were with their Grandpa McNary. Rowdy knew he would keep them there as long as he could. Abigail, born a little over a year ago, was asleep in her crib. Rowdy nodded at Lance.

"I can do that. Beth will be wondering where I am so I can stop at Slim's on the way home." Rowdy backed out of the doorway and led Smoke away from the hitching rail. Holley eased over to see what the plan was.

"Try to keep everyone calm. I am going home for a bit. I will pick up some clean clothes for Slim when I go by." Rowdy paused and added quietly, "You might want to do the same for Smiley. No good man should have a bullet hole in his shirt when he's buried."

Holley agreed and Rowdy pushed Smoke to a cantor as he left the yard.

As Slim's house came into view, anger came over Rowdy in deep waves. Slim had worked so hard on that house to make a home for Sadie. Smiley and Tiny had been there through the entire building process. Now Slim and Smiley were both dead because some men wanted cattle that were not theirs.

The chickens were clucking contentedly and were close to the pen. Rowdy pushed them in and closed the gate. He gathered the eggs and took them to the house. He lifted the shotgun from where it had been dropped on the floor and stood it beside the door. As he looked around the kitchen, he saw Sadie's cinnamon rolls on the table, freshly made that morning.

Rowdy cursed under his breath. *Life is darned unpredictable. Slim's death was so unnecessary and Smiley's too.*

Both Slim and Smiley had been shot from behind.

"I think they stole those cattle because they were there—I don't think that theft was even planned," Rowdy muttered to himself.

As he studied Sadie's kitchen, Rowdy debated what to do with the cinnamon rolls. He finally rolled them up in a towel and shoved them into his saddle bags. "Beth and I can come down and clean up here in a few days," he growled as he looked around.

Sadie had been making clothes for the baby and little garments were folded everywhere. Rowdy frowned as he stacked them in Sadie's sewing room.

"I'll stack these together. It might be easier for Sadie to find things when she comes back."

Rowdy found a new blue shirt and a black vest tucked back in Slim and Sadie's closet. He did not know Sadie had just made them. Clothes were not something Rowdy knew a lot about.

"I guess these would be Slim's," he muttered as he studied them. He held the shirt up to his own body and it was way too small. "Well, Slim is smaller than me. Surely it's his since it was in their closet."

Rowdy also did not know Doc Williams was going to be marrying Slim's sister, Josie, in just a few months. Rowdy's wife, Beth, was Doc's sister and he hadn't told her yet. Sadie had made the shirt and vest for Slim to wear to the wedding since he would be giving his sister away. She had Slim try on the shirt the night before to make sure it fit, and he preened like a peacock. They were both laughing by the time he finished prancing around the house in his new shirt, fancy boots, and no pants.

Had Rowdy known any of that, he probably would have chosen a different shirt. He didn't know much about clothes, but he did know about sad hearts and raw emotions. Rowdy was a tough man on the outside and he worked hard to hide his heart. Beth had unwrapped his heart and showed him true love.

Carefully, Rowdy rolled up the shirt and vest along with a clean pair of britches. He left Slim's fancy boots in the closet. He wasn't sure if Slim wanted to be buried with his boots on or not, but it seemed like a terrible waste to bury new boots.

Beth smiled at Rowdy as he walked in the door to their house. She stopped stirring as she looked at him again. She pointed toward Rudy and Maribelle.

"Rudy, you put up Smoke and, Mari, you help to rub him down. Your father has had a hard day."

Rowdy did not usually have the kids help him with Smoke as that was his time to talk to his horse about the day. They were delighted to be able to brush Smoke by themselves. They were arguing about who would use the brush and who would use the currycomb as they ran out of the house.

CHAPTER 5

WHAT CAN WE DO?

BETH'S PRETTY FACE WAS FULL OF CONCERN AS ROWDY slumped into a chair and dropped his saddle bags on the floor. He looked up at her. The pain in his heart showed in his eyes. "Slim is dead. Rustlers shot him and Smiley. Sadie is a wreck, and the Rocking R is a powder keg."

"Oh, Rowdy! What can we do?" Beth asked as she covered her face with her hands.

He frowned. "I'm not sure. We need to be here to do chores—we have that milk cow, you know—plus the chickens. Sadie has chickens too. Maybe we should put them all together. It will be hard to do chores at both places."

Beth slid onto his lap. "Well, the cow is easy. She calved last night so we don't have to milk her for a while. Besides, Hank is here. Since we don't have to milk, he could do the chores here and at Sadie's as well."

Rowdy looked down at his wife's earnest face. He squeezed her tightly. "You always see the bright side of everything, Beth." He kissed her cheek and whispered, "You make my heart happy."

Beth wrapped her arms tightly around Rowdy's neck and closed her eyes. "Poor Sadie," she whispered. "I don't know what I would do if you didn't come home." Beth's pretty eyes filled with tears and her lips quivered.

Rowdy thought about that. He didn't know what he would do either if something happened to Beth. He kissed his wife again. "Let's load up and get down to Lance's. I'll talk to Hank. He should be fine here for a few days."

Hank had been working for them for a little over a year. Rowdy had been his sergeant in the War Between the States and was furious when Hank had been caught up in a rustling ring. Rowdy had helped him out. Now Hank was their hired hand.

Rowdy paused and added quietly, "I really feel like I need to be there. Lance is so angry. I'm afraid that there could be a lynching. I know it's justified but I don't want the boys to do something they'll regret." Rowdy slowly stood, lifting Beth as he did. "Wagon or horses? I know Smoke is tired, but he will have a fit if I leave him."

Beth's face brightened. "Let's take the horses. I haven't had Sister out for a while, and it will be a beautiful day for a ride.

"Rudy has totally claimed the horse you let him ride. He calls it Kansas. Oh, and he brought Waldo in today to show me his leg. That mule was running and bucking with no limp at all!"

Rowdy was quiet. Waldo was Rudy's pet mule. It had broken its leg in the wagon accident that killed Rudy and Maribelle's parents almost two years ago. Rowdy was going to put the mule down. However, Rudy was so heart-broken that Beth begged him to give it a chance. Rowdy knew leg injuries on mules and horses were usually a death sentence. In fact, Doc told them Waldo had a complete fracture of the long leg bone, and that rarely healed well. Still, Rowdy gave in.

"I'll be darned!" he exclaimed. "I sure would never have ever guessed that mule would pull through, let alone heal without a limp."

Looking down at the saddle bags, he remembered the cinnamon rolls. As he pulled them out, Beth's eyes filled with tears again. They decided not to take them to Lance's. They both thought it would be too painful for Sadie.

"I can clean her kitchen while you show Hank what he needs to do for chores," Beth offered. "In fact, I'm not sure he has ever been to their house, so he needs to go along anyway."

Maribelle and Rudy were excited. Rudy even offered to let Maribelle ride with him since he now had his own horse. Even though they argued, Maribelle adored her big brother.

As they rode cross country to Slim's ranch, Rudy asked, "Are we going to a party? Is it going to be at Slim's house?" As Maribelle joined in the questioning, Rowdy stopped his horse and looked at both children intently. He pondered how to tell them about Slim.

Rudy and Maribelle both knew Sadie and Slim well. They were not only neighbors but were also part of the Rankins' small community of friends. The children loved to go to the Crandall's house. Slim was like an ornery uncle to them, and Sadie always made them some kind of sweet treats. Maribelle especially was excited that Sadie was going to have a baby.

"Kids, Slim was killed by some cattle rustlers. We are going over to your Uncle Lance's to see what we can do to help out. That's what you do when friends have hardships—you help. First, we are going to stop at Slim's and do their chores while Beth cleans up Sadie's kitchen. Then, we are going to ride on to the Rocking R and see what else we can do there." He paused and tears tried to squeeze their way out of his eyes.

"Slim was a fine man and a good friend to me when I needed one. Besides, Sadie and Slim are like brother and sister to your Uncle Lance. That makes them extra important to all of us." He tapped his reins on Smokes neck and added quietly, "Sometimes, it isn't so much what you say as what you do when folks are sad."

Rudy thought about that. *Rowdy is a smart man. I want to be like him when I grow up. He knew how to make us feel better when Ma and Pa died. Now he is helping someone else.* He watched as Beth moved her horse closer to Rowdy's and how she touched his arm. *Ma and Pa loved each other but they never really showed it.*

"I like it when Rowdy and Beth hug on each other," he whispered to himself. Mari was little. She had only been three when their parents died. She called Rowdy and Beth, Papa and Mama, but Rudy just called them Rowdy and Beth. They didn't seem to mind so that was that.

Slim and Sadie's stone house looked quiet and lonely when they rode into the yard. Sadie's little garden was just starting to produce. Rowdy had the kids pick the radishes and a little lettuce while he took Hank to the barn to look after the horses. Once they were done, they hauled buckets of water from the horse tank for Rudy to pour on the garden. Beth hurried into the kitchen to clean things up. She could see where Sadie had dropped the tea towel on the floor. Beth's eyes filled with tears and her breath caught in her throat.

"Oh, Sadie. I wish I could help you handle this," Beth whispered as she began to wash pans and scrub Sadie's workspace. Once everything was cleaned and put away, she went into Slim and Sadie's bedroom. "She might need a change of clothes," Beth stated softly as she looked around the tidy room.

Beth knew Slim well enough to know he would not want Sadie to wear black. Besides, Sadie did not own anything black. Beth chose a soft blue dress and a shawl. Early May around Cheyenne was still chilly, especially once the sun went down.

Beth spotted a nearly finished dress hanging in Sadie's sewing room. She knew instantly who it was for. *Reub and Josie are getting married,* she thought in surprise. As she touched the dress, her face lit up with joy. *Oh, I am so happy for them!*

She paused and a slight frown creased her face. *But why didn't they tell us?* Her frown turned to a smile as she remembered they were to have dinner with Reub and Josie after church on Sunday. "I am sure Reub was planning to tell us then!" she whispered.

Beth closed the door softly to Sadie's sewing room and folded Sadie's clothes into a bag she had found. As she carried them outside, she saw clothes tied behind Rowdy's saddle. She refolded them and added Slim's clothes to the bag as well. Beth was feeding the chickens when Rowdy came from the barn.

"Ready?"

Beth nodded. She had collected eggs in one of Sadie's aprons and she pointed to them. "Although I don't know what to do with these."

CHAPTER 6

A Second Chance

ROWDY TOOK THE EGGS INTO THE HOUSE. HE SET them under a shelf in the kitchen where he had put those he had gathered earlier. He hoped they would stay cooler there. He called for the children and soon they were all back on horseback. Rowdy gave Hank a few instructions and added, "We should be back in a few days."

Hank nodded. "I'll be fine here. I can take care of the chores at both places. You just go and be with your family." Rowdy gripped Hank's hand and smiled down at him. "I sure appreciate all you do for us, Hank." Hank blushed and shrugged as he gripped Rowdy's hand in return. He waved back when the kids smiled and waved at him. A smile creased his face as he watched Rowdy turn Smoke east.

Hank's smile remained on his face as he watched Beth move her horse up beside Smoke. Rowdy took Beth's hand and pressed it to his heart. They held hands as they rode down the lane.

"I sure am glad Rowdy gave me a second chance or there would be a body in that fourth grave down by the railroad tracks."

Life had never been easy for Hank in Tennessee. His pa had run out on their family when he was small, and his ma struggled to keep their family of eight fed. Cash money was scarce in the 1860's. Hank enlisted to fight for the South the day he turned fourteen.

He didn't know much about the reasons for the fighting. He just knew he was hungry, and the army promised pay and good food to anyone who could shoot. His friends had grown up shooting, and most of them signed up as well. They all lied about their ages, but no one seemed to care. Hank and his friends thought it would be a great adventure.

Unfortunately, the Confederacy was strapped for both cash and food. Bullets were sometimes even in short supply. When Hand was assigned to Sergeant Rankin's four-member unit of sharpshooters, he was finally able to eat every day because Sarge let his men make snares and scavenge in the forest. They were often moved from location to location, but he always made sure they had something in their stomachs. Since they couldn't waste their bullets on food, they had to be creative in their hunting methods.

"Shoot, we were just kids. I'm betting Sarge wasn't too happy to be handed a bunch of wet-nosed boys to babysit. We could shoot though and that's all that mattered to the captain." Hank frowned as he thought of the number of men that he had shot. He shook his head. "My old ma would sure have been ashamed of me if she'd known all the bad that I done before I came here. Maybe I'll write her a letter this week. I've been thinkin' on one. I have a little cash money saved up now. I could even send her a little somethin' to help her get by."

Hank scratched his head and slicked his unruly hair back as he tugged on the brim of his old hat. He grabbed a pitchfork and looked back toward the barn. "I just as well muck out those stalls while I'm here. And the next time Beth gives the kids haircuts, I am going to ask her to give me one too." He whistled as he strolled back to the barn.

"It sure feels good to have a place to call home," Hank muttered as he dug his pitchfork into the dirty hay.

CHAPTER 7

LET'S GO CATCH SOME FISH

ROWDY RECOGNIZED ONE OF ROOSTER'S BUGGIES BY the barn. He also recognized Doc's horse. There were several other horses tied to the corral fence he didn't recognize. Rowdy helped Beth down from her horse and lifted Maribelle from Rudy's horse. He watched as Beth hurried toward the house holding Maribelle's hand before he turned toward the barn leading Sister. Smoke followed him without being led.

Rudy led Kansas toward the barn as well. Rowdy rubbed the horses down without talking. Rudy copied his movements as he worked with Kansas. He talked to him softly as he moved around his horse.

When they finished, Rowdy pointed toward the house. "Why don't you carry a couple of buckets of water up to the house. While you're there, ask if the women need you to pack anything else? I am going to go talk to your Uncle Lance."

Lance was standing by the corral and Rowdy walked over to join him. Lance's body was still tense, and his face was tight although he acted calmer than he had that morning. Rowdy put his hand on his brother's shoulder.

Lance turned to look at Rowdy. His eyes glinted with anger.

"So unnecessary," he grated out. "Those rustlers were working up past Laramie. They were on their way back from shipping stolen cattle in Laramie. They just happened to come across Slim and his crew driving that herd. Now two good men are gone." Lance shook his head.

Rowdy squeezed Lance's shoulder but didn't say anything.

Rudy set the water down inside the kitchen door and slipped back outside. He could feel the sadness in the house, and he didn't want to stay. He dropped down on the steps and quietly watched the two brothers.

In his early years, Rudy had never been around any kind of extended family. That changed when he came to live with Beth and Rowdy. Usually, their visits to the Rocking R were filled with laughs and fun. He didn't like the anger and sadness that seemed to have settled over all the adults. It made him think of his little brothers and sister who had died, and he brushed away the tears that tried to sneak out. Rowdy had told him crying didn't mean you were weak. Still, as a twelve-year-old, he didn't intend to cry today.

Soon, Lance and Rowdy were both leaning on the top bar of the corral. Both had their right foot up on the lowest bar and their hands folded across the top. Rudy grinned at them and thought, *Same.* That was what Broken Knife, Lance's Indian brother, called Rowdy, and the name seemed appropriate. Both men were tall with dark curly hair. Both had bright blue eyes that could twinkle with humor or be as hard as glass. Rowdy was a little broader through the shoulders and a little more serious while Lance was just a bit taller. Otherwise, they really did look exactly alike. Rudy stood up and wandered over to stand beside the two men.

Lance turned to the young man. "Sammy has been asking all day if you were coming. Maybe you could take Paul and him exploring or fishing to get them out of the house." Lance tipped Rudy's hat and gave him a quick grin.

Rudy nodded. He turned toward the house. He did not have to search far as Sammy came racing out followed by Paul.

"Want to go fishin', Rudy? Old Man McNary wants to go, and he said we could go with him!"

A shy smile crossed Rudy's face. "I'd love to go fishin.' Do ya have an extra pole?"

Sammy snorted. "We have lots of poles! Come on—we're a burnin' daylight!"

As Rudy followed Sammy to the tack shed, an old man with fierce eyes appeared. He had been tall at one time but was a little bent now. Still, his arms appeared strong, and he carried himself proudly. His face looked severe but when he smiled, it became lots of happy creases. He smiled at Rudy and Rudy smiled back.

Everyone called the old man Old Man McNary. It seemed like a strange name to Rudy, but the old man did not seem to mind.

Old Man McNary reached over and squeezed Sammy's shoulder as he lifted Paul up to give him a hug. "These two fine young men call me Grandpappy sometimes. You're welcome to call me that or Old Man McNary. Either is fine with me," he stated with a wink.

Rudy looked up at the tall old man and his face broke into a huge smile. "I'd like to call you Grandpappy if you don't mind, sir."

Old Man McNary laughed as he handed the boys some hard candy. He reached back into the tack shed for the fishing poles and handed them out. Grabbing his own pole, he pointed toward the creek. "Let's go catch some fish!"

Sammy and Paul raced down the lane toward the fishing hole. Their poles waved in all directions as they ran. Rudy ran behind them. Old Man McNary followed at a slower pace, his fishing pole resting on his shoulder.

CHAPTER 8

LAY THEM DOWN

MOLLY GLANCED UP AS BETH STEPPED THROUGH THE door. She was washing dishes and the tears leaking from her eyes dropped into the soapy water. She hugged anyone who needed it and was glad to shoo the little boys outside.

Beth set the bag of clothes on the floor. Sadie was peeling potatoes. Her face was pale, and she was quiet. She looked up and smiled as Beth hurried in.

"Hello, Beth."

Beth ran to Sadie and pulled her into a hug. Neither of them talked as the quiet tears came. After a while, Beth took a deep breath, stepped back, and looked around at the busy women.

"So, what can I do to help? I'd be glad to help Sadie peel potatoes. That looks like a huge pile!"

Beth's happy face made the rest of the women smile. Soon, a quiet conversation filled the kitchen.

Lance appeared in the doorway, twisting his hat. Molly's heart broke for him. *Lance always mashes the brim of his hat when he is nervous or stressed.* He caught her eye and gave her a tight smile.

"Sadie," Lance asked quietly, "we are ready to find a place to lay Slim down. Do you want him here or would you like him buried on your ranch?"

Sadie's face paled but she answered strongly, "I would like to bury him here if you don't mind. I want him to be surrounded by his friends."

Lance nodded and stepped back outside. He took a deep breath and pointed the group of waiting men toward a grassy plot about four hundred yards from the house. A big cottonwood tree waved its branches and the leaves chattered in conversation.

Two graves were dug on the top of the rise in the shade of the big tree. They would have shade in the afternoon as well as a view. The small hill looked down across the long valley.

Martha and Josie had washed and prepared Smiley's and Slim's bodies for burial. Josie's face was streaked with tears. She was thankful she had moved to Cheyenne and reconnected with her brother. A sob escaped her as she looked down at Slim's once-smiling face, now quiet on the table before them.

They dressed Slim in the clothes Rowdy had packed. The hired hands had found a clean change of clothes for Smiley, and the women dressed him as well. Tiny made two pine boxes. When the other hands asked if they could help, he just shook his head. He carved a pair of boots on Smiley's and a hand with a rope on Slim's. While some of the cowboys dug the graves, the rest made crosses and carved names into them. By five that day, all the preparations had been made.

Beth handed Sadie the bag she had brought with clothes. While Sadie changed, the men laid the bodies of Slim and Smiley in the wooden coffins. They left the covers off until Sadie had a chance to say a private goodbye.

When Sadie saw the shirt Slim was wearing, she covered her mouth. Quiet sobs leaked out. She kissed him and gently touched Smiley's face. She then stood and waited for the men to attach the covers.

They attached the cover to Smiley's coffin first. The men saw the boots and the words underneath it that read, "Here these boots and this man found a home."

The small group stirred and waited for the lid to be applied to Slim's coffin. As Sadie read the cover, she smiled at Tiny and squeezed his arm. Beneath the hand holding a rope, Tiny had carved "These hands loved to rope but Sadie roped his heart for good."

Six men carried each coffin, and the somber group of people followed the bodies of their friends up to the small cemetery. Old Man McNary and Badger met them there with the three boys. Each carried his fishing pole as well as a large string of fish.

Doc Williams read a passage out of the Good Book, and they all recited "The Lord's Prayer." When it was over, Molly led them in singing "Amazing Grace."

As the last note faded away, Badger stepped up. He waved his hand over the open graves.

"Today, we put two durn good men ta rest. They was both our friends an' our pards, an' Slim was little Sadie's true love. We'll miss these here men, but we know they done went on ta work cattle in the sky 'cause the Good Lord shore needs cowboys up there too. We'll miss 'em an' we'll hold our mem'ries tight, an' we'll do our best ta always think of 'em with happy hearts…'cause that's what they'd want us ta do. Amen."

Lance and Doc each took one of Sadie's arms. Lance held his other arm out for Molly and Doc Williams tucked Josie's arm through his. They led the little group down the hill. The Rocking R cowboys stayed behind to fill in the graves of their friends.

Gus, the camp cook, had offered to prepare the meat. The smell of pork chops and steaks sizzling over a fire met the noses of all present.

Josie looked back at the graves as the riders filled them with dirt. She thanked the Lord she had been able to make a home in the Wyoming Territory. She smiled up at Doc, and he pressed her hand. Josie leaned into him and sighed. *Wyoming gave me back my brother. It also gave me this good man who will soon be my husband.*

During the meal that followed, Sadie sat quietly. She smiled but did not talk much to anyone. Martha sat down next to her and pulled her close. Martha was the closest person Sadie had to a mother. She let Martha hug her as she soaked up the older woman's strength and love.

The women had made a large pan of potato salad. Everyone had some of that along with a steak or a pork chop. Molly's garden was just starting to produce. With the radishes and lettuce from Sadie's garden, there was enough for everyone.

Old Man McNary helped the boys clean their fish. They were packed in salt to be cooked the next day. Gus studied the fish and nodded his approval. "You boys make sure you're here for dinner tomorrow, and we'll have these fine fish then." All three of the boys beamed with pride.

Sheriff Boswell arrived with his wagon just as they were eating their meal. Mule was still in the doorway of the smokehouse and refused to move. Badger finally whistled and Mule backed out. However, when the outlaws started to ease out, Mule charged them again. Martha appeared. Once again, she called to him. Mule slowly turned and followed her meekly to the kitchen door where she fed him an apple. The outlaws practically ran to the tumbleweed wagon, pushing over each other to climb in.

The Rocking R riders were angry. Most of them thought the outlaws should have been hung already.

Tiny promised loudly, "If those boys get off, I'll hunt 'em down my own self. I'll see to it justice is done." The other riders were silent but most of them felt the same way.

"You be in town in two days to testify, Tiny," Sheriff Boswell ordered grimly. Tiny stared at him silently, but Lance nodded.

"We will *all* be there on Wednesday. You said the trial is at one that afternoon. We'll be early."

Everyone watched as the sheriff drove the wagon out of the yard. Rowdy let out his breath.

"I'm glad they are gone," he stated with relief as he picked up his plate again. His food was cold, but he didn't care. He was pleased the outlaws were no longer there *and* that the riders had controlled their anger long enough for the sheriff to arrive.

When the meal was over, Sadie and Josie chose to go home with Martha and Badger. Rowdy and Beth took the boys' room. Rudy and the little boys had the option of staying with their Grandpappy McNary or sleeping in the barn. They chose the barn. They thought it sounded like a great adventure.

Sadie was quiet on the trip to the McCune's ranch. Josie was tired as well so there was little talking. Martha clucked over both young women like a mother hen and had them bedded down quickly once they arrived.

As Badger drank his evening cup of coffee, Martha commented softly, "I don't think Sadie plans to stay on the ranch. Otherwise, she would have buried Slim there."

Badger was quiet and Martha continued, "Maybe it's time for us to help our girl get her sewing business started in Cheyenne. She is going to need an income with the baby coming. That might work well for her now." She paused and waited for Badger's reply.

He rubbed his chin and asked Martha with a twinkle in his wise eyes, "Do ya want ta move ta Cheyenne or jist git a second house there?"

Martha beamed at this man she had married just four short years ago. "Why, I think I would like to live in Cheyenne through the winter and here when it's nice. Maybe a second house would be good." She added softly, "Of course, we need to get Sadie set up right away so that means finding something soon. Maybe we could even rent it to her until she is ready to buy—she might not want to make any quick decisions."

Badger stood up and took Martha's hand. He proceeded to dance her around the kitchen as he softly whistled "Buffalo Gals, Won't You

Come Out Tonight." Soon, he was singing it in her ear, trying not to be too loud, and they were both laughing.

Martha squeezed him tight, and Badger kissed her cheek as he winked at her. He whispered in her ear, "Oh, my Martha! Mule shore did know what he was a doin' when he done choosed you'ins!"

Martha smiled contentedly. Hand in hand, they retired for the night.

CHAPTER 9

So Much Family

MARTHA AND BADGER WERE UP EARLY. BADGER wanted to work with his mules while it was cool, and Martha wanted to fix the girls a big breakfast. She finally heard them stirring around seven-thirty. She knocked on their bedroom door and cracked it open. Her friendly face was beaming when she peeked in.

"Good morning, ladies! Would you like breakfast in bed or will you be joining us in the kitchen?"

Sadie and Josie hurried to dress while Martha rang the dinner bell.

Badger was in the house quickly, washed and sitting at the table when they came out. Both young women looked much better after a good night's rest. Martha knew it would be a long, healing road for Sadie. She wanted her to know that Badger and she would be there to help in any way they could.

Sadie was quiet at breakfast. She abruptly looked up. She cleared her throat and spoke determinedly.

"Martha, Badger—there is something I want to discuss with you." She paused as everyone looked at her. She took a deep breath and continued, "Slim told me to sell the ranch—to sell it to Rowdy. He said

I needed to move to Cheyenne and start that sewing business I have always wanted." Sadie paused again, and her voice caught.

"I love our ranch, but my heart is not there without Slim." Sadie's brown eyes filled with tears. Slim had often told her that her eyes were like chocolate, and they just made him melt. As she thought of that, more tears filled her eyes.

She took a ragged breath. "He said our house is bigger than the one Rowdy lives in now, and the barn would be good for his horse business. We already have corrals and a bunkhouse. He told me to sell it to Rowdy and to—" Sadie's voice caught as she finished, "to not pine away and be sad. He said our baby will need a happy mother, especially if he is as ornery as his daddy." Sadie smiled and sobbed at the same time, and Martha put her hand over Sadie's.

"Why, Sadie, Badger and I were just talking about a store in Cheyenne. We have lots of families around now, and there is a need for the quality of sewing you do. Having a shop and a home in town would be very handy for measuring and fitting your customers."

Sadie nodded slowly. "Do you think I could work out of my home? I'm not sure I'm ready to take on a shop."

Josie interjected, "Sadie, I think you can stay as busy as you want wherever you decide to work. People are amazed by your creations. Just look at my wedding dress!" As Badger grinned at her, Josie blushed.

"Reuben wanted to me to wait to tell everyone until he told Beth. He just is taking so long. I'm so excited I want to tell everyone now!"

Martha laughed. "Oh, we figured this day would come when Doc picked you up at the train station. In fact, I don't think anyone will be surprised, especially not Beth and Rowdy."

Martha laughed again and Sadie smiled.

Sadie knew Slim was delighted his little sister was going to stay in Cheyenne, as well as marry Doctor Reuben Williams, one of the surgeons in Cheyenne.

Martha squeezed Sadie's hand. "How soon do you want to look for some place to live? You know you can talk to Rowdy and Beth today as they will be staying with Lance and Molly until after dinner."

Sadie looked at Martha quickly. Her face became even paler.

"Do you think it is too soon? I mean, should I go back out and stay at the ranch for a while?"

Badger looked at Sadie with his bright eyes. "What do *you'ins* want ta do? Do ya want ta stay out there fer a time or do you'ins want ta move ahead with movin' on?"

Sadie was quiet as she looked down and twisted her hands nervously. Finally, she looked up.

"Slim is not coming back, and I don't want to live on the ranch without him. My life will never be the same, and there is no point pretending it will be."

Martha looked at Badger. When he nodded slightly, she leaned forward and patted Sadie's hand. "Badger and I were just talking about buying a house in Cheyenne. We are thinking we might want to move to town sometime. Would you be interested in renting from us, or do you want to buy something of your own right away?"

Sadie's eyes showed a spark of excitement. "I want my own place, but if you don't mind, I would like the option to rent from you. I'm not sure I want to look for a house right away. Besides, the ranch might not sell quickly."

Badger laughed and his sharp eyes twinkled. "Yer ranch 'ill sell. Lance is land-hungry. If'n Rowdy don't buy it, Lance 'ill snap it up! Let's jist plan ta go on in ta Cheyenne today an' check out some houses. I've shore 'nuf had my eye on a few of 'em I thought my Martha might like."

Martha beamed at her husband again before she asked, "How about you bring some water in so these girls can bathe before we go to town? I'm sure a bath would feel good!" She looked closely at Sadie.

"Do you want to go by the ranch and get a few things before we leave?"

Sadie shook her head. "No, but I do need to clean my kitchen. I left it in quite a mess. I can pick up a clean dress after I finish cleaning."

Martha squeezed Sadie's hand again. "Rowdy and Beth stopped by your house yesterday. He and the kids, along with Hank, took care of your animals while Beth cleaned your kitchen. I'm guessing she picked up a dress for you as well."

Sadie's soft eyes filled with tears again. "I am going to miss my family out here," she whispered.

Martha pulled the young widow to her feet. "Nonsense. You will always have us as family. Besides, Molly's father lives in town as well as Josie and Doc. You will be surrounded by more family than you can handle, most likely. And come winter, Badger and I will be there as well." Martha's smile was huge. She loved Sadie like her own daughter and was delighted at the thought of being closer to her.

Badger hauled water in, and Martha heated it. Soon, both Sadie and Josie had bathed and were ready for the day. The wagon was hitched and once again, they headed up the trail to the Rocking R.

CHAPTER 10

NEW BEGINNINGS

LANCE HAD HEARD SLIM TELL SADIE TO SELL THE ranch to Rowdy, but he did not say anything to his brother. He wanted that offer to come from Sadie. However, he did tell Molly at breakfast.

She was convinced Sadie was moving to Cheyenne immediately. Lance disagreed. He thought she might stay through the summer. Molly looked at him and rolled her blue eyes. "She is nearly five months along, Lance. She would be living alone, twenty-five miles from town. She is moving to Cheyenne to have her baby."

Lance pulled Molly close as he chuckled. "I guess not all women are able to birth a baby squatting on the floor."

Molly wrapped her arms around Lance. She tried not to think of what life would be like without him. Just the idea of it made her cold.

When Molly shivered, Lance whispered, "I will always watch over you, Molly, just like Slim will keep an eye on Sadie. I know he would have stayed if he could have. Sometimes the Good Lord has other plans though. Just know wherever I am, I will be watching over you."

Molly leaned into Lance and tears filled her eyes. "I don't know how to help Sadie. She is like a sister to me, but I don't know how to help her heal her heart," Molly whispered as tears ran down her face.

Lance wiped her tears with his thumbs and pulled her closer as he sat down. "Molly, you can't save everyone. We will be there for Sadie, but she is going to have to learn to be alone. And remember, she was alone when we met her. She knows how to survive." He looked over Molly's shoulder and added softly, "Besides, she has a very marketable skill here. She will be able to support herself and her baby."

Beth was laughing up at Rowdy as they walked into the kitchen for breakfast. Lance watched his brother. It was easy to see Rowdy adored Beth. Lance winked at him. Rowdy blushed and grinned at his older brother. "So, what's for breakfast? I see you've been distracting your wife too."

Lance laughed and agreed as Molly slipped off his lap and set out the griddle cakes. She knew Rowdy loved to eat so she had made way more than she thought they would need.

The kids were still asleep. Lance heard them digging for worms late in the night, and the conversation inside the barn probably went on even longer.

The two couples were just finishing breakfast when Badger's wagon rolled into the yard. Doc had slept in the bunkhouse with the Rocking R riders. He was just coming up to the house. He stopped by the wagon to help the women down.

Molly whispered to Beth, "When do you think the wedding is?"

Beth laughed. "They haven't said anything to us, but I am guessing soon! We were supposed to stop there for dinner after church on Sunday. Maybe we will hear about it today since we are all together."

Molly and Beth added more plates to the table for the new arrivals.

Martha declined. "I fed everyone before we left."

Badger was never one to turn down good food though, and he ate like he had missed three meals.

Josie was bubbling with excitement and trying to stay calm. Everyone pretended not to notice.

Finally, she blurted out, "Reuben and I are getting married!" She looked around the room expecting to see surprised faces, but everyone just laughed.

Badger was the first to speak. "See, I done told ya—that there not be news. We'uns knowed that there day were a comin' the first time Doc here picked you'ins up in his fancy buggy—once he figgered out which ol' gurl you was!"

His eyes squinted with humor as he tried to keep his face somber. Everyone laughed as they thought of the joke that had been played on Josie and Doc.

Badger had sent a telegram to Josie before Rowdy's wedding asking her to come. He made it sound like she was needed urgently. The telegram stated the town doc would pick her up. It also said he was old and crotchety. Badger then told Doc that Slim's sister was an old spinster and had no social life. That meant she should be free to stay and help out for a week or two.

Neither description could have been further from the truth. Josie was a small, petite blond with sparking blue eyes like Slim's and curves in all the right places. Doc was tall and good-looking with blond hair and hazel eyes. All the women in Cheyenne considered him quite the catch. However, he wasn't interested in anyone or anything outside his practice—until Josie hired on.

Doc needed to hire someone to replace Beth as his assistant since she was getting married. That meant Josie would only be there temporarily. She was to only stay and fill in a few weeks—but Josie never went back to Texas. Now they were getting married. Of course, that was everyone's plan from the beginning, so no one was surprised.

Sadie smiled as she watched these people tease Doc and Josie. Slim would have been in the middle of it as well had he been there. Her chest tightened as she thought of how she would miss his teasing and his sense of humor. Finally, the table quieted, and Sadie spoke.

"I have something I need to discuss with everyone." She paused and added softly, "I am moving to Cheyenne as soon as I can find a house." She looked at Rowdy.

"Rowdy, Slim told me to sell the ranch to you if you were interested. He said our home was larger than yours plus the barn and corrals would be good for your horse business."

Rowdy and Beth were stunned. Beth started to protest. "But Sadie, you don't have to sell. Someone could rent it and..."

Sadie shook her head. She looked around the table at these people she loved most in the world.

"Our house is full of memories, and I don't want to live there without Slim. It was built with love, and it needs to be home to a noisy, happy family. I can't run the ranch by myself, and I have no desire to do so.

"I do want to sell. I would like to sell immediately. I want to have the option to purchase a house in Cheyenne should one come up for sale that I like."

She looked at Martha and Badger and gave them an appreciative smile. "Martha and Badger are going to help me look at houses today."

The table was quiet. Soon, all eyes moved to Rowdy. He stood and scratched his head. "As long as Beth agrees, I would love to buy your ranch. Like she said though, we could rent for a year to make sure this is what you want to do."

Sadie shook her head. "This is what Slim *told* me to do," she answered softly but firmly as she looked around at the faces of her friends. "I want to sell and sell quickly. I know you will be fair, Rowdy. I have a baby coming in five months, and I would like to be settled as soon as possible. I plan to start a sewing business in Cheyenne and Martha offered to help." She smiled again at Martha who squeezed her hand.

Martha nodded and added, "I know everyone in this room would like to see Sadie happy. This is what she wants to do, and we all need to help her make it happen."

Molly asked gently, "Sadie, would you like us to pack up your house today? Beth and I would be glad to." Beth nodded.

"I would love to help as well." Josie's face was earnest as she looked at her sister-in-law.

Sadie looked around at the faces of her friends and tears filled her eyes. "I am so going to miss this big family," she whispered with a catch in her voice.

Lance walked around the table and pulled Sadie up.

"Sadie," he stated seriously, "you will always be part of this family. We loved you before you were Slim's wife, and we loved you even more when you married him." He added, "Besides, you will always be my little sister!" His mouth lifted in a smile and his eyes crinkled at the corners as he wrapped her up in a bear hug.

When he released her, Sadie's mouth quivered just a little as she looked at the three young women. "I would love for you to start packing my house.

"I want to keep Slim's good hat, his fancy boots, and the red-checked shirt he loved. Give the rest of his clothes to Rudy. He is outgrowing everything and could use some new clothes."

Beth's tender heart was breaking for Sadie. She was almost in tears. Rowdy squeezed her hand and answered quietly, "We would love to give Slim's clothes to Rudy, Sadie. He will be proud to wear them." He walked around the table and hugged Sadie as well.

Soon, all the women surrounded Sadie and pushed her out of the kitchen. Molly was chattering as they went through the bedroom door, "Beth picked up a dress last night and it is pressed. Let's get you changed and ready to step into this next chapter in your life." She whispered, "It will be fun to have another friend in Cheyenne whom we can visit and stay with."

Children's voices and laughter could be heard rushing toward the house. Soon the kitchen door slammed open. Four hungry children raced through the door, all talking at the same time. Rudy was the oldest, but he loved his little cousins. Rowdy caught his eye and smiled at him. Rudy's eyes were shining, and he gave Rowdy a shy smile.

Beth watched them from the bedroom door where she had stopped when she heard the children. She struggled not to cry. *It is so nice to see Rudy happy. He has struggled with the loss of his family—with his role in this new family as well.* "I am so happy he is learning to love us," Beth whispered. She slipped into the bedroom with the rest of the women and closed the door softly.

CHAPTER 11

BADGER'S INVESTMENT

AS BADGER DROVE HIS TEAM NORTH FROM THE Rocking R Ranch, he began to whistle happily. Sadie was quiet, and Martha put her arm around the young woman.

"Tell me, Sadie. Is there something special you are looking for in your new home? I know Slim built you a sewing room, so I am guessing you will want that. Do you want women to come to your house to be fitted for their dresses or would you prefer to do that someplace else?"

Sadie's forehead puckered for a moment. She nodded. "I think it would be easier to have the women come to my house. However, if men were to place shirt orders from me, I would prefer to meet them in one of the stores downtown."

Martha nodded and squeezed her. "You know, I have always wanted my own clothing and fabric shop. Maybe now is the time to get that started."

Badger didn't turn his head or stop whistling, but he grinned between notes and the whistling became louder. Martha looked around Sadie toward her ornery husband as she laughed. "And I am guessing Badger has places in mind for both of us!"

Badger looked over at the two women beside him, one his wife and the other like a daughter. He grinned at both of them, and his bright eyes sparkled.

"I reckon I jist might at that. A feller cin only sit 'round fer so long. Then he has ta be out a makin' a livin' an' hagglin' with folks ta buy 'vestments."

Sadie laughed as she watched the animated way Badger spoke and the way he waved his arms around. She knew neither Badger nor Martha needed to work to make a living. However, both chose to do so. She kissed his grizzled cheek and then kissed Martha's.

"I am so blessed to have you both for my friends, and I am so pleased this little one growing inside me will have such loving grandparents."

Badger cleared his throat loudly and began whistling again although the first several notes were a little off-key. Martha dabbed her eyes and hugged Sadie tightly.

The next mile was quiet. Slowly, Sadie began to relax. Martha and she talked about Sadie's sewing business and Martha's store the rest of the way to Cheyenne. By the time they arrived, Sadie's cheeks were flushed with anticipation.

Badger did have a house in mind for Sadie. It was about two blocks off the main street and close to the downtown businesses. It had a big front yard, and the lot next door came with it. Badger thought the extra lot might work for Sadie's garden or even an area for the little one to play in. Both the yard and the garden lot could be fenced.

The house was two stories. It was well-built and had belonged to a banker who had just moved to take a job in Laramie. There were two bedrooms upstairs and three bedrooms downstairs. One of the downstairs bedrooms had windows on two sides.

Martha pointed out how well the sunny room would work for Sadie's sewing room. The other two bedrooms were adjoining. They would be perfect for Sadie's bedroom and a child's room. The kitchen was bright and airy with more storage than the typical kitchen.

Sadie loved it instantly but was concerned about the cost. "I think it may be above what I can afford to pay though."

Badger shook his head. "That there banker were wantin' ta sell." He winked and grinned. "His wife done bought a new house in Laramie an' he didn't have time ta mess with hagglin'. Now me, I'm a hagglin' man!"

Martha beamed at her husband as he added, "I done bought it last week ta use fer an 'vestment so you'ins don' have ta take it." He grinned. "But the price is right an' it's yurs if'n ya want it! Rent or buy, yur call, Sadie Gurl. Ol' Badger is here ta please!"

Sadie smiled at Badger and Martha. She hugged each of them. "You know I love both of you so much," she whispered. "I love the house! I think I will just rent though until we finalize the sale of the ranch. I'll be more comfortable spending money once I get my business started."

Badger dropped the key to the house into her hand. "Ya make my Martha a new dress an' we'll call that the first month's rent. I saw 'er eyein' some cloth the other day. I done went an' bought it fer 'er so you'ins cin start whenever ya want."

Sadie's eyes filled with tears. As her mouth started to quiver, both Badger and Martha held out their arms. Sadie let them wrap her up in their love. She smiled as she looked over their shoulders.

Thank you, Slim. Thank you for making me part of your family.

CHAPTER 12

A Family Affair

AS SOON AS THE MCCUNES LEFT THE RANCH YARD, the women began to rush around. They wanted to get Sadie's house packed that day if possible. Since there were three of them to help, they knew they could do it quickly. The kids were excited and were in the middle of the women's preparations.

"Now you kids get your breakfast eaten. We are leaving here in just a little bit, and you won't be going with us if your chores aren't done."

Josie was amazed at how Molly could keep the kids organized and fix a lunch at the same time. She laughed as she watched the kids gobble their food down. Packing Sadie's house was going to be a family operation.

Lance and Rowdy headed to the barn to hitch up the wagons and saddle the horses. Slim's wagon was still there. They were going to take both his and Lance's wagon in case they needed two.

Sammy was the first one out the door after breakfast. He was excited to show Rudy his new horse. Unlike his father who didn't name any of his horses, Sammy had named his horse Barleycorn.

Rudy and Paul weren't far behind. Maribelle was the last to finish. She held Abigail's hand as she rushed out of the kitchen.

While the brothers worked together, Rowdy asked Lance, "Do you want to buy that five hundred acres back you gave to Slim and Sadie as a wedding gift? I know it was a nice little piece of pasture."

When Lance glanced up in surprise, Rowdy frowned. "I'm not sure this is a good idea at all. I'm afraid Sadie will regret this someday. After all, what if her baby is a boy and he wants to ranch someday?"

Lance gripped Rowdy's shoulders. "The reason Slim wanted to sell to you was to help you get established with more land. He knew you would be fair to Sadie, and you are proving him right. You are a good brother, Same. I sure am glad you made Cheyenne your home!"

Rowdy blushed and growled a response. Lance punched his shoulder as he laughed.

"Dang, I'm gettin' soft now!" Rowdy growled again as he ducked his head. Lance grinned and the two of them led the horses and teams from the barn.

Doc had hitched his buggy earlier. His saddle horse was tied behind the buggy. He poked his head into the kitchen. "I'm headed back to Cheyenne, Josie. I'll be back tomorrow night to pick you up if no one gives you a ride in."

Josie nodded happily. She waved from the doorway as Doc drove out of the yard. She blushed when the other two women smiled at her.

Molly set a basket of food in one of the wagons and Beth added a jug of root beer. The kids loved the sweet drink, and it would be a great treat for everyone after a hard morning of packing and loading.

Lance and Rowdy started to lift their wives into separate wagons, but the women all wanted to ride together. The men laughed and hopped into the first wagon. The children were all mounted on horseback and were in a hurry to get to where they were going. Lance called for the kids to slow down.

"Don't be running those horses. This is going to be a quiet ride." He looked around at the small group and grinned as he elbowed Rowdy. "Here we are, looking like a parade again." Rowdy laughed and Lance waved his arm as he led the way out of the yard and west toward Slim's ranch.

Molly had rigged a sling around her shoulders so she could drive or ride with Abigail and still keep her hands free. Abigail's dark, curly hair was just visible above the top of the sling and her bright blue eyes watched her mother. When Molly looked down at her, she wiggled and broke into a huge smile. Her little dimples were deep, and her blue eyes shined.

Molly's heart melted. She kissed her baby and the little parade moved down the road to Sadie's house.

CHAPTER 13

REMINISCING

THE MEN STARTED OUTSIDE. THEY DEBATED WHAT TO do with the chickens and finally decided to leave them there. Sadie might want them in town. If not, Rowdy would add them to the list he was buying. Lance wanted to inventory the items in the barn—from the horses and tack to the wagon and tools. He shook his head as he surveyed his friend's possessions.

Rowdy was quiet as he walked around the barn. Slim, Tiny, and Smiley had started the construction of the barn as soon as the house was finished. The rock laid up around the barn's foundation rose almost four feet. The wooden barn was built on top. The barn had a loft already, and Slim had been in the process of sectioning off stalls. Two had been built and the wood for six more was stacked inside the barn.

A trophy saddle sat on a sawhorse in the corner of the barn. Rowdy looked at Lance in surprise. His brother laughed.

"Slim was quite the bronc rider. He heard Deer Trail, Colorado was holding a competition on July 4 in '69. That was the summer after Molly and I married. He took some time off and entered.

"He won and came riding home on this new saddle. He was mighty proud of it." Lance paused as he brushed the dust off the saddle. He added softly, "I think this needs to go with Sadie. She can give it to their little one someday.

"In fact, it should probably go in her house. I'll give it a good rubbing with some tallow when we get back home."

Lance stood by the saddle for a moment. He walked to the front of the barn and looked out the doors as he cursed under his breath.

"Dang, I sure am going to miss him." His voice cracked as he leaned on one of the stalls. "Slim was my first friend when I came to work for Old Man McNary. Some of the fellas were surprised when the Old Man made me foreman four years later. Slim never let it affect our friendship though. He was true blue to the core." Lance paused and chuckled.

"One time, that first winter I was here, he short-sheeted every bed in the bunkhouse except his own. We all came in from a cold day on the range. The fire in the stove had gone out, and the bunk house was cold enough to freeze water. We all jumped into our bunks and pulled the blankets up. They just went on over our heads. All the fellas started hollering and Slim just went to sleep with a satisfied smile on his face—until Tiny dumped a bucket of cold water on him. Then he was colder than we were."

Lance laughed again. His smile slowly faded. He was quiet for a time before he added quietly, "Slim was quite the prankster, but he was as loyal as they came too.

"One time, he rode into Cheyenne in a near-blizzard to get the doc and some medicine for one of the riders who had pneumonia. That rider was Johnny O'Neil. He was just a kid. We called him Jip, and he had only been with us for about three months. The doc was gone, so Slim woke up half the town trying to find medicine. Slim brought that medicine back and sat by Jip all night. Jip didn't make it, but Slim made sure he didn't die alone."

Lance was quiet for a moment. "They just can't make a finer man or better friend than Slim was."

Rowdy remained silent and let his brother talk. He knew Lance needed to release some of the things inside him. *It's hard to always be the strong one. Sometimes, even the tough guys crack a little bit.* His mouth turned up in a wry grin. *I should know, I guess.*

Lance picked up a rope and slapped it against his leg. "We had better get busy. Those women will have that house all packed up, and we won't be done.

"How about we put what you would be willing to buy in one pile and what I would be willing to buy in another? We can make a third pile for what Sadie might want to keep."

The brothers worked well together with lots of good-natured ribbing. Slim liked things neat and anything that could be hung was on a hook on the wall.

Rowdy noticed two of the stalls had been mucked out. He commented quietly, "Hank must have cleaned those stalls out yesterday before he left. I sure am glad I hired that fellow."

Soon, the barn walls and stalls were empty. Rowdy's pile was small, but Lance's pile was quite large with a variety of items. Some of the items Lance had added were purely sentimental while other items were functional.

Rowdy let Lance claim anything he wanted. In fact, Lance could have taken everything as far as his brother was concerned. Slim had been Rowdy's friend, but he was Lance's pard.

Lance tallied the items and the brothers walked outside. Slim had five horses. Rowdy and Lance walked around them and together agreed on the value. Lance studied them a moment longer before he looked over at Rowdy.

"I wonder if Sadie will want to keep any of the horses. Slim usually brought her over in the wagon. I don't know how much she even likes to ride."

Rowdy was quiet as he listened. "Well, it will be Sadie's choice. She sure won't need more than one.

"Besides, she might not want to pay to have even one stabled. She could always rent a mount at the livery if she wanted to ride."

Lance nodded. He added the horses and wagon to the tally sheet.

As the two men walked into the house, they paused and looked around in surprise. Everything that had been in the cabinets and on the walls was now in burlap bags or wooden boxes on the floor. The women were in the bedroom cleaning out the closet. Their conversation was punctuated with laughs and sobs.

Lance shook his head. "This is just a hard job," he muttered as they moved to see what help the women needed.

Molly had laid Sadie's wedding dress on the bed and all three of the women had tears in their eyes when they turned toward the men. "Oh, Lance. We just don't know what to do with some of these things," as she gestured toward a pile of Slim's things.

The men stood there awkwardly for a moment. Finally, Rowdy spoke quietly.

"Put everything personal of Slim's in a box and give it to Sadie. She can sort through it when she feels like it. When it's time, she will appreciate having part of him with her."

Martha had sent several of her trunks over. The women filled one with Sadie's clothes and laid the baby items on top. The partially completed baby clothes and the quilt she had started were put into the second trunk. They wrapped up all Slim's small items and added them along with his hat, fancy boots, red-checked shirt, and belt.

Rowdy and Lance loaded the full trunks into the back of the wagon. They fit the kitchen items in around them.

Josie took her wedding dress down from where it had been hanging and laid it out on the bed. It was nearly done.

Molly studied it. "We can pin that hem tonight and help you stitch it in if you want. Then it will be done, and you won't have to worry Sadie with it."

Josie nodded as she fingered the beautiful dress. "Isn't it lovely?" she asked, her eyes shining with excitement.

The dress was a pale pink taffeta with a gathered waist and full skirt. The sleeves were fitted at the shoulders and were butterflied out in lace from the elbows to the wrist. A large ten-inch ruffle encircled the bottom of the dress. The off-shoulder neckline was scooped.

Sadie had added a small edge of lace around the neckline as well as around the very bottom of the skirt. Black satin ribbon trimmed the waist, the tapered sleeves, and bottom ruffle. Molly nodded her head, and Beth sucked her breath in softly.

"It is beautiful, Josie. You are going to be a lovely bride," she whispered as she hugged her future sister-in-law.

The room became quiet as they all thought about Sadie's and Slim's wedding. The Crandall's hadn't even been married two years, and now Sadie was going to raise their only child alone. All three of the women wiped their eyes as they thought about Slim never meeting his baby.

Both wagons were nearly full when Molly ran back to grab the eggs. The children had checked the garden again for ripe vegetables, and Rudy had watered it.

It was nearly two in the afternoon and everyone was hungry. Lance was grumbling about nothing to eat, and Rowdy's stomach was growling.

Molly laughed as she brought out the basket of food. Rowdy's eyes lit up, and Lance was smiling once again as they sat down to eat a picnic lunch on the ground. Everyone had some root beer as they shared stories about Slim. It was a fine way to finish a hard morning.

CHAPTER 14

ANOTHER RANCH FOR ROWDY

ROWDY WAS QUIET DURING THE MEAL, AND BETH knew something was bothering him. She put down her plate. "Rowdy, Lance said Slim had started stalls in the barn. Can you show those to me?"

Rudy started to volunteer, but Lance winked at him and shook his head slightly. Rudy was confused but he eased back to the ground.

Rowdy led Beth to the barn. He was relieved to have a chance to talk to her alone. He wanted to make sure she was okay with moving.

Beth quickly nodded her head in agreement. "It is a beautiful location, Rowdy, and Slim's house is wonderful. I love our little place on the hill, but this will be perfect for your horse business."

Rowdy nodded his head slowly. "I don't know that we need three houses though," he commented as he studied the barn.

Beth laughed, "Well, maybe we need to hire more help," she giggled.

Rowdy grinned at her and pulled her close. "You will be closer to town here, plus we are only five miles from Lance and Molly. I guess that will make visiting a little easier," he drawled.

Beth stood on her tiptoes and kissed her husband as she whispered, "Rowdy, I would stay with you no matter where you lived." Rowdy wrapped his wife up in a hug. They walked back to their family, Beth's small hand wrapped up in Rowdy's large one.

Molly smiled at them as they sat down, and Lance thumped his brother on the back. "I think I am going to like having you closer, Same!"

Rowdy grinned back and proceeded to eat enough for three men.

Lance shook his head. "I sure am glad I don't have your feed bill, Beth. That man doesn't have a bottom in his stomach at all!" They all laughed, and Rowdy made sure there were no leftovers.

Sadie and the McCunes had returned to the Rocking R from Cheyenne before Lance's group rode into the yard. As the men helped the women down, Badger came out of the house. The women were tired, and Badger helped lead the teams to the barn. The boys followed Lance and Rowdy. They knew they had to take care of their own mounts. Rudy led Mari's as well.

Lance looked at Badger. "Well?"

"Done deal," declared Badger. "Sadie liked the first house we showed 'er. I done bought it last week from a banker who was in a hurry ta get out a Cheyenne, so I got me a good deal fer it. She's a gonna rent from us fer a month or so until she gets onta 'er feet." He added, "Our Sadie be a strong gurl. She's a gonna be okay."

Lance nodded.

Rowdy was silent. The land wasn't discussed but Badger already knew Rowdy was going to buy Slim's spread.

Sadie looked up with a tired smile as the women entered the kitchen followed by Paul, Abigail, and Mari.

Beth smiled brightly and asked, "So does Cheyenne have a new resident?"

Sadie smiled again a little bigger. She answered softly, "Yes, I think I will try to move in tomorrow or the next day, depending on when I finish getting the house packed."

The men had just entered the kitchen and Lance laughed.

"Well, you can move tonight then. These women didn't mess around!"

Sadie's brown eyes were huge. "You packed the entire house this morning?" she asked in surprise.

Beth giggled and answered, "We sure did. Lance and Rowdy cleaned out the barn while we women worked in your house. The wagons are full, and Lance pulled them into the barn."

Sadie's face crumpled and she choked, "I don't know how to thank all of you."

Molly put her arm around Sadie. "That's what family does, Sadie," she murmured softly. "They step up and help with no strings attached. And I will go with you tomorrow to help you set up your new home."

Lance looked at Molly and shook his head. "Good thing we hired Gus to cook. My wife just doesn't stay home to cook for me much anymore." He pretended to complain but with a smile in his eyes.

Molly elbowed him and rolled her eyes. "And you might be eating with the men tonight as well. We have a wedding dress to hem this evening so Josie can take it home with her."

Sadie started to protest but Molly waved her off. "We three can hem it, Sadie. It looks like that is all you have left to do."

"It is. It will be nice to have that done and ready for the wedding." She smiled at her friends. "I am so tired. Thank you," she whispered softly. "You know I love all of you like sisters." The three young women surrounded Sadie as she hugged each of them.

Martha stood. "Sadie, let's go on back to our place. You need to get some rest if you are moving in the morning." She looked at the group of people gathered in the kitchen. "We will be over by eight tomorrow morning, ready to head to Cheyenne." Martha took Sadie's arm and whisked her out the door.

Badger had the team waiting in front of the house.

Lance was amazed. Even though Martha and Badger had only been married four years, they acted like they had been married forty.

"They can just read each other's minds," he muttered to himself as he followed Martha and Sadie outside.

By the time Lance came back inside, the women already had the wedding dress off the hanger and were in the bedroom helping Josie into it.

Rowdy and Lance looked at each other and headed back outside. Lance had the tally sheet, and he grabbed a pencil as they left.

"Let's get a contract written up so you can finalize that purchase. Maybe you can even sign papers after we move Sadie to Cheyenne in the morning."

Rowdy nodded in agreement, and the two men turned toward Old Man McNary's. He called to Rudy as they left, "Keep an eye on your cousins and sister. We'll be back in an hour or so. And no fishing without an adult!"

Rudy nodded and watched as the two men walked up to Old Man McNary's. He would have liked to have gone along. *Next time*, Rudy thought. He wanted to learn all he could about how to run a ranch. *After all, I am twelve years old*, he thought with pride as he headed back to the barn to play in the loft.

CHAPTER 15

THE CONTRACT

OLD MAN MCNARY HAD A MIND FOR NUMBERS AND legal documents. He was more than happy to help Rowdy write up the contract. Lance knew how much land Slim owned. He had all the legal descriptions written down. He showed the other two men on his rough map where the boundaries were.

Slim and Sadie had fifteen hundred acres. They had filed on their homestead and that was six hundred forty acres. Then they bought another three hundred sixty acres. With the five hundred acres Lance had given them as a wedding gift, they had fifteen hundred acres, including the land the buildings were on.

Old Man McNary pointed with his pencil, "That land varies from $10 to $11 per acre. Some of it is good grass and other parts won't produce much. You do have good water on the home place."

By the time they added in the improvements, it figured out to $12 per acre. Rowdy looked at Lance. "Are you sure you don't want that five hundred acres back?"

Lance grinned. "Of course I want it back, but Molly gave me strict orders not to buy. And I don't like it when my wife is mad!"

All three men laughed, and Old Man McNary added everything up.

"$18,000 for the land and $25 for the miscellaneous items you bought out of the barn. Sound all right?" he asked.

Rowdy nodded. It would strap him a little but with the government contract for horses he had acquired, he would be able to keep money coming in.

Lance's bill was $60. Lance studied the paper. "Molly said not to go over $50, but I think she will be okay with this. That woman keeps me on a short rope when it comes to money," he stated with a slight blush as he looked at the two other men.

Old Man McNary laughed and Rowdy snorted.

"She needs to. You would buy up the entire country if you could!"

Lance pretended to look shocked but he chuckled. "Sure would!" he agreed.

Rowdy thanked the Old Man, and they turned to walk back to Lance's house.

Old Man McNary watched the brothers with a smile on his face. His fierce eyes became soft when the two laughing men shoved each other as they walked.

"I sure am glad that hungry boy rode in here seven years ago. I have two sons now, two little gals I love like my own, and even grandkids."

He had just turned to go inside when Lance hollered, "Why don't you come down for supper? In fact, come down now, and we'll take the kids fishing for a little bit."

The Old Man nodded and waved. He shut his door and headed down the trail to where Lance and Rowdy were waiting for him.

As Lance went into the house to tell Molly they were taking the kids, Abigail toddled over to him with a big smile on her face. Lance lifted her up.

"How are you, Sweetheart? Do you have a kiss for your daddy?" Abigail grabbed Lance around the neck and gave him a sticky kiss. He laughed.

"We are taking the kids fishing. I will take her too so you can have some undisturbed stitching time. Oh, and I invited the Old Man down for supper."

Molly smiled at him as he headed out the door with Abigail. She grabbed a clean diaper rag and tossed it at him. "You might need this."

Lance shoved it into his pocket. "Or maybe we will just let you run around naked. Then we won't have to worry about it," he whispered to Abigail. She smiled and jabbered at him as Molly shook her head. She hurried back to the table and the dress they were working on.

Rowdy had the kids gathered and the Old Man was handing out fishing poles. Sammy and Rudy ran to get the worms they had dug the night before. Rowdy lifted Paul onto his shoulders, and the little troupe headed for their favorite fishing hole.

The Old Man put a worm on his pole while Lance and Rowdy helped the little ones.

Sammy and Rudy went down the creek, away from the rest of the kids. As they left, Sammy complained, "The little kids make too much noise! No fishes will bite with all this racket!"

CHAPTER 16

JUST A LITTLE MUD

ABIGAIL WANTED TO PLAY IN THE MUD, SO LANCE took off her dress and diaper to let her splash. Soon, she was covered in mud from nose to toes.

Rowdy looked from the little girl to Lance. "You know, you are going to have to clean her up before we go back."

Lance grinned at him, his blue eyes glinting. "Sure will. There is a little pool down the way I'll dip her in."

Abigail was delighted. Paul and Mari wanted to join her. Soon, three naked little bodies were covered in mud.

Lance checked his pocket watch, "4:00 p.m. We had better get back to the house. I want to check things over before we eat."

Rowdy was quiet as he looked over at his brother. "You do remember that trial is tomorrow afternoon. It starts at one o'clock."

Lance slowly nodded. "Yes, and all the hands want to be there." He frowned and shook his head. "I hope that judge is tough. Tiny is still mad. And this time, I don't have big rocks for him to throw around."

Lance was still frowning when he looked at Rowdy. "Are you going to keep him on? If not, I will take him back. Tiny is a heck of a worker."

Rowdy thought a moment before he answered, "I would like to keep him but let's see where he wants to work.

"Hank is darn handy with fixing things, but he is not much of a horseman. How about Spur? Would you let me have him if Tiny wants to go back to the Rocking R?"

Lance nodded slowly. "Let's see what the boys want to do." He looked sideways at his brother.

"Just don't be making it so easy they all want to leave!" he growled as his eyes twinkled.

Rowdy laughed and they picked up the muddy little ones to carry them to the pool. Old Man McNary took Paul while Rowdy carried Mari. Lance carried Abigail. They held them out from their bodies while muddy arms and legs threw splatters of mud everywhere.

When the men set them down in the pool, Abigail's blue eyes went wide. Her face started to crumple as the cold water flowed over her. Paul laughed and splashed her. Soon, the three of them were jumping around wildly in the pool. After five minutes of furious splashing, the children were almost clean. Neither of the fathers had thought to bring a blanket so they used their bandanas to "sort of" dry them off. The kids were chilly, and it wasn't long before everyone was redressed.

Neither of the older boys had any fish, and Sammy began a long story about how they had a big one, but it slipped away. Lance laughed as he watched his son. *That boy sure has the expressions*, he thought as Sammy acted out how they tried to pull the fish in and how it almost broke the pole.

"Rudy is really strong, Pa," Sammy declared. "He pulled that old fish in an' the pole was ready to break. He grabbed 'im an' if he hadn't fallen in the water, he would have had 'im too!"

Rudy blushed at the compliment as he looked up at Rowdy.

"Good for you, Rudy! We just need to make you a bigger pole!" Rowdy stated with a laugh.

Rudy smiled and ducked his head. He was not used to compliments but he liked them.

As the kids charged into the house, the women could be heard. "Don't touch that dress! Why are you so muddy? Take off your shoes!" That was followed by "Lance!" and "Rowdy!" called simultaneously.

Josie was laughing. Old Man McNary said nothing, but his fierce blue eyes were full of merriment.

The kids came racing outside again and Lance called, "Go do your chores!"

Rowdy added, "Rudy, you and Maribelle can help them."

As the men walked into the house, Molly pretended to glare at Lance. He shrugged his shoulders and gave her an ornery smile as he winked at her.

Molly stood. "It's done!" she exclaimed as she handed the dress to Josie.

Josie held it in front of her. "It is so beautiful," she murmured.

Another voice answered from the door. "Yes, it is, and so is the woman holding it."

Josie looked up with a startled look on her face. When she saw Doc standing in the doorway, she gasped. "You aren't supposed to see my dress until the wedding!"

Doc just laughed. "No one out here seems to care about that tradition," he commented. He walked across the room toward his future wife and added with an ornery smile, "Now, I will just visualize you in it."

Josie smiled and blushed as she whisked the dress into the bedroom.

CHAPTER 17

BETH'S SURPRISE

DOC GAVE BETH A BIG HUG. "I FINISHED EARLY TODAY so decided to come back out and pick up Josie." He smiled down at Beth. "How is my little sister?" Suddenly, his face took on a surprised expression and he looked down at her stomach.

Beth turned bright red while Rowdy looked from one to the other completely confused. Molly and Lance looked from brother to sister and laughed. Rowdy frowned. He had no idea what the joke was as he glared around the room.

Beth quickly turned to Molly, "So what are the plans for supper? I suppose we should get started on that right away."

Molly nodded. She smiled at Doc and waved toward an open chair. "You will stay for supper, won't you?" she asked as she turned away from Beth and tried to keep the laughter from spilling out of her.

Lance drawled, "Beth, maybe you had better take my brother for a walk. Otherwise, the rest of us are going to spill the beans over supper."

Beth blushed again. She grabbed Rowdy's arm. "Come with me. I want to take a walk." Rowdy let her drag him out the door as he frowned.

As they headed down the lane, Maribelle rushed to follow them. Old Man McNary grabbed her. "Would you like some hard candy?"

he asked with a smile on his face. Maribelle's little face broke into a shy smile as she nodded.

"Let's go find the rest of your pals, and we will all have some," he added with a grin as they headed for the barn. When he walked into the barn, Old Man McNary could see the hay forts everywhere.

"Say, kids, I don't think Lance will like his good hay scattered all over. Let's get this picked up. When this barn is cleaned up, we will all have some candy." Big and little hands were soon piling the hay while Rudy and the Old Man forked it back into piles.

As the Old Man set his pitchfork down, he looked at the children sternly. "Next time, you had better ask Lance first where you can build your hay forts. That hay will be important this winter, so we can't waste it."

As the children looked at him somberly, he smiled and winked.

"Now let's have some candy," he whispered as they all sat down on the floor of the barn.

Beth was nervous and fidgety as she rushed down the lane. Rowdy allowed himself to be dragged a little way, but he soon stopped.

"What's going on?" he growled. His eyes showed the confusion he felt, and that confusion was turning into frustration.

"I wanted to tell you this sooner, but things have been..." Beth paused and looked up at her husband. Her green eyes were alive with love and excitement.

"Rowdy, I'm pregnant. We are going to have a baby!"

Rowdy looked shocked. He stared at her face and then at her stomach. "And Doc could tell that just from hugging you?" he asked with confusion.

Beth laughed. "Well, I do have a little bit of a bump." She touched her stomach. "I think I am a little over three months along. I wanted to wait to tell you until I was sure."

She took Rowdy's hand and placed it on her stomach. His face filled with surprise as he felt the small bump that hadn't been there before.

His eyes lit up with joy. He grabbed his wife to wrap her up in hug. He frowned as he put her down. "Do I need to be careful? Can I still hug you?"

Beth giggled and pulled her husband closer. "I'm not breakable, Rowdy. I'm just pregnant."

Rowdy scooped her up and swung her around. "We are going to have a baby." he whispered loudly as he kissed his wife.

Beth wrapped her arms around his neck. "If it's a boy, may we call him Eli?"

Rowdy smiled and nodded. "Eli is a fine name. Eli he will be."

Beth giggled again as she looked up at him. "And what if it is a girl?"

Rowdy laughed as he set her down. "Well, I don't know. I reckon we have some time to ponder on that, don't we?" Beth wrapped her arm in his, and Rowdy placed a big hand on her stomach.

"A baby in there!" he exclaimed with amazement. "I can't believe there is a baby in there!"

As they walked back toward the house, Maribelle came rushing up to them. Rowdy picked her up and kissed her sticky face.

"I see your Grandpappy has been spoiling your supper again."

Old Man McNary walked out of the barn. "Do you see any candy on me?" he asked with feigned innocence.

As Rowdy stepped into the barn, Rudy popped the last piece into his mouth. He tried not to smile, but syrup started to leak down his face. Rowdy laughed.

"Kids, Beth and I have something to tell you. Rudy, Maribelle—how would you like to have a baby brother or sister?"

Maribelle grinned with excitement, but Rudy's smile left. A look of concern came over his face.

Beth stepped up to him and put her hands on his shoulders. "There is plenty of love to go around, Rudy. A baby doesn't mean you will be loved any less," she whispered as she kissed his cheek.

Rudy blushed and smiled. "I reckon a baby would be just fine, but I hope it's a boy. We need more boys at our house."

Rowdy nodded seriously, "Yes, I think so too. Let's hope it's a boy," he agreed with a wink at Rudy.

Sammy asked excitedly, "Can I tell my folks?" As Rowdy nodded, the three smaller children left on a run for the house.

Maribelle was shouting, "I get to tell! It's my baby!" Rudy hung back, and Rowdy put his arm around his shoulders.

"Rudy, I sure am glad we have a big brother in the house. Little kids need a big brother." Rudy looked up at Rowdy and a slow smile came across his face. It grew until it was a huge grin.

"Thanks, Pa," he answered as they all walked toward the house.

Rowdy squeezed his shoulder. It was the first time Rudy had called him Pa.

CHAPTER 18

BUNKING WITH THE HANDS

AS ROWDY AND BETH ENTERED THE KITCHEN, THEY could see Molly and Josie cutting thick slabs of ham while Lance ate the deviled eggs. No matter how much Molly scolded him, he did not stop. When Rowdy saw the eggs, he joined his brother. The kids were all talking at the same time, and everyone pretended to be surprised at their news.

Lance paused eating long enough to ask, "Who is having a baby? Are you sure? She doesn't look as big as Molly did when she was going to have a baby!"

Molly waved her knife at him, and Lance grinned.

I have the prettiest, sassiest wife around, he thought as he pecked her cheek, avoiding the waving knife.

Grandpappy McNary took Paul, Mari, and Sammy home with him after supper with a promise they would be back by seven in the morning. He winked at Rudy as he left.

"Rudy, where would you like to sleep?" Rowdy asked.

Rudy paused and asked tentatively, "Can I sleep in the bunkhouse with the hands?"

Lance was surprised but he nodded. "Sure can. Just have them tell you where an empty bunk is. They all have certain bunks so don't just take one."

Rudy nodded happily and headed outside.

Josie and Doc left shortly after supper. Josie wanted to help clean up, but Beth and Molly insisted she head for home.

"You have a two-hour ride in that buggy, and it will be dark before you both get there now," Molly told them.

Doc hugged Molly and Beth. He patted his sister's little tummy and kissed her cheek. "Mother would be so excited," he whispered.

Beth's tender heart was full as she smiled up at her big brother. "If it's a boy, we are going to call him Eli," she murmured softly. Doc's eyes looked a little watery as he hugged Beth again. Their brother, Eli, was killed in the War Between the States and they were both pleased to honor his memory.

Rudy had watered and fed Doc's team. They were once again tied in front of the house. Spur watched Rudy take care of the horses from the bunkhouse window.

"That Rudy is going to be a fine man someday," he commented as he turned away from the window to join the card game that was starting.

Rudy appeared in the doorway. "Lance said I could sleep in here tonight," he announced shyly as he looked around the room at the cowboys.

"Shore can," Spur answered. "Just throw your outfit on that back bunk." He paused as Rudy dropped his blankets on a bunk. "Want to play some cards before you turn in, or would you rather dig for some more worms tonight?"

As Rudy looked at him in surprise, Spur winked at him.

One of the other riders asked, "So did you find any night crawlers last night?"

Rudy's face was excited. "We found a whole pile of them. The best place was between the corral and the barn.

"I made the little kids fill all the holes back up. They just dug holes everywhere!"

The cowboys laughed and shoved each other to the side as they made a spot for Rudy to sit.

Spur began to explain how to play poker. Soon, Rudy was part of the game. Spur smiled as he watched Rudy. *The kid has a game face. He shows no emotion whatsoever and runs a fine bluff.*

Before long, the riders began to peel off and head for bed.

Tiny was one of the last ones to go. He had a bottle in front of him and was staring at it.

Spur commented dryly, "Tiny, you had better get some sleep. The trial is tomorrow, and they will be asking you questions."

Tiny hung his head. "Boys, I lost both my best pards. An' I done lost my job to boot. I jist don't know what I'm a gonna do."

Rudy looked around at the men. He spoke up tentatively.

"Tiny, I heard my pa and Uncle Lance talking. They both want you to work for them. They said you could decide where you wanted to go."

Tiny looked surprised. His face broke into a huge grin. He stood up and hollered, "I'm back, boys! Tiny is a hand at the Rockin' R again!"

Some of the men responded with hoots while others just growled. As Tiny crawled into his bunk, he leaned out and whispered loudly, "Thanks, Rudy. I shore needed to hear that."

Rudy smiled. He looked over at Spur.

"Pa said if Tiny wanted to come back here, he would sure like to have you at our place. Would you like to work with us, Spur?"

George Spurlach looked down at the sincere young man in front of him. He tugged on his big mustache and smiled, "Why, I shore would like that, Rudy. I do like to work with hosses, and yore pa is a fine man."

He held out his hand to Rudy, "Ya just hired yoreself a rider." Spur grinned as he spoke.

Rudy's smile was huge as he shook Spur's hand. He was still smiling when he drifted off to sleep.

CHAPTER 19

LOADED AND READY

EVERYONE WAS UP EARLY THE NEXT MORNING. ROWDY wanted to finalize the purchase of Slim and Sadie's ranch while the entire Rocking R was on edge because of the trial. Gus cooked breakfast for everyone so they could get on the road as soon as Badger arrived.

Molly looked at all the mud under the fingernails of Abigail and Paul. She scrubbed their hands and finally sent Lance out for more water.

"I was hoping I wouldn't have to give baths this morning since you took them swimming. I declare, Lance. Your idea of help is questionable sometimes!"

Lance met Rowdy at the spring. They both laughed as they hauled water back to the house.

Rudy protested about taking a bath in front of the women. He opted to go with Rowdy and Lance to the creek. The water was cold, so their baths were quick ones. Still, Rowdy took the time to show Rudy how to clean his fingernails with his pocketknife while the dirt was wet. Lance smiled as he watched his tough brother navigate the turns of fatherhood.

Badger arrived promptly at eight and everyone was ready to get on the road. They were able to fit all Sadie's household items and personal things in one wagon. Lance helped Molly into Sadie's wagon and jumped up beside her. Rowdy's family was all on horseback.

The smaller children decided to ride with Badger in his buggy, so Martha and Sadie made room for three more. Abigail was bouncing up and down on Molly's lap. She was always ready to go, and it didn't matter where.

Rowdy caught Sadie for just a moment before they left.

"I have the contract ready whenever you want to read it over, Sadie."

Sadie smiled and thanked Rowdy as he handed it to her. "I can let you know when I'm ready to finalize all the paperwork." She paused as she scanned the document. "Maybe we can even take care of it before you leave town."

Once they started, Rowdy rode beside the wagon and visited with Lance. Barney Ford's restaurant had burned down several months prior. The Ford House was one of the few destroyed businesses that had been covered by insurance. He had quickly rebuilt and had just reopened. Rowdy had become good friends with Barney in the few years he had lived in Cheyenne. In fact, the Fords were guests at his wedding. Barney was now talking of selling the Ford House to move to Denver.

"I will miss Barney if he moves," Rowdy commented.

Lance agreed as he tapped the lines on the back of the horses.

"Barney is a fine businessman though. He will be a success wherever he goes."

Rowdy nodded slowly. "Yes, he needs to do what is best for his family. I sure will miss his good food though."

"Who else would bring you two plates of food as soon as you sit down?" Lance asked with a laugh.

"That's true," Rowdy responded with a grin. "Let's eat there today. I haven't seen him in several months."

"The men can for sure. I'm not sure the women will take time out to eat. They are on a mission to have Sadie firmly ensconced in her new home." Lance bumped Molly's arm and added, "Although they will be glad to send the kids with us."

Molly glanced up. Beth's horse was on Molly's side of the wagon and the two women had been talking. Molly had only heard the last part of their conversation. She looked at both men. "Of course we want you to take the children with you. There might not be much time left though once you unload the wagon and move everything inside, plus carry the trunks into the bedroom, and..."

Lance rolled his eyes. "I declare, Molly. You have become a bossy woman since you had Abigail!"

He looked from Rowdy to Beth and back. "You'd better be careful, Rowdy!"

Fire was beginning to shoot from Molly's eyes, so Lance put his arm around her. "But you will always be my sweetheart," he whispered softly as he squeezed her.

Molly looked up at him and laughed. Somehow, God had picked this ornery, kind, wonderfully obnoxious man just for her, and she was blessed. She looped her arm through his and scooted a little closer.

Lance's smile became bigger. "That's my girl. That's the Molly I love. Molly Girl, you are as beautiful as the day I met you!"

Molly smiled contentedly. She had met Lance when she was pregnant. Paul was the result of her rape at the hands of Quantrill's raiders. Even before Paul was born, her widowed father had wanted her to give him away. When he put Molly on the train headed west, she was to stay with her aunt in New Orleans. Her aunt had offered to help Molly find a home for her baby.

However, Molly didn't stop. Instead, she took a steamer north and never returned home. Now she was married, precious little Paul was nearly four years old, and her father lived in Cheyenne.

Even Rowdy loves my father, Molly thought. *They have almost a father/son relationship.* Molly sighed. *My life certainly didn't turn out like I thought it would, but I have been truly blessed.*

CHAPTER 20

WHERE THE TRAIL LEADS

LEVI PARKER RODE INTO CHEYENNE THAT MORNING on a large mule. Levi was a big man and he needed a big mount. He stood over six feet five inches in his socks, and most of his nearly two hundred fifty pounds was in his shoulders and chest. Curly, brownish-red hair was cut close to his head, and a day's growth of red stubble showed on his face.

His dimples as well as the cleft in his strong chin showed clearly when he smiled, and Levi liked to smile. He saw humor in most things. However, he was cynical for his twenty-eight years when it came to justice. Still, Levi was a gentle man…most of the time.

Today, he was tracking some outlaws who had stolen three of his mules. He had trailed them to a little spread south and west of Cheyenne. There the tracks mixed in with a herd of cattle, so he rode on into Cheyenne to do some listening.

The town was abuzz over a trial of some cattle rustlers. Levi perked up and listened harder. The word was the outlaws had killed two men driving a small herd of cattle. The Rocking R, one of the larger ranches around Cheyenne, would be in town today in force. The two men had ridden for the Rocking R, and one had been the foreman for a time.

That might explain the cattle tracks that covered my tracking, he thought as he rode toward the livery.

A spry hostler with quick eyes stepped out to greet him.

"Rooster Smith is my name. Here fer the trial?" he asked as he reached for the reins to Levi's mule.

Levi shook his head. "Naw, I'm not much on trials. What are they charged with?"

"Cattle rustlin' an' murder," stated the bandy-legged hostler. "They killed a couple a fellers an' runned off with their cattle. They picked the wrong fellers though. Slim were a rider fer the Rocking R fer quite a few years an' the boss' best friend. The other feller be a new rider, but he were liked too. Gunned 'em down—shot 'em in the back.

"Those outlaws was stealin' hosses an' cows up by Laramie an' was on their way back home. They come across Slim an' his eighty head—his first herd to go to market. They shot Slim an' his boys down jist to steal his cattle. Durn foolish thing to steal that close to yer home but they was bold. Lance, the boss of the Rockin' R, was gonna hang 'em but the sheriff got there in time. Them backshooters go on trial today."

Levi was quiet a moment, "On second thought, that might be a trial I would like to see. What time does it start?"

"One o'clock this afternoon. Judge Nader 'ill hear the case, an' he don't know much more 'bout law than a durn jackass." Rooster snorted as he led the mule away.

The younger man could hear the old hostler muttering as he stomped into the barn, "Those boys should a jist hung 'em. Hard ta tell what direction that weasel Nader 'ill go."

Levi thought for a moment. *Judge Nader does have a reputation for waffling when it comes to rustling cases. However, he has higher aspirations than a district court judge. Now if someone could let him see his judgement here could affect those aspirations, why he just might put a little more time into his decision.* Levi smiled to himself and walked out of the barn.

He stepped into the closest saloon and ordered a beer. Trials were usually held in a saloon, and Cheyenne seemed to have a more than an adequate number to choose from.

Several men nodded at him as he leaned against the bar. Although Cheyenne was growing, the locals still recognized a new face in town. Besides, Levi's size helped him to stand out. The man next to him moved over to make more room. He wanted to talk, and Levi listened quietly, sipping his beer.

"Yessir, that trial 'ill be a big one today. The Gold Room Saloon is the biggest saloon in town, but I'm jist not sure if there'll be enough room fer all the folks who plan to go. Might want to get there early." The man shook his head. "One of the fellers what was shot was married less than two years. His wife is 'spectin' their first born an' that little tyke's pa ain't even gonna be 'round."

Levi could feel the ire rising in him. He downed his beer in a long swig and threw some money on the bar. "I believe I will have a talk with Judge Nader," he growled as he pushed through the saloon doors.

Judge Nader was just getting off the stage when Levi strolled down the street.

He stepped up to the judge and asked softly, "Carry your bags for you, Judge?"

Judge Nader turned. When he saw Levi, his face went tight and red creeped up his neck. "What are you doing here?" the judge demanded. "You have no business in Cheyenne."

Levi kept his face bland. "Why, Judge, just how do you know where I have business? I am a businessman with connections all over. I know folks from here to the Assembly and even on up to Governor Campbell. Yes sir, I surely do know lots of people."

Levi lifted Judge Nader's bags. The judge's face blanched when Levi spoke again.

"Let's just say I am here today to make sure you give this case the proper consideration it deserves. I want to make sure all witnesses are heard, and that there is no prejudice on the part of anyone—especially a judge who doesn't like to convict." Levi spoke softly as they walked toward the hotel.

Judge Nader thumped his walking cane on the sidewalk and his small mustache twitched. His balding head was sweating under his top hat. In addition, he was stiff from the long and bumpy ride in the stagecoach.

"I won't have you telling me, a district judge, how to rule! How dare you speak to me like this!" he sputtered. The judge slammed his stick down on the wooden boardwalk. He picked it up to wave it at Levi. "You have a lot of nerve to even talk to me!"

Levi gave him a cynical smile. "You're right. I would have to have a good reason to talk to you. You'd better consider what I said though. I will be in court today, and I will be watching you closely. Your decision will certainly be shared with people in high positions, so you listen to this case carefully." Levi leaned closer as he added, "And just know I will follow the money collected from the fines you assess. I will find out where every dollar goes." He dropped the judge's bags on the walk and sauntered on down the street without looking back.

Judge Nader glared after him. Levi Parker didn't take many cases. When he did, he was tricky and tenacious. Nader was furious the man was sniffing around this case.

He looked around furtively to see if anyone had heard their conversation. The Rollins House was close to the livery, and the only person near him was the hostler. The judge dismissed the small man working there as an insignificant underling.

Judge Nader grabbed his bags and hurried up the steps into the hotel. He stomped into the lobby and looked down his nose at the hotel clerk as he demanded, "Send my bags up to my suite. And I will expect my lunch at eleven-thirty sharp."

The clerk frowned. *Most patrons ask if their meals can be delivered to their room.* He stared after the pompous little man. He finally shrugged his shoulders. *Mr. Ford said to make sure the judge had what he needed while he was in town.* He wrote a quick note and sent it over to Ford's restaurant with a young man who ran errands for him.

Judge Nader sucked air in hard and banged on the stairs with his cane. He was used to being treated with kid gloves, and Levi Parker refused to give him the respect he deserved.

"And another thing," he muttered to himself, "I should not have to pay for my hotel stay when I come to these foul towns. The stipend I am given barely allows me a bed, let alone a quality hotel. Humph." Of course, Judge Nader had learned over the years how to direct the fines he levied back to his own pockets.

"Money solves all kinds of problems," he stated greedily as he rubbed his hands together.

Rooster Smith had excellent ears. He heard enough of the conversation between the judge and the big man who had come into the livery earlier to pique his interest. He grinned to himself. "I believe this is one trial I'm gonna attend!" he chortled with a wily grin. Rooster picked up the pace. If he was going to close the livery, he had work to be done.

CHAPTER 21

A Pro Bono Offer

LEVI WALKED INTO THE FORD HOUSE AND ORDERED a meal. It was only eleven in the morning, but it had been a long time since supper. Besides, this day had all the makings of a long one. His lips twitched with humor as he thought about the judge's face when he had mentioned the fines.

Judge Nader dismissed a lot of cases. He also fined those people heavily, but the assessed fines never seemed to be completely collected. Part of the money was accounted for. The balance just disappeared along with the party who was fined.

Levi's eyes narrowed. *This will be one trial where Judge Nader will be watched closely. Justice will be served today in Cheyenne.*

As Levi waited for his food, a group of riders rode by followed by a wagon filled with household goods. A buggy with small children bouncing in it followed behind. Levi looked closer and laughed. "Badger McCune here in Cheyenne? Well, this is going to be an interesting trial!"

While Levi watched, Badger yelled something at the riders. They moved to the side to let him drive around the wagon. The entire group turned off just up the street.

Levi pondered what he had just seen. *I guess someone is moving into Cheyenne. Shoot, I might move here myself. I like this town.* He laughed again to himself as he admitted he would rather be a muleskinner than a lawyer. *An unemployed lawyer who doesn't like to practice law.*

Barney Ford, the owner of Ford House, came out to see if his newest customer's food was satisfactory. Levi assured him it was delicious and asked for a second plate. Barney moved on to visit with the next table just as two men walked in. They were followed closely by four children. One man was carrying a baby while a tall boy held the hands of a little boy and a girl. The last young man had lots of wild, blond hair. He seemed to know everyone. At least he spoke to everyone and shook a lot of hands.

Levi studied the two men. They bore an uncanny resemblance to each other. They were obviously related. Ford hurried to greet them, and it was apparent he knew them well. The shorter of the two men grabbed his hand and laughed as he pulled the owner into a bear hug. They visited a bit and were led to a table toward the back.

A group of cowboys burst through the door. They worked their way through the full restaurant to an empty table next to the men. Barney greeted each of them as well. "I see we still have our table, Barney!" one of the riders exclaimed as he shook the owner's hand. Barney laughed and moved on to greet the next table of customers.

When the food was brought out, two plates were set in front of one of the men. The man grinned and waved toward the kitchen. All the children were busily eating except for the blond boy. He was full of questions and wanted to introduce himself to everyone around them.

The taller of the men shook his head. "Don't bother folks while they are eating, Sammy. Barney is busier than normal today with the trial, so people need to get in and out quickly."

Sammy scowled but ate his food. The baby ate off everyone's plate and no one seemed to mind.

Levi smiled. He did not have any kids, but they looked entertaining. *Shoot, I don't even have a wife. Once I almost did…but when she found out I wouldn't move to Denver to practice law with her pa, she dumped me.* Levi almost laughed out loud. *That was the best unanswered prayer I ever sent up* he mused and almost laughed aloud.

Suddenly, he realized that one of the men was speaking to him. "…salt. Could you pass that on over?" Levi handed the man both the salt and the pepper.

Just then, the restaurant door flew open and a small man almost bounced in. His bright eyes cataloged the entire room. As they came to rest on Levi, his face broke into a grin.

Levi stood. "How are you, Badger? I surely didn't know you were out this way!"

Badger winked at Levi and his eyes twinkled. "Why I shore 'nough live here," he stated with a wink. "I come in here ta eat with my family. Lance, Rowdy—this here feller is one of the toughest lawyers out there, but he'd rather skin mules than talk law!"

The little blond boy did not waste any time. He jumped out of his chair and rushed over to Levi. He put out his hand and introduced himself. "I'm Sammy Rankin. And you are?"

Levi almost laughed but he kept his face serious. "My name is Levi Parker. And who are the rest of your pals, Sammy?"

Sammy turned and pointed. "That's Paul. He's my little brother. Rudy and Maribelle are my cousins, and Abigail is my little sister. Lance is my Pa, and Rowdy is my uncle.

"What does a lawyer do? Why don't you want to be a lawyer? Isn't it fun? Do you like mules? Badger loves mules. My momma is helping Sadie move into her new house. Slim died." Sammy's bright face became sad. "I liked Slim a lot. He was my uncle too. Now Sadie's gonna have a baby and it won't have no pa."

Lance pulled Sammy back. "That's enough, Sammy. Finish your dinner. We need to be leaving here soon."

The men shook hands with Levi. As Badger sat down, he asked, "So were ya follerin' some rustlers? I seen yer travelin' mule down ta the livery. They jist might be the same ones what stoled our cows."

Levi nodded slowly. "I was but I lost their tracks under a herd of cows. They might be at that."

He stood and started to leave but turned back.

"I would sure like to question those outlaws if you boys are looking for a lawyer."

As Badger grinned at him, Levi laughed and added, "Only for today."

Lance studied the tall man in front of them. "I didn't think we needed a lawyer. We have an eyewitness."

Levi's blue eyes twinkled. "Let's just say I will do this pro bono. I want to make sure Judge Nader does his job."

Lance agreed, and the two men shook hands again. As Levi walked away, Lance looked at Badger and asked with surprise, "He seemed like an interesting fellow. Now how in Sam Hill do you know him?"

"Met 'im in Kansas City. He bought some mules from me. We dickered fer a time too." Badger gave his evil laugh.

"I watched 'im in court whilst he was there jist fer the sport of it." Badger shook his head. "That boy is like a wolf. He goes fer the throat an' hits from the side." His blue eyes sparked as he added, "Ya jist upped the entertainment level when ya hired that feller."

Lance still did not see why they needed a lawyer. However, if the man was a friend of Badger's, that was good enough for him.

Rowdy and Lance took the children back to Sadie's house. Samuel Brewster, Molly's father, was coming by to get *all* the children. Lance chuckled as he thought of quiet Samuel with all those kids. He guessed Samuel would follow Badger's lead. He would sugar them up and send them home.

Lance had invited Samuel out to visit several years before. Molly's father had reconciled with her and relocated to Cheyenne. Samuel loved Paul along with all the other children, and he loved being a grandfather.

Gus, Samuel's longtime friend and family cook, was Lance's cookie, and both were part of the Rankins' little community.

Sadie decided not to go to the trial. The women had planned to attend. Since Sadie was staying home, they were going to put Sadie's house together that afternoon. The young widow's face was pale, and her hands were trembling. Molly finally made her lie down.

"Take a nap, Sadie. There are three of us here to help you today. No need for you to wear yourself out when we can take care of this."

Sadie hugged her friends and closed the door to the room that would be her new bedroom. As she climbed into bed, she looked around. The room was bright and cheery. When she closed her eyes, she could hear the happy chatter of her friends. As she fell asleep, she saw Slim's ornery face, and the tears in her eyes dried on her cheeks.

Samuel came by around twelve thirty in the afternoon to get the children.

Beth asked, "Rudy, do you want to go with the kids, or would you like to go to the trial?"

Rudy's eyes lit up. "I would like to go to the trial if you don't mind. I think this lawyer business sounds interesting."

Beth kissed his cheek and watched as Rudy ran out the door. He seemed to know where he was going as he did not slow down when he turned the corner onto the main street.

Molly was smiling when Beth turned around.

"Rudy is a fine boy."

Beth smiled proudly. "He is, and he is finally becoming comfortable with us as his parents." She paused and added softly, "He called Rowdy 'Pa' the other day, and he has never done that before."

Molly hugged her sister-in-law. "That is wonderful, Beth. Is he excited about the baby?"

Beth hesitated before she answered.

"He wasn't at first, but he relaxed when I told him there was plenty of love to go around. This has been quite an adjustment for him. Maribelle is younger but Rudy is old enough to remember everything. We are a lot more social than his parents were as well, so he is struggling to adapt to that too."

Martha beamed at both young women, and the three of them threw themselves into cleaning and organizing Sadie's new house.

CHAPTER 22

A Trial in Cheyenne

LEVI STARED AT THE TALL MIRROR THAT STOOD IN HIS room in the Eagle Hotel. He brushed off his britches and put on a clean shirt. He glanced at the paper on the bed and smiled.

He had asked at the sheriff's office where to get a list of landowners and residents in Laramie County. The Wyoming Territory was established in 1868 and only had five counties, so Levi knew the list of county residents couldn't be too long. The sheriff had directed him to the land office.

The land agent hadn't been too happy to look up the names, but he did. Now Levi had a list of every registered resident in Laramie County.

Levi scowled at his reflection in the mirror. His arms and shoulders were so large that it was hard to find a shirt that fit. As he scrutinized himself, he muttered, "This one is darn thin but at least it's clean." He polished his boots and headed downstairs. He wanted to get to the Gold Room Saloon early. *Maybe Lance and his riders will be a little early. I'd like to talk to the fellow who was shot along with the other cowboys who helped capture those outlaws.*

Business was thriving at the Gold Room Saloon. The saloon owners all vied for the rights to have trials held in their establishments because of the business and publicity trials brought.

Nathan Baker, the local newspaperman, was to be the official court reporter. Levi introduced himself.

"It is a pleasure to meet you, Mr. Baker. My name is Levi Parker, and I am the lawyer for the prosecution. You have a reputation for reporting the truth, and I would like you to document every detail of this trial. I don't want any mistakes should questions arise later."

Baker looked at Levi coolly.

"I only report the truth, Mr. Parker. I won't enhance it, nor will I fail to disclose any details," he replied as he stared intently at the man in front of him.

Levi nodded. He was pleased. *This trial is starting on a good note.* However, when he saw the lawyer for the defense, he scowled.

"Count on Judge Nader to try to pack things for his benefit," he muttered to himself.

He nodded at Judge Nader who scowled at him. Levi held back his grin. He put his hand out to Peter Smith, the defense attorney.

"Peter."

Smith ignored Levi's hand and turned his back. The young lawyer grinned. He walked over to Lance. A large man with his arm in a sling was sitting there as well.

"I see you have your arm in a sling. Are you one of the riders who was pushing those cattle that were stolen?"

Lance nodded. "He was. Tiny Small, this is Levi Parker. He is our lawyer."

Tiny looked up at this man who was even bigger than him. His mouth opened in surprise.

"How many were there, and can you identify them?"

"There was ten of 'em. Three was shot that day, Mule killed one, an' the other six are over there." Tiny pointed at six men clustered together, laughing and talking like they hadn't a care in the world.

Levi looked hard at Tiny.

"How can you be sure? I know they killed your boss and your best friend, but how is it you are so sure?"

Tiny started to bristle up, and Levi put out his hand.

"You will receive this question today and likely in several different versions. Tell me how you know."

"'Cause they all clustered 'round Slim an' me when we was down. One of the fellers who died stood over Slim an' shot 'im point blank. Then he said, 'Make sure the big feller is dead too.' The smaller feller with the pimples shot into me, but his foot slid on a rock an' his bullet went wide. Otherwise, I would be as dead as Slim an' Smiley.

"Smiley took a load a buckshot in the back. The guy with the greasy hair was the only one carryin' a shotgun so he must a shot Smiley." Tiny glared at the men on the other side of the saloon.

"They caught us unawares. We was trailin' those cows to the railroad sidin', an' they come up behind us. Acted all friendly-like an' then jist cut loose. All of 'em had their guns out an' was a firin.'

"I'm not sure which a the two tall ones shot Slim in the back with the rifle or which one winged me, but they was all a shootin'. They bounced a bullet off my saddle, an' it hit my arm. My hoss bucked an' I fell off. That is when the little pimply feller stood over me an' shot again.

"Low-down sidewinders. The boss shoulda' let us hang 'em."

Tiny looked directly at Levi as he added quietly, "If they don't hang, I'm a gonna make sure they die."

Levi studied Tiny. The man was angry and sad. *Yes, I believe you just might.* He squeezed Tiny's shoulder.

"I will do my best. No matter what happens, don't threaten anyone today. This trial can go sideways if that judge hears anything that even sounds like a threat. And trust me, they *all* want you threaten them."

Rudy slid to a stop as he ran through the doors of the Gold Room Saloon. He paused as the doors swung back behind him and scanned the room for Rowdy. He saw two heads that looked the same from behind. He wiggled through the crowd as he pushed his way toward them. He tapped Rowdy on the shoulder.

Rowdy was surprised to see Rudy, but he moved over and made room for the young man.

Judge Nader was ready to pick the jury and Levi asked to approach the bench.

"Since this crime was committed in Laramie County, I have a list of all the residents of this county, courtesy of the land office." He paused and looked hard at the judge as he added quietly, "That means that if they aren't on this list and can't prove they are a resident, they can't be on the jury."

Judge Nader's neck grew red. He started to sputter as Levi added with an innocent smile, "Of course, women may serve on a jury now and we have plenty of women here today."

Judge Nader was furious. He had intended to pack the jury with friends of the outlaws, issue a heavy fine, and dismiss the case. *How dare Levi Parker become involved!*

Badger watched the exchange, and even though he could not hear what was being said, he was pleased. "From the side like a wolf!" he chortled with a wicked laugh.

Lance was quiet. He was beginning to see why having a lawyer was a good idea. He scowled.

"Why can't folks just be honest?" he muttered.

Rowdy gave his brother a hard look.

"I agree but folks will be folks. Some just lean a little to the side, and it doesn't take much to push them over the edge."

Jury selection began. Levi had made copies of the potential jurors. He had given both Peter Smith and Judge Nader a copy. Smith still tried to add names not on the list. Levi refused them without checking his sheet.

"Not on the list. Next."

Nathan Baker was writing furiously and trying not to smile. *This trial certainly won't be a bogus one.*

When the jury was finally picked, there were four women and eight men.

Judge Nader did not think women should serve on juries. However, in this case, he was hoping that they would be more lenient.

He told each lawyer to introduce himself and tell where he had practiced. The judge smirked when Levi stated he had practiced law for two years. However, when Levi added he had worked as a United States Marshal for four years and a Justice of the Peace for two years, the judge's face tightened.

When it was time for Peter Smith to introduce himself, he stated he had worked as a lawyer for fifteen years, practicing in Laramie for the last ten of those years.

Levi casually asked if he worked for himself or if he was part of a firm. Smith blushed a deep red and stuttered, "I work mostly free lance."

People were leaning forward to listen. They didn't know what this meant, but it was obvious Peter Smith did not want to say who he worked for.

Judge Nader slammed his gavel down. "That's enough!" he shouted. "Where Peter Smith works is not relevant to this court!"

Levi answered apologetically, "I just wanted it to be clear that he worked for you, Your Honor."

The men seated in the saloon began to mutter amongst themselves and the judge turned purple. He banged his gavel again and shouted, "Order!"

He turned to Levi and snapped, "Another outbreak like that, and I will throw you out of this courtroom."

Levi looked meek and nodded.

Badger slapped his knee and laughed out loud. "From the side!" he whispered loudly.

Tiny was the first witness called. Peter Smith asked, "Where were you when Charlie Crandall died?"

Tiny looked confused.

Levi interjected, "The witness knows Charlie Crandall as Slim Crandall."

Tiny's confusion disappeared and he began to tell the entire story.

Peter Smith shut him off as he started to talk about the men being shot while they were down.

"That is all, your honor."

Tiny turned purple and started to yell at him, but Levi was beside him quickly.

"Mr. Tiny Small, can you tell the court exactly what happened from when you first encountered the rustlers?"

Peter Smith shouted, "Cowboys!"

Levi paused and stared at the outlaws before he answered. "The gentlemen who attacked you from behind," he finished.

Tiny told his story as he had told Levi. His eyes filled with tears as he talked about the death of his friends.

Levi asked quietly, "Do either of the deceased have families?"

Peter Smith started to protest, but Tiny stood up and yelled over him.

"Slim had him a wife an' a little baby on the way! Now that baby don't have no daddy an' Sadie has to get herself a job."

The women on the jury had tears in their eyes while the men in the room stirred angrily in their chairs.

Levi patted Tiny's shoulder and stated, "I have no further questions."

Peter looked at Judge Nader. He wasn't sure who to call. This wasn't going as they had planned at all. He decided to put the leader of the outlaws, Ace Durant, on the stand. *After all, no one can prove that he actually did any shooting.*

Smith asked Ace some soft questions and nodded his approval at the answers. Then Levi moved toward the stand.

He pointed at a table to the side where ten holsters with guns in them as well as nine rifles and a shotgun lay.

"Do any of these guns belong to you, Mr. Durant?"

Ace stared from the guns to Levi and finally pointed to a black holster that held a gun with notches carved on the butt. He also pointed to one of the rifles.

"Mr. Durant, you look like a man who knows your guns," Levi stated as he turned the handgun over. The Colt Walker was well-oiled and clean.

"Would you say you reload your gun as soon as possible after you shoot it?" Levi questioned as he held the gun and admired it.

The outlaw smirked. "A gun ain't no good if it ain't loaded. I always reload."

Levi turned to the jury. He pointed to the man closest to him.

"Will you check the number of shells in these guns? I think we can all agree these guns have not been fired since the owners were incarcerated." Levi looked around the room making eye contact with each juror. His eyes settled on the sheriff.

"Am I correct, Sheriff Boswell?"

The sheriff nodded his head, and Peter Smith started to protest.

Levi put his hand on the juryman's hand to pause him.

"Is there a reason you don't want these guns checked, Mr. Smith?"

Peter Smith turned purple and sat back down. The juryman opened the chambers on both guns. The Colt was missing five shells and the Henry rifle was missing three.

Levi handed the man the remaining guns and asked him to check those as well. All the checked guns were missing bullets. The shotgun had no loads in either chamber.

The noise in the courtroom reached a crescendo as Judge Nader banged his gavel.

"Order!" the judge shouted. "Order!"

Levi stepped down and Peter Smith once again moved forward to question the witness.

"Isn't it possible you might not have reloaded after the last time you used your gun, Mr. Durant?"

Ace Durant was not the quickest thinker and when he didn't think, he answered honestly.

"'Course I reloaded. We shot at those fellers who was chasin' us up by Laramie, an' I reloaded onset we got away. Ya can't take off with a half-empty gun!"

Peter Smith's face went white, and he shot a furtive look at Judge Nader.

The judge snorted and waved his hand. "Do either of you have more witnesses?"

Levi nodded.

"I would like to call Lance Rankin."

Lance looked at Levi a little surprised but stepped up to the witness stand.

After he was sworn in, Levi asked, "Can you tell us what type of men the deceased were?"

Lance started with Smiley. He told how they had met him, almost hung him, and how he had become a valued rider and friend to all on the Rocking R. When he mentioned Slim's name, Lance's face went hard.

"Slim was my first friend when I came to the Rocking R. We remained friends even after I became foreman.

"He grew up an orphan down in Texas. He ran away from his spinster aunt at twelve years of age. He saved to buy his little ranch here, and the eighty head of cattle those fellas stole was the first load of calves he was sending to market. Slim Crandall was a fine man…and he was only married one-and-one-half years."

Lance looked from the men to the women on the jury. "Their baby is coming in just a few months." He stared hard at the outlaws and added, "Slim was looking forward to becoming a father. He loved cattle and he loved ranching, but he loved Sadie most of all."

The room was silent, and Peter indicated that he had no questions.

As Lance stepped down, one of the outlaws called out, "Yeah, but he was a coward. Ya shoulda seen the fear in his face when Stone put that gun to his chest!"

Lance went completely still. Tiny lunged to his feet with a roar. The entire bench of Rocking R riders surged out of their seats and pandemonium broke out in the room.

Judge Nader's lips moved, and the gavel banged, but no one could hear him. Levi was holding Tiny back while Rowdy and Badger were trying to control the rest of the Rocking R riders.

Lance was standing with his fists clenched and breathing hard. Old Man McNary had his hand on Lance's shoulder and was ready to pull him back if he lunged at the outlaws.

Rudy watched everything with big eyes. He tentatively touched Lance. Lance jerked and looked down at him.

"Uncle Lance, I'm kind of scared. Is there going to be a big fight?" Rudy asked as he held his hands tightly together.

Lance looked at the young boy and some of the anger seeped out of him. He patted Rudy's head.

"No, Rudy. There won't be a fight." He turned to his riders.

"Rocking R! Sit down and let's hear the verdict!" he shouted as he took a seat himself. The riders followed his lead and the room slowly calmed down.

Judge Nader was still shouting and pounding his gavel, but no one paid him any attention.

Levi patted Tiny's shoulder and stepped into the middle of the room. He raised his arms and began in a powerful voice, "Ladies and gentlemen, please let me give my closing arguments so the jury can decide this case."

As the room quieted, Levi stepped over to the jury box.

"Ladies and gentlemen of the jury. I believe you have heard undeniable testimony today as to the guilt of the six men on trial today for the murder of Slim Crandall and Smiley Johnson as well as for the theft of eighty head of Slim's cattle. While not every man stood over the dying men, all those on trial here today were shooting. It would be impossible to say which of the rifles shot Slim and Smiley. However, it is easy to see these men were of one mind—to kill those good men and take their cattle.

"As you heard today from one of the killers himself, these men have no remorse. Their only thought was to steal *more* cattle on their way home from an earlier theft. Murder was of no concern to them.

"I hope you will find the men on trial here today guilty of murder and rustling knowing both of these crimes are hanging offences in the Wyoming Territory. Thank you." As Levi stepped down, the room was quiet.

Badger squeezed Lance's knee.

Peter Smith stood. His shoulders were slumped, but he straightened himself. *I have nothing to lose. This has gone nothing like the judge and I planned.*

"Gentleman...and ladies, you heard the testimony today. No one here can say for sure that any of these accused men fired the killing shots. Why, for all we know, these men may not have even been there."

Tiny tried to lunge to his feet, and Levi jerked him back down.

Peter Smith smirked at the Rocking R riders.

"The men in front of you are surely not the first men to be accused out of anger. As you heard, those wild cowboys almost hung another innocent man.

"I believe a fine would be sufficient. That and a promise to never again return to Laramie County." He smirked again, this time at the women in the jury, and returned to his seat.

The four women stared at Peter Smith in shock. "How dare he treat us as if we're stupid," whispered one of the women jurors to the woman beside her. The other woman did not respond. However, all the women jurors sat upright in their chairs and stared straight ahead.

Judge Nader instructed the jury as to the severity of the crime and the suggested punishment. Finally, he added, "Of course, you may decide on a guilty verdict and give a lighter sentence. Sometimes fines are more effective than the barbaric methods recommended by this territory."

Several of the men on the jury glared at him, but Judge Nader was paying no attention. *If only I didn't have to come in contact with these unschooled and backwards people. I will surely need to bathe when this is over just from breathing the foul air in this room.*

As the jury went upstairs to deliberate, Badger shook Levi's hand. "Congratulations, Boy! Ya smoked 'em!"

Levi smiled. Unlike Badger, he never celebrated before the verdict came back. Too many factors could affect that decision.

The jury returned in fifteen minutes. Levi was a little nervous as that meant that there was little dissention.

Maggie Jones had been made foreman since she had served on a jury before. She handed a paper to Judge Nader. As he read the verdict, the judge's neck turned red. Only then did Levi begin to smile.

"On the charge of cattle rustling, the jury finds these six men guilty. On the charge of murder, the jury finds these six men guilty. The sentence is death by hanging." The judge banged his gavel and yelled, "Court adjourned!"

As he stomped out of the room, Levi followed him.

"It was a pleasure as always, sir," Levi commented.

Judge Nader swung his cane. Had Levi not jumped, it would have struck him. Levi smiled and waggled his finger at the judge.

"Now, now, Judge. That is no way for an officer of the court to behave!"

Levi's smile grew as he walked back to where the Rocking R riders were gathered. He shook Tiny's hand.

"You did a fine job, Tiny. I'm sure Slim and Smiley would agree."

CHAPTER 23

Meet the Family

LANCE SENT HIS RIDERS BACK TO THE RANCH. THERE was some protesting, but he shook his head.

"Nope. You will all want to be in town on Saturday night. I don't want you in here tearing things up tonight. Do your celebrating at home."

Joe headed for the livery. He had become the accepted leader of the Rocking R riders, and the men all followed him.

When Spur hung back, Lance looked at him with a question in his eyes. Spur winked at him before he put his hand out to Rowdy.

"Your son hired me last night, Rowdy. It will be a pleasure to work for the R4."

Rowdy looked surprised and then pleased. Rudy was smiling, and Rowdy clapped him on the shoulder.

"Fine job, Son! Fine job."

He grinned at Spur and added, "You go on home too. Work is piling up there and Hank could use a little help." He shook Spur's hand. "Welcome to the R4."

Lance invited Levi back to Sadie's house. "I want you to meet Slim's wife," Lance told him.

133

Levi looked surprised. "She is living in Cheyenne?"

Lance nodded slowly. "We moved her to town today. Slim told her when he was dying to sell the ranch to Rowdy. That is what she is going to do."

He turned to Rowdy. "When are you signing papers?"

Rowdy paused a moment before he answered. "I think we will do it tomorrow. I'm tired and I'm sure Beth will be tired after unpacking and cleaning all day. Sadie could use a little down time too. Tomorrow morning will be fine if that works for Sadie."

The three men walked slowly down the street when they heard the rush of feet coming from behind. Turning, they saw Badger hurrying to catch up, and he had Rudy in tow.

"Found this young man in that thar saloon tryin' ta read a couple o' law books that durn judge left a layin' on the table when he rushed out a there."

Rudy blushed as he looked up at Levi. "Mr. Parker, can you tell me what I need to do to be a lawyer? I think I would like to do what you did today."

Rowdy looked surprised and Levi laughed.

"Well, first, you need to go to school and learn everything your teacher tells you. Being smart can help you as a lawyer for sure but thinking is more important. You want to think faster *and* think around the fellows on the other side.

"And practice memorizing things. Stretch your mind and make it see all the angles."

Levi paused before he added, "And read the Bible. There are some sharp judges in there." He thought a moment as he studied the serious young man.

"You know, I have some law books I studied when I was first learning. You write down your address and I will mail them to you."

Rudy's eyes shone with excitement. "Yessir!" he exclaimed as he ran ahead to tell the other kids about his day.

Beth, Molly, and Martha watched their husbands walk toward the house with a mountain of a man.

"My stars, he is huge!" commented Molly in amazement.

Beth giggled and added, "But he is kind of cute."

When the other women turned to look at her, she blushed.

"Well, not as good-looking as Rowdy, but only Lance is as handsome as him." she explained as they all laughed.

Sadie was only half listening. She was looking for her tea kettle. "Do any of you remember where the tea kettle is?" she asked. "I could use a cup of tea."

Beth quickly pulled it out and set it on the table. Sadie grabbed the bucket from the sink and went out to draw water. As she pumped the water up from the cistern, she saw the men walking into her yard.

Rowdy reached out and took the bucket from Sadie while Lance put his arm around her.

"Levi, I want you to meet Sadie. She is the closest thing to a sister Rowdy and I have ever had. We love her to pieces," he drawled as he smiled down at Sadie. He held the front door open for Sadie to enter and the men followed her into the kitchen.

Levi felt a pang of sorrow for the young mother. Hanging the outlaws wouldn't bring her husband back, but it would keep them from committing the same crime again.

Sadie turned her brown eyes to the man beside Lance and they kept going up before they finally reached his eyes.

"Goodness, you are tall!" she exclaimed and then blushed at her rudeness.

Levi laughed, and a dimple showed on each side of his face. He put out his hand. "It is nice to meet you, Mrs. Crandall," he replied with a smile.

"Levi is a lawyer, and he *was* on our side today," Lance explained. "Quite frankly," he added dryly, "I'm glad he was on our side."

Molly's father, Samuel, herded the kids into the house. They swarmed through the kitchen while he followed them, smiling.

Molly shook her head. They were all sticky and dirty. "It looks like all of you had a fun time with Grandpa Samuel," she commented dryly.

Beth sat down and pulled Maribelle onto her lap.

"What did you do all day?" asked Beth as she tried to comb the sticky "something" out of Mari's hair.

Maribelle jumped off her lap and replied with big eyes, "We played in a *giant* barn. Rooster let us build hay forts in the loft, and Grandpa Samuel let us eat all the candy in his house! Then we dug holes in Grandpa Samuel's yard, and..."

Sammy interrupted, "And we found coins! Some feller buried a whole bunch a coins in Grandpa Samuel's yard an' fergot they was there! Probably a pirate or an ol' bandit. We dug an' dug, an' we found a *bunch* of 'em!"

Samuel laughed, and his eyes twinkled.

"Funny thing. They were all in the one area I was going to make into a flower bed. Now that ground is all dug up and ready."

Everyone laughed, and the children rushed back outside to play.

"No digging!" Molly called after them as they raced across the yard to the open lot.

Samuel studied the big tree in the front yard. "That would be a perfect tree to hang a swing, Sadie. I would be glad to do that for you if you would like one." He smiled at the quiet young woman.

As Sadie nodded, Samuel turned away with a pain in his heart. *She is just like my Molly was when I sent her away. I put her on a train all by herself because she was pregnant. How did she ever forgive me?* He felt tears form in the corners of his eyes and he rubbed his face.

Molly moved nearer to her father.

"Thank you for taking the children today, Father. I know they had a wonderful time. We were able to get Sadie's house completely set up while they were gone," she whispered as she squeezed his arm.

Samuel hugged his only child and murmured, "Molly, please forgive me. You were just like little Sadie, and I sent you off on that train by yourself. I didn't even help you handle the trauma of being raped," he choked brokenly as he held her close.

Molly kissed his wet cheek. "But, Father, if you hadn't sent me away, I would never have met Lance…and I would have missed all this!" she exclaimed as she drew her arm around the room.

She hugged him again.

"I love you, Father, and I am so happy you now live in Cheyenne."

Samuel slowly smiled. The barb that had been in his heart melted away. He looked around at these noisy people who were now Molly's family. His family too. "Yes, you would have missed all this. We both would have," he agreed softly as he caught Lance's eye. Lance smiled and Samuel walked across the room to meet the tall man beside his son-n-law.

Doc and Josie came by when they closed the office at five. One of Doc's patients had told him which house Sadie had bought.

Josie looked around in approval. "I love your house, Sadie. It is so welcoming, and the windows are wonderful!"

Sadie smiled and nodded as she looked around her new home.

"Yes, but it is really too big for just one person." She paused and smiled softly at her sister-in-law.

"You should move in with me until the wedding, Josie. It would be so much more comfortable for you than staying at the Eagle Hotel. Besides, I would love the company."

"Are you sure? I don't want to get in your way." Josie's blue eyes were wide with excitement. *The hotel room is crowded and besides, it will be nice to invite Reuben over in the evenings.*

Sadie nodded. "It would be fun to have another woman around to talk to. It will give us a chance to get to know each other better as well." She smiled and added, "I will have someone to ask for medical advice too."

Josie hugged her. "I will move in tomorrow after work. Then we will have all weekend to plant a garden or flowers if you want."

Sadie nodded as she sat down to drink her cup of tea. Molly had made coffee, and everyone was talking and laughing. Sadie smiled.

This is what you wanted, wasn't it, Slim? All your family together and happy. Oh, how I miss you, she thought as tears welled up in her eyes.

CHAPTER 24

MY OLD PARD

LEVI WATCHED SADIE. SHE WAS A LOVELY WOMAN. HIS thoughts turned to Slim, and he chuckled. Sadie glanced up, startled, and Levi smiled at her.

"May I sit down?" he asked.

Sadie nodded. Levi stretched his long legs out under the table and Sadie almost giggled. She had never seen such a tall man.

Levi looked at her seriously. "I knew Charlie when we were kids."

Sadie stared at him. Her face was shocked.

Levi added quickly, "I didn't mean to startle you. I had no idea until the trial started. When the other lawyer said Slim's name was Charlie, it caught my attention. When Lance talked about Slim's early life in Texas, I knew your Slim was my best pal, Charlie."

Levi laughed as he remembered.

"He hated the name Charlie, so we just called him Kid. Kid Crandall. We ran away together when we were both twelve. He lived with that spinster aunt, and I was in an orphanage in a little town down by San Antonio. My parents had died in a buggy accident, and my mother's only sister didn't want a bratty nine-year-old boy."

His eyes crinkled in the corners as he smiled at Sadie. "The night we left, he jumped out of a two-story window, and I was supposed to catch him." Levi chuckled.

"Kid wasn't big, but he was tough. He about killed me when he landed on me! We crawled into the back of a freight wagon and rode all night. We weren't sure what would happen to us if people knew we had run away, so we tried to stay low for those first few weeks. Then, hunger overcame us, and Kid came up with a story.

"We decided to tell people we were headed to Kansas to meet up with our folks. We said we had fallen out of a covered wagon, and the train went on without us." Levi paused and looked up as he laughed softly.

"Funny thing was people did believe us. We met lots of nice folks who fed two young boys and pointed them in the direction they needed to go. Some even arranged a ride for us. We finally made it to northcentral Texas. We had both lived on ranches before our folks died so we decided to get a job herding cows.

"No one wanted to hire two kids, but one rancher finally gave in. Dan Waggoner owned the Waggoner Ranch. He gave us some old ponies to ride.

"We took those cows out every morning and brought them back every night. We did a fairly good job. He gave us the wages of one man, split between us. Then, he hired us on for the winter."

Levi paused again, and Sadie waited for him to continue. Slim had never talked much about his early years, and it was wonderful to hear about that part of her husband's history.

"I think Waggoner's wife felt sorry for us, but we didn't care. We were happy. We had beds to sleep in and horses to ride. We stayed on that ranch for three years.

"The fellas started calling me Judge because I liked to argue. Then Dan Waggoner introduced me to a friend of his who was a lawyer, and that put the bug in my bonnet."

Levi's eyes had a faraway look in them. Slowly, they returned to Sadie.

"By the time we left, Kid was a top hand, and I was fairly good at breaking horses. Kid was a better rider though. He could ride anything you put in front of him."

Sadie thought about Slim's trophy saddle and she laughed.

"Yes, he entered a ranch competition the summer before we were married. He won the bucking horse contest and placed in several other events." She pointed at a saddle in the corner of the living room. "That is the saddle he won."

Levi stared at the saddle for a moment before he looked back at Sadie. "He did it!" Levi chuckled as he wiped his eyes. "He always told me, 'Someday, I'm goin' to find someone foolish enough to bet me a saddle I cain't ride his horse.'"

Sadie and Levi both laughed as they looked at the saddle.

"We rode for two more ranches together. Then I decided to read law with a lawyer I had met in St. Louis one time when we trailed cattle there.

"That lawyer had moved further west. He saw potential in the little town called City of Kansas, now Kansas City. I studied with him for three years.

"It was during that time I lost touch with Kid. We were supposed to meet up in five years at the stock yards in Fort Worth on the first Saturday in December. That would have been in 1867."

"I didn't make it though." Levi's voice was soft when he added, "I was working a case in Denver and couldn't get away." He looked down. His face was sad when he looked at Sadie again. "I wish I had."

Sadie put her hand over his. "Levi, Slim wouldn't have been there either. By then, he was riding for the Rocking R. There is no way he could have made it down to Texas in December of any year."

They were both quiet for a time. Finally, Levi grinned at her.

"You know, you had better not call your baby Charlie. He really did hate that name."

Sadie laughed. "I know. I have thought about that. I don't know what I should call it. Slim was convinced it would be a boy, but we really hadn't talked about names yet."

Ornery lights showed in Levi's eyes as he looked at her. "Well," he drawled, "You could give it the name that we agreed on when we were twelve."

Sadie's brown eyes opened wide as she waited for Levi to share the name.

"We decided if we ever had kids, I would call my first one Kid, and he would call his Levi."

Sadie's face lit up as she laughed. Levi felt a pang of longing surge through his chest. He knew he needed to leave. He stood.

"Sadie, it was wonderful to meet you. Best of wishes with your little one. I will stop back by one of these days when I'm passing through.

"I hope to see a miniature version of my old friend." As Levi started to walk away, he looked back, tipped his hat, and drawled, "I shore did enjoy our talk."

Sadie's eyes went wide. "He sounded just like Slim," she whispered as she waved.

Beth looked at Levi's departing back. She sat down beside Sadie.

"Mr. Parker seems like a nice man."

Sadie nodded. "He knew Slim as a child. He told me a little about those years Slim never talked about." She smiled and added softly, "It was wonderful to hear about Slim's childhood."

Beth hugged her friend and pulled her up from her chair. "Let's go outside. Everyone is in the yard, and it is a beautiful evening."

Sadie started to pull back. "What about supper? I don't know if I have enough food to feed everyone, but I am sure they are hungry."

"Barney caught Lance after the trial. He offered to send food up around six this evening." Beth laughed, and her green eyes sparkled. "Tonight, we get to sit down and let someone else cook for us! Now let's go join our family in the yard."

Levi looked back once as he headed down the street. Voices rose and fell as Sadie's family surrounded her with love. Once again, he felt a pang of loneliness, and it surprised him.

"It's been a long time since I missed family and togetherness," he muttered. He pushed himself to walk faster, but his feet dragged a little as he walked away from the happy gathering behind him.

Levi stopped at the sheriff's office. Together, they rode down to the corrals so he could claim his mules. As he mounted his large mule and headed back toward Laramie, he looked again toward Sadie's little house. He couldn't see it tucked in amongst the other houses, but he knew the yard was full of her friends and family. Levi laughed.

"Kid, you sure did find the prettiest girl around, and you managed to leave her with a great big family. I miss you too, my friend." Tears filled the corners of Levi's eyes as he rode out of town.

Rooster watched as Levi rode down the street. "I sure hope that young lawyer comes back. We need someone to keep the judges honest," the old hostler muttered as he went back inside the livery. He had to clean up all the hay forts in the loft and it was going to take him some time. He chuckled as he thought about the children's excitement as they built them.

"Ol' Sam's a softie. That's what he is. Not me though." He grinned to himself and began to whistle as he forked the hay into piles.

CHAPTER 25

SISTERS

JOSIE MOVED HER THINGS INTO SADIE'S HOUSE THE next day. She took one of the upstairs bedrooms and insisted on cooking in the evenings.

Sadie protested, "But you will have worked all day. You will be tired when you come home."

Josie smiled and her blue eyes twinkled, "Yes, but this way, Reuben will eat with us in the evening instead of taking his meals downtown. That means I will get to spend more time with him."

At Sadie's questioning look, Josie laughed.

"Reuben is all business at the office. When he isn't with patients, he is studying procedures. I truly am an employee there. Don't get me wrong—I do love working with him. I just want to be around him when the job is turned off too," she stated with a laugh.

Josie leaned toward Sadie as her blue eyes flashed. She whispered, "Perhaps, after we are married, I will have to dress more provocatively to get his attention!"

Sadie's eyes went wide, and Josie giggled. Sadie stared at her sister-in-law and a laugh bubbled out of her.

"Josie, you act so proper in public, but underneath, you are every bit as ornery as Slim!"

Josie giggled. She looked away. When she looked back, her eyes were somber.

"I miss him so much. I am so thankful that I came to Cheyenne. I just wish I had moved here sooner." She hugged Sadie and added, "I am so thankful he found you. I can't wait to meet his little boy."

Tears filled Sadie's brown eyes, but she smiled. "You are all so sure I am going to have a little boy. What if she is a wild little girl?" Tears leaked out of Sadie's eyes. "Oh Josie, I so didn't plan to raise this baby alone."

Josie pulled Sadie into a hug. "You don't have to do it alone, Sadie. You have a big, loud family to help you. Slim may not be here, but he made sure you were taken care of."

Sadie went to bed early that night. She could hear Reuben and Josie laughing through their meal. She was still awake when Reuben left.

"Oh, Slim, why did you have to die?" Sadie whispered. "I miss your smile, and I miss your arms around me at night."

She quietly climbed out of bed and pulled Slim's red-checkered shirt out of the closet. It still smelled of his scent. Sadie wrapped it around her arms with her face on it. She finally fell asleep.

That night she dreamed she saw Slim's smiling face. "Be happy, Sadie. Be happy fer me an' fer our baby." Sadie did smile and slept deeply for the first time since Slim had died.

The women of Cheyenne soon heard about Sadie's abilities, and her sewing business grew quickly. Before long, she was turning down jobs or scheduling them out two and three months in advance. Only Sadie was surprised, and all her friends were delighted.

Sadie took her work and her creations very seriously and she was trying to finish as many as she could before the baby arrived. As she paused one morning to look at her calendar, she gasped.

"It is August first, and according to Doc's calculations, our baby could arrive the end of this week." She rubbed her back and pulled herself to her feet.

Lance always told her she was beautiful. Sadie laughed to herself. "Lance thinks all pregnant women are beautiful."

Molly just rolled her eyes when he said that, but Molly *was* beautiful when she was pregnant. She had a tiny body and a little baby bump.

Sadie's full figure bloomed, and she felt huge. As she walked by Slim's saddle, she growled, "And don't you say anything. I know I'm bigger than a cow."

Slim's voice came so clearly to Sadie that she almost dropped the shirt she was working on.

"Now Sadie, ya know I think cows are beautiful an' if I was there, I'd shore tell ya that yore the most beautiful little heifer I ever seen."

Tears sprang up in Sadie's eyes. She slowly laughed. "Yes, you would," she agreed. She straightened her shoulders and took a deep breath.

"I need to purchase more pins if I am going to get all these projects completed."

Sadie grabbed her shawl and handbag. She pushed a loose curl back into the bun on the back of her head and hurried down the street toward the Union Mercantile.

"Mrs. Whipple said the pins I ordered would be in today. She was to get some new fabric in as well. She offered to let me look it over before she set it out so I'd better hurry."

Suddenly, Sadie's stomach cramped so hard it almost took her breath away. She paused and gripped the fence next to the walkway as she took deep breaths.

"Perhaps I should walk down to Doc's when I leave the store. Surely, I'm not in labor yet," she whispered as she crossed the street slowly.

Mrs. Whipple was delighted to see her.

"Sadie, the pins are in, but we have been so busy we don't even have the order unpacked. I will send one of the boys over this afternoon with them.

"Would you like to look at that new fabric while you're here?" she asked excitedly as she hurried around the counter.

Sadie's face blanched when another contraction hit her, and she gripped the counter. She tried to smile at Mrs. Whipple as she shook her head.

"I don't think I will today. I'm not feeling that well."

When Mrs. Whipple's face filled with concern, Sadie put up her hand.

"I am only a short way from Doc Williams' office. I will go ahead and walk down there now. I believe I will look at that fabric another day though." Sadie moved haltingly toward the front of the store, pausing to grip the door jamb before she walked out.

CHAPTER 26

THE BACHELOR AND THE LADY

LEVI RODE SLOWLY DOWN THE MAIN STREET OF Cheyenne on his large stallion. He had received a letter several weeks ago asking him to consider practicing law in the Wyoming Territory, specifically in Cheyenne. It was signed by several of the business leaders of Cheyenne including the mayor, H.M. Hook.

Samuel Brewster had started the petition. He presented it to the mayor with the signatures of nearly all of Cheyenne's full-time citizens. The first one to sign was the hostler, Fred Smith. Most of the signees had been at the trial of the rustlers five months prior and had seen the corruption of their legal system at its worst. The whole town had been impressed at how the young lawyer had handled himself. Now, many folks were hoping he would relocate.

I wonder if Sadie had her baby, he pondered as he rode slowly down Main Street. He pulled up in front of the Union Mercantile just as a young woman stepped down into the street. The raised walk in front of the mercantile was crowded, but the boardwalk on the opposite side of the street was nearly empty.

Sadie began to cross slowly. Another contraction came with a fury. She almost fell as she staggered a few more steps toward the other side.

Whooping and hollering sounded from down the street along with the bawling of cattle. A new herd fresh off the trail was charging down the street directly toward her, followed by whooping cowboys.

Terrified, Sadie looked up. She stumbled as she tried to get out of the way. When the cowboys saw her, they tried to push toward the front of the herd to move the cattle over. However, the longhorns were running full tilt and the street was too narrow to get around them.

Levi spurred his stallion. The horse charged into the street between the cattle and the young woman. He leaned down from his saddle and grabbed her around the middle, placing her in front of him as his horse leaped up on the boardwalk on the opposite side of the street.

The cattle rushed by followed by the cowboys. Several called out as the herd swept on down the street. Levi could feel the young woman's heart beating frantically. He realized his arm was still clenched around her and not in such an appropriate way.

He looked down as he relaxed his arm. He was ready to release her to the sidewalk when he realized he was holding Sadie. Another hard contraction hit, and Levi felt it. His eyes went wide with alarm.

"Sadie! Tell me where Doc's office is. We need to get you there now!"

She pointed down the street. Just then, her water broke drenching them both. Levi spurred the horse again. Dropping to the ground and holding her easily, he raced into Doc Williams' office, roaring for the doctor as he ran. No one answered.

A sign over one of the doors said Examination Room. Levi kicked the door open and laid Sadie on the bed. He started to step back.

She gripped his hand. "You are going to have to help me since Doc isn't here. Undo my dress and help me out of it."

Levi's face turned a deep red, and he began to stutter.

Sadie's brown eyes flashed. "Get this dress off me or I will rip it off," she panted as she struggled to remove the dress.

Levi's hands were trembling as he unhooked her dress and slid it down her shoulders.

She kicked at it. "Get it *off!*"

Levi jerked the dress down leaving Sadie in her bodice and pantaloons.

Another contraction hit her, and Sadie squeezed Levi's hand so hard she almost drew blood. As it eased off, she stared at him.

"Help me out of bed. Molly squats on the floor when she births her babies, so that is what I am going to do." Sadie began to pull on her pantaloons, but they were stuck to her. She jerked at them while Levi stared at her in shock. He quickly turned away.

"Don't you turn your back—help me get these things down!" The cotton fabric was wet and was stuck to her body. Sadie jerked Levi back around and glared at him.

"Pull them down! You don't expect me to birth a baby in britches, do you?"

As Levi began to work the wet pantaloons over her large stomach, Sadie grabbed his arms. She hung on as another contraction came. Levi's hands were shaking as he pulled on the wet pantaloons.

Sadie glared up at him and screamed loudly, "Pull them *off*—this baby is coming now!"

Levi jerked the pantaloons down and Sadie kicked them to get them out of the way. She grabbed his arms as another contraction came and began to lower herself to the floor.

Looking up at the man in front of her, Sadie grunted, "Catch it and don't let it drop or hit the floor."

As Levi stared at her in horror, she screamed at him, "Catch it! I can't do this all myself!"

Levi dropped to the floor and placed his hands under her bottom.

Sadie's hands were on Levi's shoulders. She clenched them so hard, he thought she was trying to kill him. Her eyes were closed as she strained, pushing and grunting loudly.

Levi thought about screaming himself. Sadie's nails were digging into his shoulders, and he could feel his thin shirt tearing.

Suddenly, a little wet head appeared followed by shoulders. As the baby slid out, Levi caught him in his hands. He stared at the tiny boy and then at the young woman squatting in front of him.

Sadie slowly sank back on her folded legs and tears ran down her cheeks.

"Slim, you should have been here. Why did you have to leave me?" she sobbed.

Levi lifted her up with shaking hands and helped her onto the bed. He placed the baby on her chest and pulled a blanket over both of them. Sadie was crying softly as she looked at her son, and Levi backed away from the bed.

Doc Williams rushed into the room with Josie close behind. Levi moved toward the wall to give them more room. As he looked at all the blood on the floor and on his hands, his head began to spin. The room began to weave. Levi passed out and hit the floor with a loud crash.

Sadie stared at him for a moment.

"I think I traumatized the poor man," she whispered to Josie. Her eyes were huge as they looked from the big man lying on the floor to her son. Levi was too big to move so Doc let him lay as he worked to deliver Sadie's afterbirth. He cut the cord, and Josie took the baby to clean him up. The little boy was crying loudly when Josie brought him back to Sadie. The new mother kissed her baby's curls. She pulled him close to nurse, and he began to suckle noisily.

Josie put smelling salts under Levi's nose, and he began to stir. She was trying not to laugh as she checked him over.

"You will have a bruise on your head. I also see some cuts on your arms and shoulders. Other than that, you should be fine."

Levi turned a deep red again as he sat up. He slowly climbed to his feet.

Sadie smiled sweetly at him. The crazy woman who had screamed at him as she birthed her baby was gone, and sweet Sadie was back.

Levi was confused and a little afraid, but his heart was overflowing. The entire experience had been terrifying and wonderful at the same time.

When Sadie smiled at him again, he asked, "Do you want me to leave?"

Sadie's eyes were large as she shook her head.

"Please stay until Martha and Badger arrive. They should be coming any time." She paused and touched his hand where the cut marks were bleeding. When she saw more blood spots on his shirt sleeves and shoulders, she frowned. "Did I do that?"

Levi blushed again as he shrugged. "Those are nothing, but you must have been in some powerful pain to grip as hard as you did."

Sadie's brown eyes were wide. "I don't remember gripping you that hard but thank you. Thank you for bringing me here and for helping. I'm not sure I could have managed this birthing alone."

Levi squeezed her hand. "I'm glad I was here," he whispered as he touched the baby's little head.

CHAPTER 27

Some Apologetic Cowboys

BADGER AND MARTHA ARRIVED IN A RUSH. LEVI could hear Badger's high-pitched voice hollering at the team and then at people in the waiting room.

"Move over, we's a comin' through! My gurl's back there. Now get outa the way an' quit yur starin!'"

The two excited people charged into the room. When they saw baby and mother were both fine, they relaxed. Badger looked Levi over and laughed his wicked laugh.

"So ya birthed yur first baby, did ya? An' I see ya survived ta tell!"

Levi's neck turned red. As the color moved up to his face, he looked down. His britches were wet and splattered with blood. His shirt was soaked and the cuts on his shoulders were showing through the thin fabric. He looked up at Badger and grinned.

"Well, durn. This was my best shirt too."

Sadie started giggling, and Martha laughed out loud. The shirt was so thin the fabric was almost sheer. Now it had cuts and tears all over.

Sadie smiled as she looked at her friends.

"Badger, if you look in my closet, there is a shirt in there for Levi." She smiled shyly at Levi. "I made it after the trial as a thank you—just in case you came this way again."

Her eyes filled with humor and another laugh bubbled out. "It may not fit perfectly, but it will be better than what you have on."

Levi grinned at her. "I think I earned that shirt a second time," he drawled as Josie led him out of Sadie's room and down the hall to clean up.

She pointed toward a basin of hot water. "You may wash up there."

Badger followed him.

"So who's all the cowboys in the front room there? They has flowers an' all sorts a stuff."

Levi was confused. "Are they waiting to see Sadie?"

Badger nodded his head.

"They seem ta be. Mebbie you'ins should ask 'em what they need." He added with a sly grin, "After all, you'ins be the one ta birth that there boy so that makes ya as close to a pa as that little tyke'll ever have."

Red crept up Levi's neck again. He looked down at Badger and asked seriously, "Have you ever birthed a baby, Badger? Why Sadie was just darn near crazy—and angry!"

Badger's blue eyes flashed, and he folded over as he laughed wickedly. "Why shore that's normal though some be a little madder than others. Kinda funny thing that they's willin' ta do it more'n oncet."

Levi nodded as he thought about that. Finally, with clean hands and face, he headed out to the waiting area.

Ten nervous cowboys were milling around and twisting their hats. They all turned as Levi entered the waiting area. One of the older riders stepped forward.

"We jist wanted to say we was sorry fer nearly runnin' down yur wife like that. We shore didn't mean no harm. We was glad to finally make it up here from Texas an' we come into town on a side street. We shore didn't know that route would take us right down yore main street

156

there. We jist was a little too anxious to get them cows south to the pens." The cowboy's face was sincere as he added, "We come up here to see that she was alright."

The man hesitated. His face turned red as he added, "We shore didn't know she was a gonna have a little baby till we heard all the hollerin' back there."

Levi stared at the humble riders. As red creeped back up his neck again, several of them grinned. Others looked just as uncomfortable as he felt.

"How about you just apologize to her yourselves? I think she'd appreciate that." His eyes twinkled as he added, "She's back to her sweet self so you'll be safe to go in now."

A sigh of relief filled the room and the cowboys followed Levi back to the examination room.

Levi tapped on the door. He poked his head inside when Sadie answered.

"There's a group of fellows here who want to say they're sorry."

Sadie looked startled as she pulled the light blanket up higher. Josie had given her a blouse to wear so she would be more comfortable having visitors. She nodded her head.

As the contrite riders filed into Sadie's room, she almost started laughing. Each was carrying a bouquet of wilted prairie flowers or a small package of candy.

Levi pointed from the men to Sadie.

"Fellows, this is Mrs. Sadie Crandall." The men all nodded. Most had their hats in their hands. One didn't and the man next to him slammed an elbow in his ribs.

"Take off yore durn hat. We're in the presence of a lady," he growled in a loud whisper.

Levi hid his smile and added, "These riders asked to speak with you, Sadie."

One stepped forward and cleared his throat.

"Ma'am, we want to apologize fer nearly runnin' ya over. Next time, we'll come in like we's sposed to an' not run those cows down main street. We didn't mean to hurt nobody, 'specially not a little pregnant momma."

As he held out the flowers, Sadie nodded.

"Thank you for apologizing. Had it not been for Levi, things might have ended badly." Sadie smiled at all of them as she looked around the room.

"My late husband, Slim Crandall, was a rider from Texas. I know he would appreciate you all apologizing."

Several of the riders looked at Sadie in surprise. One in the back leaned forward.

"Why I knew Slim! We rode together fer several years. In fact, he nursed my baby brother when he was sick one winter.

"Jip didn't make it, but I heard Slim did his best to get 'im medicine. He even stayed by Jip till he passed. I always wanted to thank Slim fer that." He added softly, "We shore are sad to hear of his passin'. Slim was a fine man an' a good friend."

Sadie's brown eyes filled with tears. She reached out her hand to take the flowers from the man closest to her. She smiled again at all the riders. "Thank you so much for coming by. It is always nice to meet Slim's friends."

Slowly, the riders moved forward and placed their gifts in Sadie's hands. She greeted each one graciously and thanked them in a soft voice.

As the men headed outside, the one who appeared to be the foreman looked up at Levi. "How did Slim die?" he asked quietly. "I know it had to be recently 'cause that little ol' baby looks like his daddy."

Levi's face pulled down in hard lines. "Rustlers. They stole his herd on the way to the rails and shot him while he was down. That was nearly five months ago. It has been a hard time for Sadie, but she has lots of friends here. They have all stepped up."

The rider processed what Levi said. His eyes were hard when he spoke.

"Did they hang? I hear that judge they have here is easy on outlaws and heavy on fines."

Levi studied the man. *Now how did he know that?* Levi nodded slowly.

"Slim's friends wanted to hang them right away, but they were convicted legally. They hung a week later. Good thing too. The Rocking R riders would have torn the town apart to get to those outlaws if they hadn't been convicted."

The rider studied Levi with his cool eyes. "Good to know 'cause we jist might a taken a detour on our way back to Texas as well. Slim rode with nearly ever' man in our outfit an' a finer friend they jist don't make." He shook Levi's hand.

"We'll check back in with Mrs. Crandall on our next drive." He gave Levi another hard look with his cool, blue eyes. "Thanks fer helpin' out. Slim was one a us so his wife is too."

CHAPTER 28

REASONS TO STAY

LEVI STARED AS THE GROUP OF COWBOYS WALKED away. The hair came up on his neck.

"If those outlaws hadn't been hung, they'd sure be dead by the time those boys left this territory," he muttered. "I believe this town does need a good lawyer. Maybe I will just hang up my shingle here." As he looked back toward Sadie's room, he blushed and started to argue with himself as to his reasons for staying.

Badger stepped up beside him. "So ya decided ta stay an' lawyer here, did ya?" he asked with a knowing grin.

Levi turned a darker red and started to mutter. As he looked into Badger's ornery face, he laughed. "Well, you were the upstanding citizen who knew where to send the letter to bring me here, weren't you? Now here I am."

Badger grinned at him again and his knowing eyes twinkled. He patted Levi on the back.

"Let's go find that there shirt Sadie made ya."

Levi rode his stallion down to the livery where the hostler was waiting.

"What took ya so long to come back to town?" the man asked as his bright blue eyes gleamed.

"I am guessing you were one of the citizens who signed the letter asking me to practice law here," Levi stated with a chuckle.

Rooster's eyes twinkled.

"Fred Smith at yur service, but ya cin call me Rooster. I shore did enjoy yur last performance an' I'd like to see that kind a entertainment 'round here on a more regular basis." Looking more seriously at Levi, he added, "'Sides, Cheyenne is a growin' town an' we've a need fer honest men here."

Levi nodded in agreement as he shook Rooster's hand. He walked out to where Badger was waiting with his wagon.

As Levi climbed up, Badger hollered at his mules. He looked sideways at the man beside him.

"Don't let Rooster fool ya. That there feller has lots a connections back east. He were a big help ta some big dog officer durin' the war, an' he cin make things happen."

As Levi stared at him, Badger grinned. "Good feller ta have on yur side."

Levi snorted. "Kind of like the fellow sitting beside me now, I think."

Badger laughed his evil laugh as he faced forward and turned the wagon toward Sadie's house.

Sadie's home was neat and tidy. The curtains on the windows showed a woman's touch. Once again, Levi felt a longing for a home. He pushed the feeling aside as he waited for Badger, shifting uncomfortably from foot to foot.

Badger finally came out of a bedroom carrying a large shirt.

It was dark green. As Levi held it up, he was amazed. *Those sleeves might actually be long enough.*

"I don't know I have ever had a shirt big enough through the shoulders or with sleeves long enough," he mused out loud.

Badger laughed. "Sadie is purty much a whiz with 'er needles. She cin whip up jist 'bout anythin'. 'Course, this baby may slow 'er down some. Guess we'll have ta see.

"My Martha loves 'er like a daughter an' I do too. We sure was glad when Lance picked 'er up in Julesburg. Molly likes ta rescue folks an' Sadie shore did need rescuing. Now she's part a the family an' we all love 'er."

As Levi looked up, Badger saw the longing of a man who had never had a family. Levi looked away quickly, and for once, Badger had nothing to say. His busy mind was making plans though, and they all included this young lawyer. They visited like old friends as Badger drove his wagon up to the Eagle Hotel.

"I reckon I'll see you'ins 'round some," Badger stated as he grinned and winked. "An' let me know when you'ins be ready ta look fer a buildin' fer yur lawyer buisness!"

Levi chuckled as he jumped down from the wagon.

"I sure will, Badger—if I decide to stay."

Levi could hear Badger laughing as he drove away and he shook his head.

"Ol' Badger seems mighty sure I'm putting down roots here. I guess we'll have to see." He grabbed his warbag with the new shirt folded neatly inside and headed down to take a bath. When he visited Sadie again, he intended to look a lot cleaner than he had when he first rode into town.

It was August of 1872, but Levi did not even know what day it was. As he relaxed in the tub and smoked his cigar, he pondered on where his life would go from here.

"Maybe it wasn't so much I didn't want to practice law. Maybe it was more the location of where I'd have to live to do it," he muttered to himself.

Levi liked Cheyenne. *The folks here are straight shooters, and they want this town to be more than just a wild town created by the railroad. Yep, I think I will hang my shingle up here. I might actually enjoy practicing law for once.*

As he thought about the trial five months ago, he remembered Rudy and his interest in learning more about the legal workings of the law. Levi had shipped Rudy the books he had promised to send, and he hoped Rudy was studying them. *Maybe I can even get that young man to help me some. He might be able to come over after school.*

When Levi finally climbed out of the tub, his skin was wrinkled, and the water was cold. However, his mind was clear. For the first time in years, he had a plan and knew what he wanted to do. As he buttoned his new shirt, he stared down in surprise. He was amazed at how well it fit. The fabric was soft but sturdy, and he had plenty of room through the shoulders and arms.

I might have to hire Sadie to make me a couple more shirts, he thought as he flexed his shoulders. *Now if I can just find britches long enough to tuck into my boots.*

Levi strolled up the street and stopped at the mercantile store. The sign above the doors read, Whipple and Hay's Union Mercantile. As he walked in, a woman whom he assumed was Mrs. Whipple rushed up to him.

"Thank you so much for plucking our Sadie off the street. We were all watching and not a thing we could do to save her." As Levi's neck turned red, Mrs. Whipple continued. "I saw you rush her up to Doc Williams' office. I hope she is okay."

Levi smiled. He had no intention of sharing any information, but he nodded. "She was fine when I left her."

As he pointed toward the stacks of clothing, he asked cautiously, "Do you have any britches that would be large enough for me?"

Mrs. Whipple grabbed Levi's arm and drug him toward a stack of pants. She dug through the stack until she found the ones she was looking for.

"I believe these two pairs would be large enough. See how this one has buckskin sewn to the seat and on the back of the legs? That is to help them wear better in the saddle.

"That was actually Sadie's idea. She said she was tired of mending men's britches. She said the leather could be added when they were new. John down at the saddle shop is handling that for us.

"The cowboys are loving them, so we are going to add leather to more of them now."

Levi studied the leather reinforcement. He finally nodded.

"That is a good idea. I will take both pairs along with some socks and a pair of long handles. Don't worry if the long handles aren't long enough—they never are so I cut them off."

Mrs. Whipple laughed. "You and Lance Rankin. He can't find any long enough for his legs either.

"Let me wrap those up for you. I am going to throw in a few neckerchiefs as a thank you for rescuing our Sadie. She is a lovely girl. So sad about her husband."

Mrs. Whipple looked at Levi from under her lashes, and he almost snorted. Instead, he kept his face bland and thanked her for her help.

"And thank you for the bandanas as well," he called over his shoulder as he left the store.

CHAPTER 29

BADGER'S BUILDING

MRS. WHIPPLE WATCHED LEVI GO. "MY, HE SURE IS A nice-looking young man. Does anyone know who he is?" she asked of the patrons in her store.

A young cowboy looked up and started to answer. The rider beside him jabbed him in the ribs.

"Never share information if ya don't have to," his friend hissed in his ear. "If the big feller wanted 'er ta know his name, he coulda told 'er hisself."

All the riders in the mercantile had been at Doc's and had met Levi, but no one said a word. When Mrs. Whipple did not get any more information, she rushed off to help other customers.

Levi went back to his hotel room and changed into the new britches without the leather. He polished his boots and added one of the new bandanas. As he studied himself in the mirror, he almost blushed again.

"Dang, Levi. You almost look like you're ready to go courting," he muttered to himself. "Well, I am the new lawyer in town, and I do need to find a building to work out of," he argued in his own defense.

Levi had never thought of himself as good-looking, but most women would have disagreed. His friendly face held a ready smile, and he was easy to look at. His shoulders and arms were heavy with muscle. They tapered down to his long legs. His hair was brownish-red, and the curls were tight but thick. His blue eyes were flecked with hazel and laughed most of the time. However, when he glared, those same eyes could pierce like a knife.

Levi did not like facial hair. He had grown a beard once. He thought his head looked more like a pumpkin than a head and had not grown one since. Levi Parker was a simple man with simple needs. He liked to keep his appearance that way as well.

His stomach grumbled loudly, and he realized it was nearly noon. He did a quick calculation. *No wonder I'm hungry. I haven't eaten since yesterday.*

I believe I'll walk down to see if Miss Sadie needs anything. Maybe she'd like me to bring her a little something to eat too, he thought as he strolled out of the hotel.

As Levi walked along the main street, he looked at the buildings. Most had businesses in them already although the one next to the Lucky Lady Saloon looked empty. He stopped in the saloon and ordered a beer. When the bartender brought him his change, he asked about the building.

"Feller named Badger McCune owns that. Not sure what he wants to do with it. He bought it several weeks ago."

Levi laughed into his beer. *Of course, Badger owns it. He has never been a man to leave anything to chance.* He downed his beer and thanked the barkeep. As he stepped out of the bar, he saw Badger and Martha coming up the street.

Badger waved his top hat and hollered, "Howdy there, young feller! Want ta join us fer supper? Thought I'd take my Martha out ta celebrate 'nother grandson!"

Levi grinned at the animated little man. He tipped his hat to Martha as he said, "Ma'am." He turned to Badger. "I'd be glad to, Badger. In fact, I'd like to talk to you about purchasing that building right there." Levi's eyes glinted as he pointed at the empty building.

Badger scratched his chin and pretended to be surprised. "Why shore now, that would be a plumb good location fer a lawyer now, wouldn't it?" he mused as he continued to rub his stubbly chin. "Climb on up here, Boy, an' we'll talk over dinner."

Levi swung his long legs into the wagon, and Martha smiled at him. She put out her hand. "I'm Martha McCune. We weren't formally introduced when you were here before, but I understand you have known Badger for some time."

Levi leaned forward to shake her hand. "Yes, we met in Kansas City when I first began to lawyer. I didn't really intend to practice law again but that trial here several months ago showed me the need." He looked around and added softly, "I like Cheyenne, and it's been a long time since I said that about any town."

Martha beamed at him. She liked this young man, but then, she knew she would. Any man who saved her Sadie and then helped her birth her baby was a good man in Martha's mind.

Badger had told Martha a few of the details, and she almost felt sorry for the man. She did not know Levi had fainted though until Sadie told her.

Sadie was surprised, and Badger was too. After all, the man did raise mules. He certainly had experience birthing animals.

Martha had snorted at the two of them. "Birthing an animal would only partly prepare a man for birthing a baby, especially a bachelor. I'm just thankful that he was here and willing," she told the two of them.

The Ford House was nearly full, but Badger led the way to an open table. Lance and Rowdy strolled in followed by four loud little ones. Rudy was a little ways behind.

Rudy's eyes lit up when he saw Levi. "Mr. Parker! Are you here to practice law? I have been studying the books you sent me. Can I help you after school? Ma said she might have me stay with Grandpa Samuel during the week and attend school in town this year. I sure would like to help you if I can."

Rowdy stared from Rudy to Levi and a slow grin spread across his face. He put out his hand.

"Levi, good to see you. I believe those are the most words I have ever heard Rudy say to anyone at one time," he commented as he squeezed Rudy's shoulder.

Rudy blushed but the excitement stayed in his face. He maneuvered between the men to sit close to where Levi stood. Levi shook hands with the men and sat down beside Rudy. His eyes were twinkling as he studied Rudy's face.

"Why, Rudy, I think I would like to have your help. Of course, your studies come first. You'll have to have your schoolwork done before you come by." Levi put out his hand and Rudy shook it eagerly.

"Did Badger show you the building he bought for you?" Rowdy asked.

Badger choked on his drink, and Lance started laughing. Rowdy looked confused as he looked from one man to the other.

Badger growled, "Now durn it, Rowdy. Ya know I was goin' ta sell that thar buildin' fer a whole lot more'n I paid fer it. You'ins jist went an' spoilt the whole deal."

Martha elbowed Badger as she rolled her eyes. She smiled at Levi as the men laughed.

"Actually, Levi, the building belongs to me. You may rent it or buy it, your choice."

Levi stared at Martha for a moment. He nodded.

"Martha, I would love to do business with you. It would take a special lady to keep up with Badger. The pleasure will be mine."

Martha beamed and Barney began to bring out the food. He took one look at Levi and set a second plate in front of both Rowdy and him. Levi was surprised but happy, and the food was excellent.

Sammy and Maribelle were on either side of Badger, and he sneaked candy to them all through the meal. Lance finally caught on when he realized why they were both so quiet. Paul sat between Rowdy and Lance while Abigail climbed from lap to lap eating off everyone's plate.

When she finally made it to Levi's lap, Lance reached for her. Levi shook his head. He liked kids even though he rarely ate with them. It was all a game to him.

Abigail took to the big man and stayed on his lap for the rest of the meal.

CHAPTER 30

BABY LEVI

AS THEY LEFT THE RESTAURANT, LEVI TURNED TO Martha. "When would you like to finalize the sale of your building, Martha? I'd like to get to work right away."

Martha reached in her purse and handed Levi a key. "You go ahead and do what you need to do. Badger and I will be back in town tomorrow to take Sadie home. I plan to stay with her a few days to help out.

"In fact, why don't you come by Sadie's the day after tomorrow for supper. We can close the deal then."

Levi nodded, and Badger hustled Martha into the wagon. They were gone with a clatter of hooves.

Lance turned to Levi. "Do you want to come down with us to see Sadie? She said you helped her birth her baby." Lance's eyes were twinkling, and he was trying not to laugh.

Levi stared at him suspiciously and Rowdy grinned. Lance laughed as he added, "They all go through an angry stage. Don't let it get to you. I'm sure she yelled some."

The red began to creep up Levi's neck, and Lance laughed out loud. "Dang, wish I'd been there to see the show."

Levi shook his head. "No, you don't," he declared seriously as his face turned completely red.

Rowdy stared at the two men. "Now you do know Beth is going to birth this fall. Are either of you going to share anything with me?"

Levi and Lance both said, "No!" at the same time.

Lance laughed again. He clapped Levi on the back. "Let's go see Sadie." Abigail pulled on Levi's legs and held up her arms. He lifted her and she proceeded to climb on his shoulders. Levi hung onto her legs as she squealed excitedly. The three tall men headed up the street to Doc Williams' place followed closely by Sammy, Paul, Maribelle, and Rudy.

Molly met them at the door of Doc's office with Sadie's baby in her arms. The little boy's curly, blond hair showed out of the top of the blanket. Molly's eyes were shining.

"Isn't he beautiful!" she exclaimed as she held him down for the children to see.

"What's his name?" asked Sammy.

Beth rushed out to join them. "His name is Levi. Isn't he a beautiful little boy? Just look at those blond curls."

Levi stared at the baby. He took the tiny hand in his and said softly, "Well, Kid, you kept your part of our deal. Guess I will have to name mine after you." As the small group stared at him, Levi looked away. His face was almost sad when he spoke.

"Slim and I knew each other as kids. He hated the name Charlie, so we all called him Kid. We agreed when we were twelve that we would name our first son after each other. His would be named Levi, and mine would be Kid." Levi's eyes watered a little at the corners as he looked at the happy group. "I hope he is as ornery and happy as his daddy was."

Rowdy and Lance looked away. Beth touched her heart with her hand.

Molly wasn't listening. She was focused on the baby. She whispered to him and pulled him closer to kiss his face. She turned toward the room where Sadie was.

"Come, children. Let's go see your Aunt Sadie."

Sadie was sitting in a rocking chair by the bed. She had watched the little group come up the street and saw Abigail on Levi's shoulders. She also saw that he wore the shirt she made for him. *It fits him well*, she thought proudly. As the noisy group pushed into her room, she reached out her hands for her baby.

Levi had never seen anything so beautiful as Sadie rocking her baby. When he realized he was staring, he looked away. Abigail was squirming so he set her on the floor.

All the children were talking at the same time, and they all wanted to hold the baby. Molly slid a chair across the room. She put it next to Sadie. One at a time, the children held the little boy under the watchful eyes of their parents.

Sammy looked down at the baby. He frowned as he looked from Sadie to Levi.

"His name is Levi and yur baby's name is Levi. We can't have two Levis," he stated emphatically. "I am gonna to call him Little Kid."

As the adults laughed, Sadie looked up at Levi and smiled. Levi's heart caught. He could feel panic rising in him. He started to edge toward the door. *I need to leave. I can't get too attached to Sadie or her family.*

As everyone talked and visited, Levi slipped out the door and headed back up the street.

Beth's wise eyes followed him. When she looked up, Rowdy smiled at her. They both understood how Levi felt, and Beth was determined to make sure he was always welcomed when she was around.

Rowdy looked down at his wife and he felt a tug on his heart. *Molly rescues people and Beth rescues hearts*, he thought. He moved up beside Beth and put his arm around her as he kissed her cheek. She smiled up at him but there were tears in her eyes.

CHAPTER 31

WHO WOULD YOU HIRE?

LEVI STOPPED AT HIS NEW BUILDING AND UNLOCKED the door. The building was long. There were three rooms downstairs as well as one large room upstairs. He was pleased with the size of the rooms.

"Why I can have my sleeping quarters upstairs. I can crawl out of bed and head right down the stairs to my office."

As he walked through the rooms, he calculated what he needed. "I need a desk and a bookcase in here as well as a filing cabinet of some kind. I will put a higher desk out there in case I ever hire a receptionist." His mouth twisted in a half smile. "In case I ever get really busy," he laughed.

Levi studied the third smaller room. An idea came to him, and his eyes glinted with pleasure.

"I will make that my assistant's room. I can put a smaller desk in there for Rudy. He can maybe do his schoolwork here from time to time. We can shut the doors when either of us needs privacy or quiet." He paused in his planning and muttered, "Now I just need to find someone to make me some furniture."

Levi frowned as he walked back to his room at the hotel. *It's a good thing I sold my mules and my little spread west of Laramie. I am going to need some working capital to get this all rolling.*

The hotel clerk looked like a friendly fellow, so Levi stopped to visit. They chatted about the town for a bit. As Levi headed towards the stairway, he paused. He turned and smiled at the clerk.

"Say, who would you talk to if you needed some office furniture made—like some desks, bookcases, that sort of thing?"

The clerk thought a moment.

"One of the handiest fellows I know is Tiny Small. He's a ranch hand out on the Rocking R. He made some furniture for Mrs. Crandall and does careful, detailed work. He doesn't really hire out much. You would have to ask him personal if you wanted him to help you out." The man grinned at Levi as he added, "Lance keeps his hands busy, but he might let him off if he likes you."

Levi laughed along with the man. "Well, maybe I will ride out there and talk to both of them. How about a sign for the door? Know anyone who can create one of those?"

The talkative clerk suggested the blacksmith.

"Old Smithy is mighty handy with his iron. Just tell him what you want, and he can make it up."

Levi put out his hand. "The name is Levi Parker. I'm going to practice law here. I sure appreciate your help. Mr.?"

The clerk shook Levi's hand. "Peter Strand. It's a pleasure, Mr. Parker. I watched you at that trial of those outlaws last spring. I sure am glad you came back to town." The clerk's dark eyes were friendly, and Levi grinned at him.

Levi hung up his new shirt and pulled out one of his old ones.

"Maybe Sadie will make me a few more shirts. I'd best keep this one clean for now."

He scratched out a quick sketch of what he wanted on his sign and headed for the blacksmith's shop.

Smithy studied the paper before he looked up at Levi.

"That looks a little plain. Ya want me to add a little character to it?"

Levi slowly nodded. "I hear you are a man who knows your metal so you create what you think will look good." He put out his hand. "Levi Parker. Thanks for your help, Mr.?"

The blacksmith grunted. "Just Smithy. That's what they call me. I'll have this ready for you tomorrow afternoon, Mr. Parker."

"Just call me Levi. Thanks, Smithy, and I will be in tomorrow afternoon."

Levi picked up his horse at the livery. He rode by Doc's office just as Lance and Rowdy walked out. He pulled up his horse.

"Lance, I'd like to talk to you about hiring one of your hands to make some office furniture for me. He was recommended by a fellow here in town. I want to ask him in person but thought I should make sure you could spare him for a couple of days."

"Who did they recommend?"

Levi swung one long leg up over the saddle. "Tiny Small. Said he made some furniture for Mrs. Crandall and did a fine job."

Lance nodded. "Why don't you ride on out to the ranch with me, and you can ask him this evening. I could spare him now if you could start tomorrow.

"I'm headed home as soon as I get my horse. Why don't you wait here, and I'll pick you up on my way out of town. The women are spending the night at Sadie's and just headed up there with the kids."

Lance grinned at Levi. "It's a little quieter in there now if you want to say hello."

Levi could feel the heat start to creep up his neck, but he laughed.

As he walked away, Levi called after him. "What about wood? Anything I need to buy before Tiny starts or does he have wood he likes to work with?"

Lance shrugged and replied, "Just ask him tonight. I'm not sure what he likes to work with or what he has stashed."

Sadie had her window open and heard the conversation between Levi and Lance. She watched as Levi dismounted, but he made no effort to walk up the steps to Doc's office.

She called softly, "Come on in, Levi. There is no point in you waiting for Lance out there."

Levi grinned and waved. He quickly loped up the steps. As he stepped through the door, Sadie smiled at him.

She held the baby out to him. "Would you like to hold your namesake now that things are calmer? After all, you were the first to hold him!"

Levi reached for the bundle Sadie held out to him. The baby's blond curls were soft and laid against his head. His round, little face was full, and his lips were dark red. Levi thought he was the prettiest baby he had ever seen. But then, he really had not seen any babies this young.

"He's truly beautiful, Sadie."

She nodded happily. "He snorts like a little pig when he eats, and he gulps as fast as he can. Doc said he weighed ten pounds at birth, but the way he eats, he is going to gain quickly."

The baby started to stir, and Levi quickly handed him back to his mother.

"So, you are going to stay? I heard you talking to Lance about hiring Tiny to make furniture." Sadie smile was friendly as she waited for Levi's answer.

"Yes, I am going to practice law here. I bought a building on Main Street and will close the deal with Martha in a few days." He paused. "In fact, she invited me over to your house for supper to sign papers. She said she would be staying with you for a time."

Sadie laughed softly. "Martha and Badger are wonderful. They are more like my parents than friends."

Levi studied Sadie's pretty face.

"You have a big, loving family here, Sadie. It is obvious they all care for you. You are a lucky woman."

Tears filled the corners of Sadie's eyes, but she nodded. "Yes, I am," she agreed.

"How about you, Levi? Do you have family anywhere?"

Levi pulled his eyes from Sadie's and looked out the window. He was smiling when he looked at her again.

"Naw, just me. You know my folks died when I was young. I don't have any other family that I know of."

He gave her a full grin and added. "I did almost marry one time, but the gal dumped me when I wouldn't move to Denver to practice law with her father. She sure broke my heart, but it was all for the best." He grinned bigger and his eyes sparkled. "Of course, I would be fabulously wealthy by now if I had done it."

They both laughed and were talking easily when Lance poked his head through the door.

"Ready or do I need to come back later?" he asked with a grin.

Levi blushed as he reached out to touch the baby's soft cheek. "I guess I'll see you in a few days then," he drawled as he tipped his hat to Sadie.

Sadie's face was thoughtful. She had seen the loneliness on Levi's face when she had asked him about his family.

"I guess we all have a little sadness we carry around with us," she whispered to herself as the two men mounted their horses.

CHAPTER 32

A Job for Tiny

W HEN LEVI WAS MOUNTED, LANCE LOOKED OVER AT him and grinned. Levi scowled as he felt himself blush and Lance laughed.

Once their horses were headed toward the Rocking R, Lance pointed out the spreads they passed. He told Levi who lived where, as well as who the largest operators were. He never mentioned himself, but Levi guessed Lance was one of the big dogs around Cheyenne.

"Where do Rowdy and Beth live?"

Lance pointed west.

"Rowdy bought out an outfit northwest of here. After Slim died, Sadie sold their spread to him. They moved down there about a month ago. It's been kind of a long process. Rowdy has mules and horses spread all over the country."

Lance chuckled and added, "He landed a government contract to provide riding stock for the army. That is keeping him busy. It helps with the cash flow too. I like to raise cows, but Rowdy has always liked horses."

Lance stared toward the direction of Rowdy's ranch and added quietly, "He is particular though. He won't sell to anyone he thinks will abuse them. It cost him a little business in the beginning. Now his reputation is established, and most folks appreciate that policy."

Levi nodded but did not respond. He had heard that about Rowdy and respected him for it.

Lance leveled his hard, blue eyes at Levi. "What about you? What do you want?"

Levi stared back at Lance. He shrugged and slowly looked away.

"I didn't think I would ever practice law again. It didn't really interest me as much as mules and horses. When I helped try those fellas who killed Slim, it all changed.

"I am tired of corrupt and weak judges letting the guilty off or being bought off. If we want this territory to prosper, we need to tame the wild element without punishing the good citizens. As a muleskinner, I can't do that. As a lawyer, I can." Levi looked directly at Lance.

"For the first time in a long time, I feel at home. I like Cheyenne, and I like the people. Maybe I won't be here forever. For right now though, this is where I want to settle down."

Lance's eyes glinted.

"And how about a wife? Do you have one of those or are you looking?"

Levi's neck turned red, but he returned Lance's stare. "I don't have a wife, but I am open to the idea if the right woman comes along."

Lance looked hard at Levi, and Levi stared back. Lance finally smiled and the two men rode the next five miles with little conversation. Each was wrapped in his own thoughts and voicing them was not necessary.

Gus rang the supper bell as Lance and Levi rode into the ranch yard.

Lance called to him, "One more for supper, Gus."

Gus grunted. He always fixed extra food because there was usually one extra pair of boots at the Rocking R's table.

As the hands began to trickle in, they eyed Levi curiously. Most remembered him and wondered what he was doing on the Rocking R.

When Tiny spied him, he shouted, "Why it's that lawyer feller! What're you doin' this far outa town, Judge? Somebody goin' to jail?"

As the hands began to laugh, Levi grinned.

"I actually want to talk to you, Tiny. I'm hoping you can build me some office furniture. I hear you are quite handy when it comes to wood."

Tiny cocked his head. "Now who told ya that?"

Levi's grin became bigger.

"A nice fellow at the Eagle Hotel by the name of Peter Strand. He said you were kind of notional though. He suggested I ask you myself."

Tiny turned toward the riders behind him. "What do ya think, fellers? Should I help out this here tinhorn?"

Joe was usually quiet, but he commented seriously. "Well, he did do us all a service." His eyes glinted with humor and he added, "Besides, if ya keep dancin' with that little gal who works in the Painted Lady, ya may need his help to keep from goin' to jail—what with all the drinkin' ya been doin.'"

The other riders began to hoot and Tiny turned red.

He looked over at Lance. "Boss?"

Lance nodded. "Three days, Tiny, and then I want you back out here. And you stay out of the saloons. This is a working trip."

Tiny's face fell but he agreed.

"How about wood? What do you need me to have ready for you?"

Tiny snorted. "I'll bring my own durn wood. Ya jist tell me what all ya want so's I know what an' how much to bring." He moved his eyes over to Lance.

"Boss, cin I haul my tools an' wood in yur wagon?"

Lance nodded again. He looked from Tiny to Levi.

"What time do you want to start?"

"How about seven tomorrow morning? I'll provide dinner and supper every day as well as breakfast on the second and third days. I'll also arrange for a room at the Eagle so you don't have to come back out here every night."

One of the younger riders interjected, "Don't you need more than one man? I could stand a job like that!"

Levi shrugged.

"That's up to Tiny. I am on a deadline so the faster we get done, the happier I will be." He pulled some papers out of his saddle bags and showed them to Tiny.

"These are the things I want and the dimensions. The only thing I didn't put on here was a bed. I need a big one. If it's big enough for you, it will be big enough for me."

Tiny cocked his head and peered at Levi for a moment. "I think you an' me will get on jist fine, Judge." He pointed at a quiet rider.

"Shaw, how 'bout ya help me? Yur purty good at measurin' an' such."

Shaw looked at Lance who shrugged.

"Get it done and get back out here."

Tiny took the rough drafts from Levi and headed for the barn. Shaw joined him. Levi could hear them loading wood and banging tools.

Levi turned to Lance. "Let me know what I owe you for the lumber."

Lance laughed and shook his head. "That is all Tiny. He finds wood in the darndest places and then stores it in my barn." He grinned and added, "I don't mind though. He is always building something and most of his creations are darn handy." He clapped Levi on the back.

"Let's eat while it's warm. I'm guessing you will want to get back to town this evening, and that road is easier in the daylight."

It was nearly seven when Levi rode away from the Rockin R. The air was crisp and cool in the evening, but it was still light since it was early August.

Levi Parker was a happy man. He hoped to be staying in his own place within two to three days.

"Shoot, I could be open for business in a few days. And I'm ready to get to work."

Sadie heard the horse go by around eight. She recognized Levi by how he sat his horse.

"He sure rides easy for such a big man," she murmured to little Levi. "He kind of makes me think of your daddy." She lowered the window a little and climbed into bed.

As she pulled her baby close, she dreamed of Slim laughing beside her. Then his hair changed from blond to red, but he was still laughing. Sadie stirred and frowned in her sleep.

CHAPTER 33

A New Lawyer in Cheyenne

THE FORD HOUSE OPENED FOR BUSINESS AT SIX IN THE
morning, and Levi was one of the first hungry men through the door.

Barney waved and called to Levi, "Take any table but the big one in
the back." He was beside Levi's table with two plates of food. He didn't
visit but hurried off to serve other customers.

The Ford House was known for its good food. It was also said to be
one of the quickest places to get in and out of. Barney Ford was proud
of his "Good food Fast" reputation.

Tiny and Shaw were just pulling up in Lance's wagon when Levi
unlocked his new building. As he showed them around, Tiny nodded
and grunted.

When they came to Levi's personal office, Tiny cocked an eye at him.

"Do ya want yur desk built in here 'cause the size ya drew ain't gonna
fit through this here door."

Levi studied the door and grinned.

"Build it in there. I'm not planning to go anywhere. If I do, I'll have
you fix the hole I pull it through."

Tiny and Shaw started immediately measuring and cutting. They
had unloaded a variety of wood and Levi liked the looks of all of it. He

recognized the pine and the oak, but the hawthorn and hackberry were new woods to him. Neither of the men talked more than necessary, so Levi borrowed a broom from the saloon and began to clean up.

By noon, the bookcase was up, and his desk was partly done. Levi brought them food from the Ford House before he left to pick up his sign from Smithy.

The wrought iron plaque was a work of art. It read "Levi Parker, Lawyer for the People." The outside edge was surrounded by iron scrolls, and the letters were made from twists of iron.

Levi stared at it and shook his head.

"This is the finest sign I have ever seen," he stated as looked from Smithy to the sign again.

The blacksmith pretended to glare at him but grinned when Levi paid him a little extra.

"Thanks, Smithy. This is fancier than I expected. Almost *too* nice." He shook the gruff old man's hand. They were both smiling as Levi walked away.

As Levi walked back toward his building, a man shouted at him.

"Mr. Parker!" Levi turned to see a well-dressed man waving at him from the door of the First National Bank of Cheyenne. As the man beckoned again, Levi turned back to walk toward him.

"Mr. Parker, would you be willing to read over some legal descriptions for us? I usually mail them to Laramie. If you could read them here though, it would save me almost a week of wait time.

"My name is Robert Baker. I am the president of this bank." He paused as he looked around proudly. "We were just chartered this year and have only been open for business a short time."

The man was almost cocky, and Levi eyed him carefully.

He frowned and Mr. Baker added, "We will be glad to pay what we pay the lawyer in Laramie A bonus too if you finish early. $4 per contract with a bonus of $4 if you finish in two days or less."

While Levi studied the man and ran the numbers in his head, the banker grabbed a stack of documents.

"This is the first proposal I want you to read over."

Levi flipped through the pages before he glanced up at the bank president.

"I will be glad to go through these. However, my fee is $6 per contract or proposal with a bonus of $10 if I finish in two days or less—with a day being twenty-four hours."

Robert Baker's face blanched. He had hoped this new lawyer wasn't up to date on the price of legal fees. Unfortunately, it appeared he was.

The banker's face was long as he agreed. He placed the documents in an envelope and handed them to Levi.

Levi's eyes twinkled as he took the packet.

"I will see you in forty-eight hours with my comments and suggestions attached. Full payment with the completion of the work will be fine." He held out his hand. "It is a pleasure, Mr. Baker."

Robert Baker watched Levi walk away. He was disappointed the new lawyer required more money. However, there was no way an inexperienced novice could dig through all that legal jargon in two days. He rubbed his hands together and rushed back into his office to have his son document the contract.

When Levi returned, Tiny and Shaw were still working on his desk. They had used a combination of woods and the result was beautiful.

Tiny truly was a craftsman. Shaw was sanding the drawers to make sure they slid easily while Tiny was insetting small pieces of cut wood around the top edge of the desk. He had told Levi to draw out his brand earlier. That brand was now carved into the corner of the desktop. Tiny had filled it in with hawthorn.

The big cowboy looked up as Levi stared in amazement. "Ya might want to take Lance's wagon down to the mercantile an' see what they have fer mattresses. Yur bed is done an' ya could mebbie sleep here tonight. I fixed ya up a table there too in case ya want to work there of a night. Ya 'ill need a lamp a some kind an' I think ya should put a stove in somewhere too."

Levi slowly nodded.

"Tiny, you are better than a crew of men. You boys cut it off at six tonight, and we'll go down to Ford's for supper. Then you can come back here and work or go on up to your room at the Eagle. I'll pick up some lamps." Levi studied the rooms and before he turned to Tiny again.

"Would you mind helping me pick out a stove? I have no idea what I need or where to put it."

Tiny pretended to snort, but he agreed. He liked Levi. Even though he was smart, Levi didn't pretend to know everything. As Levi walked away, Tiny pointed at his back.

"That there is the man I want on my side if'n I ever git in trouble again. He don't know wood, but he shore knows the law."

CHAPTER 34

MY OWN PLACE

LEVI DROVE THE HORSES AND WAGON DOWN TO THE mercantile. When he asked Mrs. Whipple about a bed, she became animated. She drug him upstairs to see the new mattress that had just come in.

"It is a new invention and the first one in Cheyenne! In fact, we're not even sure if we will be able to purchase any more of them. Feel those springs? They allow the bed to move with your weight."

Levi frowned. "But how much weight does it hold?"

"Why it is safe for over three hundred pounds. Surely you don't weigh three hundred pounds, Mr. Parker," she stated as she looked him up and down.

Levi could feel himself turning red, but he calmly asked, "Do you have cotton tick mattresses? I think that is more what I am looking for. And some quilts or blankets to throw on top of it. I need some oil lamps as well."

Mrs. Whipple had him fixed up in no time. She was disappointed Levi did not want the spring bed, but she was sure someone would want to buy it.

Levi saw her dragging a woman customer up to look at it as he left. He grinned as he loaded his mattress in the wagon. The cotton mattress was rolled in a coil and tied. He planned to let it fluff up some before he slept on it. He drove the wagon back to his building and jumped down.

The mattress was heavy. Tiny grabbed one end to help Levi carry it upstairs. Shaw followed with the bedding and quilts. Levi had purchased five kerosene lamps. He placed one in each downstairs room and two in the upper bedroom.

Levi had forgotten to mention chairs, but Tiny was already working on them. He planned to make two for the upstairs table. He was trying a new design that swiveled for Levi's desk in his office.

The chair for the receptionist's desk would be taller since the desk would be taller. Levi was amazed at how much Tiny and Shaw had done in just one day. They were both tired though and chose to call it a night after they ate.

Once the two men were checked into their room at the Eagle Hotel, Levi went back to his office. He opened the papers and began to study them in detail. He laughed as he read them. They were simple compared to what he had analyzed in the past.

"I can probably have these done by noon if I don't have too many interruptions," he muttered as he breezed through the documents. He worked until about ten. Levi was tired when he locked his building and returned to his room at the Eagle. He smiled as he packed his warbag.

"Tomorrow night, I will be sleeping in my own bed in my own building!" he exclaimed to the mirror. As he dozed off, a pretty face with brown eyes flitted through his mind, and Levi smiled in his sleep.

Levi was up again at six the next morning. He hurried up the street to the Ford House. Tiny and Shaw were seated at the big table toward the back. They were the only ones at the table despite the full tables around them and the nearly full restaurant. Tiny looked up as Levi wandered back to where they were seated.

"Have a chair, Judge. This here's the Rocking R table. We know we always have us a place to sit in this here eatin' house no matter how full she is. Barney takes good care a us."

The little waitress set two plates in front of Levi and rushed back to the kitchen for more orders.

As Levi began to eat, Tiny pointed at the second plate. "Now I been eatin' here fer most a seven years an' not once did ol' Barney bring me two plates."

Levi grinned at him around his griddle cakes.

"You just need to eat with Rowdy more often. He gets two or three plates of everything. I guess I look almost as hungry as him."

Tiny wanted to sand the desk and bed one more time as well as apply oil before they were finished. He planned to finish the reception desk and chair as well as the file cabinet that day.

"Do ya want a desk an' chair in that there small room? I think ya said somethin' 'bout an assistant."

When Levi nodded, Tiny studied the plans. "I think we cin finish today unless ya think a somethin' else ya need."

Levi studied the two men. "You boys are fast and efficient. Lance is lucky to have you around—although I think you could stay busy just building things if you wanted."

Tiny scowled at him. "The Rockin' R is my home," he growled. "An' I ain't leavin' till Lance throws me out."

Levi chuckled and asked, "What time this morning do you want to look at stoves?"

Tiny wrinkled his forehead. "Shaw here cin put on the oil an' I'll go with ya to look. The mercantile don't open till after seven-thirty this mornin'. How 'bout ten? We should have a good start on the rest a that stuff by then."

"That will work. I just might have the stove delivered. No point in hitching those horses twice."

Tiny studied Levi as he ate. He had never known a lawyer before, but this fellow was nothing like he expected.

The morning passed quickly and at ten o'clock sharp, Tiny and Levi were on their way to look at stoves. Tiny studied them and showed Levi the ones he thought would smoke the least, burn the most efficiently, and vent the easiest. They finally settled on a Round Oak Beckwith stove.

No one seemed to know why it was called a Round Oak stove. Mrs. Whipple was excited to sell it though. The stove was another new product, and the mercantile only carried one of them. Mr. Whipple offered to deliver it at no charge.

Levi thanked him as he muttered under his breath. "He should deliver at what that stove just cost me."

Tiny eyed the stove. "I think ya should hire Joe an' Hicks to build ya a chimney. That way ya won't have to run that durn pipe through yur roof."

Levi nodded slowly and laughed. "I'll just do that.

"Lance may get tired of sharing his hands with me though by the time I'm done with this place!"

CHAPTER 35

TINY'S CRIB

LEVI FINISHED THE BANK PAPERS WHILE TINY AND Shaw worked on the rest of the office furniture. He took the completed papers to the bank at two that afternoon.

Mr. Baker accepted them with a shocked look on his face. "You are sure you went through all these?" When Levi glared at him, the banker blushed and apologized.

"I didn't mean to question your integrity or knowledge. I have just never had anyone work so quickly before."

Levi grinned at the surprised man. "Well, I do have a little more time right now. Maybe the next job will take a little longer."

Mr. Baker nodded distractedly as he handed Levi a second envelope. "Same fees and timeframe?" he asked.

Levi nodded and took the payment Mr. Baker offered him. He extended his hand.

"It is a pleasure to work with you, Mr. Baker." He paused before he asked, "Say, can you tell me where the land office is?"

Mr. Baker looked up with interest, but Levi did not share any more information. The banker's face showed a flicker of disappointment as he pointed down the street.

"The clerk opens at eight every day except Sunday. He is usually there most mornings by seven though."

The land office door was open, and Levi strolled in. He extended his hand to the man behind the desk.

"My name is Levi Parker, and I am a new lawyer in town. I was wondering if you could tell me the going prices of buildings on your main street."

The clerk pulled out his book. "The last one to sell was next to the Painted Lady. It sold for $3000 but the value was listed at $4500. The fellow who bought it has been buying a few properties here and there. He seems to know when bargains pop up, and he's right on them."

Levi stifled a chuckle and nodded. "Well, that gives me an idea of values. Thanks for your time."

Levi laughed as he walked back to his building. "Badger is right back into acquiring properties all over Cheyenne. I am guessing he liquidated in Kansas City but who knows with him."

Tiny had finished all of Levi's furniture and piled the wood scraps in one area. He was working on what looked like a small crib. As Levi leaned over to see, Tiny looked up.

"It's fer Miss Sadie. I didn't git 'er a crib made fer the baby yet, so I thought I'd jist make one now." His eyes twinkled as he stared at Levi somberly. "Guess that means yur gonna pay me fer the time it takes to make it—an' out a yur wood too."

Levi laughed out loud and Tiny grinned.

The crib was finished in an hour, but Tiny began to carve on each end. He sanded it a second time and made sure the rockers on the bottom were smooth. When he was done, the little crib was fancier than any from a mail-order catalog.

All four woods had been used with the grain of each accenting the wood next to it. Tiny had carved a pair of boots and spurs on one end and a rope with a shooting star on the other. As he sat back on his haunches to study it, Tiny pointed at the carvings.

"Slim loved his fancy boots an' he could ride anythin' he got on. He always said Sadie was his shootin' star an' I reckon she was. He done roped her an' they was happy." Tiny wiped his eyes. "Durn, I shore miss my friend."

Badger poked his head in just then. "Ya boys ready to call 'er a day? Martha said ta invite all a you'ins over fer supper. She said she'll have 'er ready by five so you'ins cin git on back ta the Rockin' R 'fore dark."

Tiny nodded and grinned. "We'll be there. I'll git the wagon an' load up these here scraps. I wouldn't miss Martha's food fer nothin'."

He carried the little crib to the front of the building and set it inside the open door.

Several women walked by and commented. One knocked tentatively.

"Excuse me? Are you selling this? If so, I am interested in purchasing it."

Tiny started to yell at her, but Levi stepped in front of him. "Actually, that one is a special order. However, you may place an order for one here. I believe he charges $10 in case you need to know the price." As the woman looked up at him, he added, "They are one of a kind, you know. Each one will be a little different. Depending on how intricate you want the carving, they could run just a little more."

Tiny's mouth was hanging open and Levi continued to block Tiny with his body. As the woman studied the beautiful little crib, Levi closed the sale.

"Of course, if you need to think about it, we can always add your name to the bottom of his list of jobs. He is a busy man though."

The woman took some money from her purse.

"Here is $10. I would like a crib with a doll on one end and three hearts on the other. My name is Josephine Hook. My husband is the mayor here.

"You can leave it in the land office when it's finished. My husband has a small office in the back. And thank you. I might be interested in some other items as well if your friend has the time."

Levi thanked her and Mrs. Hook hurried out.

Tiny's mouth was still open.

Levi grinned at him. "See how easy it is to pick up work? You are a craftsman, Tiny. Don't sell yourself short." Levi frowned briefly. He followed it with a grin.

"Although maybe I should have waited to build you up until I paid you myself."

Tiny laughed and slapped Levi's back. "Shore 'nuf, Judge. This here job is gonna cost ya more now!"

Levi grinned and the two men began to clean up. Shaw joined them. Soon, all three men were headed for a fast bath and a shave.

Levi wanted to be clean not only for supper but to sleep in his new bed.

CHAPTER 36

A Fair Price

TINY AND SHAW WERE TRYING TO REMEMBER HOW long it had been since either of them had taken a real bath. They couldn't agree. As they argued back and forth, Levi began to laugh.

"If you can't remember when it was, I am just glad that you decided to take one today. Now Sadie won't have to smell you during supper."

As the arguing turned to who stunk worse, Levi interrupted. "I'd like to get you paid before we go for supper, Tiny. Any idea what I owe you for the wood and labor?"

Tiny was silent for a moment. "$50 should cover it."

Levi looked over at Tiny in surprise. "That might barely cover the cost of the wood, but I doubt it. I was thinking more like $100."

Tiny's mouth fell open and Shaw laughed. "Why that's mor'n I make in three months as a hand!"

Levi smiled. "Yes, craftsmen make more than laborers. You need to think on that, Tiny."

Baths were quick as everyone was hungry. As they dressed, Levi handed Tiny $100. "Talk to Molly about holding this for you. You need to start saving, especially if you have a girl.

"And get started on that crib for Mrs. Hook. A couple of cribs per month would give you an extra $20 a month to put back for your own place."

Tiny stared at the money for a moment. He pushed his hand toward Levi. "Why don't ya jist hang onto this till I head fer home? That's a passel a money to be carryin' 'round."

Levi took the money back. "How about I bring it out this next week some time?"

Tiny nodded, and the relief showed on his face.

Tiny probably doesn't own a wallet. Well, I can change that. I like to work with leather. I can make a wallet just from the scraps I have coming by train with the rest of my belongings.

The three men headed to the livery for the wagon. They picked up the crib and Levi locked his building before they hurried to Sadie's house. They could smell the food before they arrived, and their stomachs were all growling.

Tiny carried the crib up the steps, and Levi knocked on the door. A very shapely Sadie answered. Levi realized he was staring. He blushed when she greeted them.

"Hello, Tiny, Shaw, Levi. Come in, won't you? Martha has been busy all day, and there is enough food for an army!"

Tiny held out the crib. "I made somethin' fer yur baby."

As he explained the carving on each end, Sadie hugged him and kissed his cheek. "Thank you, Tiny. What a wonderful gift." She whispered softly to him, "Slim would have loved this."

Tiny's smile was huge. He adored Sadie as much as he had loved Slim, and his expression showed it.

Martha's food did not disappoint, but when Sadie pulled out the cinnamon rolls, all three men were even more delighted. Martha and Sadie both loved to feed hungry men and little food was left when they finished. The men offered to help clean up, but Martha shook her head. She shooed Tiny and Shaw out the door.

"You get on home. I don't want you to have to drive that wagon too far after dark."

Tiny and Shaw thanked the women again. They headed for the Rocking R, arguing with each other as to who could see best at night. Shaw didn't say much to other people, but he sure liked to argue with Tiny.

Sadie went to tend her baby, and Martha pushed the dishes back to make room on the table.

"I drew up a contract, Levi. I think you will find it fair." Her selling price was $3025, and Levi looked up in surprise.

Martha gave him her big smile. "I like to see young folks get off to a good start. Besides, it will be nice to have a lawyer in town whom we can trust."

Badger grinned at him from across the table, and Levi laughed.

Badger leaned forward, and his bright blue eyes sparkled with humor. "I shore did enjoy the way ya pinned that thar shyster lawyer down. Them there boys was fixin' ta walk an' ya done changed their plans."

Levi nodded slowly. "That trial really showed me the need for a lawyer here. Judge Nader likes to pack his jury. He prefers fines because he makes sure they end up in his pockets. He's a weasel, and he knows what I think of him."

He moved his eyes to Martha. "Would you like me to pull out cash or just move the money to your account?"

Martha frowned. "I don't bank here in town so why don't you just bring me a bank draft next week. I'm not in any hurry. Besides, if you time it right, you just might get another meal." Her eyes were twinkling, and Badger was grinning.

Levi laughed and nodded. "I believe I can do that," he agreed.

Sadie carried the baby in, and as Levi peered down to look at him, he could see that the little face was even rounder than it had been two days ago.

"He looks like he's growing."

"Yes, he is," Sadie murmured softly as she kissed her baby's curls. "Of course, with Martha around, I don't have to do anything but feed him!" Martha kissed the baby's round cheek and began to clear the table.

Levi carried his dishes to the washtub, and Badger followed. "Say, ya' goin' ta the weddin' tomorry? Doc an' Miss Josie is gettin' hitched. They's doin' a small service at the church an' then we's all goin' up ta the Rollin's House fer a big party."

Levi shook his head.

"No, I didn't know anything about it—."

Martha interrupted him as she explained, "Doc told us to invite you. We forgot with all the baby commotion. You need to come. You will meet more of the townspeople.

"Besides, Sadie needs to dance with someone who won't step on her toes."

Sadie's eyes opened wide as she looked up. She dropped her gaze when they met Levi's and he laughed.

"Well, I do like to dance. Maybe I will try to go. What time does the party start?"

Martha was smiling broadly, and Badger's ornery eyes were snapping.

"Jist be there by four so's you cin help move some tables. They's fixin' ta feed us 'round five an' the dancin' starts after that. "'Course, ya might have some broke cowboys want ta sleep on yur floor if'n you'ins don't mind."

Levi raised his eyebrows in surprise.

Badger shrugged and added, "Payday were last week so they's pro'bly outa money by now an' can't afford ta stay in town. Rooster only tolerates so much noise in his barn. He draws the line if'n they's been a drinkin' all night. 'Course, I have Mule in thar an' most don't want ta sleep anywhar close ta that thar big jack!"

Levi had heard Badger had jack mule folks did not want to get too close to. He assumed that was the mule Badger was referring to. He thanked the women again for the meal.

As his eyes settled on Sadie, he added, "Sadie, I sure would like you to make me a couple more shirts. I have never had a shirt that fit so well nor had sleeves that were actually long enough." He flexed his arms to show her the room he had. "It surely is a fine shirt, and I do thank you for it."

As he smiled down at her, Sadie blushed, and Levi looked away. He put out his hand to Badger.

"Badger, thanks for an enjoyable evening. Martha, Sadie—thanks for a wonderful meal."

He tipped his hat to both women and turned to leave.

Sadie followed him to the door.

"Levi, I want to thank you again for helping me."

As Levi blushed a deep red, Sadie's neck colored and she added softly, "I'm sorry Doc wasn't there, but I couldn't have done it without you. You really were wonderful."

"Sadie," Levi answered huskily, "I wouldn't have wanted to be anywhere else—although, I will say it was a little terrifying!"

"Well, let's hope you don't have to experience that again," Sadie commented with a laugh.

"I would never wish that," Levi stated quietly. He turned to lope down the steps. When he reached the end of the lane, Sadie was still standing in the doorway. Levi tipped his hat as he smiled.

Sadie gave a quick wave before she stepped back into her house.

A big smile filled Levi's face.

"A dance, huh? Well, I do like to dance!" He pushed his hands into his pockets and began to whistle as he sauntered back toward his building. As he unlocked the door and went inside, a deep sense of pride came over him. "My own place and I can pay cash for it too. I like Cheyenne already."

Levi worked on the stack of documents until nearly nine-thirty. "I'm mighty glad to have these lamps," he mused to himself as he placed the papers inside the bank case. He stripped down and blew out the lamp.

As he lay back in his bed, a smile creased his lips. He put his hands under his head and studied the darkness. *I wonder what this town holds for me*, he pondered as he drifted off to sleep.

CHAPTER 37

SMALL TALK

CHEYENNE AWAKENED EARLY, AND LEVI LISTENED TO the sounds of the growing town. Hammers pounding, men talking loudly, and the smell of food cooking brought him out of bed. He swung his long legs to the floor, stretched, and dressed.

Shaw had pounded some nails in his walls to make hooks for his clothes, and Tiny had built him a small bureau. Levi was surprised since he hadn't put one on his list. The drawers slid easily, and he was pleased.

"Now I just need to get out to Laramie to see what the holdup is with those crates I had shipped." He had arranged for the shipment of his personal items by train the day he closed on the sale of his spread there. They should have beat him to Cheyenne.

The freight office in Cheyenne told him they were still in Laramie. The office there wouldn't release them to be loaded onto the train—something about missing paperwork.

Levi scowled. "I guess I will have to make a trip to Laramie on Monday."

As Levi made his new bed, he laughed.

"I did sleep well last night. I feel fresh as a daisy. Why I believe I can dance all night." He did a jig across the floor and hurried downstairs.

Levi liked things tidy, so he swept up the lingering sawdust and wood chips. When he was finished, he moved the furniture around to where he wanted it. Only then did he open the packet of papers Robert Baker had given him.

He read and made notes until he was too hungry to think. It was nearly one when he locked his doors and headed to the Ford House.

Barney led him to a table in the back and placed two plates of food in front of him with a friendly smile. As Levi began to eat, he listened to the conversation around him.

"Have you seen the new widow woman in town? She just had herself a baby. She sure is a looker. I hear Jimmy Baker has his eye on her. Probably will work too, him bein' the son of the richest banker in town."

Levi kept a poker face, but his stomach squeezed hard. He had met Jimmy Baker, and if a weasel could walk on two feet, its name just might be Jimmy Baker.

He almost laughed out loud as he thought about what Slim would say if Sadie let Jimmy court her. "Why he might just come up out of his grave!" The man next to Levi looked at him curiously, and Levi smiled.

"I guess I commented out loud. I believe my father would enjoy this food so much he just might come up out of his grave."

The man smiled in agreement, and Levi returned to his meal hiding a smile. *I'd better quit talking to myself out loud. Guess that's what happens when you have been alone your whole darn life.*

Doc Williams came in and men began to greet him. Some were reserved and polite, but most were haranguing him about his wedding that afternoon.

"So, yore marryin' yore assistant, are ya?" asked one. Another added, "Well, that's a good way to guarantee she sticks around to help!"

Doc took the teasing good-naturedly and invited all of them to the dance to be held later at the Rollin's House.

"The Ford House is fixing the food so you know we will have plenty to eat!"

Barney stuck his head out of the kitchen. "Doc, do you want me to plan to feed the entire town?"

Doc Williams laughed.

"Just as well. If I haven't invited them, Beth has. Josie's aunt is coming up from Texas, and I hear she might be bringing some friends as well."

One of the younger men leaned forward and asked excitedly, "Is she bringing women friends? Maybe some young ones? I sure hope so. I would like to dance with a woman who won't step on my toes."

Another man banged his shoulder. "Your toes? What about her toes? You have two left feet. No gal in her right mind would dance anything with you that requires foot movement."

The young man grinned and answered, "Who said anything about moving my feet? Maybe I'll just sway back and forth in the same spot and hang on for the entire song!"

Doc laughed and moved on to Levi's table.

"Levi, do you mind if I join you?"

"Feel free, Doc. I was having a full-blown conversation with myself, and folks were beginning to stare," Levi replied with a grin.

As Doc seated himself, he looked at Levi earnestly.

"I greatly appreciate you sticking with Sadie until I arrived. She told me you were a great help."

Levi could feel his face start to color. He tried to push it down as he looked at the young doctor.

"I don't know about that, but I can tell you she had a fierce hard grip on me."

"Yes, during labor, women go through several stages, and you experienced them all," Doc agreed with a laugh. He leaned forward.

"Sadie said she squatted on the floor—she said an Indian woman had Mrs. Rankin do the same. I am intrigued by that. The position makes complete scientific sense although I am not sure about the squatting.

"I am trying to create a bed that will tilt. I haven't finished the design yet, but it is coming along nicely."

"Well, those Indian women have been birthing babies successfully with no doctors for a lot of years—I'm surprised their methods haven't been copied before," Levi stated.

Doc started to say something else but stopped. He leaned back in his chair.

"I apologize. This probably is not a desirable conversation to have over a meal, and for sure not with a bachelor."

Doc almost blushed, and Levi's eyes twinkled as he drawled, "Don't worry, Doc. This conversation is not nearly as traumatic as the actual experience was."

As they both laughed, Doc leaned forward again.

"What I really wanted to ask was who you hired to make your furniture? Do you think he would be skilled enough to help me with my birthing bed?"

Levi was surprised at the question, but he nodded.

"Tiny Small, one of Lance Rankin's riders. He is quite the craftsman. I don't know where he learned woodworking, but he knows his wood. He can build just about anything. He even built a little cradle for Sadie."

Doc's eyebrows went up.

"Is he the one who is building the cradle for Josephine Hook? I heard her telling Josie about it yesterday when she came into the office."

As Levi nodded, Doc smiled.

"It looks like I need to talk to Mr. Tiny Small."

When Levi started to answer, Doc put up his hand.

"Don't tell me he will be at the wedding. Josie made me promise I wouldn't talk business, medicine, or techniques of any kind today, let alone give advice."

Levi grinned at Doc Williams.

"I think that is probably a good plan. I don't know much about women, but it does seem they like their sweetheart's attention, especially on what they consider big days."

Doc grinned back and agreed.

"You will be there, won't you? I know Sadie loves to dance, and I hear you are quite quick on your feet."

Levi was surprised again. As he raised his eyebrows, Doc laughed and shrugged.

"Badger. He just seems to know things. In fact, he seems to know everything!"

The men visited through dinner. Finally, Levi stood to go. He stretched out his hand to Doc Williams.

"Congratulations, Doc. I am looking forward to your party."

Doc gripped Levi's hand and nodded.

"I am as well, but I don't know what I am going to do with myself today. I closed my office until Tuesday. Josie wants to go into Denver for the weekend." He frowned.

"She keeps talking about a shivaree. She said she participated in a few of them in Texas. I have never heard of such a thing, but Josie is convinced we will be tormented if we spend more than one night of our honeymoon here."

Levi laughed as he leaned over the table. "Take Josie's advice," he whispered. "I doubt it will keep you from being shivareed, but at least your honeymoon will be undisturbed!"

The young lawyer was smiling as he walked through the restaurant. He did not hear the comments that followed him across the room.

"That's the new lawyer in town. Just hung up his shingle. Hope he sticks around."

"Did you see him at the trial of those outlaws who killed Mrs. Crandall's husband?"

"Yep, I did. He's a wily one and he sure kept that judge honest."

CHAPTER 38

MIGHTY SPIFFY

WITH THE COMPLETED DOCUMENTS IN HIS HAND, Levi headed to the bank. When he asked to speak to Mr. Baker, the young receptionist batted her eyes at him.

"I will get him right away. Whom should I tell him is waiting?"

Levi was barely paying attention to her. He was looking around for Jimmy Baker. When she asked again, he was startled.

"Levi Parker. He is expecting me but probably not today."

Robert Baker rushed out of his office and grabbed Levi's arm to pull him into the privacy of the small room. As he closed the door and faced Levi, he asked quickly, "What questions do you have for me, Mr. Parker?"

"No questions." Levi extended the bank case. "I completed them this morning. I thought I would bring them over first thing so you could maybe finish what you need before the weekend."

The banker stared at Levi and then at the bank case.

"Finished? You have it *all* finished?" he asked incredulously.

"I have been involved with the law for nearly ten years, Mr. Baker," Levi stated with a smile. "I chose not to lawyer for a living, but I continued to study the law. I have a deep interest in the legal system as well as in those individuals who should be defending it."

Robert Baker turned to his desk and picked up a huge stack of documents. He handed them to Levi with a look of resignation. He did not like to pay bonuses, and it certainly looked like this new lawyer would be receiving them on a regular basis.

"This stack includes wills, deeds, land contracts, and even a divorce settlement. Bring them back when you are done." As the banker counted the payment out, Levi's mouth lifted in an ironic smile.

"Look at it this way, Mr. Baker. Since I am helping you finish these business ventures so quickly, you will be able to take on more clients and more business."

The banker's eyebrows lifted, and his greedy eyes flashed. He nodded eagerly and almost pushed Levi from his office.

The young receptionist watched Levi as he strolled out of the bank. Cora Bartels was excited to have another young man in town, especially one as good-looking as Levi Parker. The fact he was a lawyer was another perk.

All her friends had been plotting how to get him to ask them to the dance. Cora thought she had it all figured out.

She had asked Mr. Baker if she could leave work at three that day to attend a wedding. The banker grudgingly agreed.

"But only if you stay two extra hours next week," he told her. Cora tossed her head and rolled her eyes.

"Fine," she agreed. *Now if that clock would just move faster.*

Levi dropped the papers at his office. He stuffed his dirty shirt in his warbag and was soon headed down to the laundry area. He had already talked to the head laundress about washing his good shirt while he took a bath.

"Be careful with this," he instructed. "It is the only good shirt I own and the only one with long enough sleeves."

The red-faced woman snatched it from his hands as she turned away. "No problem, mister," she hollered over her shoulder as she hurried away.

"And iron it too, please," Levi called after her. He had just settled in for a long bath when Doc wandered in.

"Come on over here, Doc. Smoke a cigar with me," Levi hollered.

Doc arranged for the tub next to Levi's. The two men smoked and talked until the water was cold and they were both shivering.

Levi tried not to laugh as Doc Williams began to put on layers of clothing. When he added the cummerbund, Levi did laugh.

Doc Williams blushed as he pulled the cummerbund off and dropped it by the tub. He yanked off the bow tie at his neck and dropped it on the ground as well. He added a string tie he had in his pocket.

Levi was grinning but he had to admit that Doc did look sharp in the three-piece suit with tails. His boots had been polished and the black Stetson he placed on his head looked new.

"Spiffy. Mighty spiffy." Levi tried to sound serious as his eyes twinkled.

"Josie's aunt is pretty old school," Doc stated as he shook his head. "She wanted a real southern wedding, and she had some quite specific requests. Josie doesn't really care, but Aunt Clara cares a lot."

His face took on a pained look.

"I can just hear Slim snorting. I almost expect him to pop out somewhere and whack me one for being such a pushover."

Levi laughed and slapped Doc on the back.

"It's only for one day. If it makes your bride and her family happy, then why not go along with it. After all, Badger will be in tails so there will be two of you. Of course, he will have a top hat on as well."

Doc's face pulled into a deep scowl.

"Aunt Clara did send a top hat up, but I drew the line there. I will not wear one of those," he growled. As he looked at Levi, a smile slowly filled his face.

"Say, since Badger will be giving Josie away, I will give that top hat to him as a gift!"

Both men agreed Doc had the perfect solution.

Doc still had an hour to kill before he was to arrive at the church, so they stopped in the closest saloon for a beer. A couple of newcomers began to tease Doc about how he was dressed.

Levi turned to face them.

"Look fellas, it's his wedding day. Now if you were marrying the prettiest gal in Cheyenne, wouldn't you wear a suit with tails if she asked you?" Levi's face was bland, but his eyes were sincere.

The men stared at Doc and Levi for a moment. They were muttering as they agreed. They finally slapped Doc on the back and bought him a drink. In the end, he invited them to the wedding party. The strangers were still discussing how to make that happen when Levi and Doc walked out.

"Tell me something," Doc asked as he looked over at Levi. "Why is it big men seem to know how to get out of situations without fighting but smaller men usually fight?"

"I don't know about all big men," Levi stated with a laugh, "but I only have one good shirt. I don't want to mess it up before your wedding dance!"

Doc laughed and began to walk toward the church.

Levi hollered after him, "Don't forget your cummerbund!"

Doc kept walking. He waved his hand without turning around, and Levi grinned.

"I wonder what Aunt Clara will do when she finds out Doc 'lost' his cummerbund." As Levi thought about who might acquire it and wear it to the reception, his eyes lit up with humor.

"I hope it looks good on whoever finds it," he chuckled.

CHAPTER 39

AUNT CLARA'S WESTERN WEDDING

WHEN LEVI WALKED THROUGH THE DOORS OF THE Rollins House, the place was in full-blown wedding preparation. He grabbed one end of the heavy table Rowdy was pulling across the floor. The two men carried it to where Beth pointed them. Rowdy grinned as he looked across at Levi.

"Nice of you to keep Doc company all afternoon. Josie just knew he was going to show up at Sadie's house."

"That wasn't really my plan," Levi answered with a chuckle, "but we did end up spending the afternoon together." He looked seriously at Rowdy. "Doc Williams is a fine man. He is easy to talk to and just a heck of a nice guy."

Rowdy agreed and the men moved on to the next table.

Molly arrived in a rush with the children in tow. The women were leaving all of the children with Grandpa Samuel during the wedding. Levi wandered over to join the fun.

As Rowdy and she left, Beth looked back to see Levi scoop up the two littlest kids. He hoisted them in the air, holding one on each side, as he chased the older kids around the room. The kids were all screaming and laughing as the parents slipped away.

Doc presented Badger with the new top hat before the wedding started, and the little man was delighted. He immediately tossed the one he was wearing aside and replaced it with Doc's. He wanted to leave it on during the wedding but reluctantly removed it when Martha pointed at it.

Badger did a little dance step as he proudly led a smiling Josie Crandall up the aisle to be joined in marriage to Reuben Williams. Their friends were pleased. The plans they had put into motion just a year before had come to fruition.

One of the church ladies, Mrs. Mortenson, pumped the organ as hard as she could, and the music of "Here Comes the Bride" was deafening. When the music started, one could nearly see the smoke erupt from Aunt Clara's ears. It was so loud it was difficult to tell if the correct notes were even played. Aunt Clara gritted her teeth.

The pastor turned toward the organ. His lips moved but no sound could be heard as Mrs. Mortenson smiled and thumped her way through the song. The guests looked at each other, unsure if they should laugh or hold their ears.

When the music finally stopped, the pastor was sweating. Badger bowed deeply to both Josie and Doc. Aunt Clara's glare became deeper when she saw Reuben was wearing neither the cummerbund nor the bow tie.

Josie did not care about the music or the groom's clothing. She was marrying the man who stood before her, and he was all she cared about.

For his part, Doc thought it was a lot of fuss for fifteen minutes. However, he was willing to do whatever made the beautiful woman in front of him happy.

When it came time for the second song, Aunt Clara marched up to the organ and signaled for Mrs. Mortenson to move over. She proceeded to play Franz Schubert's "Ave Maria," and it was beautiful.

Pastor Jenkins presided over a short but animated service. When he said, "You may kiss the bride," Doc gave Josie a long kiss…until Aunt Clara cleared her throat loudly. The guests were laughing, and Doc gave Aunt Clara a broad wink.

Aunt Clara's face turned a deep red. However, she remained seated at the organ and played Mendelssohn's "Wedding March" as the happy couple exited the church. It was not quite the perfect wedding she had hoped for her only niece. Her lips were pinched together tightly as she primly left the church on the arm of the pastor.

As soon as Aunt Clara stepped away from the organ, Mrs. Mortenson promptly began to again pump and play "Goodbye, Liza Jane" for all she was worth.

Everyone was smiling as they gathered in front of the church to see the newlyweds off.

Lance whispered loudly to Molly, "Now wasn't that just a fine wedding? Seemed kind of fitting for the only niece of stuffy old maid."

Molly elbowed him and Lance grunted. He was laughing as he added, "I think Slim would have enjoyed his little sister's wedding."

Badger was quite the picture in his tails and top hat. He had rented a fine buggy, and he swung it to a stop in front of the church. He planned to take the happy couple to the Rollins House—in a roundabout way of course.

Martha waggled her finger at him when he leaned over to address Aunt Clara. Badger froze and the air went out of him for a moment.

Sadie began to giggle. She was sure she could feel Slim laughing through it all.

As Doc helped Josie into the buggy, he asked, "Would you like to ride with us, Aunt Clara? The hotel is about a half mile away."

Aunt Clara shook her head. She had hired a driver and carriage of her own. He was going to take her to the hotel when the party was over as well.

When her buggy arrived, she noticed the grinning driver was wearing a cummerbund and bow tie she recognized. His top hat was cocked at a rakish angle, and the stubble on his face had been there for a time.

Aunt Clara's lips formed a thin line. She asked him haughtily, "Tell me, sir. Where did you find your fine tie and cummerbund?"

The man, who had been recommended to her by Rooster, hiccupped and grinned. "Why shore now, I found 'em down by one a the washtubs.

"I thought I might take me a bath 'fore this here shindig. Good thing too. Some feller done lost 'em after he took 'im a bath. It were my lucky day to find 'em." The man had hooked the cummerbund around his hips, and it proved handy to hide the whisky bottle in his back pocket. The bow tie was upside down.

Aunt Clara sat back in her seat and sighed deeply. Her driver pulled his whisky bottle out of the cummerbund.

"Mebbie ya oughta take a little swig a this, Miss Clara. Might make ya relax a bit," he drawled as he held out the bottle.

Aunt Clara glared at him, but she took the bottle. She took four long swigs, wiped her mouth daintily with her handkerchief, and smiled her first smile of the day.

"Thank you, good sir. I do feel better. Now let us get over to that party."

Her driver hollered at the horses, and they moved out at a fast trot. He proceeded to tell her the history of Cheyenne as he pointed at houses and businesses. He waved his whip as he talked. When they arrived at the Rollins House, he jumped off the seat and hurried around to help Aunt Clara down.

"It shore were my pleasure to drive ya, Miss Clara. Now ya jist ask fer Jake if ya need a ride anywhere else while you's in Cheyenne. An I'll be back 'fore the party's over." As Aunt Clara took his hand, Jake asked, "Would ya like me to 'scort ya to yur table?"

Aunt Clara thought for a moment. She slowly nodded her agreement.

Jake guided her through the crowded room to a table in front. He bowed and grinned as he tipped his top hat.

"I say, Miss Clara. You shore are the prettiest woman in this here room today. I fer certain will be back to ask ya to dance!" Jake bowed again and was gone, dodging other guests as he made his way to the door.

Josie rushed up to her aunt.

"Oh, Aunt Clara—Isn't this just wonderful? Thank you for the lovely wedding!" She gave her aunt a hug. "Now let me introduce you to some of my friends."

Aunt Clara Crandall was amazed at all the people Josie knew *and* called her friends just in the short year she had been in Cheyenne.

A small blond boy sidled up beside her. He looked Aunt Clara up and down.

"Are you a grandma?"

Martha McCune grabbed Sammy before he could ask more questions. "Now Sammy, you know what your daddy told you about asking so many questions. This is Josie's aunt. Her name is Aunt Clara."

Sammy looked up at Aunt Clara somberly.

"Josie is Slim's sister, an' Slim was my uncle. He died. Do you know Slim?"

Aunt Clara's face became soft.

"Oh yes, I knew your Uncle Slim when he was just a little boy. In fact, he acted a lot like you. I loved him very much."

Sammy stared up at her.

"I guess you ain't as grumpy as my pa said you were. You kind of act like a grandma."

As he ran off to play with the other kids, Martha's face turned light pink. She laughed as she spoke.

"Sammy is precocious, but we all love him. Lance and Molly adopted him after his parents were killed. The Rankins are wonderful people. Come, let me introduce you to them."

CHAPTER 40

A DANCE AND A PARTY

SOON, EVERYONE BEGAN TO LOOK FOR CHAIRS. BETH waved at Levi. "Come sit with us, Levi! I saved you a place."

Levi walked over to her table. He nodded at Lance and Molly as well as Beth and Rowdy. Sadie smiled at him, and Beth pointed at an open chair next to Sadie.

"Sit down quickly. We may run out of seats!"

As Levi sat down, Abigail crawled from her mother's lap to Levi's leg.

"Wevi! Wevi!" She began to bounce up and down until he bounced her. As she screamed with delight, Lance leaned over to her.

"Go find your Grandpa Samuel and tell him to sit with us. Badger and Martha too."

Abigail slid down from Levi's knee and jabbered at Sammy. Sammy grumbled as he took his little sister's hand and wove through the crowd of people, looking for Samuel and the McCunes.

When Sammy and Abigail returned with Grandpa Samuel and the McCunes, Molly asked, "Where is your Grandpa McNary?"

Sammy pointed at the front table. "He's sittin' with Aunt Clara."

Sammy looked at Lance and added, "I don't think she's so grumpy, Pa. She seems kinda nice to me."

As Sammy ran off again, Lance looked over at Rowdy in surprise while Molly laughed.

"Which surprises you, Lance? That Old Man McNary is sitting with Aunt Clara or that Sammy thinks she's nice? I agree with Sammy." She added, "Although the wedding was pretty funny."

Soon, they were all laughing about the music. "Slim would have loved it," Levi agreed. He looked around for the baby. Little Levi was asleep in Sadie's arms.

"I can hold him for a while, Sadie. Or we can lay him down on the table if you want." As Levi took the baby and held him gently, he touched his cheek.

"Kid, you sure do look like your daddy," he whispered softly. He stood and looked down at Sadie. "I am going to get a beer. Do you need anything to drink?"

Sadie thought a moment before she answered.

"Water will be fine unless they have sarsaparilla. Either is good though."

Levi walked away with the baby on his arm. He stopped to talk to several people and finally made his way to the bar area. Rooster was in charge of the drinks.

"No sarsaparilla but I did make some root beer. Think Miss Sadie would like that?"

Levi didn't know. He took both root beer and water back to the table before he returned for his beer. As he picked it up, Rooster peered at the baby.

"Cute kid. Mebbie ya should git ya one a those."

Levi looked up in surprise. When he saw that Rooster was grinning, he laughed.

"Maybe I will someday. And you should too, Rooster. There might be a spinster lady out there somewhere who would just love to tie onto you."

It was Rooster's turn to be surprised, and both men were laughing when Levi returned to his seat by Sadie.

She smiled up at him as he sat down. "What is the drink? It is delicious. Would you like to taste it?"

Levi took a little sip and smacked his lips.

"Rooster made it. It's called root beer. I'm not sure what all is in it but that is some of the best I have tasted." He shifted his arm, and the baby stirred.

Sadie lifted him out of Levi's arms.

"Maybe I will lay him down on the table until we eat." Molly spread a quilt out and Sadie laid the sleeping baby down.

People were beginning to line up for food and Beth offered to stay at the table while everyone else filled their plates. She smiled up at Rowdy.

"Don't worry. Molly can fill one for me too. I'm sure yours will be so full it will take two hands to carry it."

As they joined the line, Levi looked around.

"Where did all the kids go?"

Molly laughed. "Martha took them all back to the kitchen to eat. They wouldn't slow down to eat out here. She said we could enjoy an uninterrupted meal for once."

Aunt Clara had given Barney quite specific requests for food. Fresh oysters, dumplings, roast beef, and pans of meatloaf filled the tables along with potato salad, fresh bread, and grits. A second table was filled with sweets from cakes to bread pudding and even some apple cobbler. As the hungry guests emptied the pans, Barney refilled them. He kept the food coming.

Finally, the people slowed down, and Barney strolled over to the table where Lance and Rowdy were sitting with their families.

Rowdy pulled up a chair.

"Sit down, Barney. The food was great, but you have to be tired. I think you fed nearly half the town!"

Barney laughed. "One hundred eighty-nine. I counted the plates as we set them out...and that doesn't count the kids." He looked around the room. "I didn't even recognize several of those fellas who came through the line," he added in surprise.

"Doc almost got into a fight with some strangers in the Half Dollar Saloon," Levi explained with a chuckle. "He ended up inviting them to the party. It might have been them."

Beth looked up in surprise. "Reub fight? He never fights!"

Levi shrugged. "They were just teasing him—making fun of his suit with tails. When they found out it was his wedding day, they bought him a drink. We had a good visit and he invited them to the wedding party."

The local musicians were tuning their instruments, and everyone began to push the tables to the sides of the room. Those guests who were not spending the night would be leaving shortly to be home by dark. However, many had opted to stay in town overnight.

Molly, Lance, Beth, and Rowdy were staying with Sadie while Martha and Badger took a room at the Rollins House. As the kids became tired, they were to be taken upstairs to the McCunes' room. They would be collected when the dancing was done. Samuel opened his house to any who wanted to stay, and some of the riders from the Rocking R took him up on his offer.

Tiny eased up beside Levi.

"Don't spose we cin sleep on yur floor? We left our bedrolls at the livery, but Rooster gets a little crotchety if we drink too much or come in late."

Levi nodded.

"If you want to leave before me, just ask me for the key. Otherwise, I will leave it unlocked when I turn in."

Tiny nodded his thanks. He went back to a group of five cowboys who all waved at Levi.

"Guess I will have six guests tonight," he commented to Lance as he grinned.

"Just make sure they don't take advantage of your hospitality. That number could increase." Lance frowned and added, "Be sure to tell them where they can sleep and what rooms to stay out of."

Levi nodded and grinned. *I sure didn't see my place becoming a hotel when I settled here.*

The music began and Levi stood.

"Sadie, may I have the first dance? I'm not sure I'll have another opportunity the way those cowboys are lining up behind you."

Sadie looked up in surprise and Beth reached for the baby.

"Let me hold your little one, Sadie. Rowdy and I have plenty of time for dancing since we don't have to ride home tonight."

"Goodbye, Liza Jane" was just starting when Levi swung Sadie onto the dance floor. Levi was every bit as good a dancer as Badger had told her. She barely touched the floor as he spun her around the room.

The beat was fast, and Levi was enjoying himself. As he twirled Sadie out at the end of the song and pulled her back in, she spun close to him. Levi was laughing as he looked down. He was surprised to see what looked like fear in Sadie's eyes.

Levi quietly took her arm and led her to the table. He excused himself and wandered over to where Rooster was still doling out the drinks.

CHAPTER 41

Give 'er Time

ROOSTER GRINNED AT LEVI. "YA LOOKED PURTY GOOD out there, Judge. Guess you've danced a little before."

Levi agreed absently as he watched Sadie. Men had begun to line up. It didn't look like she would be sitting down for some time.

"Women is notional," Rooster commented. "Sometimes, if they like somethin' too much, it scares 'em an' they run away."

As Levi looked at Rooster, he could see the man was sincere.

"I thought we were having fun but the look she gave me at the end of the dance was not what I expected to see." He stopped and looked at Rooster. "That's what you're talking about?"

Rooster nodded.

"Miss Sadie likes talkin' to ya an' spendin' time with ya, but then she feels like she's a bein' unfaithful ta Slim's memory. Most womenfolk 'ventually move on. 'Course, some never do."

Rooster grinned and pointed. "There's a lot more womenfolk in this place what want ta dance with a good-lookin' feller like yerself though. Git ready 'cause here they come!"

Levi turned to see a group of giggling women headed his way. He went to meet them.

"Say, ladies, I know some fellows who are just dying to dance but are too shy to ask pretty women like yourselves. Let me introduce you so some of my friends."

With a girl on each arm, he guided the group to the clustered Rocking R cowboys. "Tiny, Shaw, these girls want to dance. Why don't you boys help them out?"

As the cowboys surged forward, Levi backed up and headed across the floor to where Beth was still holding the baby.

"Beth, quick, give him to me, and you will do both of us a favor!"

Laughter bubbled out of Beth's lips as she looked at Levi's face. She handed him the little boy and Rowdy guided her out onto the dance floor with a grin over his shoulder. Levi sat down with the baby on his lap and watched the dancers.

Lance and Rowdy topped the male dancers in the room, and their wives danced well with them. Doc and Josie were quite smooth too.

Sadie was struggling to keep her feet out of the way of the clumsy cowboy she was dancing with. Levi was tempted to rescue her when the dance finally ended. As the smiling cowboy walked her back to her chair, another stepped up. Sadie shook her head.

"I need a rest. Let me catch my breath."

The cowboy wandered off, disappointed.

Levi looked at her, his eyes twinkling.

"Well, you broke his heart. How many more hearts can you break in one night?"

"My poor toes," Sadie groaned. "They will never recover!" She removed her shoe and began to rub her toes.

Levi looked at her and the twinkles in his eyes grew bigger. "There is an easy solution to that."

Sadie nodded as she flexed her toes.

"Yes, go home early."

"Naw," Levi drawled. "I was thinking you could just dance all night with me."

Sadie looked startled and a laugh bubbled out of her.

"You kept me spinning so fast that my feet barely touched the floor. If they had, maybe you would have stepped on them too."

Levi shrugged and cocked an eyebrow as he grinned.

"Choices. Life is full of choices."

Molly returned to the table out of breath.

"Levi, let me hold the baby, and you two go dance. Lance wants to dance with Josie, and I need a rest."

As Levi handed the baby to Molly, he looked down at Sadie with a smile. He held out his hand to her while inside, he was holding his breath. Sadie hesitated. She finally took his hand with a smile. Levi led her into a slow waltz.

Sadie felt like she was floating across the floor.

"You are a wonderful dancer, Levi. Where did you learn to dance?"

"The orphanage. We danced every week." Levi laughed. "The old gals who ran the place said it would help us with our coordination and our socialization. They were right although I sure didn't think much of it back then." He squeezed Sadie's hand a little tighter.

"I was nine when the folks died, and I was used to being outside all day. It was a big change to live in town, let alone learn to dance.

"We had to wear pinchy shoes and britches that just went below the knee. I hated every moment of it. I was planning how to escape when Kid moved in two houses down.

"Town kids didn't usually play with us, but Kid and I hit it off right away—probably because we were both unhappy." Levi's eyes filled with humor.

"Did you know Aunt Clara tried to make him learn to play the organ? She insisted Kid take lessons even though he hated it. One Sunday, she took him to church, planted him on the organ, and told him to play.

"Kid didn't argue with her. He just pumped that organ up as high as he could and thumped out the ugliest, loudest version of "Amazing Grace" I ever had heard." Levi laughed as he looked down at Sadie.

"In fact, the music you all talked about today reminded me of that Sunday. Aunt Clara was furious. She tried to pull Kid off the organ bench, but he wouldn't leave. He thumped that song out through seven verses as loud as that organ would squawk before she was finally able to yank him off the bench. Lucky for her too since there are thirteen verses in that song. I was trying not to laugh and doing a poor job of it.

"Kid winked at me as she dragged him by, pulling him by the ear. He was howling at the top of his voice.

"I eventually fell off my seat laughing, and I was hauled out of church right behind him. We both got a good whupping that day, but we didn't care.

"That was the end of Kid's organ lessons...and he never played in church again either." Levi laughed again as he swung Sadie into a spin.

She began to giggle and soon they were both laughing.

"Are you going to talk to Aunt Clara? I'm sure she would remember you!"

"Nope. She always said I was trouble. I'm not so sure she would be happy to see me. I think we'll just leave her memories of me in the past." He grinned at Sadie again and his eyes twinkled. He leaned toward her and whispered, "Just looking at her makes me want to do something to shake her up so I think I'd better stay away. Kid might get in my head and make me do something I shouldn't."

Sadie laughed again. She loved to hear stories of Slim's childhood. She assumed he had been ornery. It was fun to hear Levi talk about their time together.

Levi swung her right into the next song and kept her on the dance floor for nearly fifteen minutes. A slow song was starting when Sadie shook her head. Levi pulled her back.

"Just one more, Sadie. A slow song will help you cool down and catch your breath."

Sadie allowed herself to be pulled close but as she looked up at Levi, the panic came again. Her breath was coming quickly, and she pulled away.

"No, I need to sit down."

She hurried off the dance floor, and Levi followed her back to the Rankin table. Lance had joined Molly and Levi nodded at them.

"I think I will call it a night. Take care, Sadie. Lance, Molly—thanks for sharing your table." As he headed over to tell Doc goodbye, Beth and Rowdy returned to their seats.

"Where is Levi going?" Beth asked with surprise.

Sadie didn't answer but Lance spoke up.

"He said he was going to call it a night."

Beth jumped up.

"Not before I dance with him!" she exclaimed as she rushed across the floor.

Levi had just finished talking to the newlyweds and was turning toward the door when Beth grabbed his arm. "You are not leaving without dancing with me, Levi Parker!"

She smiled up at him, and Levi grinned at the friendliness in her eyes.

He laughed and agreed, "One dance but then I'm leaving. It has been a busy week."

As they moved to the dance floor Beth whispered, "Give her time, Levi. She likes you. She just isn't ready yet. Give her a little time."

Levi looked down at Beth in surprise. "Do you always offer sage advice to men after you ask them to dance?" he asked quietly.

Beth giggled. "Well, I do seem to offer lots of advice. I don't know how wise it is but sometimes I'm right."

The music changed to a fast polka and Levi swung her into a spin.

"So how is your German? Want to try this?" The rollicking polka had them spinning all over the dance floor, and they were out of breath when it ended. Beth was laughing as Levi guided her back to her seat.

"Rowdy, your wife plumb wore me out. I will see all of you another time."

Sadie watched him go but said nothing. Beth was chattering, but the rest of the table was quiet.

Lance pulled Molly up. "Come on, Sweetheart. Let's dance while we can. Who knows what the kids are getting into. We probably ought to rescue Martha soon."

As a slow waltz started, Levi glanced back at Sadie. She already had three men around her, each hoping for the next dance. When he saw that one of them was Jimmy Baker, he snorted.

"Yep, time for me to leave."

He waved at Tiny and called, "The door will be unlocked. Don't sleep in my office—that door will be shut." He waved again as the cool evening air greeted him through the open door.

"Wait, huh," he muttered to himself as he thought about what Beth had said.

"Well, I can wait. I have lots of work to do to get my business rolling. I can probably stay busy for years. Two or three for sure."

Levi was not tired, so he walked down the street and on out of town. Soon, the lights of Cheyenne were behind him. Levi stopped and stared into the night.

"Better not go any further. That walk back might take me longer."

The night was cool. Fall was beginning to make an appearance. Levi sat down on a small rise and watched the moon. The clouds glided across the sky and flitted over the orange globe. It was a beautiful night. Slowly, the anxiousness left him, and he calmed down. He stood and walked slowly back toward Cheyenne.

"Home. That's where I'm headed. Back home." He was smiling as he unlocked his door. He lit a lamp and climbed the stairs to his room.

Levi heard the riders come in. They did a poor job of staying quiet, but he still fell back asleep.

Tiny pulled out his pocket watch and groaned.

"Two-thirty in the mornin'! Today is goin' to be a killer, boys. We'd better fall asleep fast." Soon six different snores could be heard throughout the building.

The night would be short, but the party was worth it.

CHAPTER 42

JIMMY BAKER

THE NEXT TWO MONTHS WERE BUSY ONES FOR LEVI. Business picked up quickly, and soon he was skipping lunch much to the distress of his starving stomach.

Jack Coral, the owner of the Painted Lady Saloon offered to make him lunch each day, and Levi quickly agreed. If he did not come and get it, one of the girls brought it over. Usually, it was Sugar. She was a small, slender girl with big eyes and light brown hair. She always wore a shawl when she came regardless of how cool it was outside.

As she knocked tentatively on his office door, Levi looked up with a smile. "Come in, Sugar. Just set it down there." As he handed her some money, the young woman spoke shyly.

"My name is Annie. Annie Pearl. Sugar is my work name. I would like it if you would call me Annie."

Levi looked at her in surprise. "Why, sure. Annie it is." As he studied Annie's face and the way she clutched her shawl, he began to wonder just how much she liked her job.

"Do you like working at the Painted Lady, Annie?"

Annie blushed and shook her head.

"I like the men most of the time, but I hate the clothes I wear. My father would be so ashamed of me."

Levi leaned back in his chair. He wasn't sure how old Annie was, but he doubted if she was over eighteen years.

"Where is your father, Annie?"

Annie's face crumpled and tears sprang up in her eyes. "He's dead. We stopped here on our way to the gold fields in California. He wasn't feeling well, and he died of typhus a few days later. We had traveled with some buffalo hunters the last few days before we arrived here. Several of them died along the way as well. They may have died from it too—I don't know.

"After he died, I sold what I could. When my money ran out, I took a job at the Painted Lady. Mr. Coral is nice to me, but I don't like dressing immodestly or dealing with drunken men."

Annie looked down at her feet before she looked up again at Levi. "Mother would be horrified. She was a regular at church. She died in childbirth along with my baby brother. That was when my father decided to head west."

Levi's heart was heavy for the young woman.

"How old are you, Annie?"

Annie looked away as her lips trembled. She answered softly, "I just turned sixteen, but I told Mr. Coral I was eighteen so he would hire me. I was fifteen when I started, and that was nearly eight months ago." Annie backed away.

"I really need to get back to work. Mr. Coral expects me to deliver the meals quickly, and this is my favorite part of my job."

"I will come over when I'm done. Maybe Jack will let me talk to you while you are working if I buy a drink." He grinned at her.

"I have a business proposition for you, Annie."

Annie's eyes became large, and she backed out the door.

"Thank you, Mr. Parker."

Levi watched her rush out the door and toward the Painted Lady.

"I wonder if Annie would like to be my receptionist. Business is brisk enough now for me to hire one. Besides, it would save me from unnecessary interruptions."

Just then, Jimmy Baker sidled up to his door. He stepped in without knocking.

Levi was instantly irritated. He did not like Jimmy Baker. Not only that, but the man had grown up in a bank. He knew business protocol.

"Something I can help you with, Jimmy?"

Jimmy cleared his throat and tapped the toe of his boot on the floor as he studied the man in front of him.

Levi almost glared at him, his irritation growing.

Some women found Jimmy to be good-looking. Levi did not agree. Jimmy was a "leaky bucket." You couldn't count on him to keep his word, no matter how small the promise. That made him flawed in Levi's eyes.

Jimmy pulled out the chair in front of him and leaned forward across Levi's desk.

"I want to talk to you about how to set up my assets. I want to ensure my wife would not receive them if something should happen to me."

Levi's eyebrows raised and his eyes narrowed. His voice almost grated when he replied,

"I didn't know you were married, Jimmy."

Jimmy shook his head vigorously.

"Oh, I'm not but I am thinking about it. However, the woman I have in mind has no assets. I want to make sure she won't get mine should something happen to me."

Levi tried not to glare at the man in front of him when he answered.

"First of all, you shouldn't marry a woman you don't trust. That aside, what about your children? Shouldn't they be provided for in your absence?"

Jimmy stared at Levi. He shook his head and answered emphatically, "I hate kids. I would never want any kids."

Levi was losing his patience.

"Well, Jimmy, I suggest you stay single then and keep your pants zipped up. Nothing you have just shared with me makes you much of a candidate for marriage."

Jimmy Baker glared at Levi.

"Well, that shows just how much you know. The right woman would help draw the picture I need to paint for the bank. She would be someone who would accompany me to customer events and business outings. She would give our bank a more family-friendly image."

Levi stood and growled. "Hire a one of the girls south of town, Jimmy. She could do all those things and go away when you don't want her. I don't know any woman who would agree to those terms if you were honest with her."

When Jimmy glared back at him and did not answer, Levi leaned his hands on his desk. His eyes narrowed as he sarcastically added, "Oh, I see. She would come into the marriage assuming you were committing to a lifetime of love. If she wanted out when she saw it was a farce, you wouldn't be tied to her for alimony. Did I get that all right?"

Jimmy grinned. "Exactly!"

Levi pointed at the door. "Get out. I won't be part of any deal to trick some woman into making the worst decision of her life." As Jimmy backed up, Levi shoved his desk aside and started for him. He towered over the smaller man as he pointed toward his door.

"Get out! And don't ever come back here again. You are a disgrace to men everywhere."

Annie was coming into the building as Jimmy rushed out and he nearly ran her over.

"Get out of my way, you little slut," he shouted. "Stay in the saloon where you belong!"

Levi lunged for Jimmy. He grabbed him by the back of the collar and threw him through the door. He was breathing heavily, and his eyes were hard and cold.

"Jimmy, if I ever hear you speak to a woman like that again, I will break you in half. Now you stand up and apologize—or I just might do it now."

Jimmy staggered to his feet. "I would never…," and Levi hit him. Jimmy flew backwards into the street and collapsed in a pile.

Annie was backed up against the wall of Levi's building. Her palms were flat beside her. Her eyes were large and terrified, and her breathing was ragged. Levi didn't see her as he stormed inside.

He rubbed his knuckles. "I never did like that little weasel," he growled as he walked back into his office. Suddenly, he remembered the young woman. He hurried to the door and looked around.

"Did you need something, Annie?"

Annie's eyes were huge, and her breath was coming quickly.

"Mr. Coral let me off early today, so I came back over to talk to you about your business proposition." She paused and whispered hoarsely, "but I can come back another time." She was nearly halfway to the street when Levi stopped her.

"Annie, please. Come into my office. I promise I won't treat you like I did Jimmy." Levi grinned and winked at her, and Annie relaxed. She cautiously followed him into his office.

"So, Annie—here's the deal. I need a receptionist. I need someone who can make appointments and screen people as they come in. Right now, I am interrupted all the time.

"You would be here some days by yourself when I am in court. Other days, I would be here. On those days, you would be setting appointments and screening clients. There would also be some billing and bill paying. Of course, any business or conversation that takes place inside these walls would be considered confidential.

"I will be leaving for Laramie next week. I will be gone for about a week for a trial there, but I will be hiring someone when I get back. Think you might be interested?"

Annie's eyes opened wide in surprise.

"I'll take the job!" she exclaimed.

Levi laughed. "No, we need to talk salary first. You also need to tell me if there is anything you expect as part of the job." Levi's eyes were twinkling, and Annie smiled.

"I believe I would have to have at least as much as I am making now which is $11 per month plus tips." She paused and took a deep breath.

"I would be willing to work for you for $15 per month, provided you make a chamber pot of some type available." She blushed slightly but she looked directly at him.

Levi's eyebrows shot up and he laughed out loud.

"That is not what I expected you to request, but it is a reasonable requirement. Shall I plan for you to start tomorrow?"

Annie nodded eagerly. Her smile slowly faded.

"Will I be able to help Mr. Coral deliver meals over the noon hour? I enjoy it and no one else likes to do that." She paused as she sucked her breath in. Her voice was barely audible when she asked, "How many continuous hours are you wanting me to work in a day?"

Levi laughed again. "Your meal deliveries will work. After all, I still need to eat. I can't have my meals interrupted just because I hired away John Coral's best worker!

"Your hours will be from eight in the morning until five-thirty in the afternoon. You may take a break whenever you need as long as we don't have clients backed up and waiting."

Levi was smiling and Annie beamed.

"I will tell Mr. Coral right now. Thank you, Mr. Parker."

"Levi. You may call me Levi."

Annie shook her head.

"No, you are my employer. I will call you Mr. Parker." As she hurried toward the door, she turned with a smile. "Thank you, Mr. Parker. I will do my best to help your business run smoothly."

Sadie had come by Levi's office on her way home from the dry goods store. She had not seen him since the dance and was going to invite him over for supper. She heard part of the conversation between Levi and Jimmy because Levi was yelling loudly. She jumped out of the way when Levi threw Jimmy out the door. She ducked behind the corner of the building. When she saw the young woman go back into his office, Sadie quietly slipped away.

"What did you expect, Sadie?" she asked herself. "He has been nothing but kind and you acted like you were terrified of him. I am sure that young woman was glad to have him defend her honor."

As Sadie hurried toward her house, tears formed in the corners of her eyes. "Life is so confusing," she whispered. When she opened the door to her home, she was welcomed by a smiling Martha. She hugged the older woman and hurried to feed little Levi.

The word spread quickly around Cheyenne that the new lawyer had thrown the banker's son out of his office. There was lots of speculation but neither Jimmy Baker nor Levi Parker was sharing any details.

Levi didn't know Sadie was the potential wife Jimmy was discussing. Jimmy hadn't mentioned her name. Of course, that did not stop the tongue-wagging, and some of the talk wasn't too far from the truth.

Jimmy Baker was not a favorite son of Cheyenne while Levi was quickly becoming one.

CHAPTER 43

ANNIE'S FIRST DAY

ANNIE PEARL ARRIVED AT LEVI'S OFFICE THE NEXT morning at seven-fifty. She was dressed conservatively, and her hair was pinned tightly on top of her head.

Levi let her in. He opened the appointment book and explained the information he needed from each client or potential client.

"Some folks will be cautious about sharing any information with you so be subtle but persistent. Greet each person with a smile as they come through the door and ask them how you may help them." He handed her a stack of tickets.

"These need to be paid." He pointed to another pile. "That stack needs to be addressed. The ones to the businesses here in town may be dropped off. The rest will need to be mailed." He nodded toward the box of envelopes on the floor.

"Those may be used for the single sheets. I have large envelopes in my office for the packets. Just ask if you have more questions." Levi walked back into his office and shut the door leaving Annie on her own.

A young woman rushed through the door. As Annie looked up and started to speak, the woman interrupted her. "My name is Cora Bartels. I must speak to Levi right away."

"Mr. Parker is preparing for a trial and has asked not to be disturbed," Annie replied with a smile.

Cora glared at her, but Annie remained calm. She added, "Perhaps you could come back around noon. He likes to take his dinner at twelve-fifteen sharp." Annie smiled as she added sweetly, "Perhaps you could even sit with him a bit as he eats."

Levi heard the entire conversation and was grinning until he heard the last part. He almost choked and had to cough to keep from laughing.

Cora glared at Annie who continued to smile. She begrudgingly agreed to come back.

"I will be here at ten minutes after twelve. Please tell Mr. Parker to expect me."

As Cora whirled out of the office, Levi poked his head out laughing.

"That was excellent—all but the part about suggesting she eat with me! Keep in mind I am running from that woman. Don't make her efforts to snare me so painless."

Annie laughed as Levi shut his door. It was a calm morning. She had the letters separated and addressed by eleven forty-five. She knocked softly on Levi's door and held the box of envelopes in front of her.

"These are ready to be posted or delivered. You will need to sign the bank drafts before I seal the envelopes." She hesitated before she asked, "Do you glue them or use wax?"

Levi looked at Annie in surprise. He had not expected her to complete them all this morning. Now she would be able to post them that day. He pointed to the side of his desk.

"Gluing will be fine. Just set them down and I will get to them after dinner. I would like you to deliver the local ones—you don't have to glue those.

"Are you familiar with most of the businesses in town? If not, can you find them with the addresses?"

When Annie nodded, Levi pulled some papers from the pile on his desk and began to study them.

Annie shifted nervously from foot to foot as she waited and Levi looked up with a question on his face.

"Do you need something else, Annie?"

Annie backed away slightly but looked directly at Levi.

"Would it be alright if I deliver Mr. Coral's meals now?"

When Levi nodded, Annie hurried from his office to the saloon next door.

Annie was finished and back with Levi's sandwich and milk at a few minutes after twelve. As she handed him his food, she commented, "Cora is on her way." Then she grinned and added, "I hurried so I would be here when she arrived." As she closed the door, she could hear Levi laughing.

When Cora rushed through the door a second time, Annie looked up and smiled.

"Hello, Miss Bartels. Would you like me to tell Mr. Parker that you are here?"

Cora glared at her but nodded.

Annie walked to Levi's office door and knocked softly. "Mr. Parker? Miss Bartels is here to see you."

Levi rustled a few papers before he opened the door. He walked toward Cora as he asked, "Good afternoon, Miss Bartels. What can we do for you?"

Cora batted her eyes at Levi. She had marked him as her target the first time he had walked into the bank, and now she was going to invite him to the Ladies' Choice Dance being held at the Rollins House on Saturday.

The young woman in front of Levi was a pretty girl with blue eyes and a pert nose. She was just a little too aggressive for him though. She made him want to run whenever he saw her coming.

Cora smiled coyly. "Levi," she purred, "There is going to be a Ladies' Choice Dance on Saturday night. I was wondering if you would be my date?"

Levi had to admit Cora had curves in all the right places. He knew very few men turned her down. Still, he had no intention of going anywhere with her, let alone to a dance. He smiled but shook his head.

"Sorry, Cora. I already have a date. One of the other town girls beat you to it."

Cora looked surprised and then angry. She sputtered and blushed. "Well, another time then." She hurried out the door. Levi winked at Annie as he backed toward his office.

Annie shook her head. Her eyes were dancing and she commented softly, "You just lied. Mr. Honest Lawyer just lied to keep from spending the evening with a girl!"

Levi nodded somberly. "Yes, but you could change that by asking me yourself." As he grinned at her, Annie shook her head.

"I'm not going. There is a cowboy I would like to ask though. I'm just terrified he would say no."

Levi raised his eyebrows. "Now why would you think that, Annie?"

"He dances with me in the Painted Lady quite a bit, but I'm not sure he actually comes to see me. He rarely talks until he gets drunk. Then he talks up a storm. He's funny too."

Levi studied his new receptionist. "Maybe he is just shy."

Annie looked up at Levi with a startled look on her face.

"You think so? He isn't shy at all once he starts drinking."

Levi laughed.

"Liquid courage. I have used it myself a few times. You women can be mighty intimidating to us poor old cowboys."

Annie laughed out loud.

"I tell you what. I will ask you on the condition that I dump you like a hot coal if my cowboy shows up."

Levi threw back his head and laughed. He put out his hand.

"Deal! Now get those letters delivered so we can maybe finish early this week. I have to work out at the Rocking R for a few days to pay back their boss for stealing his hands. It took four of them two days each to help me get this place together."

Levi had agreed to work for Lance in return for the four days he had used the Rocking R riders. Besides Tiny and Shaw building his furniture, Joe and Hicks had installed his chimney. They were every bit as good as Tiny had said they were too.

The Rocking R was gathering for fall roundup this week, and Lance asked Levi to put in a couple of days. If all went well today, Levi was going to help out there Wednesday through Saturday.

The rest of the day flew by. Annie was efficient. She had all the letters delivered or posted and was back with the mail by two-thirty that afternoon.

She started to hand it to Levi, but he held up his hand.

"Sort it into three piles—personal, business, and questionable. Give me the business ones. Just lay the other two piles on the stairs that lead up to my living quarters."

Annie sorted the mail as Levi had told her. One letter was penned in a very neat woman's hand. It was addressed to Mr. Levi Parker, but there was no return address. She had heard a few rumors about her boss and Mrs. Crandall, but Annie was not one to gossip. Besides, she did not want to do or say anything that would hurt her boss' reputation, let alone that of Mrs. Crandall.

She laid the mail on the stairs in the two piles as instructed. As she turned away, her skirt caught the personal letter. It slipped between the stair steps and dropped to the floor behind them. Annie didn't notice as she hurried back to her desk.

The office was quiet that afternoon, and Annie ran out of work. She found a broom and began to sweep all the floors. Then she dug around until she found a rag and began dusting.

"I will bring some oil over tomorrow and clean this better," she declared as she moved the dust around.

Levi came out of his office at four. He looked around the clean reception area in surprise and smiled.

"You keep this up, Annie, and I may have to give you a raise." He nodded toward the door.

"Go on home. I will see you in the morning. Oh, and I will pay you once a week. Your first payday is on Friday." He waved as Annie hurried toward the door.

"See you tomorrow, Annie."

CHAPTER 44

THERE COULD BE A LYNCHING!

ANNIE LITERALLY SKIPPED BACK TO HER ROOM ABOVE the Painted Lady Saloon. She had heard Mrs. Crandall was advertising a room in her house, and she wanted to talk to her about renting it.

"Oh, to live in a real house where I can cook as well as smell clean air *and* not hear men cursing all the time." She stopped in the saloon to tell Mr. Coral about her new job.

The saloon owner liked little Annie, or Sugar, as they all called her. He hated to lose her as an employee, but he knew her new job was much better for her. His wise eyes twinkled.

"So when are you moving out, Sugar?"

Annie's eyes became large and she stuttered as she answered. "I—well I—um—I am talking to a lady today who has a room advertised. I don't know if I will get it or not. Hopefully, soon."

Jack Coral smiled.

"I'm sure you will, Sugar. You just let me know if you need any help moving your things."

Annie ran up the two flights of stairs to her small room and took off her only good dress. She hung it carefully on the wall hook and was just slipping into her old dress when her door burst open. Two men rushed in. They had handkerchiefs over their faces. As they grabbed her, they shoved something under her nose. The last thing she remembered was feeling herself sliding to the floor.

When Annie awoke later that evening, she was lying partly on her bed. Her naked body was scratched and bruised. When she tried to sit up, her head throbbed. Annie pulled a blanket around herself and began to cry. Once again, she passed out.

It was late night when Annie awoke the second time. The saloon was going full tilt, and loud voices drifted up the stairs.

Annie held up the old dress, but it was ripped beyond repair. She put on her only dress, placed the few items she owned in an old suitcase, and walked stiffly down the stairs. As she stood at the bottom of her stairs, she saw a light in Levi's private quarters. She slipped around the back of the saloon and ran to his door. At first, she knocked softly. When no one answered, she beat on his door.

A tired Levi jerked the door open. When he saw who it was, his anger turned to concern.

"Annie! What happened?" As he pulled her inside, she fell to the floor sobbing. Levi dropped down beside her. His face was tight with anger as Annie told what had happened through her sobs. He lifted her up.

"I am taking you to see Doc. He needs to check you over. You can spend the night there. Tomorrow, we will find you someplace else to stay."

Annie tried to protest, but Levi was already carrying her down the street. When he arrived at Doc's, he beat on the door. When no one came, Levi began to bellow loudly for someone to open the door before he kicked it in.

Doc opened the door. His hair was wild, and he was rubbing the sleep from his eyes. When he saw the young woman Levi was holding, he snapped awake.

"Follow me. Just lay her down on that bed."

Levi set Annie down on the bed and Doc pushed him toward the door.

"You wait out there. I'll call you when you can come in."

Josie hurried in with a pad and paper. She jotted down notes as Levi told her what he knew. She quickly joined Doc, and Levi could barely hear their voices as they talked to Annie.

Doc came out about twenty minutes later.

"I wanted to give her a sedative to help her sleep, but she was dosed with chloroform and way too much of it. She will have a headache for several days." He frowned as he drummed his fingers on the back of a chair. "I don't want to risk giving her any more sedatives.

"She is calmer now and Josie is sitting with her. Hopefully, she will be able to fall asleep." He looked at Levi curiously. "How did you come to find her?"

Levi's face was drawn into tight lines. "She just started to work for me. In fact, yesterday was her first day. We closed early and I sent her home at four. Whoever attacked her must have broken into her room shortly after she went home." He scowled. "She can't go back there. I will have to find her someplace to stay."

"She can stay here tonight.

"Maybe you should talk to Sadie. She was going to advertise a room. I think she would enjoy the company since Josie has moved out."

Levi rubbed his eyes. "Do you mind if I sleep here tonight, Doc? I'd like to be around when Annie wakes in the morning. Then I will talk to Sadie about renting her room."

Doc nodded. He gave Levi a sideways grin.

"I'd offer you an examination bed, but they are all short. You might be as comfortable pulling some of those chairs together and sleeping right here."

Doc went to find some quilts. When he came back, Levi was asleep. He looked curiously at the big man and shook his head.

"I am glad Annie was comfortable enough to ask you for help," he commented quietly as he pulled a quilt over Levi.

253

Annie finally fell into a heavy sleep, and Josie joined Doc in their bedroom. She had tears in her blue eyes.

"Poor little thing. Do you know she is barely sixteen years old? Why if the town hears of this, there could be a lynching. And who knows if they would get the right men.

"She said there were two men, but she barely had a look at them before she passed out."

Levi was up early the next day. He passed his hand ruefully over his rough face. *I feel like I have been on a three-day drunk, and I probably look like it too."

When he tapped on Annie's door, she answered immediately. She stared at Levi as she frowned.

"You look terrible, Mr. Parker. You had better clean yourself up before you go to work."

"Yes, I thought the same thing," Levi replied with a chuckle. "I just wanted to let you know I am headed over to Sadie's to see about a room she might have available. I don't want you to go back to where you were." He paused as he stared out the window. Finally, he turned his eyes back to Annie.

"Did you get a look at them at all, Annie? They could be hung for what they did to you."

"I couldn't see them." Annie's eyes filled with tears. "They broke into my room. As I turned around, they put a cloth under my nose and I passed out. One had black hair and the other had sandy-colored hair, but they had handkerchiefs over their faces."

Her face crumpled and she began to sob. "My cowboy will never want me now."

Levi stepped up beside the bed and put his big hand over hers.

"Annie, if your cowboy is as wonderful as you think he is, this won't change a thing." *He will probably want to kill them though.*

"You just get better. I will be back after work to take you up to Sadie's." He patted her hand and strode out of Doc's office.

254

CHAPTER 45

BREAKFAST WITH A PRETTY LADY

SADIE WAS STARTLED TO HEAR A KNOCK ON HER DOOR so early in the morning. She peeked through the curtains and saw a very tired Levi. Surprise filled her face as she pulled the door open.

"Levi! What in the world? Is everything all right?"

Levi's heart skipped at the sight of Sadie. She looked beautiful, fresh, and smelled like flowers.

She stepped aside quickly. "Come in. Have you eaten? I was just fixing myself some breakfast. Would you like to join me?"

Levi stepped in the door and smiled.

"Good morning, Sadie. You smell as pretty as you look."

Sadie could feel the red creeping up her neck. She smiled at him and turned quickly away.

"How many eggs, Levi? Griddlecakes? Are you hungry?"

Levi took her hand and pulled her down to the table.

"Sadie, I would love to eat breakfast but let me tell you why I'm here.

"I hired Annie Pearl as my receptionist and yesterday was her first day. Last night, she was raped by two men. She is up at Doc's. They drugged her. She came to me when she awoke around two this morning." Levi's face was filled with a combination of sadness and anger.

Sadie took his hands. "Oh, Levi. I'm so sorry. You bring her here to stay with me. She can't possibly go back to wherever she was staying."

Levi squeezed Sadie's hands. "I was hoping you would say that. She could use a woman around her too. Poor kid. She's barely sixteen."

Recognition washed over Sadie's face.

"She isn't the little girl who worked at the Painted Lady, is she? The one they called Sugar?" As Levi nodded, Sadie's face went white.

"Tiny is sweet on her. He hasn't talked about another girl since she started working there. Of course, he is too shy to tell her."

Levi stared at Sadie.

"Annie told me she liked a cowboy, but he only talked to her when he drank. I guess that explains why Tiny is drinking more than he used to." Levi frowned. "I had better tell Lance. He needs to know this before someone tells Tiny."

He looked across at Sadie with a tired smile. "I guess I had better take you up on your offer of breakfast. It looks like it will be a long day."

The baby began to stir, and Levi asked, "Do you mind if I pick him up?"

Sadie smiled and nodded.

"He likes to be up on your shoulder. His neck is pretty strong already and he tries to hold his head up."

Levi reached into the small crib and tickled the little boy. Bright blue eyes stared back at him. Blonde curls were sticking out everywhere.

"Good morning, Kid! You look just like your daddy looked first thing in the morning." The baby's legs began to thrash as he waited for Levi to pick him up.

Levi lifted the baby and smiled at him before he put him over his shoulder. As he walked toward the window, Sadie paused to watch them.

Levi is so kind and has such a big heart. As he looked toward her and smiled, she resisted the urge to look down. She met his smile with one of her own, and Levi's grew bigger.

He opened the door and took the baby outside. Sadie could hear him talking and pointing at things as they walked.

Samuel had hung the swing he promised, and Levi sat down in it. As they moved back and forth, the little boy looked around, whipping his head from side to side as if to see everything.

The sound of an explosion came from the direction of the baby's bottom, and Levi jumped up. The blanket was wet, and Levi could feel something leaking through his shirt. He rushed back into the house with a look of horror on his face.

"I think he just dumped all over everything!"

Sadie laughed as she took the baby.

Levi was looking at his hand and shirt. Both were covered with whatever the baby had released. It looked and smelled terrible. His throat was catching, and he was trying not to gag.

"There is a kettle of hot water on the stove, Levi. Dump it in the tub. You may wash up there," Sadie called from the bedroom.

As Levi began to wash up, she walked into the kitchen and handed him a new shirt. "I'm almost done with the second one, but you might need this one now."

Her eyes were crinkling at the corners as she added, "If only you had seen the expression on your face as you rushed in here!" she giggled.

Levi grinned back. "I reckon you did think that was funny."

He removed the dirty shirt outside, dropping it beside the steps. He held up the new one and studied it before he put it on. As he shrugged his shoulders and began to button it, he looked down with admiration. He was smiling when he entered the house.

"Sadie, you make the best shirts."

The blue of the shirt brought out the blue in Levi's eyes. Sadie quickly turned away to pick up the baby.

Once little Levi was cleaned and changed, she handed him back to the big man.

"When are you riding out to the Rocking R?"

Levi frowned as he ate. "I need to go by the office first and make sure that I don't have any appointments. Once I do that, I am heading out right away."

Sadie was silent for a moment.

"Molly may want to come back in with you. She can maybe help Annie." Sadie paused and her brow puckered as she added, "I am really worried about the riders though. Tiny has been a favorite for a long time. He's kind and gentle but can turn into a roaring mound of muscle when something happens to his friends." She added innocently, "Kind of like another big man I know."

Levi looked over at Sadie in surprise. "Now when did you see me lose my temper?"

"Why I believe that was just a few days ago." Sadie's eyes glinted as she giggled. "You threw a gentleman out of your office and then hit him."

Levi stared at her. "Where in the world were you?"

Sadie laughed and her brown eyes filled with mirth.

"I was hiding. No way was I going in there if that was how you treated your customers." Sadie laughed harder at the surprise on Levi's face.

"Let's just say if you had heard the entire conversation, you would have encouraged me to hit him again." Levi frowned. "The man is a sniveling little weasel, and I hope his father sends him down the road soon." Then he caught himself.

"What did you need? You never came back, did you?"

"It was nothing important. I was just going to invite you over for supper."

Levi stared at her, and a grin filled his face.

"A free meal with one of my favorite ladies? What could be more important than that? The answer is yes. Just tell me when."

Sadie laughed out loud. "Don't sound so eager, Levi. Maybe you should try to make your social calendar sound a little fuller."

Levi snorted. "It is a full-time job just to run away from the gals who want to fill it up. I lied to one yesterday and told her I had a date for the Ladies' Choice Dance on Saturday. Then I begged Annie to ask me." He stood up and placed his hands on the back of his chair as he rolled his eyes.

He grinned at Sadie's surprised look. His eyes were twinkling as he added, "She did on the condition she would drop me like a hot potato if her cowboy showed up." His face became somber again.

"Poor little Annie. I don't know how to help her."

Sadie put her hand on Levi's arm, and he kissed her. As he lifted his head, he saw her eyes were wide, but she did not pull back.

Levi took her by the arms. "I know I should apologize, Sadie, but it would be a lie. I've wanted to do that for almost as long as I've known you." He squeezed her arms and stepped back.

"Thank you for breakfast and for opening your home to Annie. Someone will bring her by this evening." He picked up his hat and sauntered out the door, whistling to himself as he took the steps two at a time.

Sadie touched her lips, staring after him. Levi turned around when he was by the big tree and waved his hat. She knew he couldn't see her, but he was counting on her seeing him. She laughed.

"What a precocious man!" Sadie was still smiling as she hurried to clean up the dishes. When she finished, she rushed upstairs to make sure the little room was ready for its new guest.

Later that morning, Sadie saw Levi's dirty shirt lying beside the porch. She picked it up and brought it in to wash it. As she dropped it into the wash tub, she giggled again at the thought of the big man's face when the baby pooped all over him.

CHAPTER 46

THE WORD IS OUT

LEVI STOPPED BY THE PAINTED LADY AND TOLD JACK Coral what had happened.

Jack's eyes tightened down. "If we find out who did that..."

Levi finished for him, "We will let the law take care of it. However, could you have someone watch the stairs to her place? There might be some evidence in her room. No one should have been in there since she left this morning. I am going to get the sheriff as soon as I clean up, and we will be back to go through it."

Sheriff Boswell was a methodical man. He wanted to write down everything Levi knew before they searched Annie's room. Levi was chafing to get out to the Rocking R, but he tried to be patient. Once the sheriff was satisfied he had all the preliminary information he needed, the two men headed for Annie's little room.

Annie's torn dress was on the floor. There was blood on the sheets and on the dress as well. Neither man spoke as they gathered up the evidence of the horrible crime.

The light glinted on something gold. Levi spotted a pocket watch laying on the floor, partly under a small bureau.

Sheriff Boswell picked it up. When he popped open the cover, an inscription showed. It read, "To Jimmy, With Love from Dad."

Levi's face hardened, and he stared at the sheriff.

"I guess you know who that is."

The sheriff looked at Levi coolly. "We know who it could be. A trial will give us our answers."

Levi said nothing but he knew Jimmy's father would pay whoever and whatever amount was required to get his son off. He scowled. *This situation is going to blow clean up if something doesn't slow it down.*

Levi looked hard at Sheriff Boswell.

"Annie was seeing one of the riders from the Rocking R. I am headed out there now to let Lance know about this. You had better have Jimmy Baker in jail when I get back. I will do my best to give justice time to work, and we'd better both pray it does."

Suddenly, one of the bartenders from the Painted Lady appeared at the bottom of the stairs. He hollered up, "We found this feller sneakin' around back here. You want we should hold 'im or turn 'im lose?"

The sheriff growled, "Hold him. I'm coming down. I will take him to the jail for questioning."

The man was jerking and trying to get loose so Levi hit him. He looked at the sheriff coolly.

"Now he will be easier to manage. I will even drag him for you." He grabbed the man's collar and drug him down the boardwalk, bouncing his feet over the boards and dirt as they crossed the streets.

The sheriff opened the cell, and Levi tossed the unconscious man inside. He turned hard eyes on the sheriff again as he grated out, "I will be back by evening, and you *know* I will be prosecuting this case."

However, as Levi walked to the livery, he began to worry. The chances of Jimmy getting off were good. They had his watch, but he could claim Annie had entertained him before. Most would know it was a lie, but he was the banker's son after all. *Our only hope is that someone talks. If the second fellow is smart, he will know this will all be pinned on him.*

And why was the fellow we caught hanging around those stairs? Maybe he's the second man.

As Levi saddled his horse, Rooster stood to the side and chewed on a piece of straw. He watched Levi but said nothing.

Levi looked at the old man.

"Well, what's the word? Who all knows and what do they think they know?"

Rooster shrugged his shoulders.

"Ever'one knows Sugar was attacked an' that she's at Doc's. A couple a Doc's neighbors heard ya a bellerin' this mornin' early an' looked out their windows. That an' some cowboys saw Sugar come down 'er stairs with a suitcase in the middle a the night. She was a cryin' an' went over to yur place.

"Folks is a puttin' things together. They jist don't know Jimmy Baker was in on it yet—but that won't take long now."

Levi stared at Rooster.

"Now why do you think Jimmy Baker was involved?"

Rooster snorted and spat before he spoke.

"'Cause that no 'count Beans ya jist drug down to the jail rides with Jimmy when he ain't pretendin' to be a banker. Them two boys is trouble. 'An' I think if ya checked with the sheriff in Deadwood, ya jist might find Jimmy has a reputation fer takin' favors from women without bein' invited."

Levi stared at the little man. "Would you be willing to testify in court if I need you?"

Rooster nodded.

"I like little Sugar an' 'sides, no woman should be treated the way she was. My question fer ya is how's ya gonna keep the Rockin' R from a tearin' down that jail when they hear 'bout this?"

Levi looked bleakly at Rooster.

"I don't know and that is why I want to get out there as soon as possible. Maybe Lance can head that off." He mounted his stallion, and it was running full speed when he left town.

Patrons and businessmen alike stepped onto the street and watched Levi head south. There was lots of speculation as to why the town lawyer was riding fast toward the Rocking R. Before long, the rumor mill was going full speed.

CHAPTER 47

THE MESSENGER

MOLLY WAS HANGING LAUNDRY ON THE LINE WHEN Levi rode into the yard. She could feel the hairs come up on her neck as she looked at his face and saw how lathered his horse was. She dropped the shirt she was holding and ran towards him.

Levi sat on his horse and looked down at her.

"Hello, Molly. Do you know where Lance is working today?"

Molly pointed as she told him how to get there. She touched his leg. "Is it Sadie? Has something happened?"

Levi answered grimly, "Sadie and the baby are fine. A little gal who worked at the Painted Lady was raped last night by two fellows. Her name is Annie. Sadie told me she was seeing Tiny. I'm hoping Lance will keep the Rocking R out of town for a few days. There will be a trial and it will likely be ugly." He shook his head. "The lawyers for the defense will drag Annie through all kinds of muck to get their boy off."

Molly could feel her chest begin to squeeze, and she felt faint. As she staggered back a few steps, Levi jumped from his horse and steadied her.

"Molly, are you okay? I sure didn't mean to upset you with all this."

Molly's face was pale. Her breath was coming in short gasps. As she slowly regained her color, she stifled a sob.

"I need to go see her," she whispered. "I might be able to help her a little." Her eyes were wide as she added, "I understand how she feels." She looked up at Levi through tear-filled eyes. "Isn't she quite young?"

"Just barely sixteen. She's sweet on Tiny, and it sounds like the feelings are mutual. He has been through a lot here lately, and I don't want him to do something he will pay for the rest of his life."

As Molly hugged herself and trembled, Levi wrapped a big arm around her. "I'm so sorry, Molly. I sure didn't mean to upset you," he whispered.

Molly finally pulled herself upright.

"Please let Martha and Badger know what's going on. I may need Martha to watch the children when I go into Cheyenne.

"And get a fresh horse. You may have to chase Tiny all the way back to town."

Levi quickly moved his rig to a big bay in the corral. He gave his stud horse a quick rub down and watered it before turning it loose. He did not want it in the corral with the other horses. Lance might have some staggy horses in his remuda, and they did not need fighting horses. He forked some hay out of the barn and pulled the doors closed. His stallion would not go anywhere but it did like to tear up hay piles. As he left the yard at a fast cantor, he saw the horse following Molly toward the house.

"Big baby," he grinned. "He's hoping she has some apples."

When Levi arrived at Badger's, he found Martha in the house. Badger was helping Lance with round-up.

Martha's face paled when Levi told her what had happened. She immediately rushed to the barn to hitch up her buggy. Levi hitched her mules for her and gave her a hand up. As she started her team toward Molly's, Martha called, "Now you tell Badger where I've gone. I don't want him to worry about me."

The Rocking R was gathering where Molly had told Levi they would be. Branding fires were going, and the fall roundup was in full tilt.

Lance spotted the approaching rider. He squinted his eyes but couldn't recognize the rider or the horse. Badger rode up beside him.

"Now why is that thar lawyer ridin' one a yur hosses?" he asked as he peered at the small figure riding toward them. Lance stared at Badger and shook his head.

"I see your eyes are still working fine," Lance commented dryly. He frowned. "Probably because his is played out and that means bad news."

The two men wheeled their horses toward Levi and rode to meet him. Several of the hands turned to see where their boss was going. Soon, all the Rocking R hands knew a rider was coming, and their boss was concerned enough to ride out to meet him. The hands kept working but they were looking up often to watch the approaching rider.

CHAPTER 48

BAD NEWS

LEVI SLOWED HIS HORSE TO A WALK AS HE MET LANCE and Badger. The men nodded at each other.

"Bad news?" Lance asked.

Levi nodded. "Sugar was raped last night. I knew she was sweet on one of your boys, and Sadie told me it was Tiny." He shifted his weight in the saddle as he added, "Tiny needs to be told because the word is all over Cheyenne." He paused and studied Lance. "I'm just worried about what your hands will do. I sure don't want them to take the town apart."

Lance put both of his hands over the saddle horn as his eyes bored into Levi. For the first time, Levi personally felt the cold hardness of Lance's blue eyes. "If the good sheriff doesn't catch and convict whoever did this, I just might turn the boys lose. Sugar is just a kid."

Levi stared back at Lance. "It is the sheriff's duty to capture them, but it is the court's responsibility to try, convict or exonerate, and punish the guilty."

The two powerful men stared at each other. Lance finally nodded.

"I will keep my boys under control until after the trial. I'm guessing someone powerful is involved or you wouldn't have made this trip."

Levi stared hard at Lance a second time. His face was drawn in tight lines as he grated out, "I made this trip because Tiny is my friend. I don't want him *or* his friends to do something stupid."

Lance nodded slowly. "Sorry, Levi." He gave an apologetic grin. "Molly tells me I push too hard sometimes. I will keep the Rocking R home, but you ride in with Tiny. I know I can't keep him here."

As the three men rode slowly back to the branding area, Tiny stood up and shouted. "Hello, Judge! Come to work off some of yur time?"

As several riders laughed, Lance hollered, "Tiny! Ride out with Levi—he needs to talk to you. And give me your guns."

Tiny looked surprised and then suspicious, but he handed his guns to Lance.

The men who could hear stopped working and stood up. They all looked from Lance to Levi. Other riders slowly stood and watched the three men. Lance waved at them.

"Back to work! Tiny has some business in town, and you boys have a lot of calves to brand." The men picked up where they had left off. They all stopped again when Tiny suddenly spurred his horse and headed north.

Badger looked at Lance. "I believe I'll mosey on over ta yur place. I want ta make sure my Martha made it there."

Lance swore under his breath as Badger rode away. "And right smack in the middle of fall gather."

Then he thought of Molly and his brow furrowed. He knew she would want to help and how hard it would be on her.

Rudy was helping brand and Lance hollered at him.

"Get on back to your house. Ask your ma to come over and watch our kids. Your Aunt Molly has to go to Cheyenne. And make it quick!"

Rudy nodded and took off cross country toward the R4 Ranch. He loved to ride fast. Even though he knew something was wrong, he was excited to run his horse.

Levi spurred his horse to catch Tiny.

"Slow down! You'll kill that horse!" he yelled as he raced after the angry man.

Tiny finally slowed down. There were tears in the big man's eyes. "Sweet little Annie. She didn't deserve this." He looked over at Levi and quietly promised, "If the law don't git whoever done this, I'm a gonna kill 'im—an' I won't need no gun to do it."

Levi was silent for a time. He finally put his hand on Tiny's shoulder.

"Tiny, I know that is what you want to do, and they probably deserve it. Your first duty is to Annie though. Don't be so full of anger that you can't comfort her or show her you still love her."

Tiny looked shocked.

"Why wouldn't I still love 'er? This ain't her fault."

"And she needs to hear you say that. Right now, she is mighty fragile. You put her ahead of revenge."

When they were about a mile from town, Tiny cursed and once again spurred his horse to a run.

CHAPTER 49

ANNIE'S COWBOY

TINY RACED HIS HORSE UP TO DOC'S OFFICE. HE dropped the reins as his boots hit the first step. As he burst through the door, he roared, "Annie! Annie Pearl! Where are you?"

Annie's face paled as she stood up. She pulled the robe tighter around her small body.

Doc met Tiny as the big man strode through the waiting area, still bellering.

"Annie is back here, Tiny. Now lower your voice. We have other folks in here and you will frighten everyone."

He smiled up at Tiny as he pointed at Annie's door. "Knock first. If she answers, you may go in. And try to keep your voice down."

Tiny beat on the door Doc had pointed to. Annie pulled the door open. Her face was pale, and she looked like she had been crying. Tiny picked her up and kicked the door shut. He sat down on the bed with her still in his arms.

"Little Annie. Are ya alright? Do ya hurt anywhere?"

Annie looked up at her cowboy as she shook her head. "I was afraid you wouldn't want me anymore," she whispered as a tear leaked out of her eye.

Tiny hugged her tightly. "Now that's silly talk. Nothin's changed fer me 'cept I'm a gonna tell ya straight up that ya stoled my heart months ago. I been tryin' to work up the courage to ask ya fer yer hand but I jist couldn't get the words to come out." He kissed her cheek softly and pushed her hair back. "Reckon I'd better ask quick 'fore those words sneak away again. Will ya marry me, Annie? I promise to always love ya an' care fer ya. I reckon I ain't the most handsomest cowboy 'round, but I promise I'll love ya fer as long as my heart beats in this big chest." He held her hand over his heart and Annie started to cry.

Confusion and concern washed over Tiny's face. "Now durn it, Gurl, I didn't want to make ya sad. I—"

Annie kissed his cheek as she smiled through her tears. "Tiny, that is the most wonderful thing anyone has ever said to me. I have wanted you to ask me that question since the first time I danced with you. I just couldn't understand why you only talked to me when you drank."

Tiny grinned at her and kissed her again. "I reckon 'cause the inside a me ain't near as brave as the outside a me is. You is jist so beautiful an' sweet, my tongue gets all tangled up in my mouth. I have to drink jist so's I don't choke."

Annie laughed and kissed him again. "Tiny, I would love to be your wife," she whispered.

Tiny's smile was huge as he squeezed her tighter.

Annie's face became pale again and her breath caught as she looked at him. "Tiny, since I was raped, I could be pregnant. Are you sure you will still want me if I am carrying another man's child?"

Tiny pulled her closer. "If you's pregnant, that there little kid will be mine either way. We'll git married right off an' I'll be that baby's daddy either way. After all, it's still part you."

Annie wrapped her arms around Tiny's neck and smiled up at him. "I'm so happy my cowboy loves me. I have wanted this for so long.

"I don't care where we get married. You decide. The Rocking R riders were the first friends I made here. My friends are your friends.

Tiny frowned as he stared into her face and a tear leaked from his eye.

"My best pards are in the ground out to the Rockin' R. I reckon I'd like to marry close to 'em so's they cin come too.

"I been thinkin' on buildin' a big arch. I cin put it over those tombstones where they look out into the valley. That would be a real purty spot to tie the knot if ya was willin'."

"That sounds wonderful." Annie's eyes were happy and excited.

"The Rocking R hands can stand up for both of us." She added softly, "I want to ask Mr. Coral to give me away. He offered me a job even when he knew I lied to him about my age. He's been the closest thing to a father I have had since Pa died."

Tiny stared down at Annie as he hugged her.

"How old are ya, Annie? Do we need to wait a while to marry?"

Annie laughed and her eyes sparkled.

"I will tell you how old I am when you tell me your given name. If I am to marry you, I want to know who you are besides Tiny Small."

Tiny's face turned red, and he fidgeted on the bed.

"It ain't such a bad name. I jist don't like it. I was named after my Pa an' Grandpappy. Beauford Porterhouse Small. Now who would call a little bitty ol' kid that? An' even if ya shorten it up, it still comes out BS!"

Annie started giggling and Tiny scowled at her. "Ain't no one but you knows that name an' no one is a goin' to neither. Now keep yur end a the deal an' tell me how old ya are."

"I just turned sixteen. My birthday was last week. My mama married when she was fifteen, so I reckon I'm old enough." Annie laid her head on Tiny's chest. She was quiet as she listened to his heart beat. She asked softly, "Do you have any family, Tiny? Any brothers or sisters you want to invite? We can wait longer to marry if you need to contact anyone."

Tiny shook his head. "Naa. My ma was sickly. She had more babies 'fore me, but they all come too soon. I would a had a little brother but Ma an' him both died after he was born. Pa died that winter tryin' to break ice in a pond. He went under an' my grandpappy found 'im too late. Grandpappy an' Mammie raised me. They's the ones what called me Tiny. Mammie said I was a tiny feller when I come to live with 'em but I growed fast. They was old though an' they both died the winter I turned thirteen.

"That's when I left home. I bummed 'round from one ridin' job to 'nother fer several years. I finally come to the Rockin' R. That's been my home now fer nigh on six years." Tiny looked over Annie's head and continued softly, "Slim took a job on the second ranch I was ridin' on. I was a hand, but I helped the boss fix things too. Slim, he hired on bustin' broncs. He was the first good friend I ever had. When he left, I left too. I was a little younger an' he treated me like a kid brother. If I drank too much, Slim would cut me off an' send me home.

"He was quite the ladies' man back then. Why we couldn't go nowhere but the gals jist hung on 'im. He liked it too. He made each of 'em think she were his one an' only. He might see a gal fer a few months 'fore he jist up an' disappeared. Rich gals an' poor gals—it didn't make Slim no difference. They all loved Slim an' he loved on them.

"The last ranch 'fore we come here, the boss' daughter set out after 'im. Slim told me one night to saddle our hosses—we was leavin' in a hurry right after supper. He come a runnin' down from the big house an' hollered, 'Bring those hosses! We're a leavin' *now!*'

"I raced his hoss up beside 'im an' we took off outa there. Her ol' man was a shootin' at us as we left the ranch yard. We cut fer the trees an' we didn't slow down till we had some distance twix us. We could hear the boss hollerin' at the hands to track us as we went over the first hill.

"No one tried too hard though. Shoot, ever' feller on that ranch wanted to marry up with that little black-eyed gal. She let ever' one a those boys walk out with her too till Slim come along." Tiny's eyes were misty as he shook his head.

"I miss my old pard. I didn't think he'd ever slow down fer a woman…an' then Sadie come along. I never seen Slim so taken with a woman so long as I knowed 'im, an' I knowed 'im a powerful long time.

Longer than any a the Rockin' R hands 'cept fer Judge. Yessir, Sadie done roped his heart an' she never even tried."

Tiny grinned down at Annie. "Kinda like ya did, Darlin'. One look at me from those big eyes a yores an' I was done gone. But me, I never had no gurls afore ya, jist some gals I danced with. I liked to dance an' I danced a lot at the dance halls. I took off fer home when I run out a money or they closed down. Sometimes I was 'most too drunk to ride, but I always made it back to the ranch.

"Smiley was my second pard. We both was workin' fer Slim when those fellers cut us down."

He kissed Annie gently. His voice was soft when he added, "I only been powerful mad three times that I know of. Oncet when Lance was shot, oncet when those rustlers kilt Slim an' Smiley, an' oncet when Judge told me what happened to ya.

"I want to be yur man fer always, Annie. I ain't perfect but I'll give ya my best."

Annie smiled up at him as she wrapped her arms tighter around his neck. "You're perfect for me, Tiny."

Doc tapped on the door and Annie wiggled out of Tiny's arms to stand. Tiny's arm was around her when Doc came in.

"I see you are up and feeling better, Annie. I want to check you over one more time." He frowned slightly. "Are you going to be staying with Sadie? I think that would be best for now."

Annie nodded and smiled.

"I will until Tiny and I are married. We haven't set a date yet but neither of us wants to wait too long."

Doc studied the two of them before he smiled. He put out his hand to Tiny.

"Let me be the first to congratulate you. You are marrying a fine girl, and from what I have heard, she is getting a good man."

Both Tiny and Annie blushed.

"When cin I take Annie home? Does she have to stay much longer?"

"I'd like her to stay this afternoon, but she can go home before supper. You are welcome to come back in after I check her over or you may wait in the other room while she rests."

Tiny squeezed Annie's shoulders. "I'll be right outside an' I'll be back in soon as Doc finishes with ya."

Doc Williams helped Annie back into bed.

"I want you to try to rest this afternoon. Your system is still trying to work the chloroform out so you may have headaches for a few days." He checked her over and patted her hand. He hesitated as he looked at her again.

"You are going to be sore for a while, Annie. It might be a good idea to put off the wedding and all that goes with it for a time." Annie's face turned a deep red and she looked away. She pinched her eyes shut but the tears still leaked out. Doc patted her hand again as he opened the door and stepped outside.

As Tiny turned toward the door, Doc shut it quietly and pointed toward his office. "Come with me, Tiny. I want to talk to you a bit before you go back in."

Tiny followed Doc into his office. He frowned when Doc shut the door. Doc pointed to the chair in front of him before he perched on the edge of his desk. He drummed his fingers on the desktop as he frowned. Finally, he looked directly at the man in front of him.

"The men who hurt Annie damaged her inside. She needs to heal a while." As Tiny stared at him, Doc cleared his throat and continued.

"Tiny, when a woman is hurt the way Annie was, they have to heal inside and out. Sometimes even after their body is healed, their heart isn't whole yet. You will need to be gentle with Annie. She never knew a man completely until this happened. Sometimes, women will push away those they love after they have been raped. You need to be ready for that." He hesitated and added quietly, "I suggest you put off the wedding for a time."

Tiny stared at Doc as he frowned. He shook his head.

"Naa, I don't reckon we'll do that 'less Annie wants to. We both know she might have a little ol' baby a growin' inside a her, an' I want it to be mine one way or the other. As far as all the pleasures that come with marriage, I reckon I cin wait on those. All I care 'bout is lovin' Annie an' makin' sure she's safe."

Doc studied Tiny's sincere face. He smiled as he stood up.

"I have heard many good things about you, Tiny, and I am guessing they are all true. You go ahead and marry little Annie. I believe you are just the right man to be her husband." He was still smiling when he shook Tiny's hand again and led him back to Annie's room.

CHAPTER 50

A POWDER KEG

LEVI WATCHED TINY'S DEPARTING BACK AS HE RACED toward Cheyenne. He shook his head and scowled. He followed Tiny at a slow trot. When he stopped in front of Doc's house, Tiny's horse was standing there with its head down. The horse's heaving and lathered sides showed the speed of Tiny's last mile. Levi picked up the reins and led the animal down to the livery.

Rooster met him and took the reins to Tiny's horse. As the men stripped the gear off both horses, Rooster asked, "Tiny at Doc's?"

Levi nodded.

Rooster paused in his rub down. "Think Lance'll be able to keep those boys home?"

Levi shrugged as he looked over his horse's head. "He said he would until after the trial." He looked sideways at Rooster. "Did Sheriff Boswell arrest anyone yet?"

Rooster nodded and his wise old eyes snapped.

"Sure did an' Banker Bob is madder'n hops. Jimmy'll try ta pin it on Beans an' Beans'll start talkin'. Word is Banker Bob sent back east for some powerful big lawyer. They intend to drag Sugar through as much slop as they cin."

Levi shook his head. "It will be a nasty trial. Poor little Annie. I'm not sure she is up for all this."

Rooster took the reins of the bay from Levi. "Why don't ya go get a bath an' a shave. See if that little widow woman 'ill feed ya supper." Rooster's eyes were twinkling, and his face looked overly innocent.

Levi scowled at him but eventually laughed.

"Rooster, you sure seem to know a lot about everything here, right down to relationships that haven't even happened. Why a man could accuse you of caring about other people."

Rooster grinned. "Only *some* folks," he corrected as he led the horses to water, whistling as he strutted across the barn.

Levi grinned as he watched the little man talk to the horses. "Cheyenne is plumb full of characters."

Levi took Rooster's advice on the bath though. It felt good. As he put his dirty shirt back on, he looked at it with remorse.

"Two good shirts and I still can't keep them clean." He remembered he had left a dirty shirt at Sadie's and he grinned. "I'd better get that one. I'll at least have one clean shirt once I get it washed," he told himself as he strode toward her house.

When Levi arrived, he heard women's voices in the kitchen. He knocked on the door and a smiling Martha opened it.

"Why, Levi, how good to see you! You are early for supper but come on in." Sadie looked up and smiled. Molly's pretty face was pale, but she smiled as well as she asked, "Did Tiny make it in?"

Levi nodded. "We rode in together part of the way. He is up there now.

"Will Annie be staying here tonight or is Doc going to keep her another night?"

Martha replied without turning away from the stove, "Tiny is bringing her here. Badger just went down to get them in the wagon."

Sadie handed Levi a clean shirt, and he took it with surprise.

"I remembered I left my dirty one here when I took a bath. Thanks for washing it. I sure didn't expect you to do that."

Sadie smiled as he took the shirt from her and hurried to help Martha at the stove.

Levi stepped outside and changed. As he tucked the clean shirt into his britches, he heard Badger's distinctive voice. Soon Badger's wagon appeared on the street.

"Now, Tiny, ya hep Miss Annie get 'er things up ta her new room. I'm a gonna take this here wagon down ta the livery an' make sure it were Levi what done took you'ins hoss."

Levi walked out to meet the wagon. Tiny jumped down and lifted a pale Annie from the seat. One big hand carried her case, and the other pulled her close to him.

"Welcome home, Annie." Levi smiled at her. "I'm guessing those women fussed over your room all day long."

Annie smiled shyly at Levi. "Thank you, Mr. Parker, for helping me last night."

Levi grinned at the surprised look on Tiny's face.

"Annie refuses to call me Levi since she works for me. She will only call me Mr. Parker. I kind of like it. Maybe you could refer to me that way as well, Tiny," Levi drawled, his eyes sparkling with humor.

Badger snorted. Tiny started to curse but caught himself.

"Like He…I ain't gonna call ya nothin' but Judge. Ya shore are good with words an' ya like to boss folks around like a durned ol' judge."

Badger began to laugh, and Levi grinned at both men. He took Annie's case from Tiny and followed them to the house. Badger called from the street. "I'm a gonna take this here team ta the livery. Want ta ride with me, Levi?"

Levi waved in agreement. He set the case inside the door. There were a lot of women in there, and he preferred to avoid high emotions whenever possible. He loped back down the steps and jumped up on the wagon seat. His stomach growled loudly as he sat down. Badger grinned.

"Been a long day, ain't it, Boy?"

Levi nodded.

Badger continued, "I hear they arrested Banker Bob's boy. That thar's gonna be one messy trial."

Levi nodded in agreement, "And they will drag Annie through all the mud they can. That will infuriate Tiny and the Rocking R. This is a powder keg."

The men rode in silence the rest of the way to the livery.

CHAPTER 51

Somebody's Mule

Rooster came out to take the wagon and Badger hollered, "Got any more a that thar root beer ya made? Thought I might have Judge here carry some back ta Sadie's house. We got us a house full a folks fer supper."

Rooster grinned as he tied the team. He disappeared. When he returned, he staggered under the weight of a full, five-gallon jug.

Levi stared at the jug and then at Badger. "Now I know why you wanted me to ride down here with you."

"Shore 'nuf," Badger answered as the devils danced in his eyes. "Ya can't 'spect a feller as old as me ta tote this here jug all the way back ta Sadie's." His grin became bigger. "Put 'er on Judge's bill. It cin be his pay fer all the food he's a gonna eat fer supper."

Levi choked and laughed. He lifted the huge jug onto his shoulder, and the two men started back up the street.

The women had outdone themselves on the meal. There was meatloaf, mashed potatoes, corn, and apple pie.

Sadie filled Levi's plate a second time when he did not do it himself. She knew he had missed dinner and wanted to make sure he left full.

Levi was quiet as he listened to the chatter and conversation around the table. Tiny was quieter than normal as well. Levi smiled as he watched how protective the big cowboy was of little Annie.

Badger opened the root beer after supper. They were all drinking when they heard a loud commotion to the east. The sound died as quickly as it had begun. It was followed by a short period of silence before men's voices sounded loudly.

"That sounds like it came from around the jail," Levi stated as he stood. "I think I will go check."

Badger jumped up as well. "I'll go with ya."

Tiny grabbed his hat, and the three men headed for the jail. A crowd had started to gather but no one seemed to be overly concerned.

As they walked up, Sheriff Boswell glared at them. "Where were the three of you this evening?"

Levi shoved Tiny back when he tried to lunge forward. His eyes narrowed as he looked at the sheriff.

"We can account for our whereabouts all evening. Now what is this about?"

Sheriff Boswell gestured toward the back of the jail. "Somebody left the back door to the jail unlocked. Somehow, Beans and Jimmy escaped. They were attacked by something as they ran out. It looks like it could have been a mule, but no one saw anything. We can't even find a mule."

As the sheriff looked at Badger, Levi spoke. "I rode with Badger down to the livery before we ate. Mule wasn't in the barn nor was he part of the team we left with Rooster." He looked at the sheriff as he commented dryly, "Just because it might have been a mule doesn't mean it was Badger's mule. That is pure speculation on your part."

The sheriff's face was dark. "Speculation, yes, but I'd bet my life I'm right."

As the men walked to the back of the jail, the scene was bloody. Several men were holding lamps over the bodies of the two men. Jimmy was barely recognizable, and Beans' forehead showed the distinct print of a mule hoof. Both men had been stomped and kicked, but Jimmy's body was the most savaged.

Sheriff Boswell muttered, "I'm could lose my job. Robert Baker will never let this rest."

Levi looked at the sheriff coolly.

"Robert Baker worships at the altar of money and position. I would have to think on which he loves more, that or his son."

The sheriff stared at Levi. He jerked his head away and hollered, "Did anyone notify Robert Baker? We need to get these boys off the street, but I want him here before we move anything."

Tiny was breathing hard, and Levi patted his back as the three men walked back to Sadie's house.

Levi frowned as he looked at Badger, and the little man winked at him.

"Looks like somebody's mule jist saved this city a lot a grief. An' Miss Annie too," he suggested innocently.

Levi did not answer. He was quite sure that Badger had something to do with the death of the two men, but they had all been eating when it happened.

He finally commented, "I am guessing that the sheriff will be out at your place at first light to see if Mule is locked up."

"Yep, he shore will," Badger agreed. An' he'll find 'ol Mule right whar I left 'im, pinned up next ta the barn. I let 'im run loose whilst I'm 'round but if'n I'm a gonna be gone of a night, I pin 'im up. He likes ta foller me. He be a notional feller, ya know."

Badger winked at the two men and did a short jig as he walked faster.

"Guess I better get us a room down to the Rollins House so's that thar sheriff cin find me in the mornin'." He was whistling as they climbed the steps to Sadie's house.

The women looked up as the men came in, but the three said nothing.

Annie's face was pale once again. "I think I will go to bed if you don't mind."

Tiny moved forward and gave her his arm to the top of the stairs. When he came back down, he grabbed his hat and headed for the door.

Levi grabbed his arm. "Huh uh. You are staying in town tonight. I don't want there to be any question as to where any of us were this evening. Tell Peter at the Eagle to put your room on my bill." He grinned as he added, "But you are only staying one night so don't get too comfortable."

Badger grabbed Martha's arm. "Come on, Sweetheart. We's a stayin' in town too. Judge over there wants ta make sure us boys keep our noses clean an' be handy-like fer the sheriff ta find us in the mornin'." He nodded at Tiny. "We'll give ya a ride, Tiny, so's ya don't have ta do no more walkin'. Levi there seems ta enjoy it, but I prefer ta have my feet a restin'."

As Badger and his party moved out of the house, Sadie and Molly looked over at Levi. Molly grabbed his arm and led him to the table while Sadie put a big piece of apple pie in front of him. Molly stood in front of him. Her hands were on her hips as she glared at him. Levi grinned around his dessert.

No wonder Lance tries not to make her mad, he laughed to himself.

"My, this apple pie is tasty," he commented innocently as he chewed. As the fire in Molly's eyes became more pronounced, he put his fork down and laughed up at her. Sadie was smiling too.

Levi's face became serious.

"Jimmy and Beans escaped. As they went out the back door of the jail, it looks like they were attached by a mule, maybe more than one. Not much left of Jimmy. Beans had a hoof print in the middle of his forehead. Both had been kicked and stomped but Jimmy was the worse." He looked at the women as he talked, and their faces showed shock.

Molly turned away. She almost snorted as she nodded.

"Good. Saves a lot of trouble. I know Robert Baker's lawyers would have torn Annie apart. This makes it easier for everyone."

Levi nodded slowly.

"I am pleased your husband kept his hands home today. That could have sure muddied the waters."

Molly stared at Levi. Fire flashed in her blue eyes.

"Tiny has been part of the Rocking R for a long time, and most of those men would do anything for him. He has a kind heart and we all love him."

Levi shook his head as he tried not to grin.

"I am thinking we kept the men home but maybe let the most dangerous member of the Rocking R come to town."

Molly stared at him. She rolled her eyes as she turned away.

"If you only knew!" Sadie laughed out loud. "Yes, Molly can certainly take care of herself." Sadie put her arm around her friend. The fire slowly died in Molly's eyes until finally, she laughed.

Levi put the last bite of pie in his mouth. He stood to go. When he reached for his dirty shirt, Sadie shook her head.

"I know how hard they are on clothes down there at the laundry. Let me wash this for you."

Levi was surprised but he slowly nodded.

"If you are sure. That does mean I will have to come back and pick it up," he drawled. He tipped his hat to both women and took the stairs two at a time as he headed for the street, whistling as he strolled back toward his place.

Sadie watched him go. When he got to the big tree, he turned and doffed his hat. This time, he saw Sadie standing in the doorway, and he paused before he turned around.

"If Molly wasn't there, I'd probably run back and give her a big kiss," he commented to himself. His walk was just a little jauntier as he resumed his trip.

Molly looked at Sadie and tried not to laugh.

Sadie shook her head. "I tried to push him away. He was gone for about two months. Then I missed him." She blushed as she looked at Molly. "I really do like having him around," she murmured.

Molly hugged her friend. "Oh, Sadie. I'm so happy for you. I think Levi is a fine man. He has given you the space you needed. Now you are falling in love on your own time."

Sadie was quiet a moment as she stared out the window. "Sometimes I feel so disloyal to Slim though," she whispered as she looked from the saddle to the sleeping baby.

"And Slim told you to be happy and not pine away over him. You've told me how Levi talks to little Levi and tells him stories about his father. What more could you ask for?"

Sadie smiled through her tears, and the two women retired for the night.

CHAPTER 52

HELLO, KID

PEOPLE WERE AT LEVI'S OFFICE DOOR EARLY THE NEXT morning and business was brisk until noon. Jack Coral delivered the noon meal himself.

"How is Sugar?"

"As best as she can be. We moved her in with Mrs. Crandall last night." Levi paused and added with a chuckle, "Those women just might smother her with all their love."

"Good. That's what she needs." Jack was silent as he looked around Levi's office. He finally asked, "Do you think she will come back to work for you?"

Levi thought for a moment before he nodded.

"I think so. Annie likes to pull her own weight." He grinned at Jack. "I sure am glad I stole her from you. She is quite the little worker!"

"I hated to lose her but I'm glad you stole her too. She didn't have any business working in a saloon." Jack clapped Levi on the back. "I need to get moving. I have quite a few meals to deliver.

"I sure hope she takes these lunch deliveries back. She is a lot faster than I am, and she just keeps picking up new customers."

"I'm sure she will but it may cost you more," Levi agreed as he laughed. "She is a sharp little gal. After spending some time around Martha and Molly, you just may be in trouble!"

Levi did not finish his work in the office until nearly seven that evening. He assumed he had missed supper but went to pick up his shirt anyway. As he lifted his hand to knock on the door, he could hear women laughing and talking. He stood there for a time and listened before he knocked. Levi liked the sound of family, and sometimes, the pangs of loneliness just overcame him.

Sadie answered the door. As she pulled it wide, she smiled.

"I thought maybe you weren't coming this evening."

Molly spoke sarcastically from the table where the women were working on a dress.

"Sure she did. That's why she saved half of the food and wouldn't let us have seconds."

Levi's eyes lit up.

"So there is food left? I would sure eat if there is. A fellow could get used to eating you ladies' cooking."

Sadie had left the food on top of the stove where it would stay warmer. She soon had a plate filled and set in front of Levi.

As he began to eat, his eyes almost rolled back in his head with pleasure.

Molly laughed.

"You men. Food is your everything."

Levi looked up and his eyes moved to Sadie. He started to respond but he changed his mind. Instead, he took another bite and remained silent. However, Sadie saw the response in his eyes. Her face turned a light pink and she busied herself at the washpan.

When he was finished, Levi leaned back in his chair and watched the women. He liked the sounds they made and the way they filled the room with color and warmth. Soon, little Levi started to fuss, and Levi picked him up.

"Hello, Kid. How was your day?"

Molly frowned when she heard Levi call the baby "Kid" but Sadie was smiling so she remained silent.

Levi forgot about the rest of the people in the room as he talked to the baby. "Did you poop all over anyone today? You really need to learn to poop in a pot. It was pretty bad, but you smell good tonight.

"So how was dinner? Did Mommy feed you enough? I hear you are a little pig. That's okay. Your daddy was too. He never turned down a meal, no matter if he had just eaten."

He pushed the baby's blond curls back and kissed his cheek. "You sure look like your daddy, Kid. I wonder if you will be as ornery as he was."

The baby stared at Levi a little longer. He suddenly squinted up his face. He began to cry. His face turned dark red as the fussing turned instantly to screaming. Levi quickly handed him to Sadie.

"Yep, you act like your daddy too!"

Levi did not notice the women watching him. When he finally looked up, Molly was intensely focused on her sewing.

Annie stared at him for a moment.

"Do you have little brothers or sisters, Mr. Parker?"

"No, but there were always little babies coming to the orphanage. They usually didn't stay too long. I always liked to hold them."

Molly and Annie both looked surprised, but Sadie smiled as she kissed her son.

"You do seem to have a way with babies. At least with this one," she murmured softly as she smiled into the face of her son.

Levi grabbed his hat.

"Thanks, ladies. The food was delicious." He looked over at Annie.

"Annie, I have to help out at the Rocking R for the next few days, but I hope you will be back at work next week."

As she nodded, Levi's eyes began to twinkle.

"So, do we still have a date for Saturday night or are you ditching me for that cowboy you talked about?"

Annie blushed furiously and looked down. When she looked up, she was smiling.

"Sorry, you are on your own, boss. You have officially been dumped."

"Well, let's keep that a secret." Levi chuckled as he looked at Molly and Sadie. "Maybe I can convince one of you ladies to save me.

"How about it, Sadie? Want to go with me to the dance on Saturday? I know it's Ladies' Choice so how about you choose me?" As he smiled down at her, Sadie's heart lurched.

"Well…maybe I could just meet you there."

Levi beamed.

"It's a date! I will pick you and Kid up at seven. See you Saturday evening!"

As he pulled his hat on and winked at Sadie, Molly laughed out loud.

Sadie stood in the doorway. When Levi turned around to doff his hat, she waved at him. His smile nearly split his face as he headed across town to his own building.

Molly was laughing as Sadie closed the door.

"He doesn't really take no for an answer, does he?"

Sadie laughed, her face turning light pink.

"He seems to know when I don't really mean what I say," she mused, and even Annie laughed.

Molly frowned. "It still bothers me he calls your baby Kid. That seems so impersonal."

Sadie laughed softly.

"Levi thinks the baby looks just like Slim. Sometimes, he reverts back to the name he knew Slim by when they were young. I don't mind. It is getting a little confusing with two Levi's around anyway."

"Why did you name your baby Levi, Sadie? Is it a family name?" Annie asked.

As Molly glanced up at Sadie and waited for an answer, Sadie looked towards Slim's saddle. Her voice was soft as she answered.

"I met Levi when he came by after the trial of the men who killed Slim. He didn't even know who he was defending until it came out in the questioning. He stopped by because he wanted to say how sorry he was. We talked for a little while and he shared some stories of when Slim and he were together in Texas—Levi in an orphanage and Slim with his aunt. Neither was happy and they became best friends."

Sadie smiled through her tears.

"As boys, they promised when they had kids, they would name their first sons after each other. Slim would call his first son Levi, and Levi would call his first son Kid.

"After Levi saved me the day I went into labor in front of those longhorns, I decided to honor Slim's childhood wish. Of course, I had no idea Levi would move to Cheyenne and become part of our lives."

Annie stared at Sadie.

"What a beautiful story, Sadie. So romantic."

Even Molly wiped her eyes before clapping her hands.

"Back to work. We have lots of sewing to do if Annie is going to have a new dress to wear on Sunday."

CHAPTER 53

THE END OF ANOTHER SEASON

LEVI LEFT FOR THE ROCKING R THE NEXT DAY BEFORE daylight. He rode into the ranch yard just as Gus banged on the bell for breakfast. Lance was tucking in his shirt as he walked out of the house and Levi grinned at him.

"Looks like my timing was good today."

Lance chuckled. His face became more serious as he asked, "What became of the investigation?"

"Both men are dead. They broke jail the night they were arrested—escaped through the back door of the jail. The sheriff has it bricked shut now. It is kind of fuzzy after that." Levi looked perplexed as he frowned.

"They appeared to have been attacked by a mule, maybe more than one. There were lots of tracks but nothing clear enough to tell how many. They were both killed, and a mule print was on the forehead of Beans. There wasn't much left of Jimmy."

Lance's face broke into a slow grin and he laughed. His blue eyes were twinkling.

"A conundrum, isn't it?" Lance asked innocently. "None of the likely suspects could have done it. Rocking R was branding thirty miles away, and nobody knows how the men got out of their cells."

Levi nodded.

"I thought Badger was in on it, but he was with me all evening. In fact, we were at Sadie's house for supper along with Tiny. The mule or mules were never seen. Badger's big jack was in his pen when Sheriff Boswell rode out the next morning.

"I had Tiny stay in town. Badger and Martha did as well. Robert Baker had hired the best lawyers money could buy, but he canceled them."

Levi looked at Lance in disgust.

"Banker Bob had to make a choice between investigating a possible rape by his dead son or walk away with the integrity of the bank intact. He chose to walk away. Guess he didn't want to know what he would probably find."

Lance listened as he ate.

"Tiny didn't talk much when he came home. He just said the two men in jail had tried to break out and were dead.

"He was out here the next morning in time for breakfast, but he is going back into Cheyenne Friday night." He looked at Levi with a question on his face. "What do you know about Tiny getting married?"

Levi was surprised.

"He is? When?"

Lance shrugged.

"Not real sure. He gave me notice—said he would work through Friday. He is moving to Cheyenne to start a carpentry business right away."

"Well, I'll be. I told him he needed to do that, but he had no intention of quitting a month ago. Guess that little gal changed his mind." Levi chuckled and the two men were quiet as they finished their meal.

The next two days were hard work and long hours, but Levi enjoyed it. He could only stand to be inside for so long. He liked to feel the fresh air and sun on his back.

They finished branding on Friday afternoon, and Lance gave six men the night off. The rest would have Saturday night off. The six who chose Friday did not even ride back to the ranch. They rode directly to town.

"So long, boys! We'll think about ya while we soak in the tub."

Lance's riders didn't have to be back until noon on Saturday, and four of them had already asked Levi if they could bunk on his floor. He laughed and agreed.

As Levi saddled his horse to ride to Cheyenne, Lance joined him.

"Molly should be home this evening. I sure miss my wife when she's gone." He complained good-naturedly, "I think maybe she enjoys her long stays in Cheyenne just a little too much."

Levi laughed.

"Your wife is a sassy one. She drilled into me the other night. I can see why you like to keep her happy."

Lance's eyes were soft as he replied, "Molly is the best decision I ever made. I love that little gal to pieces. I just don't know how I would handle it if something took her away from me."

Levi thought about that as he studied the man next to him. *Lance is a tough man and Molly is a strong woman, but they seem to make each other better people. I guess that is what marriage is supposed to do.*

Beth came out just as Levi mounted to leave. She waved at him. He stared at her as she held Abigail, smiling.

"Why, Beth, I didn't know you were expecting!"

Beth patted her large stomach.

"Just one more month to go," she giggled. "Rowdy thinks I am going to explode, but somehow I just keep getting bigger."

Levi nodded somberly. She did look like she might explode but she was still pretty.

"You tell Rowdy he is a lucky man. His wife may be ready to explode but she is still as pretty as she ever was."

Beth giggled again and put Abigail down. "Will we see you Saturday night, Levi?"

Levi nodded and his eyes twinkled.

"Yes, I convinced Sadie to choose me, so I even have a date."

Beth clapped her hands together excitedly.

"That is wonderful, Levi. I love Sadie to pieces, and you dance so beautifully together."

Levi laughed and waved as he rode out of the yard. Even though he had enjoyed the last two days, he was excited to get back to Cheyenne. He was excited to see Sadie too.

He had intended to clean up first but decided to just stop by her house instead. He rode his horse into her yard and knocked on her window. She was rocking the baby and was startled to see him. He grinned at her and stepped down. As she opened the door, he kissed her. Her eyes went wide with surprise. Levi laughed softly as he stepped back.

"You know, I have been thinking about doing that since the last time. You sure taste good, Sadie." As she blushed, Levi grinned at her and mounted his horse. "See you tomorrow!" he called as he rode out of her yard. He stopped by the tree and raised his hat. Sadie was laughing as she waved back.

The livery was almost full when Levi rode in on his horse. He looked around in surprise.

Rooster shrugged. "Dances, weddin's, an' funerals bring folks out. An' I don't know where they's all gonna eat what with Ford's bein' closed."

Levi looked at Rooster in surprise.

Rooster nodded somberly, "Yep, Barney pulled out yesterday. "He's a movin' his rest'ernt an' hotel ventures to Denver. Ol' Barney likes to get in on the ground floor 'fore all the other folks get the same idea."

All of Cheyenne was sad to see him go, especially the Rocking R and Rowdy. They mournfully looked at the closed door and could see "their" table through the window. Rowdy had wanted to give him a farewell party, but the decision to move was a quick one. He did not even get to tell Barney goodbye.

Beth kissed Rowdy's sad face.

"Don't worry, Rowdy. We can take the train to Denver and see him there." Rowdy perked up, and Beth began to plan a trip for their growing family.

For the town of Cheyenne, the closure of the Ford House meant not only the loss of the town's most popular restaurant, but also no more of Barney's treats at the town functions. His absence was noticed immediately as plans for Saturday night commenced. The Ford House always sent some kind of food over for every event, and that would be missed.

Of course, the citizens of Cheyenne were not to be deterred. Everyone was to bring a dish to the dance.

Levi worked a deal with Rooster for more root beer. Rooster even offered to deliver it for him.

As Levi rubbed his horse down, Rooster pointed at the new buggy he had purchased. He looked at the young lawyer slyly.

"Ya might want to rent it fer Saturday night. I hear ya have a date."

Rooster's face looked innocent, but his eyes were dancing.

"So what else do you know about my life that I might not?" Levi asked as he laughed.

The ornery hostler answered, "Oh, that she's the purtiest gurl in Cheyenne, that yore rollin' in the dough—an' that yur little Annie is gettin' married on Sunday."

Levi was laughing as he listened, but the last comment caught him off guard.

"She—What? Getting married Sunday? Lance thought it would be soon, but I am guessing even he didn't know it would be this fast."

"Well, mebbie they's a waitin' to tell ya tomorrow night. Word is yous an' Miss Sadie be standin' up with 'em. Oh, an' the weddin' an' reception be out to the Rockin' R. Tiny wants to git hitched close to all his friends. "'Sides, Mrs. Rankin wouldn't have it no other way."

Levi stared at Rooster in amazement. "Shoot, Rooster, this town doesn't need a newspaper with you around. I was only out of town for two days!" Levi laughed again. "And I'm betting Lance won't know about any of this until tonight. I think those women just make their plans and do their own things."

Rooster nodded wisely. "An' it's best not to interfere."

CHAPTER 54

A SMALL VILLAIN

LEVI WALKED DOWN TO THE BATH AREA AND TOOK A soaking bath. He had to put his dirty clothes back on but at least he was clean. As he unlocked his door, he pulled off the note that was pushed over a nail.

Come see me when you get back in town.
Sheriff Boswell

Levi frowned as he read the note.

"Now what?" He rubbed his hand over his face and slowly walked down to the sheriff's office.

"You wanted to see me? If this is going to take a while, I will come back tomorrow."

Sheriff Boswell shook his head.

"There's a young man in jail who needs your help. I know you have a big trial in Laramie next week, so I wanted you to see him today."

As the sheriff unlocked the door, a young boy about ten years old looked up and glared at Levi.

"Is this a joke?" Levi asked incredulously as he stared from the boy to Sheriff Boswell.

The sheriff shook his head again.

"No joke. Robert Baker needed a scapegoat. We found this kid digging in the trash behind the jail when we were scooping up the bodies. He accused the kid of killing his son. He intends to hang him."

Levi's eyebrows raised and his eyes became hard.

"He's a kid. Not even a rich man can get away with that."

"That banker thinks he can," the sheriff answered quietly.

Levi looked at the young man. "Why does Mr. Baker think you killed his son?"

The boy looked defiantly at Levi.

"I don't have to answer no questions from you," he scoffed defiantly.

Levi stared hard at the young man. "You're right, you don't. But right now, I'm your only hope of getting out of here. I suggest that you quit playing tough and tell me why."

As the sheriff backed out and shut the door, the boy began to talk.

"I was hungry an' I was diggin' in the trash. I seen this big mule charge out of the dark an' tear into those two men who was killed. I hid behind the trash can, quiet as a mouse. When they was dead, I swear that mule looked right at me. He didn't bother me none though. He just turned an' runned away."

"Only one mule? Did you see any people with him? Anyone giving orders?"

The boy shook his head.

"Just the mule an' that's why the banker accused me of killin' those fellers. He said there ain't no mule out there smart enough to do somethin' like that unless somebody was there givin' orders."

Levi stared at the young man. "What's your name, Boy?"

"Strauss. Leonard Strauss but I go by Leo."

"Leo, where are your parents?"

"I ain't got none," Leo replied with a frown. "I was on one of them there orphan trains headed west. The folks I was passed off on tied me up at night 'cause they said I'd steal their stuff. I might of stoled some food 'cause they barely fed me, but I didn't steal nothin' else.

"I got loose one evenin' an' hitched a ride on a train. The conductor caught me just before we got into this here town and threw me off." He gave Levi an ornery grin. "I done rode it all the way from Omaha 'fore they caught me."

Levi repressed a grin. He liked this kid.

"When was your last good meal, Leo?"

Leo squinted his eyes. "I ain't real sure. I just ate scraps on the train, and those old folks wouldn't feed me. Probably in the orphanage on Sunday's when the new parents came."

Levi felt the wrath rising in his chest. "Sheriff, unlock this door. I'm taking this kid to get something to eat."

Sheriff Boswell frowned.

"I don't think I can do that. He was legally arrested and—."

"And I'm bailing him out. I'll be responsible for him while we eat. I'll bring him back here when we're done."

As the sheriff unlocked the cell, Levi looked at his pocket watch. *Nine o'clock at night. All the eating houses are closed. Where am I going to find food at this hour?* He grinned as he thought of Sadie.

"Come on, Leo. I am going to introduce you to one of the best cooks in Cheyenne."

When Levi knocked on Sadie's door, she opened it with an expectant smile that changed to surprise.

Levi looked at her seriously.

"Leo here hasn't had a full meal in longer than he can remember, Sadie. Any chance you have some leftovers you could give him?"

Sadie smiled at the young man and pulled him inside.

"You sit down right there, Leo. I just happen to have some fried chicken. I was expecting a friend for supper, but he didn't show up."

Her eyes were laughing as she saw the surprise on Levi's face. She put a plate in front of each of them.

Levi had never in his life worked so hard to eat so little. The chicken was delicious, but the boy seemed to have no bottom in his stomach.

Sadie could barely keep from laughing at the tiny bites Levi took and the mournful way he looked at the chicken wing on his plate.

When the young man was finally full, nothing was left. Potatoes, gravy, fresh tomatoes, and fried chicken—all of it was gone.

Levi looked at Leo in amazement.

"Leo, I think I will send you out to live with Beth. She is used to feeding fellows who eat like you."

As Leo grinned, Sadie asked, "Where are you from, Leo?"

"Pennsylvania, ma'am. I plan to just be here for a few days. I want to move on to California."

Sadie looked at him in surprise.

"But you are only a child! How old are you?"

Leo looked from Sadie to Levi. He was going to lie. Instead, his shoulders slumped, and the truth came out.

"I'm nine, ma'am. I ain't got nobody in California but I hear it's warm there. I'm tired of bein' cold. If I have to sleep outside, at least I won't be cold."

Sadie's eyes filled with tears as she looked at Levi. When his eyes met hers, they both knew this young boy was never going to sleep outside again unless he was playing.

Levi stood and reached for his hat.

"Thanks for supper, Sadie. It surely was good." He could feel his heart hammering in his chest. He knew he dared not kiss her because it would be a long one.

Sadie put her arm around Leo's shoulders.

"Leo, why don't you have Levi bring you back for breakfast in the morning? I am fixing biscuits and gravy, and I always make too much."

Leo's eyes shined as he looked over at Levi. The big man was almost as excited as Leo about breakfast.

"We'll be over at seven in the morning…better make it eight." Levi did not know how long it took to cook biscuits and gravy, and he sure didn't want Sadie to have to get up earlier than she normally did.

She smiled at the two of them.

"I will see you both at eight tomorrow morning. Now come hungry."

As they walked towards the street, both looked back at her when they reached the tree. Levi waved his hat, and Leo copied him.

Sadie put her hand over her heart and tears filled her eyes. "Children are such a gift, and Leo is such a fine boy." As she closed her door, little Levi stirred and smiled in his sleep. Sadie's heart melted a second time.

CHAPTER 55

THE BIGGEST JACKASS

LEVI STARTED FOR THE JAIL. HE HADN'T WALKED FAR when he slowed down.

"Leo, we are going to make a detour. I am going to visit a man, and I want you to stay back where he can't see you."

As Leo ducked his head, Levi added, "It's the banker. I want to see if I can talk some sense into him."

Leo nodded and the two of them walked the quarter mile to a large house on the corner of a well-groomed lot. Leo let out a low whistle and Levi signaled to him to be quiet. Leo ducked down by the large porch, and Levi continued up the steps.

No one came when he knocked, so he knocked again. When no one answered the second time, Levi yelled, "I know you're in there, Robert. Open this door or I will wake all your neighbors!"

Robert Baker jerked the door open. He wanted to intimidate Levi Parker, but the man was so big he had to look up at him.

"What do you want? How dare you come to my home this time of night!"

Levi stared down at the man.

"And how dare you jail a nine-year-old boy, especially for a crime he didn't commit."

As the two men glared at each other, Levi asked casually, "Tell me, Robert, what do you know about mules?"

When the man did not answer, Levi continued, "I can tell you a lot about mules. I can tell you the commands to use with them. I can also tell you they are very smart. I can tell you they have different temperaments. Some are jackasses, just like some people I know, while others are as calm and tame as kittens.

"I can also tell you a mule will not take orders unless those orders are given in the way it was trained. Now what do you think the chances are that a kid digging in a trash can would know the right way to order a strange mule to kill someone?"

As Robert Baker's face blanched white, Levi spoke softly, "Here is what's going to happen.

"I am going to take this case. I am going to drag you up one end of that courtroom and down the other. I am going to bring in mules to make my point, and I am going to make you look like the biggest jackass of them all."

As the banker turned even whiter, Levi added, "Or, you can write out a statement, here and now, dropping all charges. And it had better be right now because I am going to start preparing my case tonight.

"I will sue you for damages, for court costs, and for endangering a child. Your reputation as a banker will be destroyed. Then I will ask for part of your assets to be set aside for a child with no parents whom you tried to railroad into a guilty sentence—just because a mule killed your son."

Levi stared hard at the man. His voice was hard when he added, "I will also bring up your son's reputation and the caliber of people whom he fraternized with during his off hours." He paused to let that sink in.

"Or you can give me that statement now, and this will all go away."

310

Robert Baker was seething. He knew Levi well enough to know the man would do exactly what he had just stated. He also knew Levi was smart. In addition, the man was a master in the courtroom.

What the banker really wanted was to tell Levi that he, Robert Baker, the president of First National Bank of Cheyenne, would no longer need his services. However, Levi had made the bank a lot of money. That meant the stockholders were pleased with his work, and Robert dared not dismiss him.

He glared at Levi and stomped to his study. He was back in a few minutes with a statement dropping all charges. His signature was large and bold, but the man before Levi was neither.

Levi took the statement, read it, and smiled.

"Thank you, Robert. I will drop off those papers you need on Monday before I leave for Laramie."

As Robert Baker slammed the door, Leo stood up and grinned.

"You sure made him eat crow! Is that what you do for a livin'? Was all that stuff you said about mules true? My pa didn't like mules. I ain't never been close to any till the other night."

Leo's face slowly changed.

"Am I goin' back to jail? Could you maybe loan me a blanket for the night? It is kinda chilly in that ol' jailhouse."

Levi stopped and took Leo by the shoulders.

"Leo, I'm not married, and I have never been a dad. I did live in an orphanage though for three years, so I know what it's like to not have a family.

"If you decide to stay with me, I am going to promise you will never have to sleep outside unless you want to. I will also try to make sure you never leave the table hungry.

"You will have to sleep on my floor until we get you a bed, but I will give you as many blankets at night as you want."

"You mean stay with you like I was your kid or something?" Leo's eyes were big as he stared up at Levi.

When Levi nodded, Leo frowned.

"'Course, I couldn't ride the cars on to California, could I?"

Levi shook his head and answered seriously, "Not until you are seventeen and have enough money to ride them with a ticket."

Leo looked up and smiled as he asked hopefully, "Can we eat Sadie's food from time to time?"

"I surely hope so," Levi answered as he smiled into the dark. "Now let's get home. I need to get some sleep if we are going to be ready for breakfast."

Once Leo was settled on the floor with four blankets, Levi walked up to the sheriff's office. Sheriff Boswell was waiting for him.

"About time you came back. My wife will have my hide for being so late."

Levi handed him the statement and the sheriff looked at Levi in surprise. He slowly whistled and nodded.

"Looks like you just inherited a kid. Guess your next job will be to find a home for him."

"He already has a home," Levi answered quietly as he left the jail.

CHAPTER 56

COOKING FOR THE BOYS

SADIE WAS UP EARLY. SHE HAD DECIDED TO MAKE cinnamon rolls as well as biscuits and gravy. Badger had shared a hog with her and now she even had smoked pork.

She was humming as she worked. She realized for the first time in a long time, she was excited. She was excited to see a big man with a gentle heart. She was excited to fix him breakfast, and she was excited to see the young boy who was coming with him. She paused as she looked at the pans of rolls ready to go into the oven. For just a moment, her heart clutched.

Sadie looked at the saddle and whispered softly, "Slim, I so want you to approve."

She stopped as she felt his presence. All sound disappeared and the kitchen felt warm, happy, and peaceful. The feeling was gone as quickly as it came. Once again, she heard the birds calling in the tree. Sadie smiled as she wiped her eyes.

"Thank you, Slim. Thank you for listening."

Once the rolls were in the oven, Sadie picked up her baby. She sat outside while she nursed him in the swing. It was a beautiful fall morning and she felt lucky to experience it. When he was done, she hurried back into the house and rolled out the biscuits. They went into the oven when the rolls came out. The gravy was just finishing when she heard voices on her porch.

When Sadie pulled open the door, both Levi and Leo sniffed. They looked past her to stare at the rolls. Leo walked closer and smelled them.

His eyes were big as he asked, "Are those cinneymon rolls? My momma used to make cinneymon rolls."

Sadie smiled and laughed as she nodded.

Levi leaned over to breathe in the aroma, and his eyes rolled in delight.

"You bet they are, Leo, and they surely do smell good!"

Sadie filled their plates and set them on the table. The large man and young boy lifted their forks, eyeing the food in anticipation.

"Would you like to lead us in grace, Levi?" Sadie's voice was soft when she spoke.

Levi was startled and just a little ashamed as he dropped his fork.

"Lord, we thank you for this fine food and for the love in this house. We pray you keep the people who eat here safe as they go about their chores and their work. Thank you for bringing Leo into our lives and keep little Levi healthy. Amen."

Leo was staring at his plate. He leaned over to Levi and whispered loudly, "Is this all mine?"

Levi nodded, and the young man began to eat. He gripped his fork and shoveled the food in quickly.

Levi noticed but decided not to correct him. *I'll have plenty of time to teach him manners when he isn't so hungry.*

When the baby cried, Leo looked around in surprise. "You have a baby? Where's the daddy?"

Sadie's face paled. Levi started to answer, but Sadie shook her head slightly as she looked at Leo. Turning her eyes to little Levi, she spoke softly.

"His name is Levi, and his daddy died before he was born."

Leo's face became sad. "So he won't have no daddy? I had a daddy a long time ago but now I don't have a momma or a daddy." He looked from Levi to Sadie and a slow smile spread across his face. He leaned toward Sadie and whispered, "Levi said I could stay with him and be his kid."

Sadie's brown eyes opened wide, and the tears in the corners of them sparkled.

"Why, Leo, that is wonderful!"

Levi grinned at Leo and tousled his hair. Leo's smile was huge. He started to say something else. Instead, he lowered his head and began to eat again.

"So, Sadie, how is your sewing business going? Are the ladies of Cheyenne keeping you busy?"

Sadie began to tell Levi about all her projects. She showed him the dress she was making for Annie.

Levi stared from the dress to Sadie.

"How did you make that so fast? The word is they are getting married on Sunday. You have only had a few days to work on it."

"Oh, I'm quite fast when I set my mind to it. Besides, Martha and Molly helped while they were here," Sadie stated with a laugh.

She handed him the shirt she had washed. "Do let me wash your shirts, Levi. I know how they are handled at the laundries."

Levi looked embarrassed.

"Sadie, now and then is okay, but I can't..."

Sadie interrupted him. "Levi, please. I was a laundress in Julesburg when Lance found me. I know how clothes are washed in those places. I put a lot of time and effort into the clothing I make. I want your shirts to last longer than a few months."

Levi was quiet for a moment. He turned his head to wink at Leo and grinned.

"What do you think, Leo? If Sadie washes my shirts for me, we might get to eat supper here every night. Of course, I might have to get a second job to pay for all the groceries we would eat up!"

Sadie laughed. "Or I could just make you more shirts," she stated dryly.

Levi's face fell, and Sadie laughed again.

Levi and Leo helped carry the dirty dishes to the sideboard. To Sadie's surprise, Levi rolled up his sleeves to wash them. She started to argue, but he rested his hands on the wash tub.

"Sadie, I love eating meals here, but it can't be all one-sided. If you are going to feed us, you have to let us help clean up. Now show me how you want this done."

Sadie tried to show Levi how she liked the dishes washed and rinsed. Levi managed to be right behind her at every step, bumping into her as she moved. Finally, she sent Leo outside to get a bucket of water from the well, and she turned to scold Levi. As she started to talk, he kissed her and backed away with a grin.

Sadie's heart was pounding, and she was almost dizzy. Her brown eyes were huge as she backed up against the wash tub and hung onto the sides.

Levi laughed and went to open the door for Leo.

"Just dump it in the kettle on the stove," he instructed.

The baby began to fuss, and Levi lifted him out of the crib. "Hello there, Kid. I wondered if I would get to see you today." The baby wiggled his legs as Levi talked and watched his face closely. Suddenly, the little boy's face lit up in a huge smile. Levi laughed excitedly.

"Sadie, he just smiled at me!"

Sadie rushed forward and the baby smiled again. Both of them talked to him and the smiles kept coming. Then he pushed his fist into his mouth and his face crinkled up. Levi quickly handed him to his mother before the cries turned to screams.

Sadie nursed her baby while Levi and Leo washed all the dishes. Levi had found an apron. He put it on to keep his clothes from getting too wet. Leo kept looking at him. Finally, he laughed out loud.

Levi looked down at the apron and grinned back. It was pink with a ruffle around the outer edge and had three hearts on the pocket.

"You don't like my apron, Leo? I am guessing it looks a lot better on Sadie."

Sadie came out to see what they were laughing about and began to giggle.

The apron was way too small. That, combined with the ruffles, made Levi look ridiculous.

After the dishes were done, Levi and Leo left. Sadie watched them from the doorway. Again, they both turned around at the big tree to look back. She waved and shut the door.

As she nursed her baby, she murmured. "What do you think, little one? Do you like big Levi?" The baby stopped nursing long enough to smile before he latched back on. Sadie smiled at him as she stroked his soft cheek.

"Levi confuses me, but I think I like it."

CHAPTER 57

CHEYENNE'S NEWEST RESIDENT

LEVI STOPPED AT THE DRY GOODS STORE. HE BOUGHT Leo two pairs of britches, two shirts, some used boots, and a hat.

As Leo stared at them, he asked quietly, "When do I have to give them back?"

Levi's mouth tightened. He remembered asking that question himself. The answer was usually "tonight when the parents leave."

The children in the orphanage had to dress nicely whenever potential parents came to look the children over. Folks were rarely interested in the older ones though. Once the adults left, the new clothes were put away, and the children were given their shabby clothes again.

Levi put his hand on Leo's shoulder as they walked. He answered softly, "They are yours, Leo, until you get too big for them. Now let's go take baths so you are clean when you put on your new clothes."

The bath area was busy, and they had to wait for two tubs. When Leo took off his clothes, Levi saw how thin the boy was. He truly was just skin and bones. Anger rose in Levi again.

"Scrub yourself all over, Leo. We are going to a dance tonight and you need to be clean. And your hair too," he added as he tossed Leo a bar of soap.

Levi was shaved and dressed before Leo finally climbed out of the tub. He looked up at Levi. "I ain't never took a bath in that much water."

"Feels good, doesn't it?"

Leo smiled and dressed quickly. As he tucked in his shirt, he looked around. "What are we doing now?"

Levi had intended to finish prepping for the trial in Laramie, but work would have to wait.

"What would you like to do?" he asked curiously.

"Well, I like to ride horses," Leo responded hopefully.

Levi grinned at him. "So do I. Let's go for a ride."

Rooster met them as they walked into the livery. Levi was sure Rooster knew all about Leo already, but the ornery hostler pretended to be surprised. "So, who is this young sprout? What's yer name, Sonny?"

Leo put out his hand. "Leo, Leo Strauss, sir."

Rooster beamed. "Rooster's the name. Jist Rooster is good enough fer me. Please to meet ya, Leo Strauss."

Rooster looked at Levi. "So what ya boys doin' today? 'Fore the dance, that is."

Leo spoke up excitedly, "We're a goin' for a ride, but I don't have a horse. Do you have any exters, Mr. Rooster?"

Rooster's eyes twinkled as he studied Leo's face. "Well, let's see. How much have ya ridden hosses, Leo?"

Leo puckered his brow. "I rode a lot when my dad was alive but I ain't ridden since then."

Rooster looked at Levi. "Horse or pony?"

Levi studied the available horses. "Let's start with a pony and see how he does."

Rooster watched Leo saddle the pony and made sure he tightened the cinch. He adjusted the stirrups, and they were ready to go.

As they rode out of town, Levi talked to the boy.

"Look around you, Leo. Notice things. Pay attention to the sounds and the people around you. Animals talk all the time but most of us don't take the time to listen."

Leo looked around as Levi talked. He liked to listen to Levi. The man's voice was pleasant, and he didn't yell at him.

Leo looked over at Levi. "Do you like Miss Sadie?"

Levi laughed and his eyes twinkled. "What do you think?"

Leo looked sideways at Levi. "I think you like her. I saw you kissin' on her."

Levi looked at him in surprise, and Leo grinned.

"I like her a lot but I'm not sure how much she likes me."

Leo looked at Levi seriously. "I think she still misses her baby's daddy."

Levi was quiet for a moment as he stared down at the boy beside him. "You are mighty perceptive for a nine-year-old, Leo."

"I think about things a lot. I watch folks too. I try to think what I would do was I them. When I was in the orphanage, we didn't play much. We mostly sat, so a feller learns to think."

Levi could once again feel the ire rise in his chest, but it was soon replaced with wonder. *This young man has had a tough childhood and yet he still loves and cares about people.*

Levi looked down at Leo. "You know, Leo, there are going to be lots of kids to play with at the dance tonight. Some of them will be close to your age. Have you played much with other kids?"

Leo shook his head. "Naa. Mostly I worked. Pa said we didn't have time to play—there was too much work to do. 'Sides, I was the only kid at our house. And nobody played at the orphanage."

He stared across the grassy pasture beside the road. "I was really glad to leave there, an' I tried hard to be a good kid so those old folks would like me." He added softly, "I heard them talkin' one night 'bout how I was a mistake."

Levi's mouth tightened into a hard line. "You know what, Leo? God made all of us, and He doesn't make mistakes. I myself am glad you ran away *and* that you were kicked off the train at Cheyenne."

As Leo looked up at him quickly, Levi smiled broadly. Then he winked. "Shall we see how fast these horses can run?"

Leo clapped his heals into the sides of the pony and Levi yelled, "Ride 'im, cowboy!" Leo whooped and the two of them were off, racing down the road.

Levi slowed his horse when he saw a wagon coming towards them. "Whoa him down, Leo. We can't run into folks." They slowed their horses to a trot. Levi recognized Lance and Molly, along with their children.

Levi and Leo moved their horses to the side of the road, and Lance stopped the wagon. "Good morning, Levi. I see you just got whipped by a short horse." He was grinning, and Molly was laughing.

Levi grinned in return. "Lance, Molly, I want you to meet Cheyenne's newest resident. Just came in on the train yesterday," he stated somberly with a wink at Leo.

Sammy was craning his neck from the back of the wagon, and Leo looked back at him curiously.

"This is Leo Strauss, originally from Pennsylvania but now from Cheyenne. Lance and Molly Rankin, Sammy, Paul and Abigail."

Sammy promptly thrust out his hand. "My name is Sammy Rankin." Leo shook it, and Sammy began to talk excitedly.

"We are goin' to the dance tonight. I don't know how to dance but lots a kids will be there. You cin play with us if ya want. Sometimes Rooster lets us build hay forts in his loft. Have ya ever built a hay fort?"

Lance patted Sammy's head. "Slow down, Sammy. You have to let him answer the first question before you bombard him with another."

He looked at Levi and his blue eyes were full of orneriness. "Have a date tonight, Levi?"

Levi rested his hands on the saddle horn and looked innocently at Lance. "There are an awful lot of folks who seem to have a great concern about my personal life. Guess you will just have to wait and see."

Molly burst out laughing. "Oh, please, Levi. Everyone knows you are taking Sadie to the dance.

"Men. You all think you are so tough, but you know so little about women."

Levi stared at her, surprise showing on his face. He chuckled as he agreed.

"You're right, Molly. I know darn little about women. I have tried to avoid them most of my life. You and young Leo here seem to know things I don't see."

Lance laughed. "Where are you headed? Riding somewhere in particular? If not, we are headed over to Sadie's and then on to Samuel's for dinner."

Levi looked at Leo. "That is up to my young friend. What would you like to do, Leo?"

Sammy was waiting expectedly, and Leo grinned.

"I might like to ride in the wagon with those kids." Sammy and Paul began to talk excitedly as they made room for their new friend.

Levi lifted Leo off his horse and dropped him into the wagon. He handed the reins to Leo. "Tie your horse to the wagon, Leo." The pony pulled back and Levi popped its rump.

Leo quickly tied the horse and sat down with the Rankins. Sammy was never short on words and soon the back of the wagon was filled with happy chatter and laughing.

CHAPTER 58

Happy Memories

LEVI RODE HIS HORSE BESIDE LANCE, AND MOLLY leaned across him to talk.

"What is the story with Leo?"

Levi frowned.

"Long story but the short of it is, he's an orphan. He has had a hard time, and I took him in."

Molly sat up in surprise.

"But how will you take care of him when you are gone so much?"

Levi grinned at her with twinkles in his eyes.

"Maybe I will have to find a wife. Any suggestions, Molly? You seem to know lots of women around Cheyenne."

Lance looked over at Molly and commented dryly, "You are gone a lot and we manage without you."

Molly's blue eyes flashed. She started to retort. When Lance started laughing, she elbowed him and sat back in her seat.

"Lance, you just try to make me mad."

"Sure do. I love those blue eyes when they get fiery." Lance was still laughing as he squeezed her.

Molly glared at him. Finally, she laughed. She scooted closer and took his arm.

"You just have to know how to handle them!" Lance winked at Levi as he chuckled.

Molly banged him with her elbow again. The fire was back in her eyes as she shook her finger and began to tell Lance all the things he did not know about women.

Levi and Lance were both laughing by then. The little group continued on to Sadie's house. As they drove up, the children were all talking at once. When they began to climb out of the wagon, Molly grabbed Sammy before he could get away.

"Sadie, would you have time to trim Sammy's hair? He is starting to look like a caveman."

Sammy protested, "I don't need no haircut. I can still see if I shake my head."

Molly's grip was firm and up the steps they went. Sadie brought a chair out of the house and Sammy climbed up, still protesting. Sadie slipped him a cookie as she put the tea towel around his shoulders and the complaining stopped. She was done in no time and looked over at Leo.

"How about you, Leo? Want to trade a cookie for a haircut?"

Leo frowned and Levi nodded.

"Shorten him up and make him look like the fine young man he is."

Leo was quiet as the straw-colored hair dropped to the ground. When Sadie was done, he felt his head.

"Not much up there," he commented.

Sadie went into the house and brought a mirror out for him to see.

Leo looked in the mirror. He smiled at Sadie.

"Thanks, Sadie. That's real fine. Folks usually just put a bowl on my head."

Sadie brushed the loose hair from Leo's neck and shook out the towel. She gave him another cookie and kissed his cheek. Leo looked at her in surprise as he turned a dark red. Sammy was hollering for him from the top of the tree and Leo ran to join him. Sadie watched him go.

"Such a sweet boy." She looked over at Levi. "You didn't ever tell me what his story was. How did he come to be in Cheyenne?"

As Levi told Leo's story, the little group became silent. Both Sadie and Molly had tears in their eyes. Lance's eyes were an icy blue.

Lance asked quietly, "So now what?"

Levi grinned.

"Let's just say I had a conversation with Banker Bob last night after I left Sadie's, and he came around to my way of thinking. In fact, he was mighty agreeable."

Lance laughed as he looked at Levi.

"I sure would have liked to have heard that conversation."

Levi answered innocently, "Oh it was nothing much. I just talked about mules—and jackasses."

Laughter bubbled from Molly's mouth, and Sadie laughed behind her hand.

Lance grinned again, and slapped Levi on the back.

"I sure am glad you made Cheyenne your home, Levi."

Levi looked at Sadie. The smile remained on his lips, but the look in his eyes became intense. "Me too," he answered quietly.

Molly pulled out Lance's pocket watch.

"We need to be going. Father is planning for dinner at one, and I am not sure what I will need to make for him." She laughed as she continued, "He pretends to know how to cook but he doesn't. When I was growing up, Gus did all the cooking. I'm not sure what to expect."

Sadie stared at Molly in surprise.

"You do know your father has a lady friend? He has been seeing Mrs. Monte. She helps out at the bakery just up from the livery. Her husband died in a blizzard several years ago."

Molly's mouth dropped open. Lance began to laugh, and Molly grabbed his arm.

"Let's go. Kids! Load up!" As she pulled Lance out the door, she called over her shoulder, "Leo can come with us if he wants."

Leo was walking slowly toward the house when Molly invited him. His eyes lit up, and he looked hopefully at Levi. Levi nodded, and Leo raced to their wagon. He waved as they headed down the street.

The house was suddenly quiet. Levi looked around.

"Where is Annie? She still lives here, doesn't she?"

"She does but she has not been here much." Sadie smiled. "Badger found them a little house on the north side of town, and Tiny is working to fix it up. Annie has been cleaning there a few hours every day. Badger introduced her to the woman who lives next door so she'd be comfortable there alone.

"She is up there with Tiny today. He is making their furniture and Annie is helping him. Yesterday was his last day on the Rocking R. He is in Cheyenne full time now."

"Good for him. He is a true craftsman and will do just fine here." He looked out the window as he asked, "Annie doing all right?"

"She is pretty skittish around men she doesn't know, but Tiny makes her feel safe."

Levi thought for a moment.

"I keep a six shooter in my bedroom. I will bring that down and put it in her desk. That might make her feel a little safer."

"She would probably appreciate that." She smiled softly as she looked at Levi.

"Annie is so young, and Tiny is so big and gruff. He just adores her. He will do anything to make her happy. They are just the cutest couple." She sighed as she looked away. "Love is a wonderful thing," she whispered as she looked at Slim's saddle.

Levi was quiet as he watched Sadie. He looked over at Slim's saddle and could almost feel his old friend smiling. He walked across the room and stood staring down at it. The seat was worn smooth and Levi ran his hand over it. His eyes were misty as he looked at Sadie. "We were both blessed to have Slim as part of our lives."

He moved to the kitchen window. When he turned around, he was smiling.

"Slim was such a prankster. He messed with that old aunt all the time. One time, several months before we ran away, I was in trouble. I was sitting on the steps of the orphanage. I had ripped my britches. The darn things were too small, but it didn't matter.

"Slim hissed at me from up in a big tree close to where I sat. He was holding a basket nearly full of little bull snakes. He slid down the tree and sat beside me. He had dumped some in his old aunt's bed and offered to share the rest with me. I couldn't leave or I'd get a whupping, so he climbed back up the tree. He jumped onto the roof of the orphanage and proceeded to scatter those snakes all over the upstairs. He was back in his tree in no time…and then the shrieking started.

"Those cranky old gals came *pouring* out of that house. Some didn't stop running until they were almost a mile out of town, their old skirts just a flapping. I jumped up and ran with them until we passed a creek. Then I cut out.

"Slim and I went fishing the rest of the day. We ate baked fish that night for supper. In fact, we fished and talked most of the night. That was when we started planning our escape. I sneaked back in through the same window Slim used and was in bed before daylight.

"Those old gals didn't even miss me that night. After that, we sneaked out almost every night. I didn't have so much trouble sitting around during the day doing nothing after being up late every night!"

Sadie's brown eyes were sparkling as she listened, and they were both laughing by the time Levi finished his story.

CHAPTER 59

I HAD A COW LIKE THAT ONCE

LEVI TRIED TO HIDE THE EXCITEMENT ON HIS FACE AS he asked Sadie, "Want to go for a buggy ride? I have something I would like to show you."

"I would love to, but I need to feed little Levi first."

"No problem. I will take the horses back to the livery and pick up the buggy. I have one rented for this evening but I'm sure Rooster will let me have it early. I'll be back in about fifteen minutes. Don't wake Kid up. We can take our time."

Sadie watched Levi as he loped down the steps. He waved at her from the big tree. His face was so excited and happy that Sadie had to laugh. As he rode down the street, she hurried to change.

Maybe Levi will wake on his own if I change first. She heard the baby stirring and she sang softly as she slipped on a new dress.

Levi rode into the livery. As he began to rub down the horses, Rooster strolled over.

"Any chance I can get that buggy early? I want to take Sadie for a ride."

Rooster nodded and was back quickly with a team. As the two men hitched the horses, the old hostler casually mentioned, "Been an uppity-lookin' gal in here this mornin' lookin' fer ya."

Levi looked up in surprise.

Rooster added too innocently, "Real purty but kinda reminded me of a cow I culled one time. Always had 'er head up, a lookin' fer trouble an' kicked anythin' that come close to 'er."

Levi stared at Rooster for a moment before he laughed.

"Well, I guess I'd better not let myself be found then, had I?"

Rooster was smiling as Levi drove the buggy out into the street. He saw that uppity young woman crossing the street. He walked back into the barn and began to clean out a stall. As she came around the corner, he tossed a fork of dirty hay her way and she screamed.

He stopped to lean on his fork as he spit. "Didn't see ya, ma'am. Chancy thing to walk into a livery unannounced."

Mariah Morgan stared down her nose at the small man and asked coldly, "Have you seen Levi Parker this morning? If so, I hope you told him I was in town."

Rooster squinted at the woman.

"Now let's see. There is a feller what come in last night late an' is sleepin' off a drunk in the back stall. Could be him. Wouldn't know."

He spat again and as it arched in her direction, Mariah jumped back. She glared at him and Rooster grinned.

Mariah held up her skirts. She tiptoed toward the back stall, dodging the horse dung and muttering under her breath, "Good grief. Levi drunk and sleeping in a barn?"

Rooster chuckled when he heard old Pete Patterson's voice hollering from the back of the barn.

"What ya doin' wakin' me up? Don't ya know this here is my bed? Git out an' quit a botherin' me. I ain't a goin' ta leave till noon."

Rooster's face became a bland picture of innocence. He began to whistle as Mariah ran out of the stall in a huff.

She glared at Rooster as she rushed by.

"You are a terrible, disgusting old man. You knew that drunk back there wasn't Levi!"

Rooster grinned without answering. His next fork of manure was tossed directly at Mariah. She screamed as it landed on her shoes and splattered up on her dress. She stomped her feet and rushed toward the open door of the barn. She was calling Rooster all sorts of unladylike names as she tried to wipe the manure from her shoes. She paused to smooth her hair and straighten her dress before she stepped onto the street.

CHAPTER 60

AN OLD FLAME

LEVI HELPED SADIE INTO THE BUGGY AND HANDED her the baby. He paused and smiled at her before he climbed in.

"You are a picture of pretty, Sadie. Purple is my favorite color, but I have never seen it so pretty as today."

Sadie's eyes were bright as she smiled down at him. He jumped up beside her and turned the horses toward the main street. He was whistling and waved at Rooster as they drove by.

Levi turned his head when he heard a someone calling his name. He slowed the buggy and stopped it as a woman lifted her skirts and hurried daintily into the street.

Mariah Morgan was a beautiful woman. Her ash-blond hair was pulled up in a coif on back of her head in the latest fashion. Her dress was from Paris, and she looked quite out of place on the dusty street of Cheyenne.

Levi watched her pick her way across the street.

"Hello, Mariah. It's a surprise to see you here."

Mariah tossed her head with impatience.

"Don't tell me that. I wrote you and told you I was coming."

When Levi stared at her in surprise, she frowned.

"You didn't receive my letter? Oh, these western towns. Mail service is so unreliable."

She leaned forward and looked at baby Levi. "Your baby?" she asked sarcastically.

Sadie blushed. When she felt Levi's muscles tense beside her, she smiled at Mariah as only Sadie could. She hooked her arm through his and replied sweetly, "No, my husband passed away before our baby was born. He and Levi were childhood friends." She smiled at Levi and added, "Levi has been a wonderful friend to me as well."

The smile Sadie gave Levi looked buttery sweet, but her eyes were laughing. Levi almost laughed himself.

Sadie gave Mariah the same buttery smile.

Mariah stared at Sadie. Irritation showed briefly on her face. She hid it before she turned her eyes to Levi, and uncorked her charm.

"Levi, I will only be here for the weekend. Would you show me around this evening?"

Levi shook his head.

"Sorry, I have plans tonight." He looked around. "Is your father here or did you come by yourself?"

Mariah rolled her eyes.

"Father thinks Cheyenne will be an important city down the road. He wants to invest in real estate. I heard you were practicing law here, so I came along."

She put her hand on Levi's arm and whispered seductively, "I really want to see you, Levi. Surely you can make a little time for me."

Levi gently released his arm and popped the whip over the horses' backs.

"I am busy, Mariah, but there is a dance in town tonight. I'm sure you'll find lots of willing young men who would love to show you around town."

As they rode down the street, Sadie commented sarcastically, "Please don't tell me that was the woman who broke your heart."

Levi grinned at her.

"Sure was but I was a lot younger and greener then—and she wasn't quite as mean."

Sadie's had left her arm looped through his and he patted her hand as he drawled, "Sure am glad I'm busy tonight!"

Laughter bubbled out of Sadie. They were both smiling as they drove out of town and turned east up a gently rolling hill. As they topped the hill, a small ranch stretched out below them. The two-story house was well-kept, and the pens were solid. A large barn stood to the right of the pens and two more small sheds stood on the other side. Levi pointed the whip toward the small buildings.

"One of those sheds is set up for smithing and the other is tight enough to be used for tack." He looked at Sadie seriously.

"I think my place is too small for Leo. He needs more room, and he likes horses. There are six hundred forty acres here so it's small, but it would work for me. A couple of horses and a few mules. Maybe some chickens and a milk cow—although I've never milked a cow." Levi's eyes were excited as he studied Sadie's face. "What do you think?"

Sadie was looking down at the ranch as she answered.

"It's beautiful, Levi. Even though it's further than you go now, the location is perfect for your work." As she turned toward him smiling, she almost laughed at the excitement in his face.

He squeezed her hand as he grinned. "Well, let's go see what Lester Johnson wants for this place. I did some paperwork for the bank yesterday. That is how I knew it was coming up for sale."

Lester came out to greet them as they drove up.

Levi stepped down and shook his hand. "Mr. Johnson, I'm Levi Parker. I'm one of the new lawyers in town."

Lester shook Levi's hand seriously and asked, "This your missus?"

Levi shook his head. "No, this is Sadie Crandall. Slim Crandall was her husband."

Lester's face changed as he stepped toward the buggy.

"Mrs. Crandall, your husband was a fine man. My wife, bless her soul, was ailin' four or five winters ago. I had used up all my wood supply and couldn't get away to cut any. Your husband and one of his friends showed up here with a wagon full of wood and cowchips. They stacked it all in the woodshed and even built the fire up before they left. Wouldn't take a thing for it. That load lasted me until my Lucille was up and around." He squeezed Sadie's hand. "He was a fine man."

Sadie's eyes filled with tears as she smiled at him. "Thank you, Mr. Johnson."

Lester looked back at Levi. "So, what can I help you with, Mr. Lawyer?"

Levi looked seriously at Lester as he answered. "Mr. Johnson, I do legal work for one of the banks in town. I saw your place was coming up for sale in some of the documents I handled yesterday. The size and location is exactly what I've been looking for. I was wondering if you would sell it to me?"

Lester's eyes twinkled. "You kinda used some insider information, didn't you, Boy?"

Levi blushed but agreed. "Yes, I did. Places this close to town are not that common so I did act on it."

Lester studied Levi for a moment. "Fellow from Denver was out here yesterday with a pocket full of cash. I told him I'd have to think on it. He's comin' back this afternoon." He folded his arms across his chest. "So, what do you want to do with the place?"

Levi was animated as he pointed at the buildings and described what he wanted to do.

Lester already knew he was going to sell to Levi, but he decided to have a little fun with the young couple.

"How about you, Sadie? Think I should sell to this here fellow?"

Sadie's pretty face broke into a smile. "Yes, I do. Levi is an asset to Cheyenne."

Lester grinned at her.

"And how about you? Is he an asset to you too?"

Sadie turned a deep red. She looked at the two men. Lester was grinning and Levi was trying to keep a poker face as they both waited for her response. Her brown eyes flashed.

"I swear. It's like the two of you talked before you even met!"

Lester laughed and shook Levi's hand.

"Let's go draw up those papers. That feller from Denver brought a woman with him too. She reminded me of a heifer I had one time. Fine lookin' animal but she carried her head high, broke ever' fence I had, and kicked anything or anybody who came close to her. After the second year of no calves, I cut her out of my herd and we ate her."

Levi laughed as he lifted Sadie down. They followed Lester into the house.

"Yes, Rooster mentioned meeting a woman with pretty much that same disposition. In fact, he described her almost the same way!"

Sadie's breath caught as she stepped into the house. "Mr. Johnson, did you do the woodwork? It is beautiful."

Lester looked around and smiled. "I like to work with wood. Often thought of startin' my own business but I'm an old man. What do I need more work for?"

Sadie ran her hands over the finish of the china cabinet and sideboard.

"These are lovely, Mr. Johnson."

"They go with the house. I made them for my Lucille, and she is no longer with me." Lester smiled. "We never had any children. With Lucille gone, it's just me. I'm considering going to the far edge of this country. I'm just plain tired of snow. My old bones would like to soak up some sunshine. That means when you buy it, you buy it lock, stock, and barrel." He looked over at Levi as he added, "I have a list of things I am going to take with me, but the rest is yours."

He rolled his eyes toward Sadie and winked as he looked back toward Levi. "'Course, this is purty nice for a bachelor. Probably should find you a wife."

Lester's face turned into a sea of wrinkles as he added, "I hear that Denver gal is available if Sadie here ain't interested."

Sadie turned a deep red, and even Levi blushed. Lester laughed out loud at the looks on both their faces.

He handed Levi the deed.

"I wrote on the bottom what I'm asking. You can bring me out the cash on Monday morning."

Levi stared at the amount and then at Lester.

The old man waved his hand and looked seriously at the two of them. "Yeah, I know it's less than I told that banker, but I like you. And Miss Sadie, I sure hope you marry this cowboy and make my house a home again."

Sadie blushed again but before she could respond, Lester added, "Now let me see the little fellow who might be sliding down my banisters."

As Sadie showed him the baby, he touched the little boy's soft cheek and whispered softly, "Ain't never been kids in this house. I hope you fill it up." The old man had tears in his eyes when Sadie hugged him.

"Thank you, Mr. Johnson. I promise I will visit, and make sure your house hears little feet."

As Lester wiped his eyes, he growled at her, "Lester. Just call me Lester."

Sadie smiled at him again. As she left the house, Lester looked hard at Levi. "Boy, if you let her get away, I will sure be disappointed. I'll be thinking I made a big character mistake with you."

Levi grinned but he answered seriously, "I'm doing my best, Lester. And you are welcome to come back and visit any time."

CHAPTER 61

A DATE WITH THE PRETTIEST GAL IN CHEYENNE

BOTH LEVI AND SADIE WERE QUIET ON THE RIDE BACK to town. Sadie stole sideways glances at Levi, but she could tell he was in heavy thought. They met Rooster's oldest buggy as they turned up the main street. Levi recognized Mariah's father. The man was having so much trouble with his team that he did not look up.

Levi laughed and nodded his head toward the buggy.

"Rooster sent Mariah's father out with the oldest buggy and the worst team of horses in the barn. Basil Morgan will be lucky if they don't run away with him." He grinned and added quietly, "Too bad Mariah didn't go along. That would have been a sight to see!"

Sadie giggled and they turned down the street to her house.

As Levi helped her down, Sadie asked, "Are you hungry, Levi? I don't have much prepared, but I can make you a cold beef sandwich."

Levi grinned as he agreed. He drawled, "So what am I going to do with myself between now and the dance?"

She laughed as she turned around. "You are going to do some of that work you didn't get done today. And you had better not show up here before six this evening!"

Levi carried the baby outside and sat down on the swing.

"I might have to put up one of these, Kid. This is just plumb pleasant." He turned sideways in the swing. When Sadie came out of the house, both were asleep as the fall sun shone down on the swing.

She went back inside and lay down on her bed. "I will just rest a moment," she told herself before she fell asleep."

Levi awoke when the baby wet all over him. As he sat up, little Levi gave him a glorious smile and Levi laughed. Then, the baby tensed his body and began to push. Levi charged the house shouting for Sadie. She rushed out of her bedroom as the baby exploded, once again covering Levi in yellow goo. He looked down and began to heave as Sadie grabbed her baby.

"For Pete's Sake, Levi. It's just poop. Why, you have spent half your life covered in cow dung."

Levi continued to gag. He rushed outside to strip off his shirt. When he stepped back in, Sadie caught her breath before she turned her back.

"Your clean shirt is on the back of the chair," she stated as calmly as she could. Her face was a light pink, and she busied herself cleaning up the baby. Levi finally quit gagging and was able to put his shirt on. Sadie turned to face him.

"Did you have a nice nap?"

He grinned at her. "Feel like a new man."

He pulled out his watch and stared at the time in surprise.

"I will just take that sandwich with me. I can get a little work done before I come back."

Levi drove the buggy back to the livery. Rooster grinned at him as Levi jumped down.

"Met your newest customer with your finest buggy and best team," Levi stated innocently.

Rooster gave an evil laugh.

"An' when he gets out there, he's gonna find some feller already bought it, ain't he?"

As Levi nodded, Rooster slapped his leg and laughed gleefully.

"Why don't I jist pick ya up an' take ya to the dance? That way, my team won't be a standin' there all night. You cin always walk that little gal home."

"That should work. Pick me up around six and we'll go get Sadie."

As soon as Rooster agreed, Levi turned down the street to take a bath. "I smell like baby poop," he muttered as he hurried to the bath area.

After a quick bath and shave, Levi headed to his office to make his final preparations for his case in Laramie. *I'm leaving on the nine o'clock train Monday morning. With Tiny's wedding tomorrow, that won't leave much time to finish this.*

He looked at the white shirt Sadie had made him and smiled. He had never looked too polished in court so this would be a big change. As he admired the shirt, he realized he hadn't paid her for any of his shirts. He frowned.

"I'm starting to act more and more like a freeloader."

Levi stared around his room with the frown still on his face. His eyes came to rest on Leo's blankets. He cursed under his breath.

"Leo! What am I going to do with Leo while I'm gone?"

He hated to ask Molly to take care of Leo but that might be his best option. Beth's baby was coming soon, and he didn't think he should ask Sadie.

Levi finished his paperwork and packed his bag for the trip. As he changed into clean britches, he checked himself in the mirror. His reddish-brown hair curled down over a broad forehead. Blue eyes with brown flecks smiled back at him. The cleft in his square chin showed more when he smiled, and he was smiling now. "I'm going to a dance with the prettiest gal in Cheyenne. Maybe tonight, she will finally let her guard down and not be afraid to like me."

He was just going down the stairs when he heard a whistle outside. He opened the door and stopped to stare. It was Rooster but not a Rooster he had ever seen.

The man wore a three-piece suit with tails. The top hat on his head looked a lot like one Badger used to wear. Rooster stood and bowed dramatically. "Yur ride, Mr. Parker."

Levi laughed and stepped into the surrey. "You outdid yourself, Rooster. The top hat is a nice touch."

Rooster looked over his shoulder and grinned.

That was when Levi noticed the large rooster feather in the brim of the hat, and he began to laugh.

"I think you should offer rides tonight. After all the work you've gone to here, you just as well capitalize on it."

Rooster laughed as he tapped the horses.

"I been thinkin' on that. Not a big fan of sittin' 'round an' waitin' on folks though. 'Course, if I show up tonight 'round eleven-thirty or so, there's bound to be some little mommas who jist cain't take it no more."

As Rooster pulled up in front of Sadie's house, Levi jumped down. He loped up to her door. She opened it as he was about to knock.

Levi stared at her—for a moment he was tongue-tied.

Her thick brown hair was in a loose twist on her head. Her dress was pink with ruffles at the neck and on the bottom of the sleeves. She smiled up at Levi. She caught her breath when she spotted Rooster.

Sadie began to giggle. She looked up at Levi.

"Did you set this up or did he do this on his own?"

"Nope, this was all Rooster." He whispered in her ear, "I think he likes you."

Sadie's eyes were sparkling, and she whispered back, "I like him too."

Levi laughed and took the baby as they walked to the surrey.

Rooster hopped down. "At your service, Miz Sadie. Any place ya want to go 'fore we take ya to the dance?"

Sadie was giggling as Levi helped her in.

"No thank you, Rooster. You certainly look spiffy though."

Levi glanced across at Sadie.

"Are you okay with walking home? Otherwise, Rooster will come and get us when the dance is over."

"I think a walk home would be nice."

CHAPTER 62

Two is Even Better

THE TABLES WERE ALREADY FULL OF FOOD WHEN LEVI
and Sadie arrived at the dance. Sadie set her cookies on the table.
Molly slapped Lance's hand as he reached one. He grinned and used the
other hand to get a second.

Leo rushed up to Levi.

"Levi, can I stay at the Rankin's while you are in Laramie? They said
it would be all right. We had so much fun today!"

Levi smiled down at him.

"Let me talk to them first, but I think that would be a good idea."

Lots of cowboys were milling around talking when suddenly, there
was a roar from the kitchen area. Rowdy charged out carrying Beth. Her
face was flushed, and she was gasping for air.

"Rudy! Get the wagon!" Rowdy shouted.

As Rudy ran towards the door, Rooster stepped forward in his long
tails. "Put her in my surrey, Rowdy."

Rowdy hollered behind him, "Lance! You are coming with me!"

Lance started laughing as he followed his brother to the surrey.
Josie grabbed her cloak and hurried outside. Molly rolled her eyes but
followed as well.

Doc jumped in beside Beth. "Just breathe deeply, Beth."

She glared at him. "You breathe deep. You don't have a giant ball stuck in you and trying to come out!"

Rowdy's face was concerned, and Beth grabbed his arm as a contraction came.

Lance handed Josie up into the back seat of the surrey.

"Somebody better watch the kids!" Molly called as Lance lifted her up beside Josie.

Lance squeezed in and looked calmly at Rooster.

"I suggest you get this team moving or there is going to be a birthing right here."

Rooster raced the horses down the street, hollering and cracking his whip. He was standing up and the tails of his coat were flying. He lost his top hat, much to his dismay, but he did not slow down.

Doc was down before the wagon came to a stop. He had the door to his clinic open, and Rowdy charged through, carrying Beth.

Lance helped Josie down. She shook her head as she hurried inside.

"I have always thought Reuben was unflappable, but I guess not where his little sister is concerned," she laughed.

Molly was still sitting in the surrey, and Lance climbed back in. He looked over at her and winked as he drawled, "Sure no need to waste a fancy surrey and a nice night." He pulled Molly close to him.

"Why don't you take us for a drive, Rooster, while I cuddle with my wife back here in the dark."

Molly started to say something but soon she was giggling, and Lance was laughing.

Rooster took them through the darkest streets of Cheyenne and had them back at Doc's about twenty minutes later.

The three of them entered Doc's waiting area. They heard Doc say, "This new bed is working great!"

Beth yelled an answer. Although they couldn't hear all of it, the part that they did hear was not complimentary. Rowdy was saying nothing at all. They heard Beth yell again as she pushed and then the sound of a baby's cry. Molly smiled. When the noise started again, and the sound of a second baby crying came to them, Molly's eyes opened widely.

Lance was laughing loudly, and Rooster was grinning.

"Shore now, one little ol' baby is good but two is even better!"

The noise calmed down and before long, Rowdy appeared carrying two babies. "Meet Ellie Elizabeth and Eli August. We had two names picked—we just didn't know we would need them both." He looked tired, but he was proud.

"Any scars, brother?" Lance asked innocently.

Rowdy looked behind him furtively and whispered, "She about killed me. She turned into this crazy person I didn't even know—but now she is back to my sweet Beth."

Molly was looking at the babies and ignored him.

Lance nodded his head seriously. "Yep, that's how it is."

Rooster slapped his whip against his leg. "This here surrey is headed back to the dance. If anybody is ridin', they better get loaded."

Molly hurried in to talk to Beth, and Lance patted his brother's back. "You made some fine kids, Same!"

Rowdy grinned.

"Doc told Beth last week he thought there were two. She debated how to tell me and decided to wait till after the dance tonight. We sure didn't expect them this soon. I'm not sure how I would have reacted if she had told me earlier, but they are mighty special."

As Rowdy turned to take the babies back to Beth, Molly stepped away from Beth's bed. She took Lance's arm and whispered to him, "I just love babies."

"And I love pregnant mommies," Lance replied softly as they walked outside.

Molly gave him her glorious smile and he lifted her into the surrey.

Levi and Sadie were watching for Lance and Mollie when they entered the Rollin's House. They hurried over to hear the news.

Lance held up two fingers, and Sadie gasped.

Levi stared. He didn't even know a woman could have two babies in her at one time.

"No wonder Beth looked like she was going to pop," he muttered. Sadie elbowed him while she maintained a sweet smile. He grunted and laughed as he rubbed his ribs.

Molly looked around for their children.

"Samuel took yours home along with Leo. Badger and Martha took the rest to Sadie's house." Levi grinned and added, "And you know they will *all* be sugared up and wild when we get there."

CHAPTER 63

BROKEN HEARTS

THE DANCE WAS GOING FULL SPEED AND THEY ALL enjoyed themselves for the next hour. Baby Levi was asleep on the floor by the wall and Sadie wouldn't dance too far from him. Before long, he began to squirm, and she left to nurse him. Levi wandered over to the food table and Mariah appeared.

"Finally, I can talk to you without that widow woman hanging all over you."

Levi looked at her coldly as he answered, "I can tell you if she did hang on me, I would be happy. What do you want, Mariah?"

"I want to dance with you, Levi. Just one dance. Please?"

Levi stared at her with complete irritation. Finally, he took her arm and guided her across the floor to where Spur was standing with some other riders.

"Spur, this lady would like to dance with a southern gentleman. Why don't you show her some of your deep south dance moves."

As Spur grinned and stepped forward to take Mariah's arm, Levi backed away. Mariah started to protest but Spur was already spinning her around the floor at a dizzying speed.

Sadie came back in just as Levi guided Mariah across the floor. She watched them for a moment. Then she gathered her baby and slipped out the door.

Levi wandered over to the food table. He watched the kitchen for Sadie. Finally, he asked one of the women if Sadie was in the kitchen. She shook her head and pointed toward the door. The music was loud. Levi could not hear what she said but he understood the pointing. As he hurried through the door, he saw Sadie about a block away, walking rapidly.

"Sadie!" he called as he ran to catch up. He grabbed her elbow and turned her around. Sadie's pretty eyes were full of tears and Levi's face tightened.

"Sadie, tell me what's wrong." He put both hands on her shoulders as he studied her face.

"Levi, do you want a family?" Sadie asked as she looked up at him.

Levi looked confused but he nodded.

"Have you always?" she continued.

Levi looked at Sadie intently. He wasn't sure where this conversation was leading or why it would bring tears, but he answered honestly.

"When I was little, I wanted a family more than anything in the world. After I met Kid, he became my family, and I didn't yearn for it so much. The years after that were wild and busy. I thought about it from time to time, but it wasn't so important anymore.

"That changed when I came to Cheyenne. I saw you surrounded by your family, and I knew then exactly what I wanted."

Sadie's eyes were large, and the tears were leaking down her face.

"That is what I am talking about, Levi. I think you are mistaking the loneliness and want you have for a family for love."

Levi stared at her, and his face slowly turned red.

"Sadie, I have had many opportunities to be part of a family. There have been lots of women in my past, but I don't want just any family. I want *this* family. I want little Levi and Leo, yes, but even if they weren't here, I would still want you. I wanted you the first night I met you. That's why I left. I knew those feelings were inappropriate but there they were."

He stepped toward her and lifted her fingers to his lips.

"Sadie, I love you. I don't want another woman or another family. I want you."

"I don't think I'm ready for that," Sadie whispered. "When I think of falling in love again, I panic."

"Real love is scary, Sadie." Levi gently squeezed her shoulders. "It is like walking off a cliff and not knowing where the next step is or when you will catch your feet. It lifts you up like you have wings and pounds your face in the dirt. It is the greatest and scariest thing you could ever consider."

Tears ran down Sadie's face as she shook her head.

"But I didn't feel that way with Slim. I knew it was right from the first time I met him. I was never afraid or unsure. I always knew he was what I wanted. I can't love you, Levi. It just doesn't feel right."

Levi let his arms drop as Sadie stepped back. His stomach twisted into a knot, and he felt like he'd been stabbed with a hot iron. He nodded his head slowly.

"I will walk you home. At least let me do that."

Neither of them spoke as he walked beside her. His mouth twisted as he thought ruefully, *here's that part about pounding your face in the dirt.*

He did not walk onto the porch, but he waited until she was inside.

"Goodbye, Sadie," were his only words before he walked away. He didn't stop at the tree to wave either. Sadie knew because she watched. She laid the baby down in his crib and threw herself on her bed. She cried until she had no tears left.

"If I don't love him and I don't want him, then why am I so sad?" she whispered in the dark. She fell asleep in her clothes and only awoke when the baby cried.

CHAPTER 64

No Room in Her Heart

LEVI PAUSED ON THE STREET. HE TURNED TO WALK toward Samuel's house. When he was close, he could hear the laughing and talking from inside the house. Once again, Levi's heart squeezed in his chest. He took a deep breath and knocked on Samuel's door.

Lance answered quickly. He had a cookie in one hand and was smiling. The smile left his face as he looked closely at Levi.

"Lance, I was wondering if you would keep Leo this next week while I'm in Laramie." As Lance nodded, Levi added, "I'm leaving tomorrow so tell Tiny I'm sorry to miss the wedding. I'm sure one of your hands will be glad to stand up with him." Lance nodded again. Levi spoke bleakly as he started to turn away, "Thanks, Lance."

"Levi!" Lance stepped outside and closed the door. "Want to talk about this?"

The big man shook his head. His wounded heart showed in his eyes as he looked around at Lance.

"She doesn't have room for me in her heart."

Lance watched Levi walk away. He turned slowly back into the house. Molly and Samuel were laughing as they talked.

Molly looked up and the smile left her face as she studied Lance's expression.

He gave her a tight smile as he moved toward the table and studied the food stacked there.

"I'm heading to bed," Samuel stated. "Your kids wore me out tonight." He smiled at his only daughter and this man she loved so deeply as he added, "And I'm sure I'll have some little ones in bed with me by early morning."

As her father headed upstairs, Molly moved up beside Lance. She took his arm as she studied his face.

"Who was at the door, Lance? What is wrong?"

Lance hugged his wife. He frowned slightly as he looked into her face.

"It was Levi. Something happened between Sadie and him. He's leaving tomorrow for Laramie for the trial instead of waiting to go on Monday. He asked if we would keep Leo this week."

Molly's blue eyes opened wide.

Lance began to smile as his eyes twinkled.

"Now, Molly, you stay out of this. You can't fix everyone's problems—even if you think you have all the answers."

Molly started to glare but instead, she snuggled closer.

"I won't do anything—at least not tonight," she promised sweetly as she smiled up at Lance.

Lance rolled his eyes. "And you have all night to make plans," he stated dryly. He took her arm and they walked up the stairs.

Levi worked most of the night leaving notes for Annie. Her first job was to present his signed letter to the bank for cash. She was to give the cash to Rooster. He would deliver it to Lester Johnson.

He made a list of the clients to deliver letters or bills to, as well as another list of people to be paid. He signed five bank drafts to be delivered or mailed. It was after two in the morning when he heard the cowboys come in quietly, but he continued to work. Finally, a little after three, he crawled into his bed. The train would be through in six short hours, and he wanted to talk to Rooster before he left. *Annie offered to work Monday. I'll give her the rest of the week off. That will give her some time with Tiny.*

Levi put his hands behind his head and stared at the ceiling. He was exhausted but he still couldn't sleep. *My business is busy and continuing to grow. I just bought my own little ranch in the location I wanted. I even paid cash for it. My life is going right down the line I had hoped it would follow. Yet, the most important part of it is missing.*

"Ah, Sadie," he sighed. "You are everything I have ever wanted. And your heart is still so full of my best friend that there is no room for me in there." His mouth twisted in a bitter smile. "Well, love has never really been a part of my life, and it doesn't look like it is supposed to be."

When Levi finally fell asleep, the sadness was a dull ache. A bitterness and sense of loss welled up in his heart. He knew he was going to prosecute with a vengeance. This trial would have no joking or bantering.

Rooster was not around when Levi stopped at the livery. He pushed his letter over a nail on the stable door and boarded the train. As he sat back in his seat, a cute little redhead across from him gave him a bright smile. He simply nodded his head, pulled his hat down, and went to sleep.

Badger and Martha stopped by Sadie's house on their way to Tiny's wedding. They were going to offer to give her a ride since she was to stand up with Annie. Instead, they found a sick momma and baby.

No one knew what had happened between Sadie and Levi after the dance the night before, but Levi had left a day early and Sadie looked like she had cried all night.

Martha's kind eyes were full of tears, and she decided to skip the wedding.

"You go on, Badger. I will stay with Sadie this week. You can pick me up on Friday. I think our girl needs me."

Martha promptly put Sadie to bed and took over the care of the baby. When he was hungry, she slipped him in bed with his mother.

She took him back when he was finished. She made sure Sadie drank lots of water and made her a variety of soups to eat.

CHAPTER 65

A Gruff Man's Soft Heart

JACK CORAL TIED HIS FAVORITE WILD RAG AROUND his neck. Actually, it was the only one he owned without holes, and he saved it for important occasions—of which he had few. He put on clean britches and a fresh shirt and spit-polished his old boots. He was giving little Sugar away today and he wanted to look his best.

The old man's hard eyes softened as he thought about the first time he had met Annie. She had walked through the doors of his saloon with trembling hands and big eyes. She had asked if he had a dishwashing job. Jack knew she was young, so he asked her age. Annie had paused and whispered, "I'm eighteen."

Jack knew she was lying but he could tell she was desperate, so he didn't push. Instead, he looked hard at her and said, "The only job I have available is a dance partner. The dresses are cut a little low, but ya don't have to do nothin' but dance—an' if the cowboys get fresh with ya, slap 'em an' we'll throw 'em out." Annie agreed.

The men paid to dance with the girls. Jack's cut was sixty percent and the girls made forty percent. The dances were 25¢ each so it didn't add up to much unless one danced all night, every night.

Annie started her job that night. Sugar, as the men called her, was careful who she danced with. She wouldn't let them hold her tightly.

Some of the men complained to Jack. "That little ol' gal won't cuddle a'tall."

Jack shrugged and pointed to one of the other girls. "Dance with Nancy. Sugar's more interested in conversation, so ya get what ya pay fer."

Still, Jack worried about Sugar. She had no family, and she was too young to be dancing in a saloon.

Then the Rocking R cowboys showed up one night and Tiny spotted her. From that point on, she became part of the Rocking R. Tiny danced until his money ran out. Of course, he had to drink to keep his courage up so his nights in town were expensive ones. The rest of the Rocking R hands made sure the other men Sugar danced with were gentlemen, and Jack smiled.

Sugar didn't just have one protector—she had an entire crew of cowboys from one of the biggest spreads around Cheyenne. He could tell Tiny was sweet on Sugar, but the big cowboy was too shy to tell her how he felt.

Jack straightened his wild rag and pulled his old hat down over his bald head. He stared at the small ring in his hand and a tiny tear formed in the corner of one eye. He cleared his throat before he shoved it into his pocket.

"Well, Ma, I didn't need this fer long, but I reckon you would approve of the little gal who'll be wearin' it now. She's the kind a little gal Janie an' me always hoped to have as a daughter. I reckon she's as close to that as I will ever come."

Tiny had stopped by the Lucky Lady the day before and all the men at the bar hollered at him. He grinned and turned a deep red. He refused the beer Jack offered him and asked if they could talk in the back.

"Jack, my little Annie wants me to ask if ya would give her hand in marriage. Ya been the closest thing to a pa she has had these last months, an' she'd sure like ya ta do it."

Jack was surprised and then proud. Tears filled his eyes as he put his gnarled hand in Tiny's big one.

"Tiny, I'd be proud to offer little Sugar's hand in marriage to ya. She's a special little gal an' I shore do approve of her a marryin' ya."

He had opened his safe and showed Tiny the small ring.

"I'll bring this with me tomorrow an' I want ya to put this on our gurl's finger. My ma wore it an' then she give it to me. My wife only wore it fer a short time 'fore she died. It's jist a little gold band but it's seen lots a love. Between the two of 'em, this ring was worn nearly thirty years."

When Tiny started to shake his head, Jack's old eyes turned fierce.

"It ain't fer ya—it's fer Sugar an' I guess I can give that little gal a gift if I want."

Tiny slowly grinned and nodded his head.

"I shore did ferget all about a ring. Annie wouldn't a cared, but she'll be proud to wear this. I reckon I'll let it be a surprise."

Jack wrapped the younger man up in a bear hug.

"Now ya git out a here so's no one else knows I'm an ol' softie at heart."

Tiny grinned again and strutted out of the saloon. As he left, he hollered back to the men drinking at the bar, "Eat yur hearts out, Boys! I won Annie over an' I ain't never sharin' 'er again."

CHAPTER 66

AN UNUSUAL WEDDING

THE WEDDING WAS SMALL. ANNIE DIDN'T WANT A LOT of people there and Tiny didn't care as long as his friends from the Rocking R and R4 could come. He had built a huge arch from a cottonwood tree, and it stood in front of the little cemetery overlooking the valley. Mr. and Mrs. Tiny Small were to be married between the large tree trunks.

Jack Coral walked Annie up the hill from the Rocking R ranch house and the guests followed. Tiny was waiting at the cemetery to take her hand, and the Rocking R riders surrounded the young couple. The fall sun shone brightly as Annie and Tiny made their vows.

Annie cried when Jack pulled the small ring out of his pocket and handed it to Tiny. It slipped easily on her third finger and Tiny kissed it after he slid it on. Meadowlarks sang happily behind them. As Tiny said, "I do," a cluster of prairie chickens exploded from the grass beside them.

The riders began laughing and Tiny hollered, "See, boys, ol' Slim jist wanted to be the first to say 'Congratulations!'"

Annie was smiling and Tiny lifted her up. As he swung her around, he whispered, "Forever an' ever, Annie. I'll be yur man forever."

One by one, the riders came forward to congratulate the happy couple. As Mr. and Mrs. Tiny Small walked down the hill, several of the hands studied the huge arch Tiny had built.

One of the new hands asked, "Where'd he get the wood? Ain't no trees 'round here this big."

"There used to be a big cottonwood tree down on Slim's place. It grew up in that little creek that runs between his place an' this one. Slim didn't want it there 'cause it sucked up all the water so Tiny, Smiley, and him went to work cuttin' it down shortly after Slim married." Jonesy laughed. "Slim was goin' to cut it up for firewood, but Tiny convinced him to jist trim the smaller branches.

"They cut that big tree into three parts an' it lay out there on the ground. It stayed right there till Tiny come back to work here. A few days ago, he talked Rowdy into loanin' 'im a heavy wagon an' team. The two a them loaded those tree trunks up an' hauled 'em up here. Tiny had some kind a winch he used to lift 'em. I wasn't there so I didn't see it.

"Rowdy said each a those trunks was close to two thousand pounds. He knowed that 'cause he knowed how far the wagon went down with the weight. Took a hole three feet across an' four feet deep to plant 'em here. I know that 'cause I helped dig the holes.

"Tiny always talked 'bout puttin' an arch in front a the cemetery, but he didn't do it till he decided to marry little Annie."

Jonesy voice was soft as he added, "Tiny wanted his two best pards to come to his weddin' so that's why they was married right here, in front a the tombstones. I reckon Slim and Smiley liked that just fine.

"Shoot, Slim was always tryin' to scare up prairie chickens 'cause that was one a his favorite meals. I reckon those birds flyin' up was jist him a lettin' us know he was here."

The riders were quiet as they looked from the giant arch to the small stones that bore the names of their friends. One of the riders patted the stone with Sim's name.

"Glad you could come," he commented softly, "an' you too, Smiley," as he looked over at the second stone. The little cemetery was quiet as the three riders strolled down the hill to join their friends.

Everyone noticed Levi and Sadie were missing as well as Martha. Jonesy started to ask where they were, but Joe bumped him.

"Keep yer mouth shut. Ain't nothin' goin' to ruin this here day." No one else spoke of it but all wondered why two of the young couple's best friends had missed their big day.

CHAPTER 67

LOVE IS A FUNNY THING

SADIE SPENT THREE DAYS IN BED. SHE ALTERNATED between crying and coughing. Martha was worried and she sent for Doc Williams.

Doc checked both Sadie and her baby. The little boy was cutting teeth and Sadie was run down. She also had a bad cold. He told her to stay in bed.

"Drink lots of fluids and sleep when the baby sleeps."

By the end of the third day, Sadie was up. She was pale and weak but acted more like herself.

"Martha, you can go on home now. I know Badger misses you when you aren't there and I'm fine now." She gave Martha a little smile as she sank down in her rocking chair.

Martha took Sadie by her shoulders and pulled her to her feet. She led her to the kitchen table and turned her around so they were face to face. She took Sadie's face between her hands and kissed her forehead.

"Sadie, you know I love you like the daughter I never had. I am going to stay here until your pretty face starts smiling again."

Sadie let Martha wrap her up in her big arms as she sobbed.

"I miss Slim so much. Sometimes at night, I go from crying to being really angry with him for dying."

Martha patted Sadie's back and let her talk.

Sadie talked about how Slim had made her laugh and how her heart had run over with love when he looked at her.

"It's like I am waiting for him to come back, Martha. In my heart, I know that isn't going to happen, but I just want it so bad. I keep hoping."

Sadie shared some of her favorite memories. Finally, she became quiet.

Martha held her back to look at her.

"Now, Sadie, we both know there is more to how you are feeling. I know you miss Slim, but you didn't get sick until you told Levi you didn't want him to come around anymore." She held Sadie's face between her hands again and kissed her on both cheeks "You need to be honest with yourself. Why else are you so sad?"

Sadie collapsed into Martha's arms as she sobbed.

"I fell in love with Slim when he wandered into my laundry area with his cut-off button." Sadie smiled as she stared out the window and her smile stayed as she turned her eyes back to Martha. "I never doubted my feelings for him. Not once. It was like I knew from the beginning he was the one I wanted to spend my life with."

She took a deep breath as she continued softly.

"It's not like that with Levi. I'm comfortable when he's around. He makes me laugh. I love to be with him. Then I start to feel guilty when we have fun.

"At the dance, I saw him talking to a woman from his past. He had told me about her, and she showed up there." Sadie frowned.

"She was a very unpleasant woman, and she was clinging to him. Levi didn't return any of her advances, but suddenly, I questioned our relationship. What if more than loving me, he loved the idea of being part of a family? I panicked. I rushed out of the dance and started home.

He caught up with me and we argued. I told him I wasn't ready for a relationship. And I said maybe he just wanted a family."

Sadie paused and slow tears leaked out of her eyes as she looked up at Martha. "I hurt him badly. His big heart was broken, and it hurt my heart to know I had done it. He walked me home and left the next day."

Martha was silent as Sadie spoke. When she finished, Martha gathered the young woman into her arms.

As Sadie sobbed, Martha patted her back.

"Love is a funny thing, Sadie. It never comes along when it is convenient, and it shows up in crazy ways.

"Take Badger and me. I was married to my first husband for thirty-two years. It was a loveless marriage, completely out of convenience. I wasn't sad, but I never knew true love or joy until Badger stepped on my toes in church one morning." Martha laughed softly at the memory.

"And I certainly didn't see love in my future when I met him that first time. I just liked his ornery eyes and his pure zest for life." She added quietly, "How I wish I had met him forty years ago."

Martha smiled at Sadie and hugged her. "No love will ever be the same. No people are the same so the way they fall in love and show love is going to be different.

"You are going to have to decide what your feelings are. The Good Lord can take it from there." She took a hankie from her pocket and wiped Sadie's wet face.

Martha pulled Sadie close again as she whispered, "You can't control your heart any more than you can control the stars in the sky—and if you try, you will be frustrated and unhappy.

"Levi is a good man, and he loves you deeply. We have all seen that for some time. You, on the other hand, must decide what you feel for him. If you love him, turn your heart lose. Unbridled love can be terrifying, but it can be wonderful too." Martha held Sadie back and smiled again at her.

"Just remember, you don't have to reciprocate feelings you don't have. If you don't love him, walk away. Just be happy with your decision either way."

Sadie smiled up at Martha and hugged her hard.

"What would I do without you, Martha? I love you like a mother and a friend all tied up together!"

Martha smiled over Sadie's head as she patted her back. "And I am happy to be both, Sadie," she whispered into her hair.

That night, Sadie dreamed Slim came to talk to her.

He was leaning on his saddle and was worried about Levi.

"Make room in yore heart, Sadie. You was my one true love, but I only need a little corner of yore heart now. Yore pinin' away fer me an' I asked ya not to do that. Open yore heart to the love right in front of ya.

"Levi was right. Love is like a cliff. I was terrified ya wouldn't love me, an' it was scary to step off—but y'all was worth it.

"He's worth it too. Don't break my old pard's heart jist 'cause ya cain't let go a me.

"Now if ya don't love 'im, why shore that's different. But if yore tryin' *not* to, why that's not good a'tall. Ya have to give love a chance if yore ever gonna be happy again."

When Sadie awoke, she was crying, and Slim's shirt was in her arms. She pulled off a strand of curly, blond hair and cried some more.

CHAPTER 68

You Have to Fight This

THE TRIAL IN LARAMIE ONLY LASTED THREE DAYS. LEVI came out swinging and buried the defense in the opening statement. It was downhill from there. The judge called both sides to the bench.

Levi was harsh when the defending lawyer called foul. He stared at the defense lawyer and shrugged his shoulders.

"You have a weak defense, your client isn't helping any with his outbursts, and resorting to whining will get you nowhere."

The lawyer stared at Levi. He had heard Parker was tough, but this man was completely cold. The judge sent them back and the trial ended quickly.

The defendant shouted as he was led away, "I'll be back, and I will kill your family—first your wife and then your kids."

Levi laughed sarcastically.

"Good luck with that. I don't have a wife and never will."

As Levi walked out of the courtroom and stepped off the boardwalk, he did not see the rifle pointed at him from the roof across the street.

He felt the bullet hit and stared down at his chest as he staggered and fell. Bystanders began to yell and point toward the gunman. Guns were soon firing in the shooter's direction, and the street was loud with gunfire for a time. When it was over, the bushwacker was dead. Levi was still alive, but he was wounded badly.

The city doctor rushed into the street. It took four men to lift and carry Levi into the doctor's office. The doctor examined him and probed inside the wound. He shook his head.

"I can't remove that bullet. It's too deep. We are going to need a surgeon, and the closest is in Cheyenne."

The redhead from the train had acted as the court reporter, and she rushed to the telegraph office to wire for a surgeon.

Doc Williams received the telegram at four-thirty on Wednesday afternoon. The next train did not leave until the following morning. He hurried to the livery and had Rooster saddle his horse.

Josie wanted to go with him, but he refused. "This is going to be a hard ride. If I go alone, I only have me to worry about."

It was almost nine that evening when Doc arrived in Laramie. He had changed horses twice along the way. His horse was still winded, and he was tired himself. He dropped the reins at the livery and asked the hostler to rub down the animal.

"I'm the surgeon from Cheyenne. Can you tell me where the patient is?"

The hostler pointed him to Doc O'Grady's office.

When Doc Williams entered, he was appalled. The room and the bed where the man lay were both dirty. The examination equipment was standing in tepid water.

The large man on the bed was breathing roughly. Doc leaned over to examine him and saw it was Levi. His face paled as he studied the wound and the marks around it where the town doctor had probed.

Doc Williams rushed across the street to the hotel. He shouted at the clerk, "Do you have any clean rooms on the first floor?" The startled clerk thrust out a key. Doc grabbed it and ran to the room. He stripped the bed of all but the sheet and pulled the small stand closer to the bed. He raced out of the hotel shouting as he left, "I need three lamps in there and I need them *now!*" He grabbed four men off the street and had them carry Levi to the clean room.

Doc glared at the people gathered around the hotel. "Is there a competent nurse in this town?" An older woman stepped forward, and he thrust the cleaning solution toward her.

"Scrub with this and hand me instruments as I ask for them."

Doc's instruments were already soaking in sterile solution. He ordered the onlookers out of the room as he put on a clean white coat. He handed a second one to the nurse. The lamps were moved as close as he could get them to the wounded man on the bed, and Doc began to search for the trajectory of the bullet. Once he determined where the bullet was, he began to operate. Levi started to come to once, and Doc gave him more chloroform to keep him quiet.

The surgery lasted nearly four hours. After he sutured the incision, Doc sat down on the bed.

"Levi, you are going to have to help me here. This can go either way and I need you to want to pull through."

CHAPTER 69

NO ONE WILL MISS ME

DOC WILLIAMS SAT WITH LEVI ALL NIGHT AND through the next morning. By noon, the wound was inflamed, and he opened it up to drain. As the infection tried to take over, Doc fought with every tool he had. Levi had still not regained consciousness and Doc was worried.

Levi finally woke at five on Thursday afternoon. He stared at Doc Williams and frowned. His breathing was labored, and Doc measured his fever.

"Levi, you have to fight this. You have people counting on you."

Levi stared at Doc Williams. His eyes were glazed but they cleared for a moment as he answered roughly, "No one will miss me, Doc. Not anyone, anywhere."

The little redhead from the train stepped up.

"I will sit with him tonight, Doctor, if you would like to get some sleep. I arranged for you to use the connecting room. I can leave the door open so you can hear if you like. Of course, I will call you if he becomes worse."

Doc stared at her for a moment. He nodded dully. He squeezed Levi's shoulder as he stood.

"I have done all I can for you, buddy. You are going to have to decide to live if you want to beat this."

The little redhead's name was Rachel and she sat with Levi Thursday night. Sometimes, she read to him or sang. Other times she prayed and talked to him. He began to thrash in the early morning, and she called Doc to give him a sedative.

Before he drifted off, Levi stared at Rachel.

"You broke my heart, you know." Several times, he called out for Sadie. Rachel wiped his brow and tried to make him drink water.

When morning finally arrived, Doc was relieved. He smiled at Rachel.

"Each day is a win for us. If he makes it through today, he should recover."

Levi swam in and out of consciousness that day. He frowned at Rachel and told her to go home. Then, he asked her where her baby was. When Doc Williams walked in, Levi smiled and tried to get out of bed.

"Kid! I knew you would come back! Where have you been hiding all this time?" Then he frowned. "Sadie is sad, you know. You need to help her to be happy."

Rachel's heart broke for the big man. Obviously, he cared for this Sadie very much. She asked who Sadie was, but Doc just shrugged.

"People talk about funny things when they are delirious."

Around six Friday evening, Levi told Rachel he was hungry.

"Can you run down to Barney's and get me some food? Barney always gives me two plates."

Rachel told the doctor when he came in, but Doc shook his head.

"No food until tomorrow. He can have water but no food."

CHAPTER 70

I'M GOING HOME

LEVI AWOKE AT FOUR-THIRTY SATURDAY MORNING. His fever was gone, and he was hungry. As Doc walked in rubbing his eyes, Levi looked at him in surprise.

"What are you doing here, Doc? How is Beth? Are the babies okay?"

Doc gave Levi a tired smile.

"You were shot, and they needed a surgeon. That was nearly four days ago. I operated on you Wednesday night. It was touch and go for a time, but you are on the road to recovery."

"I want to thank you for coming, Doc. I know that ride and your time here was a big inconvenience for you."

"That's what I do." Doc laughed and added, "Much to Josie's dismay, I jump and run when folks need me."

He looked somberly at Levi.

"I didn't know who was shot until I examined you.

"Evidentially, the brothers of the man you convicted decided to get revenge. They almost did too, but the good people of Laramie caught them. One died in gunfire, and the second was hanged this morning."

Doc looked away and was quiet for a time before he glanced back at Levi.

"I'm heading home on the train this afternoon at one. You should stay down for a couple more days."

Levi frowned and shook his head.

"I'm going with you. I have been gone long enough. I will rest better at home than here." He grinned and added, "Besides, I heard some of what was said. I think I would be much safer traveling with you than being left in that sawbones' hands."

Doc did not answer. He knew Levi should not be moved, but he also knew the town doctor would be of no help. Since Levi was leaving with or without him, he consented. He warned him, "Just know if you move this soon, the infection may come back, or you may reopen the wound."

Levi nodded and Doc made arrangements for their trip to Cheyenne.

Rachel watched Levi pull himself up and out of the bed. She offered to help but he refused.

She whispered softly, "If it doesn't work out with Sadie, come back. My name is Rachel."

Levi looked startled and slowly turned a deep red. He didn't remember talking but he must have. As he hobbled out of the room, he stopped to turn around.

"Thanks for the songs and the prayers. You have a kind voice." He smiled at her and Rachel smiled back.

"I hope he comes back," she whispered to herself.

CHAPTER 71

BADGER'S POTION

THE TRAIN RIDE TO CHEYENNE WAS LONG AND PAINFUL for Levi. His face was pale when they arrived in Cheyenne. Rooster met the two men as they stepped down.

"Doc, ya go on home. I'll git Levi up to his place."

Rooster took Levi's arm. "Now ya jist loop that arm over me an' lean on my shoulders. I'm stronger than I look."

Levi was exhausted when they finally made it up the stairs to his room.

Rooster looked down at the big man lying on the bed. He felt Levi's head and could tell he was running a fever. He hitched his wagon and raced to Sadie's house. He was surprised when Martha answered the door.

"Martha, I need to talk to Miss Sadie. Levi was shot an' is in a bad way. Doc done the surgery already but Levi's a fightin' fever now. I think someone needs to sit with 'im an' Doc can't stay there all day. I was hopin' Miss Sadie might want to sit with 'im."

Sadie was standing behind Martha when Rooster shared his news. Her face paled and she covered her mouth.

Martha turned to Sadie and stated quietly, "I can sit with him, Sadie. I will ride back with Rooster."

Sadie's heart was pounding. She shook her head.

"I will go. I just fed baby Levi and he is asleep. Will you bring him down when he wakes?"

Martha agreed and despite her concern, she almost smiled. *Oh, Sadie, you do love that big man.*

Sadie rode with Rooster and rushed up to Levi's room. She knelt down by his bed and touched his head.

"I'm here, Levi. I will be here when you awake," she whispered.

Rooster pulled an old rocker out of his living area and carried it up to Levi's room. Sadie sat down in the rocker and began sponging Levi's head. She tried to give him water, but he refused.

As Levi tossed on his bed, he dreamed he saw Sadie and he smiled. Then he frowned.

"Sadie doesn't have room for me in her heart. My best friend lives there, and there's no room for me."

Levi awoke shortly after seven Saturday evening. He thought he saw a woman in a rocking chair. He squeezed his eyes tight.

"The old woman is coming for me!" he shouted as he tried to get out of bed.

About an hour and a half later, he was awake again. He staggered out of bed. He flung open the window and peed over the sill. He thought he felt someone touch his arm and he jerked it back.

"I'm not going with you!" he shouted. "I'm staying here with my family."

As he fell into bed, he saw a pretty face and big, brown eyes. Levi leaned up and sniffed the shadowy figure. He laid back in his bed with a smile on his face. "You smell just like my Sadie." He stared at the woman covering him up.

"Thanks, Momma. I sure have missed you. And Papa too. You shouldn't have gone on that trip. Your mean old sister didn't like me. She beat me with a switch because I ate too much. The folks here at the orphanage don't like me much either. They say I have a smart mouth.

They don't give us any clothes. I am tired of wearing dirty britches with holes in them, and I'm always hungry. They told me I should leave the table hungry and I sure do."

Around ten that evening, Lance hollered from below. He followed Badger and Martha up the stairs. Sadie met them at the top of the stairs. Martha handed her the baby as they followed her into Levi's bedroom. Lance stared down the man and looked at Sadie.

"Maybe you had better let Martha sit with him through the night. I know you're tired. Besides, it's not right for you to spend the night here alone. I don't want anyone to question your behavior.

"Badger even offered to stay. He brought some of his potion. It should help break the fever."

Sadie looked up in surprise at the dark-colored liquid Badger was carrying. Badger's eyes were serious as he poured some in a cup and lifted Levi's head.

"Here now, Judge. Ya drink this up. I brung ya some a that thar root beer ya like. It'll help ya break this here fever."

Sadie caught a whiff of the concoction and almost gagged, but Levi drank the entire cup down. He shuddered when he was done and tried to fix his eyes on Badger. His voice was slurred as he spoke.

"I think Rooster went and ruined that batch. That stuff was terrible."

Badger grinned and patted his shoulder. "Yore gonna be alright, Judge. Now ya rest up an' git stronger 'cause yore shore gonna need it with what ya have comin'.

He winked at Sadie and she blushed even though she had no idea what Badger was referring to.

CHAPTER 72

A Big Brother's Help

SADIE LOOKED DOWN AT THE SLEEPING LEVI. SHE knew it was not proper for her to spend the night in Levi's room, but she didn't want to leave.

Martha sat down beside him, and Sadie followed Lance down the stairs.

"I don't want to leave, Lance," she stated softly. "I'm worried about him, and I want to be here when he awakens."

Lance studied Sadie's face for a moment and his eyes were serious.

"You really shouldn't spend the night. And if you do spend the night, you should get married right away. I won't have my sister's reputation smudged in a town she will live in for the rest of her life." He paused as he looked down at Sadie and smiled. "I reckon you are the only one who can make that decision."

Sadie caught her breath as she stared at the floor. When she looked up, she was smiling.

"Well, if that is the way it has to be, then so be it." She laughed and her brown eyes sparkled.

Lance wrapped her up in a hug and grinned at her.

"Sadie, not many women have the opportunity to be loved by two men as good as the two you chose. You help Levi get well and I'll see you in the morning." He chucked her chin and winked at her. "You just leave the rest up to me. We will have that feller hog-tied and hitched before noon tommorrow!"

For the first time in days, Sadie's heart felt light. She rushed back upstairs and hurried to Levi's side.

"I'm going to stay, Martha. Lance will give you a ride home. He brought Molly and the kids in to pick up supplies today. They didn't think they should bring the kids up, so they are all at Samuels. They will spend the night there. I will see all of you in the morning."

As her family quietly left, Sadie sat down beside Levi. She nursed her baby and sang softly to the big man, mopping his face to help him cool down. Once the baby went to sleep, she laid him down on a blanket on the floor.

She had barely fallen asleep when she heard Levi talking to someone.

"Kid, let's run away together. You ain't happy an' I ain't happy. You jump out the window an' I'll catch ya." He seemed to be listening to someone before he continued.

"It ain't that high. No higher than the loft of yore ol' barn. Let's run away together like true blue friends. Levi an' Kid—the best hands in Texas."

Levi was thirsty and Sadie gave him another cup of Badger's concoction. Badger had left the rest of the jar with instructions for no more than three cups.

"It'll give 'im a headache an' that's a fact, but it'll shore 'nough cure 'im."

Levi frowned as he drank it. He started to speak and but fell asleep.

Later as he thrashed in his sleep, he argued, "But I don't want you to go and Sadie doesn't want you to go. She's sad, and I don't want her to be sad. Come back, please? You can make her heart happy. I can't do it.

I tried but it didn't work. Only you can make her heart happy, Kid. You come on back here and I'll go away. Nobody here will miss me anyway."

Sadie sat by Levi's bed and cried as she sponged his brow. His big heart was broken, and she had done it. He was right. There had not been room in her heart for him. She had been too full of grief and memories to let anyone else in.

"Stay with me, Levi. I want you to stay," she whispered.

Levi stared at Sadie out of feverish eyes. "You look like a girl I know. She's pretty and has the most beautiful brown eyes." As Sadie leaned forward to sponge his face, he caught her arm.

"Why are you here? Can you go find Sadie for me? I need to talk to her."

Sadie murmured to him and tried to get him to drink some water.

"I don't want water!" he shouted, "I only want Sadie!" He looked at Sadie closely.

"You kind of look like Sadie. You have been crying. I don't like it when Sadie cries. It makes my heart hurt."

He slowly grew quiet. Finally, he winked at her.

"How about we get married? If we were married, you could cuddle in this bed with me. You look like you would be soft and warm."

Sadie was surprised. She tried not to laugh as she answered, "But what would Sadie think?"

Levi looked confused. He pointed his finger at her.

"I know you're Sadie. You are just trying to trick me!"

By three o'clock Sunday morning, Levi was trying to get out of bed. Sadie poured a third cup of Badger's potion. Levi didn't want to drink it.

"Rooster went and ruined that batch. I don't want any more."

"Just one more cup, Levi. It will help your fever to go down. Please drink it. Sadie wants you to drink it."

Levi grabbed the cup and drank it quickly. He shuddered violently and frowned at Sadie. His eyes slowly glassed over. He leaned forward to stare into her face. He gave her a loose grin.

"I know who you are. Did you come to visit me? Help me out of this bed so we can spoon a little. Maybe then you'll marry me."

Sadie was surprised but she pointed at him as she tried not to laugh. "Levi Parker, you stay in that bed. I am not going to spoon with you… at least not until you sleep a while!"

Levi gave Sadie another loose grin and clamped his eyes shut. He soon opened one eye and winked at her. "Was that long enough?"

Sadie laughed in spite of herself and Levi slowly relaxed. He fell asleep with a smile on his face.

A Shotgun Wedding

LEVI AWOKE JUST BEFORE SUNRISE. THE FIRST THING he saw was Sadie sitting by his bed. She was holding her baby, and both were asleep. She had tear streaks on her face, and he frowned.

He reached for the little boy and finally slid him onto the bed. He lifted him to lie below his chest and the baby sighed as he settled in. Levi watched him and his heart squeezed tight.

"Hello, Kid. I sure am going to miss seeing you and your mother," he whispered. The baby smiled in his sleep and Levi dozed off.

Sadie awoke about an hour later. She almost cried again when she saw her baby on Levi's stomach.

"You are such a good man," she whispered.

When she awoke again, the sun had risen and was shining through the windows. Levi was watching her from his bed.

"Good morning, Sadie." He smiled at her. His face slowly creased into a frown.

"You had better get home. You shouldn't be here. It's not appropriate for you to be in my room, and for sure not alone with me. You need to go home before the entire town wakes.

"Besides, I don't think you slept very well in that chair. You look tired this morning."

Levi's frown grew deeper. He sniffed and wrinkled his nose.

"What is that terrible smell? Did something die in here while I was asleep?"

Sadie sat up and smiled at him. "Welcome back, Levi. Yes, it was a long night," she agreed. She held up the nearly empty jar of Badger's concoction.

"This is what you smell, and you drank three full cups of it!" Her eyes were sparkling with humor as she spoke, and Levi frowned again. She laughed as she added, "Actually, *you* are the one who should be tired. You were quite chatty last night."

"What did I say? I hope I wasn't rude. If I was, I apologize."

Sadie laughed again as she blushed.

"Not all your conversation was appropriate so you probably should apologize." She looked at him with overly innocent eyes as she lifted the baby onto her lap.

"I'm not sure I will be able to face the town of Cheyenne after spending all night in your room and you talking the way you did." She leaned forward and whispered, "We will probably *have* to get married now. You have completely ruined my reputation."

Levi stared at Sadie in stunned silence. Before he could respond, lots of loud voices carried up the stairs, and people poured into the room. Leo pushed forward with a huge smile. Samuel and Molly followed with a bevy of children behind them.

Lance directed the man he was walking with toward the bed. He waved the shotgun he was carrying and announced loudly, "There they are, Padre. You need to marry them *now*. That fellow convinced my sister to spend the night in his room. I want this wedding to take place immediately!" Lance tossed the shotgun to his other hand as he glared at Levi.

"And you, Judge—get out of that bed. This is going to be a proper wedding."

Levi stared around the room in shock. His face began to turn red.

Sadie touched his arm. "You *did* propose to me last night," she whispered. "Didn't you mean it?"

As he stared from Sadie to the room full of people, Levi scowled. They were all smiling and laughing. Rooster winked at him and began to laugh. Tiny was grinning as he held a smiling Annie's hand.

Levi rested his eyes on the sky pilot. The man was sweating and flipping furiously through the Bible he was holding for just the right passages.

Sadie's face was happy. Her eyes were sparkling, and she was laughing.

Levi slowly broke into a grin. He tried to laugh but it made his chest hurt.

"Well, at least let me put my pants on. I don't want to get hitched without my britches." The women faced away from the bed and Lance handed Levi his pants.

The sky pilot clutched his Bible and continued to flip through the pages frantically. His face was red, and he was muttering, "Why they are all so crass. This is like a big joke to them."

He could hear the man who was to marry trying to button his britches and he seemed to be having trouble. His chest was bandaged, and he could hardly bend over to look down. Finally, the preacher turned around.

"Would you like me to help you, sir?"

Levi turned red and glared at the preacher. Lance was bent over laughing as Badger and Martha came charging into the room followed by Doc and Josie.

"Need some rope, Judge? I might have some in my wagon," offered Badger. Levi growled at him, and Badger laughed evilly.

Finally, Levi was ready. Sadie moved to stand beside him. Martha put her arm around Sadie while Lance stood next to Levi.

Badger shouted, "I give this here woman jist in case ya need ta know!"

The preacher wiped his brow and began. He talked about fornication and proper moral behavior.

Sammy whispered loudly, "What is he talkin' 'bout? What's fornycation?"

Molly couldn't speak. She didn't know if she should laugh or be horrified. Lance whispered back to Sammy, "The Good Book is chalk full of stories. I think maybe that preacher forgot and read the wrong one."

The sermon was short, probably shorter because Badger hollered "Amen!" after every point the preacher made. He stomped his feet too, and when Badger stomped his feet, both Sammy and Paul stomped theirs. Finally, the vows were made. Before the preacher announced, "You may kiss the bride," Levi pulled Sadie close.

"I'm glad you made room in your heart for me," he whispered as he kissed her. Everyone clapped and cheered.

Leo whispered loudly, "Does this mean Sadie will be livin' with us now? And we can eat at her house all the time instead of just at night an' sometimes for breakfast?"

The preacher sank to the floor. No one noticed though until Sammy asked, "Why are ya sittin' on the floor? Are ya sick?"

Lance handed the man some money, and the preacher fled down the stairs muttering about sin and abominable behavior.

Levi watched him go. He looked around the room. His face was serious, but his eyes were full of amusement as he held his new bride close.

"Now that was just a fine thing you did—smearing the reputation of the finest widow in Cheyenne—and with a traveling preacher, no less!"

Lance laughed as he drawled, "Ah, he's headed east on the next train. This country is too wild for him. Besides, I never told him your last names. He was so rattled, he forgot to ask.

"You'd better make sure this marriage certificate is filled out right though!" Lance grinned as he shoved a paper toward Levi.

Sadie's family surrounded her, and they pulled Levi into their circle of love as well.

Molly giggled and kissed Levi's cheek. "Welcome to the family, Levi!"

Levi kissed Sadie again and lifted the baby from her arms. "What do you think, Kid? This is quite the family you have here."

Leo slid up beside them. He grinned when Sadie kissed his cheek.

Levi's smile was huge as he pulled his new wife closer. He kissed the baby's head and handed him to Leo. When Sadie smiled up at him, he whispered, "This is what love feels like."

Happy tears filled Sadie's eyes, and the noise in the room grew louder.

CPSIA information can be obtained
at www.ICGtesting.com
Printed in the USA
LVHW070034260623
750570LV00003BA/10